Have You Met My Succubus?

Tales of Th'eia

Allan A. Williams

Published in Australia in 2015 by Allan Williams
Redcliffe Qld 4020

Website: www.feuery.net

National Library of Australia Cataloguing-in-Publication entry:

Williams, Allan A. – author.
Have you met my succubus?: tales of Th'eia / by Allan A.
Williams.

9780992578107 (paperback)

Short stories
Fantasy fiction

A823.408

Edited by Epiphany Editing & Publishing
Typesetting by Epiphany Editing & Publishing
Cover design by Sukubus Studios
Printed in Australia by SOS Print + Media

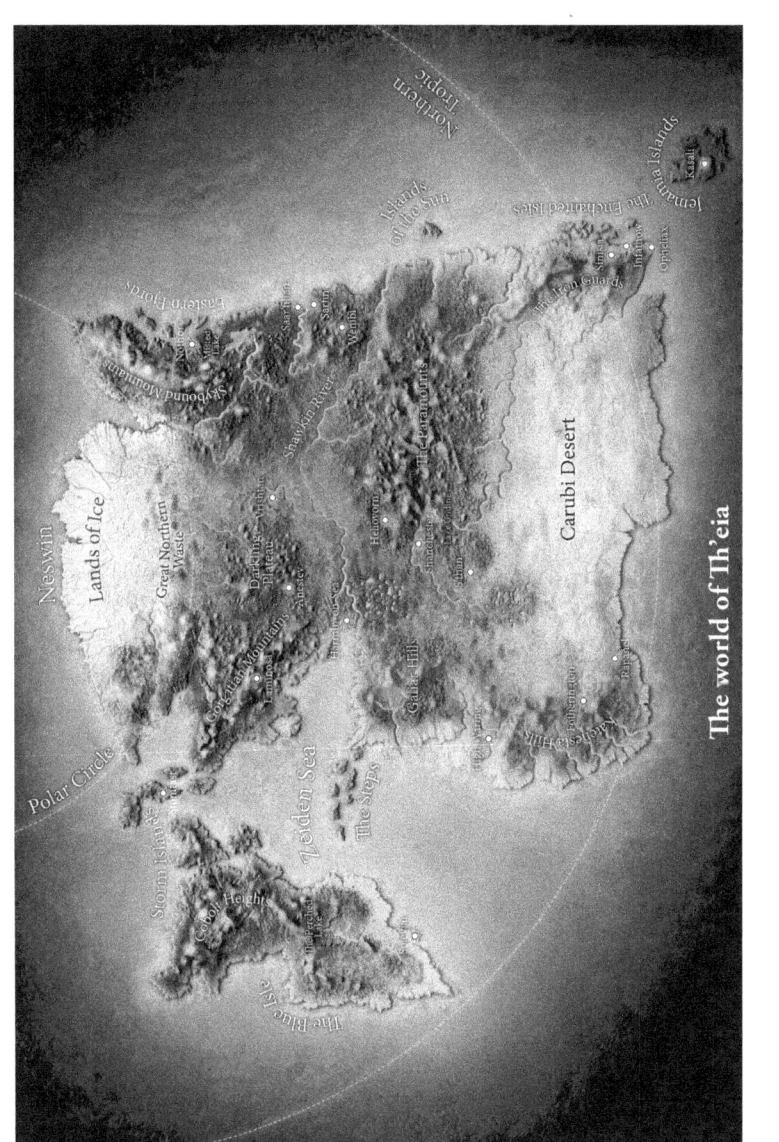

The world of Th'eia

Contents

Thank You   vii

Introduction   1

Miss-spelling   5

The Lady in Green   31

The Enchanted Fleet   57

The Empty Streets of Rapanel   85

Night Watch   111

Meeting my Succubus   131

The Golden Marigold   155

The Azure Needle   181

Anthor   207

Islands of the Sun   227

Glossary   291

About the Author   307

Thank You

Isaac Newton attributed his insights into science and mathematics to '… standing on the shoulders of giants …' Yet, this simile that our achievements are founded on the previous work of others goes much further back in time.

This concept also applies to more than just the sciences and to more than building on other's work. 'Giants' support and encourage us whenever we reach up and out to create something that hasn't existed in the world before. And the truly wonderful thing is that those giants of the spirit are the folk who are around us.

My sincere thanks to:

- Deb and Leigh for encouraging me to publish
- Laia at Sukubus Studio for her beautiful illustrations from the ever-so-sketchy drawings I provided to her
- Christie, Robin, Tasha and Pat for bearing with me as I sailed into my previously uncharted waters of writing (where, indeed, dragons dwell)
- Suzanna for introducing me to Feuery
- Kirsty at Epiphany Editing and Publishing for editing my stories and for so patiently steering me to a better understanding of the relationship between authors, editors and readers

- Linda for The Final Proofread
- Interesting beings great and small, whomever, wherever and whatever you may be, for filling my life with richness.

Introduction

Have You Met My Succubus? is a collection of short stories set in the fantasy world of Th'eia. Th'eia is recovering from the devastating millennia of the Mage Wars that, by the time they ended a few centuries later, had nearly destroyed civilisation and threatened the very fabric of this magical realm.

In the folklore of most cultures across our world of Gaia, succubi appear under many names and are generally acknowledged as being powerful, exotic predators drawn by erotic dreams to feast on the dreamer. However, in *Have You Met My Succubus?* this being serves to illustrate that life is what you make of it, and that you can choose the company you wish to keep, regardless of powerful forces trying to shoehorn you into a stereotypical viewpoint. This is especially true on Th'eia, for Th'eia is a crossroads of many worlds.

Th'eia is the sister world to our own world of Gaia. Th'eia is so infused with magic that folk of many worlds may cross to and from it: a situation which is both a blessing and a curse for the folk of Th'eia.

Our homeworld of Gaia, on the other hand, is so magically impoverished that supernatural folk regard our realm as a dead end: a boring trap rather than a holiday destination or a place suitable for business opportunities!

Nevertheless, our myths and legends abound with Th'eia's many and diverse folk. Clearly, this is the result of some traffic between the worlds. Or perhaps, as much folklore alleges, it is simply because dreams cross readily between the worlds.

Th'eia is home to all sorts of folk: both human and non-human, as well as a range of magical and bizarre creatures. Even the non-magical have complex personalities and fascinating histories and aspirations.

In these pages, not all the demons are hideous evil beings, nor are the fairies and unicorns necessarily sweet and noble respectively. On Th'eia, be prepared to expect the unexpected!

Besides a non-conforming succubus named Rielar, these stories mostly involve the adventures of the multifaceted gnome Feuery. Rielar migrated to, and has now quietly settled on, Th'eia; however, she enjoys chronicling Feuery's escapades as the gnome has chosen the often-dangerous profession of adventuring wizardess.

The world that Feuery inhabits is mostly peaceful; with cities and towns flourishing as trade and learning are re-established across Th'eia following the Mage Wars. However, many treasures, mysteries and forgotten secrets await discovery by those intrepid enough to brave the left-over hazards from the past. All in all, it is an excellent time to be an adventuring wizardess, and Feuery is more intrepid than most.

The stories are written specifically for fantasy-tragics (I admit to being one). However, they are also for those people who have never really understood why *anyone* would bother with 'all that fairies and unicorns stuff'.

For ardent fantasy fans, a warning: these stories aren't grand epic tales of flashing swords, thundering armies and devious intrigues in a world dominated by humans with the occasional mage. Nor will they please those for whom succubi equal sex. These stories are exotic rather than erotic.

For those of you who may be interested in learning more about the background of the kindreds and the creatures of Th'eia that appear – and more – in *Have You Met My Succubus?*, I've provided an alphabetical glossary at the beginning of the book.

Personally, I've enjoyed discovering all about Feuery's adventures: may you have as much fun reading them.

Allan Williams

AFTERWORD: So why do I like writing fantasy stories? Isn't the world we live in intriguing enough?

Fantasy takes us out of the ordinary aspects of our lives and allows us to re-look at that which we thought we knew from a perspective that is, well, simply magical:

> *Feuery found her way into the hall barred by a crystal-clear barrier. She could easily see through it into the impressive, marbled atrium that she needed to pass through, but the barrier wouldn't yield to her pushing and the old man had warned her that breaking through it would set off alarm spells. She took from her pouch the talisman he'd given her. It was a small card, only two inches across and four deep, but he had promised it would gain her access 'by appeasing the lone eye'. Glancing around, she saw a single, red gleam glaring at her from a small niche beside the barrier. Unsure what else to do, she held the card up to the eye. It changed from red to green, and the crystal barrier slid aside …*

Feuery had more fun with her 'talisman' than we do with a swipe card, and Th'eia has guardians that are more ferocious than Front Desk Security. But, she also has invisibility and fire-ball spells at her fingertips. I'm sure there are days when we'd all like to have access to those sorts of powers!

Miss-spelling

The hammer struck the anvil like a thunderbolt, sending sparks streaking gleefully in all directions.

'Damn you nine ways to 'ell 'n' back! Don't dare threaten me in mine own forge!'

'Then repair the axle!'

'Please, please … no need for this, I'm sure we can sort out this misunderstanding.'

The blacksmith glowered at the Darkling, whose hand kept twitching toward his serrated sword. Between them, a short, balding human – a little on the plump side and dressed in travel-stained breeches, tunic and short cape – tried to catch the eye of one or other of the two adversaries. He failed miserably.

'I'm telling you, that axle are muck-iron. Yes, I kin repair it. But no, I wo'n. 'Tis poorly cast; as porous as are a sponge. If'n I was to repair it, you'd travel no more than three, maybe four leagues afore it fails again, 'n' that wi' a light load. Your load in't light by the seeming o' it. Don't blame me. Blame the fool what made the axle, 'n' the bigger fool what bought it.'

The Darkling's aggression – so easy to trigger, so difficult to curb – eased a little. Someone had to be to blame. Someone always had to be blamed. Blame was important, but perhaps this huge human wasn't the right one to focus it on. *Very well,* thought the Darkling. *Retribution can wait. Deal with the problem at hand.*

'Can you replace it with good metal?'

'Course I kin, but 'twill have to be brought in. No call for tempered iron to keep on hand here. Best I kin do is send the boys into Heliovorn 'n' get a new one. Heavy load – it'll need the draught horse. Maybe a day there, two back? I kin fix the fit in a day. If we kin settle on'er a price.'

'Four days! I don't know if we can afford that much time ...' The short human was almost wringing his hands, worry etching his face.

'We can. We have no choice. Settle on a price with this tradesman. Then arrange lodgings for us.' The Darkling turned on his heel and stalked out.

'Unpleasant bug'rs,' the blacksmith grumbled. 'Dealt with Darklings afore. Hope I don't have to agin.'

'Oh, he's not that bad,' the man said, untruthfully.

* * * *

A mile or so north of the village, a footsore gnome rested at the side of the road. Beneath the tiredness and travel-grime, she was beautiful, with deep blue eyes, a clear complexion and auburn hair. Of course, for best effect, her foul mood after two days of tramping would also have to improve.

Her name was Feuery. For those who really knew her – and they were few – it was very apt on occasion. She wore a royal blue skirted tunic over dark blue trousers, with blue-grey boots. A flask and a shapeless bag hung from her wide belt. However, an observer's attention would most likely be drawn to her staff which was made from smoky-grey mage-metal capped with a blue gem the size of her fist. A wizard's battle-staff. And Feuery looked like she'd welcome the opportunity to use it.

There's supposed to be a village just south of here, but I really need a nap, she thought irritably. *Somewhere I won't be disturbed.*

Looking around, she spied a copse on top of a nearby hill. *Off the road, and no sign of anyone. That'll have to do,* she decided.

A few more minutes of weary trudging brought her to the spinney. She glanced around, and carefully parted the bushes, making her way in toward the centre through the thick foliage.

And then she stopped abruptly. A ring of mushrooms circled a beautiful green turf, in the centre of which was a standing stone.

She backed away slowly and cautiously, trying to make as little sound as possible. Once clear of the bushes, she turned and quickly made her way back to the road, frequently glancing behind her.

Setting a cracking pace, she arrived at the village just as the blacksmith was negotiating what *he* considered to be a very satisfactory price for supplying and fixing an axle. (Of course, the price did reflect having to work with Darklings!)

* * * *

Feuery entered the village cautiously. Recent events were likely to have made her very unpopular in the north, as earlier ones here in the south certainly had. Nevertheless, she hoped enough time had passed that the Wizards' Guild here might be more interested in pursuits other than her. And, anyway, it was too darn cold and wet in the north, and had altogether too many Darklings, who were bad enough even without her having given them cause for annoyance.

She chuckled to herself. Still, she had had fun doing what was reputed to be impossible – and profitable also. Or would be, when the Guild – her *other* Guild, not the Wizards' Guild – paid her share.

In the meantime, she wasn't exactly flush with funds, but she had enough to tide her over if she was careful. Plus, the world was full of ways for her to top up her purse. From a quick glance around the village though, it might have to involve something completely new. The place was too small to get away with card-sharping, and there probably wouldn't be a lot of call for her specialist potions. Her need for haste in order to get across the Great River Shawkin, away from the Darkling lands, had prevented her from exploring several promising ruins. They were usually reliable for a treasure or two, but anything between here and Heliovorn, further to the south, was likely to have been picked clean. Too many humans and dwarfs with their own fondness for treasure.

Musing over a range of possible opportunities, she very nearly stepped into the main square without looking first. Only her natural caution led her to peer around the corner. What she saw set her heart racing, and she quickly pressed back against the wall before taking a more careful look.

A huge crate sat in the middle of the town square, canted at an angle on a battered wagon with the two rear wheels splayed out drunkenly from a snapped rear axle. The crate itself was strong – heavy timber, reinforced at the corners and across all sides. That part was interesting and invited better acquaintance, but the dozen or so Darklings manhandling the crate off the wrecked dray didn't.

Something in the crate was very upset, and wanted everyone to know about it.

They couldn't have got ahead of me, she thought. *I'd have seen 'em. Maybe they were ordered up from further south to intercept me?*

It took a moment or two of nasty conjecture to trip over the possibility that their presence might not actually have anything to do with her at all. If they were looking to imprison and transport her, then the crate was definitely overkill for a captured Feuery. Besides, they already had something in it – something that probably wouldn't want to share, by the sound of it. Still, it was best not to take unnecessary chances until she knew more. Anyway, she needed food and badly needed a safe and preferably comfortable place to sleep. A good wash would help too.

The village inn was out, of course. The Darklings were thoughtlessly in the way, and would most likely be staying there themselves. Their wagon with its menacing cargo sure wasn't going anywhere for a while. Feuery wasn't all that fond of inns – not for accommodation anyway. They were usually noisy and drunks tended to take an annoying, if transient, interest in her. And when you've skinned a card table or picked a few pockets, it isn't the best plan to be cooped up in the same building as those people who know (or can make a pretty shrewd guess) where their money has gone.

Mostly though, Feuery considered that inns weren't usually homely-comfortable. Any real home has a special feel of acceptance and security that few inns can match.

But lodgings would have to wait. She needed to know what was going on with the Darklings. Her eye settled on the smithy as a grubby, weary little man walked out of it. He looked distracted and careworn as he hurried over to the inn. On the way, he briefly exchanged a few words with the Darklings. However, whatever was said didn't improve his mood, and even from here she could see the contempt with which they treated him. Not that that meant much – with Darklings, contempt or fear were the two main alternatives for most interpersonal relationships.

If the wagon had a busted axle, the Darklings would have sought the services of the village blacksmith. He might know why the Darklings were here. Smiths also tended to be upright citizens, and upright citizens usually knew which homes were safe and comfortable. *It's worth a go*, thought Feuery

It took a few moments for the smith to realise he had someone quietly waiting to speak to him. Events that morning had put him well behind his daily schedule, and having had to

9

burr up with Darklings hadn't improved the day either. All in all, he wasn't in the best of moods.

'What kin I do for you Miss? I don't do pots 'n' pans, nor sharpen knives nor scissors. Bobern the tinker down near the water mill is your man for that.'

To his great surprise, the pretty little gnome answered with the Sign: a complex twist of the fingers of the left hand signifying she was at least an Artificer of the Guild. It took him a moment to collect his thoughts sufficiently to give the return Sign.

'Well met, Master,' she said formally and respectfully. 'I'm travelling an' seek your advice.'

Well, advice is free, and it's nice to have another of the Great Art asking my professional opinion, the blacksmith thought to himself. That didn't often happen – barring his occasional visits to Heliovorn which always made him feel a little uncomfortable with so many other masters present. Especially those from the big towns like Heliovorn and Shanchester.

'A pleasure, little Miss.' He glanced at the pile of scythes that needed his attention. *Sod 'em. They could wait.* He was curious to know more about this strange visitor.

'I accidentally came across a fairy ring on my way here. I know iron can ward, but I can't remember what type Faerie folk fear the most. We don't get many fairy rings where I'm from.'

'Lodestone,' he said immediately. He looked her over enquiringly, his gaze fixing on her battle-staff.

'Thanks. Do you like my staff?'

''N' why would you be carrying a staff? 'Tis clear 'tis more'n a traveller's.'

'I'm a wizard as well as an Initiate of the Guild.'

'Well, would you be so? I'm thinking you have a story to tell.' He banked the furnace and led them over to two benches on the far side of the smithy.

'… an' so I walked into your village this morning,' Feuery finished half an hour later.

'N' why would you come here to me?'

'I like forges', she answered truthfully, although her preference was for work that involved a strong magnifying glass and fine touch. 'An' was hoping you might have the iron that wards Faerie.'

'Aye, I have that 'n' you're welcome to one. Good, strong one too. 'Tis a rare fine story you've told. Kin understand you not liking Darklings.' He spat into the furnace. 'You made my day the brighter for knowing you poked 'em in the eye!'

'I didn't expect to see so many here.'

'Arr. They traipsed in early morn. Seem to have bin travellin' all night. When they stopped to water 'n' feed their mounts, the wagon up and died on them. Wonder it come so far as here. Utter rubbish workmanship.'

'But why are they here? An' what's in the crate?'

'Headin' back to their own lands, I'm of a notion. 'N' can't be soon 'nough for me. As for the crate – don't know. Wo'n talk on it, but what is in't are heavy 'n' are alive. What's in it must be fearsome too, if'n the care they show in handlin' it an' the ructions from it tell a true tale.'

He regretfully looked back at the scythes. 'Work wan's me. But you'll have the lodestone from me afore you go. No charge, one smith t'other. Anyways, your story is 'nough to pay for it!'

'Thank you so much. I'll feel much safer now. By the way, do you know of anyone who might rent me lodging for a day or two? I don't want to stay at the inn.'

'Can understand that. I'd put you up at mine own home, but the wife has gone to Heliovorn with the boys, 'n' eyebrows would rise, as they say. Try ol' Missus Larmin. Say I sent you 'n' would be obliged. Some say she's a witch, but don't let that faze you.'

She followed his directions to a low but ramblingly large house on the road south to Heliovorn. One look at the garden convinced her that 'some' said correctly, for apart from a thriving vegetable garden, nearly every plant visible had properties for potions and brews. So, when the door opened to her knock, she gave the traditional silent greeting between witches to 'Missus Larmin' – offering a handshake with the thumb turned into the palm. She was quickly ushered into the kitchen where, over a cup of invigorating herbs, they soon became acquainted and settled on a price for several nights' lodging and two meals a day.

'I mostly sleeps aft'noons,' Missus Larmin warned her. 'On account I don't sleep well o' nights. I likes to go for walks o' the eve'ing to try to settle.'

'What a coincidence,' replied Feuery, and they exchanged knowing smiles.

Missus Larmin's face suddenly became serious, 'Truth to tell, of late I gets little time to meself. Faerie has drifted near here just recently, 'n' they've opened the fairy-ring you seen in the woods. In close-by weeks, there been no end of troublemakers visiting. Been pressed to keep all sort of mischief from happenin'. None of the bigger, badder ones have come through as yet, but I fear me the portal through gets stronger all the time. We may have trouble afore the worlds drift away agin 'n' this door to Faerie closes.'

Feuery nodded understandingly. Their world and Faerie frequently nudged up against one another, and when that happened a wizard wasn't needed to bridge between the worlds – not that many wizards would willingly open a way into Faerie anyway. No one ever knew what the mood was like on that side at any given moment. If you were lucky, you'd find them in a good phase, and the experience could be for the better. However, it was more likely to be mischievous and troublesome in petty ways, but it could also be sheer evil. The tone of Faerie waxed and waned to some strong, strange rhythm unknown to those of this world. Even some fairies despaired of it and fled to this world – usually the nicer and wiser ones.

* * * *

Feuery spent that afternoon enjoying a nice long bath and good sleep in a comfortable bed in a cosy room at the back of the house. After preparing and sharing a meal together with her hostess, Feuery slipped out into the gathering evening. She left Missus Larmin busy with a broom in the kitchen, arranging a comfy seat and collector's saddlebags on it. She'd been grateful to be told of the whereabouts of some rare plants, minerals and other ingredients Feuery had noticed on her journey from the north.

The town square was dimly lit, mainly by lights from the inn. Nevertheless, it seemed quieter and more subdued than one would expect. Evidently many of the townsfolk didn't enjoy the thought of having Darklings as drinking companions. Not surprising really!

Three of the Darklings wouldn't have been drinking anyway. They were guarding the crate, which had now been successfully off-loaded from the sad-looking wagon.

Feuery studied the scene from the deep shadows of the village's Court House veranda. She was curious to see inside that crate, and intended to find a way of getting past the Darkling guards. Following a few moments of deft handiwork, she'd fashioned a miniature figure out of straw she had found beside the veranda. While it wasn't essential, it would help the spell focus more easily, seem stronger and last longer.

Leaving the straw manikin in the shadows of the court house, she slipped unobserved to a shadow near the inn – the closest shadow convenient to the crate.

One of the guards glanced toward her several times. He was suspicious, but not quite suspicious enough to raise alarm or investigate. The other two were having a conversation in low voices. From the few words she caught, Feuery gathered they were complaining about being chosen for guard duty. They seemed to feel they did more than their fair share. She paid little attention to their complaints. In her experience, every guard of every kindred always had exactly the same grievance.

As softly as possible, so as not to attract the attention of the suspicious guard, she chanted the spell under her breath.

The grumbling abruptly stopped. The guard furthest from Feuery gave a startled cry. The suspicious guard, who had appeared about to look more closely at her hiding place, ran to join the others.

There was no time to waste. Feuery dashed over to the crate while the Darkling guards' attention was focused on the vision at the court house. While the guards were engaged in conversation and speaking in urgent, low tones to one another about it, she caught a quick glimpse of her handiwork– a tall, graceful figure, cloaked and hooded in the silver-green of a Fair Elven warrior, and holding a long spear with a silver, gleaming head was standing ominously in the shadows.

Then she was at the crate! She pressed an eye close to a rough join in the wood, and saw …

A horrible burning red eye turned toward her. For a moment she froze in loathing and disgust before shaking herself free, and running back to the shadows. Behind her, the crate shook as the occupant flung itself in rage against the sides, trying to break out. The Darkling guards ran to the crate, while behind them the image of the Fair Elf dissipated like smoke in a breeze.

Feuery disappeared again into the shadows and then kept running until she reached the edge of the village. She sat down to try to collect her thoughts.

How could anyone do that? It's so totally wrong! These thoughts kept repeating in her head and made thinking difficult.

Eventually she stood up, her face grim with determination.

Well, someone needs to do sum'it 'bout it, so I will. But I'll need a special piece of magic, an' there's only one place around here that will have it. She headed off again, striding angrily northward.

* * * *

The fairy ring was as she'd previously left it. Taking a deep breath, Feuery stepped into the ring of mushrooms and quickly ran three circuits widdershins. With each circuit she completed, the standing stone in the centre shone brighter and its outline became more insubstantial until, at the end of her last circuit, it seemed to silently explode, filling the ring with glittering motes of gaily dancing light and creating a tunnel-like passageway where it had stood.

A passageway into Faerie …

* * * *

After about thirty paces into the low tunnel, Feuery met two goblins playing a game of knucklebones. They were using real knuckles – fresh ones – from which the winner of each round was gnawing any remaining gristle.

'No admittance!' one shrilled at her. 'No admittance 'less you play us and win.'

'Penalty if you lose,' added the other with a snide predatory grin.

'I'll play the winner,' she said, ''n' winner takes all. But to ensure I play the best of you, you must have twenty sets so that it's clear who won because of skill, not chance. While you do that, I'll visit the Lord and Queen.'

Feuery swept past them while they tried to figure her conditions out, and how to keep track of twenty games. For a goblin, it was advanced math.

* * * *

After only a few more paces, the passage opened into Faerie. Taking a deep breath to calm herself, she stepped forward.

It was a glorious wonderland. The stars in the sky flickered in brilliant colours, each star much bigger than in the skies she was familiar with. Swirls of pulsing, coloured mist like auroras drifted across the sky, altering the radiance of the stars and intensifying colours; sometimes magnifying their vivacity, sometimes diminishing it. The trees and bushes of Faerie gleamed in greens and reds and silver, and in colours for which her world had no names. Clouds of fireflies of gold and glistening blue clustered and dispersed randomly across the landscape. Flowers of exquisite forms and colours blossomed everywhere, and gentle breezes rippled the grasses and emerald-green ferns.

Pity the folk here can be such nasty sods, she reflected sourly. *I'd better get on with it before I lose my nerve.*

'I attend on the mighty Lord Oberon an' the gracious Queen Titania from a far place. Grant me an audience if you will,' she called the formal greeting in a loud clear voice.

Heads – all sorts of heads – immediately began to pop up from the foliage, and all eyes turned to her.

Ignore 'em. They're just minor Faerie folk, she reassured herself.

Then the air on the sward before her seemed to break into a cloud of glittering motes of light. A tall, regal man and an almost equally tall and imperious woman materialised. A multitude of Faerie-folk appeared around them at a respectful distance.

'Who calls upon the Rulers of Faerie?' the woman – Titania – enquired in a serene, commanding voice. Oberon gazed at her, his face a mask.

''Tis I, Feuery. For I seek a boon of you,' said Feuery respectfully.

'Indeed!' said Oberon. His voice was deep and resonant; the surrounding landscape seemed to move to its tones. 'And what is this boon sought by one of such beauty, and what have you to offer for it?'

Titania shot a glare at him.

'I have unique gifts of fine crafting I have prepared for you,' said Feuery quickly, reaching into her pouch before Titania saw fit to act on her obvious displeasure. Feuery drew out two finely crafted balls of gleaming bronze, the outer shell cut to reveal within more pierced layers of copper, electrum, silver, gold and brass. Each layer moved within the others, and both balls were lit by a brightly-glowing gem in the centre. 'May I approach to present them to you?' asked Feuery.

'You may,' Oberon said eagerly. Titania seemed about to say something to the contrary, but was clearly captivated by what she could see of the spheres and so held her objections.

Feuery walked slowly forward and placed them in the air before the royal couple, reaching as high as she could so that the globes hung spinning and casting beams of light, close to their eye level.

There was a collective sigh of wonder and appreciation from the Faerie courtiers, and many admiring comments.

Oberon reached out and gently took one of the orbs, holding it so that it spun and danced on his palm. After a moment of hesitation, Titania could no longer resist and took hers as well.

'You say that you crafted these marvellous items yourself?' Oberon asked.

'I did, your most Highness. Hope you find them amusing.'

'I do, I truly do. I am of a mind to make you Our Royal Artificer of Diverting Treasures ...' Then he caught the look that Titania gave him. 'But perhaps not. What is the boon you would ask of us?'

'I would like a rope of moonbeams.'

'A rope of moonbeams?!' Titania looked up sharply. 'That is no small gift, nor one of mean powers.' She looked shrewdly at her royal partner. 'But I will grant you your wish if you can answer one question for me.' She glanced sideways at the commotion that had broken out among the courtiers. 'What agitates you so, Peggy-Bole?'

'Her hair, Mistress, her lovely red hair. I wants it,' said a pretty fairy with long blonde tresses.

'I likes her eyen,' said a goblin. 'May you swap mine for hers?'

A clamour began, with others from the court coveting various aspects of Feuery's features.

A malicious smile crossed Titania's face. 'Silence all, my sweets! What may be is yet to be.' She looked back to Feuery. 'Will you accept my question?'

'An' if I can't answer it?'

'Then many from my court will be granted boons, and with what you then have, my Lord may have his Royal Artefact of Divided Treasures.'

'Royal Artificer of Diverting Treasures,' Oberon corrected. But his nicety was barely heard as the court – especially those who had laid claim to different parts of Feuery – shouted and carolled their approval of the Queen's idea. Amid the general jubilation, he looked troubled.

'May I hear your question before I decide?'

'No, you may not in any wise.'

So, I guess there is no way out, thought Feuery. 'I accept.'

The court went wild with enthusiasm. Oberon looked glum at their response while Titania appeared triumphant.

'My question is this: What is the secret of Faerie-magic? You have one minute to answer.'

Amid the excitement of the court, Feuery thought furiously. The seconds ticked by.

It would help if I could get some quiet, she thought testily. A boisterous sprite near the Queen was one of those who was the most annoying. She cast a silence spell on him.

The sprite started, and Feuery felt something strange in the magic currents. Titania glared at the sprite and hissed at him as Feuery's spell dissipated.

What happened then? She tried again with an even more powerful spell cast on a toad-like fairy near Oberon, paying careful attention to the flows of magic. The same thing happened as she'd sensed before. She felt the gathering of magic to ward off her spell, where it came from, and the startled annoyance of those around the targeted fairy.

And then Feuery knew the answer.

'Your time's up, my dear. Have you a true answer for me?' Titania asked softly with a nasty smile.

'I do,' said Feuery clearly over the clamour, which abruptly turned to surprised attentiveness. 'The secret of Faerie-magic is that it is collective magic. The folk of Faerie can draw magic energies from those around them with which to work spells that are greater than those they could work alone. So, in this your Kingdom you may draw on all of your subjects to create truly mighty magic. Around the fairy-rings you may also draw on your subjects, but the further away you go from a fairy-ring an' your Kingdom, the less powerful your magic becomes. A fairy separated from Faerie-land is no different to anyone else of the kindreds, an' is able to rely only on the magic power inside themselves.'

There was stunned silence. Oberon tried (with some success) not to smile. Titania (with almost no success at all) attempted not to look furious.

'We must be gracious and acknowledge a true answer,' Oberon stated with just a trace of malice towards Titania.

'Yes. We must,' she said tightly. She reached into the air and drew a long, slim strand of rope from out of it. It was about a dozen feet long, and shone with a milky-white inner glow.

'Here is your prize, little gnome. Approach us so that we may present it to you.'

Cautiously, Feuery stepped forward, her left hand in her pouch, her right reaching out for her prize. Titania handed her the coil of rope, almost thrusting it at her ungraciously.

'Thank y …' Feuery began, but was cut short by a jubilant Titania.

'Now, our bargain is complete. On another matter – the penalty for an Outsider to know the secret of Faerie-magic is death.' She glanced around with an indulgent half-smile as the court cheered, jeered and otherwise noisily expressed their approval. 'Be patient, my sweets. We will give to each we deem as deserving a favour as soon as the sentence is carried out.'

Feuery swiftly threw a bight of the rope of moonbeams over Oberon's head, drawing it tight around his shoulders. She pulled him close to her before he or anyone else could react.

'Quiet, all of you!' She held up her left hand, displaying the lodestone.

'Now, here's what we're going to do,' she said into the horrified silence. 'Lord Oberon an' I are going to slowly an' quietly go back up the passageway. When we reach the fairy-ring, we're going to walk a little bit more away from Faerie's influence, an' then I'll take the rope off so we can go our various ways. If anyone thinks otherwise, then I touch the lodestone to Oberon, an' foof! – the Lord of Faerie loses his magic. Might mean troubled times for Faerie, but doesn't have to happen, does it Titania?'

Oberon looked stunned, trying to come to terms with the situation. Titania darted a look of pure venom at Feuery. Then she straightened, casting a complex spell of banishment that ended with a rune of power. The entire court disappeared.

'Good idea! We don't want any heroes makin' a mess of things, do we?' Feuery said approvingly. She suspected the spell had been for her, but if it was, then it had been thwarted by the lodestone. 'By the way, there's a couple of goblins in the passageway also. I don't think they're really hero material, but let's not take chances.'

Titania snapped her fingers angrily. In the silence left by the departure of the court, Feuery thought she heard a faint clatter of knucklebones falling onto a board.

Watching Titania carefully, Feuery directed the docile Oberon into the passage. Its ceiling rose to accommodate his height. There was a sound behind them like the gnashing of teeth. Ahead of them, a faint greyness at the entrance hinted at the first blushes of dawn.

* * * *

About half-way back to the village, Feuery released the now indignant and belligerent Lord.

'I've still got the lodestone, remember. So nothing silly! Your magic won't work while I'm holding it. Must disrupt the way you draw your magic from other Faerie-folk an' use it.'

'Spiked galumpers and yompers will bound on your trail when evening next falls, gnome. Shrieking jiingans will fall upon you from the night sky. You cannot run far enough, nor ever hide so deep. You will be dragged back screaming in fear and terror to my realm. I shall transform you into a potted plant, a pretty little flower that must bide in one place while all of the world goes on around it, and I shall enjoy your writhing when I trim you back to size each week.'

'Careful! Right now I still have the rope of moonbeams. I can lasso you again if you aren't nice.' She flung up the arm with the rope, and enjoyed his panicked flight from her back toward the fairy-ring. Indulgent, but she doubted he could possibly feel more vindictive toward her than he – and Titania – already did.

21

What about tomorrow? she wondered. If she was right (and if her hope was well-placed) then it wouldn't be a problem. Oberon and Titania would just have to get over it and move on. If she was wrong … Well, then it wouldn't matter anyway, would it?

* * * *

There was a lot of activity as she finally turned back into the village square. Complaints must have been made about the noise and disruption of the crate. There had evidently been a scene between the village council and the Darklings, which Feuery regretted missing, but an agreement seemed to have been reached to move the crate to the side of the inn.

At least, that's what a mixed gang of villagers and Darklings were currently struggling to do, watched on by some older villagers, a stone-faced Darkling in full battle-armour and the petulant inn-keeper who was, as it were, alongside the resolution only grudgingly.

The crate wasn't cooperating as it was dragged on the rough cobbles: at times appearing to bend out of shape. Whatever was inside objected strongly to being moved by thrashing fiercely, causing the crate to shudder violently.

Then, what Feuery had feared would happen, did. The workers made a strenuous effort to force the crate over a slightly higher patch of cobbles, and a great force within simultaneously struck the crate where it was distorted.

Heavy planks sprayed outward like confetti, knocking down several of the workers and shattering windows at the inn.

For an instant, the scene appeared to freeze in mid-action. Everyone looked with horrified fascination at what had emerged from the crate.

It was huge. The crate had been none too big for it. It was the size and shape of a great horse – but one that had been steeped in evil and rolled in nightmares. Its hide was like tiger-striping:

a dark grey (one shade off black) over a hideous purple-red. Its legs ended in black talons rather than hooves, and on its forehead a misshapen cluster of long, heavy spikes thrust forward like a many-pronged fishing spear. Fangs gleamed in its mouth, and red glaring eyes glowered at the spectators.

The creature broke the hiatus. It reared onto its back legs, shattering what was left of the crate, and screamed in deep anguish that chilled the blood.

The sound pierced the ears and minds of everyone watching. It hurtled past all rational thought; straight to the part of each being's mind that decides on fight or flight, where it threw all the switches to flight.

Everyone ran. In all directions, bar one – where the creature from Hell was.

Everyone, that is, except for Feuery.

* * * *

She'd been aware of what to expect when the crate broke open. That didn't help a lot, but it helped enough for her to stand firm and to hold her will together. And will was all that was preventing her from fleeing to anywhere far away as fast as she could.

She closed her eyes as she fought to control the part of her screaming to run – to run until this village, this land and that monstrous abomination were far, far behind. As if from a great distance, she heard screams of terror, and ones of pain and death. Running feet pelted past her, and she felt a great rush of air gust past, followed by a hideous shriek that lapsed into a gurgling whimper and then a death rattle.

She opened her eyes. Two Darklings – pierced and trampled – lay on the square in front of her. Just to her left lay the little man who had been with the Darklings: now a pathetic, deflated pile from which blood oozed onto the cobblestones.

Looking up, she saw the creature impaling someone on the run, then rearing up to cast the body high into the air.

23

Taking a deep breath, she whistled as loudly and shrilly as she could.

The beast spun wildly and saw her. She stood her ground, her staff hanging from her hand, and whistled derisively at it again.

It reared, and charged at her. Time seemed to slow to almost a standstill. She saw the dust flung up from the creature's charge. She saw the breath hot from its nostrils and the glare of the red eyes aligning her on its horn-tines; now bright red with the blood that also dappled its hide.

She waited for what seemed like an eternity as the pounding of its charge echoed through the ground and ran up her body, filling the air with its doom-laden drumming.

As the beast and the noise of its charge seemed to fill her entire world, she held up a hand, palm outward toward it.

It screamed, and dug its talons into the roadway. Dust swirled around them, while, all the time, the scream went on and on and on …

* * * *

The scream stopped abruptly, leaving a silence broken only by the ragged breathing of the creature as it stood before her, its flanks heaving, its eyes fixed on hers over the blood-stained tines just touching her upraised palm. The touch was so light she barely felt it.

Feuery slipped to one side and gently fitted a halter made of the rope of moonbeams over the creature's head, careful to avoid its horns.

Then she petted and soothed the tortured beast while the redness of its eyes slowly changed to a softly glowing silver; while the tiger-striping faded to the purest white; while the talons transformed into delicate hooves and the fangs disappeared; and the hideous pronged horns merged together to form a single, long, graceful spiral-shaped horn of gleaming gold.

She gently cleaned the blood from the creature, and then led it docilely out of the village while the crowd silently watched them pass.

At the edge of a field leading up to a grassy hill, Feuery took the halter off and set the unicorn free.

It ran lightly across the field to the top of the hill. There it reared up, and trumpeted a call of exultation, of joy and of thankfulness before disappearing into the woods.

After that there were no more pressing reasons for Feuery not to pass out, so she did …

* * * *

The world slowly came back into focus, and Feuery looked up into the concerned face of Missus Larmin. She was gently wiping Feuery's face with a cool, damp cloth.

'Shhh. Rest you. Took much out of you, I've a mind. But 'twas a fine thing you done.'

Feuery looked around and gingerly sat up.

The smith had taken command in the village square, ordering for the injured to be attended to, the dead bodies respectfully collected and the wreckage cleared. There was frantic activity everywhere.

'Does 'em good to have some'at to do,' Missus Larmin observed. 'Saves having to think about what just happened. N' on that, what did just happen?'

'Where are the Darklings?' Feuery asked.

'Gorn. High-tailed it out as soon as you let the unicorn free. Now you gonna tell us about it?'

'Us?'

'We've not yet met, but I'm pleased to make your acquaintance', said a voice behind her.

She looked back. She realised she'd been lying with her head in the lap of a small woman wearing a long red and black robe and an elaborate crested helm. The scarred and pitted battlestaff crowned with a black metal dragon lying beside her completed the picture.

'Trecina. Sorceress and Wizards' Guild Field Agent,' she introduced herself evenly, offering a hand as she stood up. 'I'm much obliged to you for having freed the unicorn from the spell. I would've had to kill it.' She looked levelly at Feuery. 'How'd you know how to cure it?'

Feuery took the offered hand reluctantly, looking at the woman carefully. She had sharp, angular features and the blackest eyes Feuery had ever seen. For a human, she was tiny – barely taller than a gnome. There was no doubt whatsoever though that she was powerful. Feuery could feel the magical energy around her and her staff. She was probably one of the most powerful wizards Feuery had ever met. There are very few mages capable of killing a unicorn, but it was quite believable this sorceress was one of them.

'I has a powerful curiosity 'bout what jest happened too,' Missus Larmin reminded them. 'Be nice to know if'n it'll turn back into … what were.'

Feuery took a deep breath. 'There's an old legend among the gnomes. A long time ago, the First Folk were worried about intruders coming into this world. I think Faerie had a lot to do with it, but there were probably worse – what we call demons now. Must have been bad, 'cos they did sum'it 'bout it that must've taken a lot of courage an' soul-searching an' heartache.'

'The Folk took some of the great horses from the plains, an' the very best of their own – mostly young ones, keen an' eager to make the world better. Unselfish folk who felt an' cared for others all the way down deep inside themselves. Brave too, an' smart enough to know bad things don't get fixed by just wishing, 'cos there had to be hardness too. They mixed the great horses an' the best of their own folk together, adding a lot of magic along the way. They made a new type of critter, bright as people, an' as pure in intent and thought as it was possible to get. But powerful an' willing to use that power to deal with almost anything – 'cept maybe a dragon or a Demon Lord – that was evil. Those were the first unicorns, an' I guess there'll still be some of them around, 'cos unicorns are one of the magic creatures that don't age.'

'This was one of them,' Trecina said. 'One of the First Unicorns; though that's just old wives' tales to explain unicorns.'

Feuery shrugged. 'Maybe. An' maybe sometimes it's a good idea to wonder why old wives tell tales, an' where the ideas came from. You're obviously a great sorceress, Mistress Trecina. Probably well-learned, but right now if I hadn't listened to old wives' tales we might have a destroyed village an' a dead unicorn, which would be tragic. Or a dead me, an' I sorta feel from a pers'nal point of view that would've been terrible tragic too.'

Trecina said nothing.

'But what happened to make it as it were?' Missus Larmin asked determinedly.

'Someone – most likely that little wizard there,' Feuery pointed to where some villagers were lifting the body of the plump little man, 'foolishly tried to bind the unicorn. Don't know why, an' probably never will now. But the spell – strong one too – went wrong. It had to go wrong, even if the binding was cast perfect. No one can put a compulsion on a unicorn. Unicorns by their nature have higher imperatives built into 'em. There's no room for more compulsion, an' it would interfere with what an' why they are. An' in this case, it interfered with most everything.'

'So the compulsion spell changed it from be'n a unicorn into be'n – what it were?'

'That's it. But deep down inside, under all that madness, was still a unicorn. Once it remembered that, it could break through the horrible spell it had on it an' go back to being itself.'

'Why bring it here? Why did the Darklings want it?' asked Missus Larmin.

'I'm guessing, but I'd bet the Darkling Empress heard about a wizard who had a truly terrible critter an' who didn't know what to do with it. She keeps a private menagerie of fearsome beasties; thinks it helps her reputation, an' maybe it does with Darklings. She'd have been prepared to pay a lot for it. She's not a very nice person. Guess the wizard figured he'd get something out of the mess he'd made.'

Trecina said. 'Have you heard enough, Missus Larmin? I'd like Feuery and I to go now while folk are busy.'

'The unicorn will stay here now, an' protect this land while Faerie is near. The folk of Faerie – leastways any you'd worry about – won't dare to come through while it's standing guard', said Feuery as if she hadn't heard Trecina. *Thank goodness*, she added to herself.

She turned suddenly to the sorceress. 'Are you taking me back to the Wizards' Guild to stand trial?'

Trecina looked surprised. 'Of course not! I'm taking you back with me to a safe place, and, if you agree, I'll continue your training. But no, I'm not taking you back to the Guild.'

'But don't you work for the Wizards' Guild?'

'I came here to deal with a bungled spell and all the repercussions that could have occurred. I don't need to now because you did a better job with a far more satisfactory outcome than I could have. No one asked me to capture a rogue wizard. But having found you, I have more sense than to let you keep on running aimlessly, always looking over your shoulder concerned about the Guild pursuing you. Anyway, I don't consider that anything you've done should warrant expulsion. I may work for the Guild, but they don't own me. I form my own views.'

She looked thoughtfully at the field where the unicorn had been released. 'In any case, I've never had an apprentice with such an impeccable character reference.'

'You'd best go then,' said Missus Larmin. 'But there is one thing I doesn't get the understanding of yet. How'd you know it wouldn't hurt you?' she asked.

'I didn't, right up to the second it touched me. But I guess I passed the test. A unicorn can't hurt … some folk,' replied Feuery.

Comprehension dawned on Missus Larmin. 'Ah! So you're a virg …'

'That's pers'nal, an' none your business.' Feuery interrupted. 'Don't think unicorns care about physical things too much anyways. What they do care about is whether you belong here, an' whether you're evil. Maybe has to be both. Evil to a unicorn – maybe true always – is someone who does what they want without caring about how it affects or hurts others.'

She turned to Trecina. 'Hope you're a good teacher, 'cos there's lots I want to know.'

Me too, thought Trecina.

The Lady in Green

The snuffling and footpads on the rich, damp leaf litter of the forest behind her were definitely getting closer.

Damn! *Probably a werewolf. A ghoul wouldn't likely sniff so much,* reflected Feuery.

Whatever it was, she didn't want the bother. It was the third night she'd followed the Lady in Green into the Wild Wood, and tonight she'd trailed her further into the Wood than ever before. Being attacked by *anything* at this point was going to be a nuisance.

It must be very hungry, she mused. Normally, werewolves weren't particularly active until both moons had risen, and the silvery blue moonshine of Oberon was at least half an hour from being complemented by the lustrous pearly-pink of the much smaller, but brighter, Titania.

Why do we call the moons after the rulers of Faerie? she wondered idly. She'd meet the real Oberon and Titania. Once was definitely enough!

More to the point now, what to do about her pursuer? Last night it *had* been ghouls, but she was fairly sure this was a werewolf, albeit a big one. At least that would be easier to deal with than ghouls.

Ahead was a narrow crevice between a rocky wall and a tree on the lip of a steep gully. She slipped through easily and, just past the gap, quickly cast a small spell of her own devising, right where her pursuer would be sure to snuffle about to see what direction she'd taken.

It would have been fun to watch, but she'd already lost sight of the Lady. She'd have to hurry now to pick up the trail. She'd lost the track last night by indulging in watching the ghouls rush at her, slavering and gibbering with excitement. Right into her zero-gravity spell. She giggled. *Almost worth it though!*

She hurried along the edge of the gully, taking care not to slip on patches of exposed clay while avoiding the fern leaves, still wet from the evening rain shower. She briefly glimpsed the deep green of the Lady's flowing skirt through the foliage ahead of her.

There was a muffled yelp behind her, followed by a staccato string of the sort of wet and messy sneezes that are associated with concussion and headaches.

Yep, she thought with satisfaction, trying to suppress another giggle. *That sounds like a werewolf.* Those woofs must have been heard across much of the Wild Wood, if not on the streets of the adjoining town. That was one werewolf who'd be more careful of gnome-scent in future.

Senses alert, she scampered through the thick foliage, emerging suddenly into a park-like opening. There was about an acre of beautifully-trimmed lawn adjoining a small, shimmering pool into which the veil of a waterfall fell mistily. Five magnificent trees, tall and slender, with silvery-grey bark and leaves of a deep, almost iridescent green, were evenly spaced in a semi-circle around the pool.

It was the last thing she would have expected to find in the Wild Wood. A blasted heath, a lich's lair, a den of orcs – all would have seemed more likely than the elegant beauty and peacefulness of this garden in the moonlight. But there was no sign of the Lady.

Surely she couldn't have crossed the lawn in that time. I was too close, thought Feuery.

She nervously glanced left and right along the line where the forest met the garden in case the Lady had slipped to one side. *No sign of her. Could she have doubled back? It was unlikely.*

Warily, she moved toward the five soaring trees. Nothing. She gazed around in frustration. *So near! How had the Lady managed to slip away?* Feuery fumed for a few moments, contemplating the scene. Well, it was too dangerous to wait lest one of the many nasties that lived in the woods was stalking her. She turned to go back to Shanchester, grumpy at being evaded – again.

A tinkling peal of almost silent laughter? She spun around. Nothing. The scene remained as serenely beautiful as before.

She made her way back through the woods in a foul temper. Flickers of magic fire across the head of her staff expressed her vexation. If anyone or anything saw her, they'd let her pass.

*　*　*　*

Feuery lithely climbed the trellis to her rooms in the house where she had taken lodgings. The human couple and their three children had been delighted to have such a charming and quiet guest, and it would be unkind to expose them to her less conventional activities, as well as very inconvenient. They assumed – and in this she encouraged them and everyone else – that she was a scholar, or possibly a trainee librarian at the Wizards' Guild. Few knew the last place that would welcome Feuery was the Wizards' Guild, even though she was a full wizardess.

Indeed, Feuery's presence in the town of Shanchester was something of an embarrassment to the local Guild. She was decidedly *persona non grata* with the Wizards' Guild after an unfortunate incident had compelled her to flee from the Academy at High Waring. Escaping via the Guild Armoury to 'pick up a few things' hadn't improved her relations with them, even though she'd only been able to select a few choice items before exiting hastily when caught *in flagrante* by a high-level battle-mage. Following on from various adventures, Feuery had made her way here to Shanchester.

The problem for the local wizards was that Feuery was – the Wizards' Guild aside – very popular. She charmed everyone, she made the best – ahem – 'personal health and wellbeing' potions available, and included amongst her numerous customers many influential town people. She was also a significant contributor to the local economy due to her success in adventuring, and her connections to various local businesses. The local wizards also had a sneaking suspicion that calling Feuery out could turn nasty; among the items she had stolen was a renowned battle-staff. Then there were also the rumours that, despite being effectively outlawed by the Wizards' Guild, Feuery continued to be tutored – and possibly protected – by a very senior sorceress.

So the local wizards took the expedient course of simply pretending she wasn't there – at least in her capacity as a wizard. It was a stance that caused no end of amusement among the other guilds that were in the know, but one that suited Feuery perfectly. By and large, Shanchester was a reasonably prosperous town that was quite happy for anything that might disturb normal daily life to happen somewhere else, and the local wizards were no exception.

Although, of course, there was the Wild Wood.

The Wild Wood sprawled into Shanchester like a big bite out of the side of a pancake. From the east almost into the town centre, the Wood nestled in a wide, gentle depression that continued on into the neighbouring forests. Covering an area almost as great as the town itself, it was a heavily overgrown, vigorous forest laced with small streams, the gullies they'd carved and numerous ruins from much earlier times.

It was also home to all manner of creatures, ranging from the conventional wolves, bears, leopards and giant wolverine through to the so-called Children of the Dark – trolls, ghouls, were-creatures – to name only some of the more savoury. Oddly, however, Feuery had discovered from her private research into the old Town and Guild records that undead such as liches were almost unknown in the Wood. It should have been prime territory for them. Sometimes, alone in the dark of the early hours, she wondered if it was because they were scared of it – and wished she hadn't thought of *that* as a possible answer.

Much of the local Wizards' Guild business involved maintaining wards and barriers to keep the Wood's inhabitants out of Shanchester. They were generally successful, but every few years the Guild made a concerted effort to reduce the number of creatures in the Wood. The entire constituency of the Town Guard and Wizards' Hall would turn out to send seeking-death spells into the Wood and slay anything that tried to flee into the town. This periodic slaughter was known locally as a 'Cleansing'.

Newcomers to Shanchester sometimes suggested setting the Wood on fire, or progressively destroying it piecemeal from the fringes. Locals would shudder and tell them of earlier attempts along those lines, including vivid tales of trees and bushes wildly seizing passers-by, or vines that writhed out of the Wood and tore down buildings in Shanchester in retaliation. Something in the Wild Wood tolerated no harm to the Wood itself, but appeared unconcerned about the creatures in it.

There were, of course, numerous folktales of, legends about and explanations for the Wild Wood. They were all wrong, but only two people knew that. Feuery knew they were wrong because she'd figured out what the Wood really was and why it existed.

What she didn't know – yet – was who was behind it. But she had her suspicions. She just needed to be sure she'd found the *other* person who knew the widely-held stories were wrong.

* * * *

The next morning Feuery slept late, which wasn't unusual as it would be assumed that she had been studying well into the night. She often did – but even when she didn't, if Feuery felt like sleeping in, Feuery did.

She regarded herself in the mirror before going to bid good morning to whoever was around. At this hour, that usually meant the lady of the house and possibly an elderly maid assisting with chores. The husband would be at his joinery business and the children at school.

Anyone would describe Feuery as being delicately pretty, and everyone did. With her fine features, bright blue eyes, clear, tanned complexion and the tips of her little pointed ears just showing through a mass of well-groomed auburn hair, she had an elfin-like beauty that many elfesses would envy. Her attractive appearance, however, belied Feuery's usual state of being. Her ground zero, so to speak, was a general disgruntlement with a world she felt could at least *try* to do as she wanted without her having to continually push it into the shape that suited her. She had long since learned not to let her viewpoint show, but rather to use on an often unsuspecting world the abundant charm with which a possibly mischievous fate had seen fit to liberally endow her.

She usually wore a blue, skirted tunic over dark blue trousers, with light, blue-grey boots. The dark metal battle-staff with an intensely blue sapphire the size of her fist at the top rarely left her hand. It was the main prize she had 'requisitioned' from the Guild Armoury during her hasty exit, and Feuery had become quite fond of it.

In her boots, she stood about four and a half feet tall. However, in curiosity, self-assurance, smarts and magical skill, she was a giant.

Ok, all the bits are there, let's get on with the day. Feuery deliberated.

According to the maid, the lady of the house had gone shopping. So after chatting briefly over tea and freshly-baked bread rolls smothered in fresh butter and honey, Feuery also left to attend to some 'unfinished business'.

She returned to the edge of the Wild Wood by a circuitous route. The boundary between the Wood and the town of Shanchester was well defined by a wide, circular roadway with a high brick wall on the side facing the Wood. The road and wall completely enclosed that part of the Wood, and curved at the ends to terminate against sheer drop-offs into the larger forest. Pairs of guardsmen were stationed at intervals along the drive in small, elevated guardhouses overlooking the wall. At least two wizards were on stand-by duty, probably in a tavern somewhere. It had been some months now since a troll had lumbered out of the Woods, so the watch was currently enjoying the more relaxed mode that characterises such routine duties.

Even so, anything bigger than a mouse would be seen, intercepted and sent back to town with 'a flea in both ears' if there was the even vaguest hint of the intention to go over that wall.

Gnomes are bigger than mice by a long shot. Gnomes are also more resourceful. And they usually have money. This one certainly was, and did.

If it had been evening, Feuery would have been able to slip through the shadows. As it was a bright, hot morning, she slipped into the nearest inn: the Delver's Rest, proprietor 'Winkle' Kherimen.

'Hi fellas', she called as she returned to the nearest guardhouse with two mugs of foaming weak ale. 'I was on my way to the library an' thought you might like a li'l refreshment!'

Strictly against orders, of course – but hey, this was Feuery. Everyone knew and liked Feuery, including their mothers and partners and senior officers. She was just incredibly likeable. Everyone knew she was prone to random acts of kindness such as this. Of course, they happily accepted her offer.

'Oh! Almos' forgot. A warm cheese loaf for you too. Careful how you cut it or it will get over everything. Sorry can't stay an' chat, but I'll be late to the Library if I don't hurry. Make sure you return the mugs please. Ol' Winkle'll be angry otherwise!'

A swift look around to make sure no one was watching, and with a cheery wave she left the two of them to wrestle with the sticky cheese loaf. She ducked under the supports of the guardhouse and nipped over the wall while they argued good-naturedly as to who would tackle her gift.

Travelling through the Wild Wood in daylight was usually a lot safer than at night, but Feuery still took care as she followed the previous night's path back to the garden. In the bright daylight, the garden looked the same as she had last seen it in the moonlight.

Or was it? She mentally kicked herself. Of course it wasn't! There were now only four trees present whereas last night there had been five. The one in the middle had vanished without a trace.

Cautiously, she crossed the lawn, pausing for a moment as a distant hooting silenced the Wood. She pressed on as whatever it was fell silent.

There was now a slight mound of rich brown soil where the tree had previously stood, from which tiny green shoots were just emerging.

At about twenty yards from the mound, she began to feel distinctly uneasy; a sense of foreboding that weighed heavily on her as she slowly moved forward.

At ten yards, she was sweating with fear and felt faint and nauseous. Since it was impossible to go on, she retreated with dignity, with every step gamely fighting the urge to turn and run helter-skelter for the shelter of the forest.

Her terror gradually eased as the pounding of her heart and the butterflies in her stomach settled. She contemplated the garden, the trees and the mound from the edge of the Wood.

So, she thought, *you're a mage of some sort also. That's a damn powerful revulsion spell.* She returned to Shanchester, easily slipping over the wall unnoticed under a guard tower. She then casually sauntered along the road to the Wizards' Guild library, where she spent an interesting afternoon in the closed records section. The Guild would have had a fit if they'd known she was there.

The Lady in Green appeared neither that night, nor the next two, so Feuery didn't venture into the Wood. She continued her research in various Guild libraries and records rooms – occasionally with permission.

On the third day after her visit to the Woods, however, she noticed preparations around its boundary. A new Town Councillor was demanding decisive action against the 'night-stalking terrors of the Wood that so imperil our dear children'. The Mayor and Senior Wizard had agreed that an early Cleansing would be the easiest way to satisfy most of the good citizens of Shanchester. And so it was to be held that night, for the Cleansing was most effective at night when the various creatures left their lairs in the ruins and went hunting.

Sipping her tea while sitting in a secluded booth in an almost empty café, Feuery shuddered at the thought of what the Wood would be like tonight. She hoped the Lady would not choose tonight to make one of her sallies into it as there was no way that Feuery would be willing to follow her through a Cleansing. There would be chaos in the Wood.

She sat deep in thought. The café was one of the few places where she felt really at ease. The proprietor, Raphen, a fellow gnome, was a retired, successful adventurer who had had the good sense to take up a less dangerous vocation as soon as he was comfortably placed in life. He recognised in Feuery a kindred spirit and treated her like a favoured niece. Here at least she felt safe to relax with her thoughts rather than always keeping one eye open for danger.

She thought she knew who the Lady in Green might be (improbable though it seemed), but what was her connection with the garden? How had she simply vanished so completely last time? And what of the mound with the green shoots where a great, mature tree had previously stood? She frowned. She felt so close to knowing the answers, but a key piece of the puzzle was obviously missing. Still, it was relaxing to be sitting in the café, and she began to feel comfortably drowsy.

* * * *

The Lady in Green seated herself opposite Feuery, gazing at her with big, green eyes flecked with gold.

Feuery almost swallowed her tonsils, and spilt her tea.

'Good afternoon to you, little nuisance,' the Lady said quietly, holding Feuery's gaze. Green eyes met blue, and neither wavered. After a moment the Lady smiled, and turned to call to Raphen. 'Please bring us two teas. Whatever our friend here is having', before turning back to Feuery.

'Is there any particular reason you've been following me?' she asked in a friendly tone, 'or are you simply a nosey busybody?'

Feuery contemplated her. The Lady was almost impossibly slender, although only a little taller than an average human woman. She had dark brown hair with more than a suggestion of green highlights and beautiful features – again, with a slight green tint to her flawless skin. Her voice was soft but firm, and, despite her vexatious words, Feuery sensed more that was inquisitive than antagonistic in her voice and posture. But a strange tension was just discernible in her.

'I'm not *simply* a nosey busybody,' Feuery replied evenly, as Raphen brought their teas. 'I'm an *expert* busybody. Knowing what other people don't bother to think 'bout is often interesting an' can lead to unusual opportunities.'

The Lady laughed softly. 'I thought as much, and so it may be now. How much have you discovered about me?'

Feuery considered the Lady's question. Although it didn't happen often, it was always a little embarrassing when someone she was snooping on quizzed her before she was ready.

'You're a wealthy an' respected lady of Shanchester listed on the town rolls as Avilera, but more commonly called the Lady in Green by the townsfolk. Or mostly they just call you the Lady, as if you are the only one in Shanchester. Maybe you are. I know you're a mage of some sort, but there's no record of any of those names with the Wizards' Guild. The Thieves and Assassins' Guilds have declared you strictly off-limits, but there's no record of why. And strangely, no one else seems to know about your visits to the Wild Wood. Always at night, but sometimes you'll be there for a coupla days.'

'Please continue. I am interested in finding out what you make of this.'

Feuery drew a deep breath and gripped her staff under the table so she'd be ready if things turned nasty. She was far from being a devotee of the truth, but there were times when it could be useful.

'I'm fairly sure you're Alivelia fan Yryss: Sorceress of the estate once known as Shanivelia, the ruins of which now lie buried in the Wild Wood. If you are, then you must have survived not only the destruction of the estate during the Mage Wars, but also the devastation afterwards. I sorta hope you're not undead', she added, very sincerely. 'But if you're not, I don't know how you can be at least 900 years old.'

The Lady's eyes had a far-away look. 'I've not heard those names from another living soul for so long,' she murmured, seeing long-gone sights that were hers alone in her mind's eye.

She snapped back to the present. 'How did you find out about me?'

Guess I got it right, Feuery thought. *Now there's just the little detail of the undead bit. An' whatever her personal views were regarding nosey busybodies. Is the reason that there are no undead in the Wild Wood because it's the territory for one very powerful undead – The Lady?* she wondered.

'I pieced it together from hints here an' there,' she said. 'I'm good at that.'

'Very good indeed! Is your battle magic as good?'

Here we go, Feuery thought as she gripped her staff and brought a powerful protective spell to mind.

The Lady, Avilera, Alivelia fan Yryss laughed. 'Relax! You needn't fear me. Not yet, at least. You're mostly correct, but Shanivelia was more than an estate. It was the town I built and loved. We held out for the first half of the Mage Wars, but it eventually fell, and I fled. When the focus of the Wars shifted, I returned to begin anew, building the town mainly under-ground – the so-called 'crypts' under the Wood today. But as you rightly surmise, the Wars returned and again I had to flee in defeat. I knew then that I needed a different way to survive the Wars and the chaos I knew would follow.'

'You're not a lich?' Feuery asked hopefully.

'Bless you, no! I abhor the undead. I won't tolerate them in my Wood. The Mages who warred against me favoured their foul kind. Some preferred them by inclination; some of necessity once their ambition had caused their living armies to be destroyed.'

My Wood, Feuery reflected. 'So, there're stories …'

'Of timeless Mages, yes. There are so many stories one would think there must be some truth to be found in the tales.

If so, the spells must be so complex that few succeed, else the world would be made up of mages.'

'But you …'

'There's more than one way to live past your allocated span and cheat the Spinners of Fate. Some great mages walked to death on what they thought were their own terms, and became liches. Some perhaps mastered some great spell, 'though the risks must have been high. And others find another way. As have I. Each choice has its own price. For the young, much of the world is free. For the elderly, each step or breath taken may seem to have too high a price. Longevity, let alone immortality, comes at a very high price indeed. Remember that, little gnome as you search through the mysteries of the world. Make sure you know the price before you seize an opportunity.

'And having said that, I wish to offer you an opportunity to earn my gratitude, and much more. Tonight there will be a Cleansing. I have … something very dear to me in the Wood. At worst, that something may attract the death spells. But at best, it is at grave risk from creatures fleeing willy-nilly in the Wood as *they* seek to avoid the spells.'

The Lady drew a deep breath, and Feuery was astonished to see a deeply troubled and worried woman. 'I didn't think there'd be a Cleansing so soon. I can't go into the Wood tonight myself without exposing my relationship to it, and then neither I nor the Wood are safe. But in the Wood – in my beautiful garden – there is something so precious to me that I must go – unless someone else will act for me. Please it is much I ask of you, but will you go into the Wood and bring out my greatest treasures from the garden?'

Now, although Feuery was mercenary and calculating, there was an undertone in the Lady's plea that moved her deeply. Even so, she automatically asked, 'What treasures?'

'Valueless to you, or anyone else other than me. However, I will risk everything if I must. But then, even if I succeed, I will have to flee – again.'

'You do understand how dangerous what you ask is?'

'I do.'

Feuery thought fast.

'I take your word that it will be worth my while.' *You can promise me anything anyway,* she thought. *How could I make good a false promise by an Arch-sorceress?* 'But if I'm going to do it, I need to go now, afore the spelling begins. Do you have a long cloak?'

* * * *

Half an hour later, the Lady in Green stood at the wall gazing across the Wild Wood. Behind her, the full Town Guard and all of the wizards were assembling.

The Lady glanced backwards as footsteps approached her from behind. She saw it was Huanthal, the Senior Wizard of the local Guild.

'My Lady, I must ask with all respect that you clear the area. We are about to Cleanse the Wood, and a spell sometimes goes astray, even with our best care. Besides, the sights you may see can be quite distressing.'

She smiled slightly to him. 'I know, old friend. The Wood looks so peaceful just now. I wish this weren't necessary.'

'But we all know it is. Please come away now.'

'Of course.' As The Lady turned to go, she spread her arms and the cloak wide as if to adjust the fit. Feuery nipped over the wall lithely from under the cloak.

'May fortune go with you, for both our sakes,' murmured the Lady as she turned back to the town, where many of the folk were gathering to watch the Cleansing as dusk settled.

* * * *

Feuery hit the ground running. If she was lucky, she might get to the garden before the Cleansing began, and only have to run the gauntlet of the seeking-death spells on her return. Assuming, of course, that she was able to find this treasure – or treasures. The Lady tended to use both terms.

The Lady in Green hadn't told Feuery what it – or they – was or were. Instead, she had given her a small basket with a thin layer of soil in the bottom, on which was placed a sprig of the dark green, gleaming leaves of the trees in the garden. Her instructions had been to go to the small mound of earth where the tree had been, to place the opened basket beside it and to leave it for at least thirty seconds. Feuery was then to close the basket without looking into it, and return immediately.

When Feuery had asked about the aversion spell around the mound, the Lady had given her another sprig of the same leaves to wear in order to counteract the spell. She had then refused to give further information. Rather, she told Feuery that she knew all that was necessary, and that she should simply concentrate on her assignment.

Feuery hated secrets she wasn't in on, and resolved to make sure she discovered everything on her return, Arch-sorceress or not. That was, of course, assuming she did actually return …

* * * *

Altogether Feuery estimated she would have to venture about a mile to the garden, although it would be a little further through the twisted gullies and thick forest. An easy enough feat in a town, but the dangers of the Wood were as challenging as they had been during her last expedition. A nasty wind was blowing up as well. Glancing up, she saw the sky was darkening with thick clouds swirling angrily above the Wood.

Not a storm on top of everything else, she grumbled to herself. It would make a bad situation much worse.

The storm was brewing with unnatural speed and ferocity. Feuery looked up grimly at the sullen clouds, within which lightning was beginning to flicker.

Too compact, too fast – that's a magically-summoned storm. Then the purpose of the storm suddenly occurred to her. While the natural creatures would seek shelter from the storm, most of the Children of the Dark would revel in it and eagerly set out hunting, making them ready targets for the death spells. The wind and rain would also ensure there was little warning before the spells latched onto their victims.

And she would be right there in the middle of it.

The first raindrops – big, fat and cold – began to fall as she ran down the faint path. There was a rushing, tearing sound of the rain on the leaves, and the deluge then hit with a roar. The forest was plunged into darkness, sporadically lit nightmarishly with crackling lightning.

Within seconds, Feuery was soaked. Gnomes are naturally good at seeing in the dark. Nevertheless, she cast a night vision spell, while blessing her sure-footedness on the now slippery ground. She paused. Something was ahead of her.

A bristle-furred, dark figure about the size of a small, wiry human pushed aside the foliage to step onto the trail. Pale eyes, glistening teeth like those of a shark and long talons gleamed in a flash of lightning.

Another appeared beside the first one.

Gaunts! Feuery felt sick. Vicious predators that hunted in small packs and which were notorious for feeding on their victims as soon as they'd grasped them.

She turned and ran back along the trail, hearing them grunting and splashing through the puddles behind her. She knew she couldn't outrun them. She found what she'd noticed on her path earlier – a tree trunk that had toppled across a deep gully over a stream. Here they would only be able to come at her from one direction, and so she could cast one of her spells on them.

She ran lightly across the slippery log, stopping to turn about two-thirds of the way across. As she did, the first gaunt leaped onto the trunk. It caught a fireball full on, shrieked, and ran smouldering back to the others and on into the Wood.

The rest of the pack – about seven gaunts – barely hesitated. Two clambered onto the log and prepared to rush at Feuery. Darn! She had enough energy left for one major and two more minor spells. But, if they came at her piecemeal …

Out of the corner of her eye, Feuery caught a colourful flash of light upstream. Glancing at it while warily watching the gaunts, her heart skipped a beat.

Three seeking-death spells were coming down along the stream at eye level. If she hadn't recognised them for what they were, they would have looked beautiful: globes like ball lightning sparkling in shades of green, purple and orange.

Feuery leapt off the log into the stream, aiming for a widening that seemed to indicate a pool.

It did, but the pool wasn't very deep. Her boots hit the bottom as she plummeted in, but it was deep enough to take the force of the fall, and to submerge her by about three feet.

Stay down, she thought, frantically holding her breath. It wouldn't do to pop up to encounter one of the death spells.

Through the bubbles of her dive, a luminous feminine face appeared before her.

'Breathe little gnome. I grant you this boon so that we may talk.' The rusalki's voice was silken soft.

With little other alternative, Feuery tried a small breath – and took in air. She wasn't buoyed up either. Her boots rested easily on the stream bed, and the basket, glowing faintly, hung naturally at her side as if she still stood on the trail. She regarded the rusalki. She realised she had absolutely no spell that would help her in this situation.

47

The rusalki was like an attractive girl who was just blossoming to womanhood. Her long, pale hair and clothing swirled from her head and body to merge with the surrounding water. Her movements were smooth and graceful – fluid. The watery ghosts of women drowned by false lovers bound eternally to streams and pools, rusalki were supernaturally strong and vindictive towards the living – especially males.

Feuery took it as a hopeful sign that the apparition was smiling.

'If you had been a male of any kindred, I would have made sure you were in the deepest pool of this stream now. I have no special grievance against any sister though.'

'How come I'm breathing here?' Feuery asked.

The rusalki shrugged dismissively. 'This is my element. But that is what I want to speak to you about. Are you a servant of the Lady? You carry her favour,' she gestured to the sprig of leaves Feuery had pinned to the front of her tunic.

'We're friends,' Feuery replied, stretching the truth a little. 'She asked me to do sum'it for her.'

'Which is why you are here tonight of all nights. I suspect that she has asked you to collect something for her from her garden?'

'Yes, but how'd you know that? An' do you know what it is?'

'Just a few nights ago many of us felt happy for the Lady. For she had achieved something she had long desired, and for that we were pleased. Even a being such as I, whom she would banish or destroy if she knew I was here.'

'Oh. 'Cos you're undead?'

'Yes, since you put it so bluntly. My element lies within her element, and she is far more powerful than me. I too would like her friendship, or at least her knowing tolerance. I will help you achieve your mission toward that.'

'I can't make any promises for her. You must know that.'

'I know, but in truth I would assist in this matter in any case given the circumstances. I must trust you to be discrete and to tell her about me only if it seems likely to be favourable. I think it will be if you succeed, for you and for any who helped you. Obviously she trusts you, otherwise she would have come herself to rescue her treasure.'

'You haven't told me what it is,' Feuery pointed out. 'Yet,' she added hopefully.

'The most valuable thing of all to her and to anyone in her position. If she chose not to tell you, she had a good reason. Now, do you want my help?'

I'm three foot underwater and in the company of a powerful ghost with a reputation for being extremely malicious, who wants to help me to help her. How can the answer be anything but 'Yes'?

'Yes. We have a deal. You help me help the Lady, an' I'll do my best to represent you.'

The rusalki flowed closer. 'More than that; it is to be part of your reward from her.'

'Ok. You want her to accept your place here in this Wood 'gainst her intolerance of undead. I can't be responsible for any conditions she might put on it though.'

'Fair enough. Now, crouch down and close your eyes. When I say 'now' you may stand and continue on with your mission. Return when you have achieved it, and I will take you and your prize to a place outside the Wood from where you will be able to walk into town unobserved.'

Feeling very exposed, Feuery crouched. She mustered all her resources. If this thing played foul, the last thing Feuery did would be to make this pool boil with a fire spell.

'Now!' exclaimed the rusalki.

Feuery stood. She was waist deep in the pool facing the four trees and mound of soil. The waterfall thundered behind her, swollen by the rain, and the trees writhed in the gale-force winds of the storm. As she watched, a bolt of lightning accompanied by a terrifying, deafening crackling speared at the trees, but was deflected away into the Wood.

She ran to the mound, placing the opened basket beside it. She counted time, willing herself to look away.

A huge rock-troll blundered into the clearing, two death spells fastened to its hide. It bellowed; tearing at them and extinguishing one before crashing once more into the forest leaving a trail of shattered trees and bushes behind it.

Feuery willed herself to wait a few seconds longer, and then closed the basket. There was a faint rustling from it.

Could she trust the rusalki? Or would she just be delivering herself and the Lady's treasure into its power? As she pondered over this dilemma, a death spell appeared at the edge of the Wood and drifted toward her, followed by two others.

Decision made. She ran and leapt into the pool again.

'Well done. Now close your eyes again. I will take you to safety.'

'Wait! What's your name? The Lady will wanna know. I sure do.'

The rusalki appraised her. 'You were willing to trust me', she said thoughtfully. 'I'll trust you not to magic my name against me. I was Elphoria.'

'I'm …'

'Feuery. I know. I hear some things from the Town.'

Feuery closed her eyes. There was a feeling of movement around her and the water felt even colder.

'Now, Shanchester is over to your right through the woods. You should be able to climb up the bank safely. Please don't fall back in, as I'm not sure I can control my urge for warm blood again.'

Not much of that in me at the moment, Feuery reflected.

She stood and clambered up the slippery bank, grasping at any root or twig she could. At the top, she turned to look back into the stream. The rusalki half-surfaced, appearing as a young woman.

'Don't forget our agreement,' Elphoria warned before submerging again.

* * * *

Here in the forest on the southern outskirts of Shanchester, the rain was only a light drizzle, but the storm still raged over the Wild Wood. Feuery knew it would continue until dawn, as would the steady stream of death spells.

Soaking wet, frozen and near exhaustion, she hurried through the woodland toward the lights of Shanchester. Almost there, at the edge of the forest, she tripped on a stone and fell heavily. Her staff went one way, the basket another. Dazed and gasping for breath, she seized her staff and limped to the basket.

The rustling inside it seemed agitated. As she approached to find out what was going on, something inside the basket lifted the lid gently and looked up at her.

She stared at a little face like the bud of a flower, with big, clear eyes that transformed into the colour of her own as they gazed at each other.

* * * *

Raphen's café had been doing a roaring trade all night, catering to the many spectators of the Cleansing and offering early breakfasts to the more hardy stayers.

Now Raphen was keen to close up for a little while and get some sleep. That was until a barely recognisable and only semi-conscious Feuery knocked on his back door.

He dried her with a towel as best he could, and insisted she sit in front of the oven in the kitchen, well wrapped in a warm if tatty old blanket. There had been an argument about boots and socks – but Feuery was tired, and had to admit the warmth of the oven on her bare feet did feel wonderful. The brandy in warmed milk helped too. However, through it all she refused to let the basket leave her side, even though she put her staff down – albeit within easy reach.

Odd, Raphen thought, *the basket is the only dry thing she has*. But Raphen was an adventurer too, and knew when to let events run their course.

And run their course they did. There was another knock on the door. He took one look at the Lady standing in the alley and ushered her into the kitchen.

She rushed straight to the basket. She opened it, and nine little figures like tiny saplings climbed out and swarmed across her arms. Eight of them gained wide green eyes and went the vivid green and brown of a forest in springtime as he watched. One already had blue eyes and foliage the russet tones of autumn.

Raphen was surprised to see that although she was smiling, the Lady was also crying softly. He was at a complete loss as to what to do. He felt like an intruder in his own kitchen.

After a moment, the Lady stood, wiping her eyes as best she could while holding the Twiglings. She went to Feuery sitting by the kitchen oven.

Feuery looked up at her. 'Belated congratulations,' she managed to croak hoarsely.

The Lady reached out her hand and touched Feuery, drying her clothing and removing her chill.

'Sleep now,' she said gently. 'And thank you so much more than I can say.'

Feuery nodded, and fell into a deep sleep.

* * * *

'You owe me an explanation', Raphen pointed out.

They were sharing an early morning tea before the café opened. It was the second day after the Cleansing, which the townsfolk generally agreed had been a great success. Best in living memory, in fact.

'Guess I do,' Feuery conceded. 'It's just hard for me to know where to start.'

'I've delved into some of those ruins,' Raphen said. 'That's how I got lucky and bought this place. I know it's a buried town, not a necropolis. Start there.'

Feuery sipped her tea. 'It was the second town the Lady built. Both of them were overrun during the Mage Wars.'

'She was directly involved in them? But that was centuries ago!'

'I don't think she wanted to be. However, some of the warring mages thought that anyone not with them would be 'gainst them, sooner or later, an' made their fears true.'

'But that was centuries ago!' he repeated.

'Do you want me to tell you 'bout it? It's gonna take a lot longer this way.'

Raphen grumbled, but let her continue.

'Anyways, after the second defeat, she retreated into the forests. They were still hunting for her an', after she decided she couldn't resist them as things were, she – changed. Not sure what the magic she used was, but she became a dryad. They barely age with time. But the magic was still in her, so she remained a powerful sorceress. After a time, she returned to the ruins, an' fostered a great forest to grow – what we know now as the Wild Wood. Outside the forest, she's still a sorceress in human form, but inside it she is the Queen of the Wood, with vast power. But she can't venture far from it. It's now the centre of her power, an' more than a few leagues away from it, her power is almost non-existent. She's at her most powerful in her garden when she alters her form to a tree. That's why I couldn't find her when I followed her. I didn't recognise her in that form.'

Feuery drained her cup and gazed into it thoughtfully. 'Feel like another? I do. No, stay! Let me get it for a change.'

She disappeared into the kitchen, pottered for several minutes and returned with a tray. 'Made us each a pot', she said. 'By the way, the re-furbished kitchen looks nice.'

'Yes, thanks to you. That was very generous.'

'You're welcome. Least I could do for you after spending time convalescing in it. Where was I? Oh yes. After the Wars an' the Troubled Times that followed, word got around that there were rich ruins here. Many parties of adventurers went into the ruins, an' over time someone built an inn for them, then shops followed, farmers settled around an' Shanchester developed. That suited the Lady – leastways her human side – an' eventually she had her own home built here as the town matured.'

'Are you telling me my café is bought from her old treasure?' Raphen interrupted.

'Probably not. Lot of rich folk settled in her towns. She doesn't particularly care about the treasure in the Wood. Nor 'bout the creatures in it much – excepting maybe a certain rusalki she's now indebted to. But she does care greatly about the Wild Wood.'

'So what were those things you brought back? Nice tea by the way.'

'Thank you.'

'Tea's always nicer when someone else makes it.'

'I'm sure that one will be,' Feuery replied.

'It does have a slightly unusual flavour; quite pleasant really.'

'Special, secret spice. They're her Twiglings – baby dryads. Something she's been wanting for a very long time. She'll raise them here, an' then find each of them a territory of their own when they're old 'nough. Some of them – maybe all of them

– will possess magic, maybe even wizardess-class magic. The woods they settle in will be well protected.'

She finished her cup. 'I'm keeping you from opening the café, an' really must be getting on. We can talk more later.'

But we won't, she thought as she left the café. *Not after that potion I put in your tea. Now you'll be satisfied you know all about the affair, but just won't recall any of the details – or want to.*

She felt a little guilty about tricking Raphen, but it was for the best. The Lady had shown her how to mix the forget-potion, mentioning she had intended to give it to Feuery – before circumstances changed.

But she couldn't possibly do that now; not to her Twiglings' Good-mother. Especially considering the bright, blue-eyed, inquisitive little one whose foliage was the colours of autumn. Twiglings pattern themselves on the first person they take a liking to after germination and so she was the very image of Feuery.

The Enchanted Fleet

A frigate, billowing sails set full, scarlet and gold pennants fluttering gloriously in the gentle breeze, slid smoothly past a cluster of cutters before executing an elegant pirouette around a great ship-of-the-line and passing under a brigantine. A massive cargo hulk, the converted shell of a once fearsome flagship, lumbered through the twisting, gyrating vessels while two ketches sped over it as if anxious to challenge a wisp of cloud that had strayed in amongst the fleet like a genial, slightly bemused drunk wandering onto a dance floor.

Feuery lay in the warm sunshine on the park lawn overlooking the harbour, comfortably watching the spectacle of the Enchanted Warfleet of Infathow above her. To any onlooker, she seemed to be idly enjoying the constant ballet of the warships – as did many visitors to Infathow.

In fact, her enjoyment was anything but idle. She'd just worked out the complex pattern associated with the seemingly random movements of the vessels.

She felt quite chuffed about that. She'd satisfied herself that the popular opinion that the fleet's movements were random was wrong – and Feuery loved to know things other people didn't. Moreover, she'd discovered that the pattern of the sky-bound vessels – while intricate – was the result of a spell of true aesthetic beauty.

Of course, what made her happiest of all was that her plan to plunder the fleet was now feasible. Understanding the pattern was essential, which was probably the reason why, to this point, no one had succeeded in plundering the war chests and valuables idly floating around up there.

Good ol' Ivarn, she thought indulgently. *It's nice when someone does you a favour.*

* * * *

Ivarn of the 3 Rs (as he was known among the Great Mages) had played a prominent part in the Mage Wars; however, his role had been protectively defensive. Early on in the Wars, he had allied himself with the Fair Elves and made it widely known that his formidable magic would be used in combination with the Elves' on anybody who sought to bring strife to that realm.

He'd made good on that promise too – several times. As a result of Ivarn's mastery, the Mage Wars never came into the lands of the Fair Elves.

Ivarn had also established a number of sanctuary areas, and was a leading figure in the formation of the Wizards' Guild after the Wars. The Guild had two purposes: to salvage what learning could be saved following the Wars and their terrible aftermath, and to seek to ensure Mages did not war among themselves ever again. He had moved from the war-ravaged north to the relative isolation of the idyllic Jemamia Islands, where the inhabitants were known for their black skin, white hair, delicate features and peaceful disposition.

There, he made it known that he intended to play no further part in the affairs of the world.

Three hundred years later most of the world had all but forgotten Ivarn, other than as a distant memory from 'the Olden Days'. Perhaps this oversight was a factor in the decision of the expansionist Empire of Infathow to invade and annex the Jemamia Islands. Certainly, the fleet they'd assembled was impressive – far more than was needed to conquer a group of people who relied on local militia to deal with the occasional pirate vessel. Conquering the Jemamians was clearly only the start of the Empire's plans.

The Emperor and all his court had gathered at the harbour of Infathow to view the sailing of the Great Warfleet. Also present were numerous representatives from other powerful lands who had been invited to witness the might of Infathow as the fleet was blessed, given its Imperial instructions and majestically set sail.

No one had thought to invite Ivarn, or indeed, anyone else from the Jemamia Islands. However, he'd decided to attend the ceremony anyway.

As the Empire's fleet sailed from the harbour it unexpectedly lifted from the sea, circled around at a height of about two hundred feet, and then sailed back over to the port. Here it stopped and dropped to twenty feet above the waves while the Emperor, his court, the invited dignitaries and the good citizens of the Empire of Infathow stared in amazement and disbelief. Likewise, the fleet's crew were more than a little emotional by then.

One thunderous word echoed across the harbour: 'OUT!' To emphasise this suggestion, the ships began to shake and shiver as if caught in an earthquake. Officers, sailors, marines and the garrison and civil administrators intended for the Islands were quick to comply, leaping from the ships until the harbour seemed full of bobbing heads.

Once Ivarn was satisfied all those willing to leave had, the entire fleet soared up to two thousand feet above the harbour and began the stately dance it had performed ever since. Not satisfied with merely rendering the fleet impotent militarily, Ivarn had placed a preserving spell on it, sealing it from intrusion, and serving as a perpetual reminder to any others of similar belligerence. Then he returned to enjoy his retirement in the Jemamia Islands.

The Empire soon collapsed. A Protectorate comprising the Guilds and representatives of the citizens – similar to that of most other cities – took its place. The new Protectorate was manifestly pacifistic.

* * * *

Feuery had let it be known she was in Infathow convalescing from an illness. That wasn't unusual as many visitors came to enjoy the prosperous port-city's benign climate and easy-going lifestyle. It explained her long 'dozing' in the sun, and was, in a manner of speaking, absolutely true. From birth, Feuery had been afflicted with abundant curiosity and a strong streak of avarice; the best treatment for both she'd decided was to indulge them to the fullest extent possible.

However, her new acquaintances worried about the captivating little red-haired, blue-eyed gnome in her customary tunic and skirted trousers of royal blue.

'Feuery, child,' her landlady cornered her in the stairwell one morning as Feuery thought she was slipping in unobserved. 'We bin fretting for you. You sech a lovely person, yet you've no boyfriends. All hours you bin studying books and making with the calculations. None of our business, but we bin fretting for what you missing, you being young and sech a pretty being.'

Feuery refrained from agreeing it was, indeed, none of their darn business. She liked her landlady – a half-gnome with a heart of gold and no discernible malice.

'Please don't worry, Mrs Gubbons. I *am* very busy,' Feuery remarked leaning closer and lowering her voice conspiratorially. 'Wizard's business, you know. I'm quite enjoying myself really. I'm trying to calculate how a random variable can be inserted into a complex pattern without disrupting that pattern, and what the parameters of that random variable need to be. It really is quite fascinating. I must show you the math!'

'Ah, well, um. That be nice, I'm sure. The folks here be glad to hearing you enjoying yours-self.'

Such conversations tended not to go very far. Feuery continued her calculations, and read everything she could find about Ivarn in the public libraries (and a lot of private collections as well, although the owners didn't usually know about that). Eventually folk decided, as so many folk before them had, that Feuery was to be accepted as she was.

Anyway, Feuery always seemed more or less contented, and if there were times when she was moody – well, she was convalescing, wasn't she? You had to expect that she'd have her ups and downs.

In fact, Feuery's occasional moodiness was mainly due to the fact she was steadily running out of money. She was managing her finances (and she'd started from a considerable personal fortune), but her expenses – maybe speculative investments would be a better term – were high.

For a long time she'd wanted to own a magic carpet but, like many of us who yearn for something, had dithered over actually getting around to buying that deeply desired item: Is it *really* what I need? Is *that* one more suitable? Maybe something at a better price would be preferable? Does this one *feel* right?

Now she needed not one, but two magic carpets (well, sort of) and was having to pay a high price for them.

Magic carpets are always expensive and Feuery needed one made to her precise specifications, and a second that exactly mirrored the first in all but one key respect. With her dubious standing within the Wizards' Guild, she couldn't just order a carpet from the small circle of mages who specialised in weaving and spelling them. Instead, she had to go through credible intermediaries, each of whom added more than a 'little something extra' onto the price. Added a *lot* more actually. What was more, the first carpet then had to be delivered surreptitiously to those she'd arranged to make and enchant the second one. Both the smugglers and *those* little buggers *really* knew how to gouge.

But eventually the two flying carpets were delivered. In privacy – and she knew all the tricks to ensure her privacy from long experience snooping into that of others – she inspected them.

They were perfect. They were woven in shades of blue-grey – darker above, lighter below – with an erratic pattern that suggested camouflage (because it was). The first carpet was just big enough for her and, should the need arise, one other person. The second one: she held up a fine film of cellophane to the light. By looking carefully, she could just make out the second magic carpet. It matched the first one perfectly. The Fairy-folk at Heliovorn – a community of the exiled and self-exiled from Faerie with whom Feuery kept close links – had done a fine job.

Should have for the price, she grumbled to herself, but she was very pleased to have her carpets at last.

And just in time. She spilled out the remaining contents of her purse: a gold sovereign, four silver reals and a couple of triangular copper bits.

She sighed. At least nearly everything had been paid for this expedition, but she'd have to sell most of her remaining jewels for travelling expenses. She brightened. There was always a good profit to be made from gems, and she enjoyed the haggling. You had to take life's little pleasures where you found them.

* * * *

No one was surprised when she bought a ticket for the voyage to the Jemamia Islands. The islands were renowned for their healthy climate and the herbal treatments of their druids.

Foreigners, however, were usually only permitted to visit the main city of Kasali.

That was fine by Feuery. She was quite happy to abide by any law that didn't try to stop her doing what she wanted. Since she hadn't even reached Kasali yet, she was quite willing to respect this decree at least until she arrived there. Later was later, and who knew what the future held?

* * * *

The voyage on the Jemamian sambuk that regularly plied between the Islands and the mainland ports was delightful. The *Blue Roebuck* was a beautifully seaworthy vessel, handled by an experienced and friendly crew. The trip was also blessed with perfect seas and weather.

By the time they docked at Kasali, Feuery had invitations to stay with the families of most of the crew and assurances that if she ever wanted to see the outer islands, that could be arranged as well.

While accommodation wasn't a problem, sharing her time became difficult. There was something about the little gnome that appealed greatly to the Jemamians and her circle of new friends grew daily. Every available moment of every day involved a friendly, guided tour of the many notable features of Kasali and long evenings spent at parties and functions organised, it seemed, mainly to show her off.

Not that she minded terribly. They were a nice folk, and all the attention was most enjoyable. But she unexpectedly discovered a dark side to the Jemamians also. On a sandspit in one of the harbour bays she'd noticed long rows of fixed stakes. Thinking they were probably a fishing device, she'd casually enquired about them. However, she's been surprised to hear that the answer was 'that's where we tie up pirates and raiders; they come from the sea and go back to the sea'.

Within Jemamia, crime simply wasn't tolerated. Even relatively minor crimes, such as theft or cheating, could earn a public lashing. Repeated wrong-doing or major crimes such as murder or abuse of cultural relics resulted in a choice: death or perpetual exile. Of course, since exile meant little to foreigners, they had only the one option. Feuery took quiet but careful note …

One place she was shown frequently, and didn't mind at all how often she went, was the Exposium – a magnificent white-marble museum. It was like no other museum she'd ever seen – not even the justifiably famous Guild Museums of Heliovorn. The Exposium housed the long, proud history of the Jemamians from what was reputed to be one of the first vessels on which their ancestors had come to the islands three thousand years earlier, to fine examples of the wondrous crystalware they had begun to produce only twenty years ago.

But in pride of place in a courtyard in the middle of the museum stood a relatively recent display. It had been presented to the Jemamians by Ivarn himself – a miniature replica of the Enchanted Warfleet of Infathow, complete in every detail and mirroring the twining dancing of the original to perfection.

Well, it would, wouldn't it? It had to otherwise Ivarn's spell on the Enchanted Fleet wouldn't work.

Feuery showed her appreciation of the miniature warships display, but her attention invariably quickly turned to other exhibits. She didn't want anyone to notice her special interest in Ivarn's display, because it was the reason she'd come to Kasali in the first place and she had plans for it.

* * * *

After spending three weeks at Kasali, Feuery regretfully announced she'd have to leave for the northern port city of Sarfin the following week. She booked her passage on an elegant Sea Elf barque, the *Sea Swift*.

This sparked an even greater round of socialising until even Feuery began to look forward to some time alone. But timing was important.

Everything hinged on the evening two nights prior to her departure. The night before she left she was booked to attend a celebration of the First Arrivals at which the whole of the Jemamian Islands would be carousing most of the night. *Everywhere* would be full of life, fun and action so she'd find it difficult to get any time alone if she left what she had to do until the last night. There'd be too many eyes watching …

So, in the last hour or two before dawn on that second last night, a small figure with a bulky bundle across its back slipped easily through the Kasali streets; so quietly that even wary guard-dogs didn't notice. It made its way to the Exposium, entering through a side window with a faulty latch – something only an observant visitor might have noticed or an adroit visitor may have rendered faulty on an earlier visit.

At the miniature display of the Enchanted Fleet, the dark figure took the bundle from its back and rolled it out across the smooth white tiles before stepping gingerly onto it. The magic carpet rose toward (but not quite to the top of) the display and hovered beside it.

If anyone else had been present, they may have seen the dark figure carefully compare a stopwatch to a list of figures it held in its other hand.

They might even have heard a muffled swear word, and seen a frantic re-calculation occur just before the carpet was guided a little lower and several feet further to one side.

They'd probably have been mystified to hear a sharp intake of breath and then to observe a swift movement of a hand that seemed to deftly slip something into the display.

They'd certainly have been impressed to see the sudden flare of magical energies as two spells met and one merged with the other. At this point, the carpet then glided away, over the walls of the courtyard, and disappeared into the night. In its wake, it left the greatest possible abuse of the Jemamians' most respected and valued cultural relic.

* * * *

Of course, the Jemamians gave Feuery a spectacular farewell. She waved good-bye from the ship's railing until the ship turned around a headland. Then she went down to her cabin to sort through the many departure gifts she'd been given. It was a pity she would be able to only keep some of them. Even bottomless bags have a limit and she would need the storage capacity if the imminent fulfilment of her venture was successful.

* * * *

The *Sea Swift* lived up to its name. In the expert hands of the Sea Elves, it seemed to skim the crests of the waves, running smoothly to a following wind almost from the moment they left Kasali.

While on-board, Feuery lazed much of the time, enjoying the quiet reserve of the Sea Elves as a welcome break from the, well, admittedly wonderful time she'd had with the Jemamians.

But she kept a careful track of their course; regularly comparing her calculations to those of the First Mate, much to the latter's amusement.

When the time came for her to 'disembark' only a day or so into the voyage, she left a polite 'thank you' note in her cabin, explaining that she'd been unexpectedly summoned by the Wizards' Guild, and apologising for having to leave so abruptly. Then she furtively loaded all her gear topside onto the magic carpet, and slipped away in the darkness of a clear night.

She sped west-nor'-west just above the waves for half an hour until she was confident even the keen-eyed Sea Elf watch wouldn't be able to see her. The carpet rose to about a thousand feet above the sea, continuing its course. It was beautiful in the starlight, with only a gentle breeze ruffling her hair and clothes.

Nevertheless, she felt a little troubled. The carpet should have been responding to her commands better than it was. Now that she thought about it, the carpet *had* handled better on her previous flights.

She glanced back, and noticed a bundle behind her she couldn't recall previously loading. Carefully, she gave the bundle a tentative poke with her staff, as if prodding it would help to prod her memory.

'Oi! Easy! I'm not a sack of spuds you know,' the bundle protested.

Feuery very nearly sent a fireball loose that would have taken the back off the carpet and everything on it.

'Whatever you are, you'd better have a really darn-fine reason for being here. Come out slow-like, an' if I see a weapon I won't see it for long.'

'No need to be all jumpity. Ah – there's a problem. Um, can you restrain yourself while I pass out my staff?'

'Your staff?'

'Yep, that's what I said. It's just that I'll have to take it out to unwrap me, and I don't want you thinking I'm pointing it at you. You seem a bit edgy.'

'Your *staff*?'

'You ok there? It isn't as if having a staff is that unusual for a wizard …'

'You're a *wizard*?'

'That's hardly illegal is it? I mean, I don't know what the laws on magic carpets are, but I'd have thought they were a good place to find wizards.'

'They're a good place to find *one* wizard. That'll be this one over here, on this side of the battlestaff. The one who owns the carpet.'

'Ok, point made. Can I pass out my staff now?'

Two dainty hands emerged from the bundle holding out a slim staff about four feet long to Feuery.

'Ok. Drop it there an' let's see you.'

The staff was lowered to the carpet gently. The hands lifted the folds of the bundle revealing a tiny figure with a mass of tawny blonde hair tied back in a ponytail and a chubby little face with bright green eyes.

'You're a brownie! An' you're using an owls' eyes spell to see in the dark!' exclaimed Feuery.

'So are you! Well, the spell bit anyway,' replied the brownie.

'You're a brownie!'

'Is there an echo around here or do you always repeat yourself? Let's get this nailed down so we can move on. I'm a brownie. I'm a wizard and since we'll no doubt get to it eventually, I'm a girl as well. I'm Elusive.'

'I'm getting that. What's your name?'

'That's it – Elusive. It's what everyone called me at the Academy and it sort of stuck.'

'You studied at the Wizards' Academy? At High Waring?'

'Sure did. To second-level wizard. Then I decided it was time for me to see what the world has to offer. Quite interesting so far I might add.'

'I don't remember you.'

'It's a big place. I don't remember you either. There was a girl gnome a few years ahead of me, but she left under very mysterious ... Oh!' Her mouth made a little 'o' of surprise and her eyes widened. 'Are *you Feuery*?'

'Still am. What'd you hear 'bout me, back then?'

'Only that she – you – was very, very good, but had a falling out with the Wizards' Guild that no one wanted to talk about', Elusive said quickly with a desperate smile. 'Have you sorted things out with the Guild yet?'

68

'They haven't seen their way clear to falling back in with me yet, so no. That's all?'

'Well, there were stories among the students of course …'

'They'd probably be mostly true. That can wait. What do you think you're doing here? An' don't say chatting with me.'

'Um, can't think of a good way to say this …'

'Try. Anyways is fine so long as it's afore I get an uncontrollable urge to send a fireball your way. To the point would be best.'

'There's no need to be mean.' Elusive took a deep breath. 'I stole a consignment of gems from the *Sea Swift*. Getting away seemed like a good idea.'

Feuery's eyes narrowed. 'Show me! But no sudden movements.'

The brownie girl carefully took out a green velvet pouch, loosened the drawstrings and tipped the contents onto the carpet.

In spite of herself, Feuery whistled softly. A small fortune of cut and uncut jewels sparkled in the sunlight.

'Someone's not going to be very pleased with you. Nor me neither. They'll think we were in on this together. Sea Elves aren't very forgiving,' she said sharply.

'No, no. It wasn't from the Sea Elves. Darnoth (do you remember the tall, sour-faced human on the ship?) is a gem-trader. This lot is his recent purchases from the Jemamian mines. The Sea Elves weren't involved. I'll pay you a share for the carpet ride,' Elusive added quickly.

'Hmm. How'd you know I was leaving the ship?'

'I saw your interest in the navigation. Then, this morning you looked really pleased after you'd done your calculations. When I saw you collecting all your things last night, I stole the pouch from Darnoth's hiding place in his cabin, replaced it with a substitute which I'd spelled to look the same and waited for you.' She almost giggled. 'You were so busy keeping an eye on the ship's watch you didn't notice when I hopped on-board at the last moment.'

Feuery looked at her thoughtfully. If what Elusive said was true – and it probably mostly was given that the jewels were evidence – then this girl was good. If it wasn't, she still got points for a monumental fib. Either way, the fact that she'd watched her so attentively without Feuery noticing her was unnerving. That was the sort of thing Feuery did to other people.

'What were you going to do if I hadn't left?' Feuery asked the brownie.

'Taken a ship's boat,' said Elusive promptly. 'There was no way I could stay ship-board once I'd lifted the gems. But I hoped it wouldn't come to that. I'm allergic to exposure and shark-bite.'

'Umph. Now, 'bout this share for providing the get-away. 70–30?'

'Yes, that's sort of what I had in mind. But I'll bet we're thinking differently about who gets the 70 and who gets the 30.'

'My carpet. Lots of water.'

'My gems. Also lots of water.'

Feuery winced at the thought of the gems glittering as they fell all the way down to the sea below.

'Thing is, you being here isn't terribly convenient. There are other things I have to do, an' time is important.'

'So maybe I can help.'

'...?'

Feuery did a double-take. Maybe she could. Truth was, Feuery hadn't worked with others often, but that was mostly due to circumstance. Very few people could keep up with her. This confident brownie lass just might be able to.

Strange Feuery thought. *Last partner I had on a job was a brownie also – Ifraim – when I went looking for the tears of an undine. Nice enough, but not very capable. But then, he was a bard. They're not made very capable, usually.*

Generally speaking, brownies – humans usually called them halflings – and gnomes tended not to get along very well. However, Feuery wasn't big on tradition unless it suited her. She took people as they came since she figured that the differences between people didn't come close to the many more things they had in common.

'What sort of name is Elusive anyway?'

'Mine. What sort of name is Feuery?'

Feuery looked at the brownie thoughtfully. If she stood on tip-toes, her head would just about be level with Feuery's shoulder. She suddenly smiled. 'Ok, best offer you're going to get. I get forty per cent of the jewels. Magic carpets aren't cheap, take it from me who knows. But, if you like, you're welcome to join me on my venture. If you're any good and we succeed with a little number I've been working on for *ages*, you get a third of the profits. Note *profits,*' she said gesturing around. 'Everything you see here, near 'nough, is what I have left after setting this up. Mind you, the profits should be pretty good.'

Elusive considered quickly. 'Deal!'

'Ok. Now, here's the plan …'

* * * *

They came in toward the Enchanted Fleet with the rising sun in front of them. Feuery carefully slid the carpet high to one side of the great globe of twisting ships, a stopwatch in her hand, counting under her breath. Elusive watched, taking pains to do nothing to disturb Feuery's concentration.

'Now!' said Feuery suddenly to herself as she cast a short but complex spell and made Elusive jump nervously at the same time.

The magic carpet shot forward, and was now positioned within the maze of dancing warships.

Feuery turned to Elusive with a beaming smile.

'It worked! We're in! An' 'cos we're a random element the pattern can accommodate, we can go anywhere we like in here!'

'How about a nice fat treasure galleon then?' Elusive suggested while looking nervously at a warship which was bearing down – very literally – on them. 'Just to start with.'

'Personally I was thinking of the flagship', said Feuery. 'The really valuable treasure is more likely to be where the Admiral can put his hands on it. Very soothing, knowing where a big treasure you can put your hands on any time is. Sure to ease the burdens of high command.'

'I thought they had mistresses for that.'

'You just behave yourself! No call to cast aspersions on long-gone admirals. Anyways, probably no mistresses allowed on invasion fleets.'

'True! Might have cramped his style with the Jemamian ladies.'

'I tol' you to behave! One thing – we don't get to take much, so what we take has to be really worth it. Taking too much might make the pattern in here go wrong. Now, let me concentrate, 'cos we don't want to collide with anything. That'd be going wrong in a way we don't want neither.'

It took quite a time for Feuery to get the measure of gliding within the fleet. During this procedure, Elusive clung for all she was worth to whatever she could of the carpet and kept her eyes tightly closed.

'Got it!' Feuery eventually exclaimed with satisfaction. 'You ok there? Trying to dig through the carpet don't count toward your share, you know.'

Elusive looked up, her face pale even against her blonde hair. 'I'm fine. Absolutely fine. That bit where you just managed to slip us under the barge was a bit – confronting, is all.'

'Good! 'Cos you've got to get the hang of this too. No telling if there won't be call for you to fly the carpet. Don't get fancy ideas of bugging out on me neither. I can call the carpet back to me.' She couldn't, but bluff was sometimes as useful as the real thing. 'Anyways, you don't know the spell to get us out.'

'I wasn't thinking anything of the sort,' Elusive replied primly. That much was true. She had previously considered the idea and decided against it. 'Anyway, how come you seem to know how all this works?'

'Lots of preparation. You know sympathetic magic?'

'Of course. It's mostly what they use in voodoo. If you make a true copy of something, and then link it to that something magically, you control the original through the copy. Witches do it a lot, but it's pretty low-grade magic.'

'Usually is, but I found a history manuscript that mentioned how Ivarn had studied sympathetic magic lots. He must have found a way to make it into really powerful magic – enough, for example to control a fleet of ships. Not only that, but he found a way to get the effect to continue while he probably went off to read a good book or two.'

'Eh?'

'Yep. The miniature model of the Fleet in the Exposium at Kasali is the controller. Brilliant! Put it out in plain sight but where the Jemamians will make sure no one tinkers with it. Well, most anyone, present company exempted of course.'

'Hmm. Now what?'

'Like I said, we need the flagship. It's that big brute down toward the middle of the Fleet with all the red flags an' blue pennants an' curly carving all gilded up pretty. Sit over here with me and watch what I do with this carpet.'

* * * *

They closed from astern on the great galleon that had once been the proud flagship of the Fleet. The rest of the fleet seemed almost to be trying to guard it. One vessel after the other swooped or rose as if to block their way, but Feuery adroitly twisted and steered the carpet around every obstacle.

'I guess it's just because the boats are clustered more tightly here in the middle,' Elusive said nervously. She was determined to sit the ride out beside Feuery, even though her body insisted that burrowing into the carpet with her eyes closed was a much better idea.

Feuery didn't reply. She was too busy making sure that they didn't get trapped in the rigging of a schooner that abruptly rose toward them.

Then, suddenly, they were coming in on the deck of the flagship.

'I'll cast a securing spell …' Elusive began.

'NO! No casting magic! It's likely to upset the fixed spells Ivarn put on this lot. Mess them up and there'll most-like be the strangest rain these – or any other parts – ever saw. Or the ships might start colliding or …'

'I get the general idea. Mental note to self: don't cast magic within the Enchanted Fleet. But we're both carrying spelled items …?'

'Pre-spelled stuff makes no never-mind. It's the casting of fresh magic that's the dodgy bit in here.'

She brought them into a smooth landing on the main deck of the flagship, right in front of the doors leading into the Admiral and Captains' cabins. Elusive breathed a small sigh of relief.

* * * *

'Master?' said the sylph respectfully.

Ivarn looked up from his book at the wispy semblance of a person, his eyebrow rising quizzically.

'The spell-sphere of the Enchanted Fleet has been breached. You requested to be told should that occur.'

The mage stood up, nodded in thanks to the sylph, and strode to the special workroom he'd not entered for many years.

It had to happen sometime. One of the remaining Great Sorcerers? Ivarn wondered. Unlikely. They'd know what to expect for intruding on my works. A new one? Possible. Enough time has elapsed since the Wars for some of the newer sorcerers to have reached great status. They'd know of me only by shadowy repute – or perhaps not at all. He frowned as a thought struck him. Please, let it not be a darn dragon. One of them would really bollix up the magic. It's been a long time since I had to go toe-to-toe with a dragon. Never easy …

He was annoyed. Whoever it was could only have got into the Fleet by breaking into his spells. How much damage had been done was yet to be seen, but it would be a mess. Someone would have to pay dearly.

* * * *

'It's locked.'

'Shouldn't think so. Doubt locking doors behind 'em was much on their minds when Ivarn tol' 'em to git.'

'It *is* locked.'

'Well, open it then.'

Elusive gave Feuery a look, shrugged and pulled a lock-pick out of her pocket.

'Good girl,' said Feuery approvingly. 'Always have a set of lock-picks with you an' know how to use 'em. The world's full of inconsiderate people locking doors to keep us out.'

Elusive grunted, fiddled for a moment with the lock, then stood up and opened the door.

The cabin was in darkness, the sun now towards their left. Feuery stepped forward, but Elusive put a hand on her arm.

'Wait a moment. The boat's swinging and in a moment the sun will come directly through those big stained glass windows at the back.'

Sure enough, after only a minute or two the ship was facing sternwards to the sun, and the cabin lit up. It was huge, with a surprisingly high ceiling, and richly outfitted with mahogany furniture against walls panelled with a strange, amber-coloured wood.

'Feuery! There's someone in there!'

'Huh?'

'Over there – in that big chair, looking out the window!'

'Oh.'

There was a long silence during which nothing happened.

'Excuse us. Are you the Cap'ain?' called Feuery suddenly, making Elusive's heart, which had just settled down, start pounding all over again.

When there was no answer, Feuery abruptly strode forward.

''S ok,' she called. 'He won't be bothering us.'

A very old man sat in the red velvet-upholstered chair, gazing out through the windows on the Fleet. A *very* dead old man.

'He can't have been gone for long,' Elusive said in a hushed voice. 'It looks like it happened within the last few hours.'

'Last few centuries, more likely,' replied Feuery.

'But, he's …'

'Ivarn's preservation spell, remember? Wouldn't have stopped him aging with the years. There'd have been heaps of food and water under the preservation spell for him to be fed. But once he died, he just became another thing to be preserved.'

'But how … ?'

'Look, haven't you ever wondered why we have to attack things with a magic fireball 'stead of just reaching inside 'em with magic to make their heart stop?'

'No, not really …'

'You should've. Never take anything for granted just 'cos everyone else does. Always find out why. Reason is things that are alive resist being got at by magic. Leastways, magic that'll hurt them. That's why we have to use magic to make something like a fireball or an icefall or a shearing wind, that'll do harm to living things, rather than just doing it direct. Life protects itself best it can. Usually that's pretty good, considering all the things that can go wrong.'

Elusive considered this. 'So,' she said slowly, 'how come the preservation spell works on all those little things that make bodies go yucky after they're dead? If a preservation spell didn't make them stop working, then it wouldn't preserve them. They're alive but the magic must stop them.'

Feuery looked at her approvingly. 'Now you're thinkin'. Reason being, they do resist the magic. But those little critters, too small to see even, don't have much room in 'em to make much push-back so the magic wins. Exact same as how healing spells work. Making rains of fire and floating castles is showy magic. But healing magic – most folk don't appreciate how hard it is to do sound healing magic. Mind you though, magic don't need to be powerful if'n it's clever.'

'Yes, but there's a lot of those little thingeys. Together they must make a pretty good push-back.'

'Fifty pounds of lots an' lots of each-one invisible critters in't the same as fifty pounds of one gnome. Fifty pounds of gnome all works together to resist magic; reason being it's used to having to work together.'

'Are you fifty pounds?' asked Elusive, a smile waiting at the edges of her lips.

'Never you mind how much Feuery there is. I'm just telling you a what-if. Now, we have a job to do.'

Elusive looked at the corpse, still dressed in a fine, if somewhat threadbare, uniform.

'Poor old man,' she said slowly. 'What a way to end up. Sitting here, day after day, looking at an empty fleet endlessly circling.'

'He chose to go up with his ship,' said Feuery brusquely. 'Let's get on with it.'

* * * *

Ivarn was puzzled. There was an intruder into the Enchanted Fleet, no doubt about that. However, his spells were intact and functioning just as they had been since he'd cast them. Instead of the great gaping hole he had expected to find torn through them to gain entry, everything was as it should be. How could this be?

It took him more than an hour of tracing with wizard's sight through the substance of his spells to finally find the fine filaments of a subtle but powerful spell that had been laid alongside parts of his own, like a gossamer thread delicately weaving through the cables of his enchantment. It had been ever so cleverly crafted. Instead of breaking through his spells, it had augmented them while, at the same time, allowing just the right keyword at just the right time and place to gain entry by becoming part of his magic.

He was impressed. He'd have credited only a few of the Great Wizards of his time to be so subtle, and most of them had perished in the Wars. Could one of those few survivors be seeking to lay a trap for him? Certainly some had sufficient reason to hold a grudge against him. Or was it someone completely new? Unfortunately, it still left open the possibility of one of the Great Dragons as well. Some of them were both subtle and highly skilled in magic.

Slowly, he withdrew out of the spell and sat quietly until his normal vision returned. Then he picked up a large crystal ball and concentrated. He was going to have to find the intruder the hard way.

* * * *

'Anything over there?' queried Feuery.

'Nothing. No sign of any lockers and no sign of any hidden compartments. Are you sure a simple little seeker spell is out of the question?' asked Elusive.

'No, too risky. Darn! This is what being without magic all the time must feel like.'

'Then let's stop thinking like wizards and try using our heads.'

'Meaning wizards don't use their heads?'

'No, silly! They need something to keep their hats on. Seriously, wizards and dragons usually keep their wealth close by, because they have the power to personally protect it with their magic. Teeth, claws and nasty breath for dragons too, of course. But if you don't have magic available, then what would you use to protect it?'

'Guards?'

'Exactly! And you make sure the guards watch each other. Organisation; makes sense, because if you *don't* have powerful magic, you wouldn't want to be the last thing between your treasure and a thief. Anyway, it wasn't *his* valuables, we found them.' She gestured to a small but very nice pile of items they'd ferretted out while searching. 'It was the Fleet's. I think we're looking in the wrong place.'

Feuery stood thoughtfully for a moment. 'Yyyeesss, you might be right. Somewhere where the marines are betwixt it an' the sailors an' any passengers, but where there's a lot of officers 'round most times day or night to watch the marines.'

'Now you're thinking,' Elusive said mildly.

Feuery shot her a glance, but failed to find any trace of the smile that would have most likely led to a sharp retort. The brownie's face was innocence itself.

'Let's see what we can find below. Better bring a couple of lanterns. We won't be able to cast seeing spells, an' it'll likely be a tad gloomy down there.'

* * * *

They found the heavily secured strongroom on the deck below the Captain's cabin, beside the Officers Wardroom.

'Darn good locks,' said Elusive grudgingly after trying to unpick them. 'Have you had any experience with *difficult* locks?'

'Been occasions,' conceded Feuery. 'Let's see.'

'They're very complex. I hope you can sort them out.'

'Should be able to. Can you hold this please?' asked Feuery, handing Elusive the first lock.

'How did you do that so fas ...'

'An' here's the other. Now, let's see what we have. Hope it isn't just the Armoury.'

It wasn't. The room was relatively small, but it was full to overflowing. Two sets of shelves ran along each wall, and the end of the room was stacked with locked chests – the pay chests for the invasion fleet.

The shelves held numerous sacks, each tightly corded and sealed with a wax seal.

'I'll see what's in the chests. You start going through those bags. Most likely they'll contain what we're after – small, light, high-value things like jewels. If they do, start sorting out the best ones. We can only take the very best.'

The chests contained mostly silver, copper and bronze coins, but even one of gold coins Feuery dismissed. However, she was pleased to find several rolls of rare and very valuable white gold coins, which she put aside for their loot. Then she went to help Elusive, who was becoming dazed by all of the riches she'd found.

Most of the sacks were personal treasures, probably belonging to the administrators who had been sent to govern the Jemamian Islands once they'd been annexed. Clearly the travellers were well-off and had probably purchased their civil government positions with the aim of becoming even wealthier during their term of office. Now, their legacy was a rich booty of jewellery and finely crafted jewelled items.

'We don't have time now to sort through it all,' Feuery said eventually. 'There're two sacks of jewels an' the white gold coins. Let's just put what we think is most valuable in with 'em, an' call it quits. Comes a point when there's too much of a good thing, so let's be satisfied with more'n several kings' ransoms.'

'But ...' began Elusive.

'No buts about it. I tol' you we'd do well an' we have. Better'n even I expected, an' I have some pretty fancy s'pectations at times, believe you me. Now let's just get away so we can enjoy it.'

'Feuery?' Elusive asked suddenly as they packed the choicest valuables into their bottomless bags.

'Um?'

'This Ivarn? Is he well educated, even by mage standards?'

'Guess so. Why are you asking?' Feuery tucked the last item, a jewel-encrusted crystal candlestick, into her bag.

'I was just thinking of the name the other mages gave him: Ivarn of the 3 Rs. Strange nickname for a mage. Sounds almost school-masterish.'

'You thinking 3 Rs as in Readin', Riting, 'Rithmetic?'

'Of course. Isn't that what they stand for?'

'Not in Ivarn's case. His peers said his 3 Rs stand for Revengeful, Relentless and Remorseless. Guess mages knew him differently to how those folk he sheltered during the Mage Wars saw him. Some folks who are so good as to be almost saintly for some causes, like ol' Ivarn, don't take kindly to being crossed personally. Can see why he fitted in so well with the Jemamians actually.'

'Oh. Aren't we sort of robbing him? That's a bit personal isn't it?'

'He'd probably see it that way. Might be for the best if he don't see it t'all. Leastways, best for us.'

* * * *

What was going on with the Flagship?

Ivarn's gaze through the crystal ball veered over and down. A hatch opened as he closed in on the great galleon. Got you, he exulted. *Clearly not a dragon, thankfully. Now to measure for the cut to follow …*

His jaw dropped.

Two girls. Two gnome girls. No, a gnome and … a brownie?

He waited for the Mage whom they must be serving to emerge from the ship. Instead, the brownie carefully and neatly closed the hatch behind her and the two of them then seated themselves comfortably on a carpet, bickering good-naturedly.

To his astonishment, it looked like two little girls preparing to have a pretend tea-party.

Then the magic carpet lifted off, soaring through the Fleet to pause only briefly before emerging from the spell and heading northward.

* * * *

'Feuery! Over there! There's something glittering in the sunlight ahead.'

Feuery steered the carpet in the direction Elusive was pointing. Stationary objects glittering in the sunlight weren't a common sight at several thousand feet.

'It's a silver tray. Just sitting suspended in mid-air.'

'Yep. With a' envelope on it. Don't know these parts well, but I'd be surprised if they're common up here for the time o' year.'

Elusive guided the carpet close enough for Feuery to pick up the envelope. She read the note inside and wordlessly handed it to Elusive.

Ivarn greets you, and sends you his compliments for your skill to circumvent his magic, your wisdom to keep your avarice in check and your good fortune withal in not damaging his spells.

He retains your miniature carpet as a keepsake, and against future need should you return.

Don't try it again!

I

The Empty Streets of Rapanel

The view from the rose-marble pavilion looking out towards the sea was always magnificent.

Feuery had found the best vantage point on the cliffs above the abandoned city of Rapanel during her many searches of the city. She'd taken to finishing off her day's work by spending a little time during the late afternoon gazing over the sea. It relaxed her and helped her to think.

Today, as usual, she'd made her way up the beautifully made, gracefully curved carriageway lined with great stone columns and statues of forgotten heroes (each in its own shrine). She glanced at one tableau in passing; an elegant, regal lady fearlessly confronting a spear-wielding barbarian. The burnished sun lit both figures with a coppery light. *What was their story?* Feuery wondered. So much had taken place on her world of Th'eia since the devastating Mage Wars had erupted, and no doubt in the shadowy past before that.

The road was still sound, as were the buildings. However, many of the once beautiful trees along the carriageway had died or were dying, and those that weren't, straggled every which-way. Around the pavilion, dry, spindly weeds filled the once-loved gardens and, here and there, sought hold in the exposed surfaces of the roads and buildings. At least up here there were none of the thick drifts of leaves and debris that so clearly signalled abandonment and neglect throughout the city.

Plus, the daily flexing of the storms out to sea was dynamic and vigorous, unlike the listless mouldering of Rapanel and the calm, oily-looking sea near it. At this time of year, the fierce sun caused towering clouds to rise from the distant ocean and generated huge, dark thunderheads from the masses of fluffy clouds that formed from the initial haze. By late afternoon, spears of lightning danced over agitated waves against the background of huge downpours. All in silence. The storms were so distant that barely the whisper of a rumble of thunder carried to shore.

It was strange to watch the thick clouds and colossal deluges while the abandoned ruins and streets of Rapanel baked in the hot, drying sun and each day, the land became more parched. The storms stayed at sea until the winds shifted and drove them over the land. And nowadays, the winds rarely blew the storms shoreward.

Today, Feuery watched the scene with detachment. Her thoughts were directed to her own dilemma.

She drew the parchment from her pocket, spread it out over the pink marble bench and stared at the map yet again. It seemed to stare defiantly back at her.

There appeared to be nothing more to the map than she'd observed many times previously. If she was missing something – and she must be – what was it?

* * * *

It had all begun several months ago when she'd been searching old records in distant S'Than. These days, S'Than was a minor hub on the western foothills that skirted the great central mountain ranges known as the Paramounts. S'Than was now a shadow of its former status and size when it had been the major overland transhipment centre of the south-western seaboard. Now, the main reminders of those heady days were the derelict warehouses, the acres of empty markets and a population notable for the number of Wood Elves and half elves; the latter the descendants of earlier traders.

Feuery had discovered a map among a bundle of old trade records. It had been folded so as to be inconspicuous but evidently had been pushed in hastily, for there were caravan receipts torn and crumpled around it.

It was exactly the sort of thing Feuery sought in her frequent dabbling with 'boring' old records, and *because* it seemed too good to be true, she treated it warily.

The map purported to show the hiding place of the manuscripts of a once-acclaimed sorcerer, Wesithar the Cautious. He had left the city of Rapanel during the Great Exodus. He had probably intended travelling light and reclaiming his hidden belongings later.

Feuery was dubious, but from her research had discovered that such a mage *had* once lived in Rapanel before the city had been abandoned. Furthermore, he had died soon after in an encounter with a rival. This occurrence had taken place in the town where the commercial records of the caravans had been made – only a few years after the end of the Mage Wars (about three hundred and seventy years ago).

Despite the then newly-formed Wizards' Guild prohibiting such vendettas, there were still a lot of scores being settled from the time of the Wars. Even today, wizards' duels were quite common, albeit over less weighty matters to the world generally. While officially frowned on, they were accepted as being inevitable among wizards, given that they were fiercely competitive, individualistic and, by definition, *powerful* personalities.

Nevertheless, Wesithar's death had been curious. By all accounts, it had been a fair duel. However, at least one spectator recorded Wesithar as having difficulties with his staff, noting that 'he shaked ite vexaciously'. Most people were aware that a wizards' duel wasn't the time to sort out essential equipment, such as staves. And Wesithar must have quickly realised it as well.

It was quite possible the map *could* be genuine. Nevertheless, Feuery conducted her own tests of the parchment's age and of the ink. When they tallied with the stated time, she resolved to see what she could find out. Apparently, the sorcerer had been a renowned collector of manuscripts. And so was Feuery.

* * * *

These days, no ships – not even fishing boats – called in to the ruined city of Rapanel, although its port had once been one of the busiest on the south-western seaboard. The reason for this stemmed from the problem responsible for the city's abandonment. Although Rapanel had been affected far less by the Mage Wars than most cities, the winds had shifted their patterns, and so in Rapanel an ill-wind now blew. The once-regular seasonal rains now rarely reached the coast. For many leagues, where vigorous winds had previously driven graceful clippers, wallowing cargo ships and, no doubt, more than a few corsairs, offshore vessels were now frequently becalmed.

Without the influence of winds, the sea remained calm for months on end, so the vast shoals of fish that had once swarmed inshore when the winds and currents raised nutrients to the coastal shallows moved elsewhere. Without trade, without fish and without rain, the city of Rapanel had been doomed. By all accounts, the city's demise had been swift: six wet seasons failed one after the other so there was neither enough food nor water to sustain the population. A certain percentage had joined caravans west and north; others had set sail for ports to the east. Few – very few – had stayed beyond the time needed to strip the city of any moveable valuables.

* * * *

Fotherington was the nearest town to the ruined city of Rapanel: a farming centre on the eastern side of the sprawling range of hills that lined the south-west of the continent. On the coastal side of the range there were thick forests interspersed with fertile valleys, for the rains there were heavy and the soils rich. The population was mixed, but consisted predominantly of Wood Elves in the forests, villages of humans and brownies farming the valleys, and several small enclaves of Sea Elves on the coastal inlets. Undoubtedly there were dwarfs in the hills as well, but dwarfs generally kept to themselves. Enough rain carried over the hills to support farming around the township of Fotherington, which visitors were inclined to describe as being 'relaxed and quaint'.

Neither relaxation nor antiquation particularly appealed to Feuery, but she made no secret of arranging travel to Fotherington 'to visit relatives'.

Actually, she had no idea or interest in whether she had relations in Fotherington, or even if there were *any* gnomes there. In fact, she had no intention of going to Fotherington at all, but it would serve as a useful decoy to confuse her real destination and purpose.

Feuery lived a watchful life in which death or worse could be lurking around any corner. A part of her was always wary, and she had every reason to be. There were a number of people who would welcome what they would consider as 'quality time' with her. Reflecting on the matter, she had to admit that she'd upset quite a few folk in the course of her adventures. She giggled. Mostly it had been a lot of fun. And while those adventures during which she'd gained friends and admirers had also been fun (admittedly, usually after the event), it had been those in which she'd left ire and vengefulness behind her that had proved to be most profitable. She loved it.

* * * *

It was fairly easy for Feuery to take precautions when she settled for a while (but never for too long) in one place. The real risks occurred during her travels, when she wasn't buffered by a network of informants, couldn't prepare escape contingencies and was in strange surroundings where the discordant was barely distinguishable from the simply unfamiliar. Few people on meeting her would believe the pretty, petite gnome with her big blue eyes and well-groomed auburn hair lived such a clandestine life. But then, most had difficulty accepting her as a wizard, despite the clear evidence of the great metal battle-staff she carried, which frequent use had made into a treasured companion.

So, while making no secrets of her phantom travel plans, she conjured and bargained with an air elemental in the small hours late one night while crickets chirped in the dark and bats hawked the seasonally early moths – and was carried safely and comfortably direct to Rapanel before the following dawn.

* * * *

Now she'd been in the abandoned city nearly a month. The whereabouts of the stash (if, in fact, there was one) continued to elude her, while the hot, dry days and nights were becoming an irritation. Occasionally, she thought she heard or saw the traces of other folk, but if so, they were as circumspect as she was and evidently disinclined to socialising. That suited her fine.

She looked again at the map in annoyance. Its directions had been less than precise; consistent with an *aide d' memoir* for the writer rather than instructions for someone else. However, she was sure she'd narrowed down the possibilities to two adjoining buildings.

The map had a small notation on the side as well – the archaic symbol for an opening spell. It wasn't a difficult spell, but jotted near it was a word in faint spindly script: '*Neaotark*'. She suspected the word needed to be said as part of the spell, but, after what seemed like endless attempts on her part, she'd failed to open *anything* in the city with it.

And that was that. No matter what she did – and she was very skilled at searching and solving riddles – she wasn't able to uncover anything.

Rolling up the parchment, she strolled over to the parapet. It had been built to slightly overhang the cliff, which thrust forward to the sea like the prow of a ship, and from it she commanded a full 270 degree view of the coastline. To her right, the docks of the city were spread out like a detailed model, the river around which they had been built now dry and cracked save for a thick, sludgy stream choked with parched rushes and drying ponds. To her left stretched grand, weathered cliffs as far as the eye could see, veiled by shimmering heat haze that almost obscured the pebbly beaches below.

She glanced straight down. The sea beneath was crystal clear, more so each day as the monotonous dry period extended. The skeletons of two wrecks lay in the shallows a little off the beach, just before the submerged shelf abruptly plunged deep into the sea.

She smiled slightly to herself. *It's strange how just the right time reveals new sights,* she reflected. For a moment she wondered about the story of the wrecks. Had they been work-weary wrecks scuttled simply to avoid the cost of breaking them up? Or had there been some now long-forgotten tragedy one stormy night? Did the ghosts of those who sailed on that last voyage wander the beach? Or was it only the ghosts of the vessels themselves that trod the shallows, reminiscing of ancient voyages, storms survived and strange ports?

She frowned as a thought struck her. *The right time!* Returning to the pavilion, she spread the map out again. She did have one spell left that she hadn't yet tried on it. For good reason: it could only be used very sparingly. A friend, Janice the Time-Witch, had gifted it to her along with one other spell, plus the warning that using them other than very rarely would be dangerous.

The spells wove through time itself. One altered time briefly for the user, giving them an unnatural speed compared to those around them. The other sped backwards through images of the life of a person or item, allowing glimpses of events pertaining to them or it. Janice's warning though was clear: over-use of either spell could disrupt time permanently for the user, or would more likely attract the attention of her Mothers – the three Fates – Clotho, Lakesis and Atropos. Either could have dire consequences.

Still, if she didn't do something, she may as well go home: wherever that was, but it assuredly wasn't here. She was getting nowhere with her search, and she'd come a long way to try to find the stash.

Concentrating very carefully, she cast the spell over the parchment. A jumble of images, starting with the map on the rose-marble bench and finishing with a clean sheet of parchment on a stained wooden table, sped past.

Feuery shook herself, and looked up. Darkness had fallen during (what for her had been) the briefest instant of time engaged with the spell. The two moons – big blue Oberon and petite pink Titania – were now rising over the headlands to the west, throwing long, eerie shadows across the landscape. Somewhere far out in the desert something howled. She could just hear the chittering of seabirds against the gentle wash of the sea along the beaches.

Feuery had her answer – or at least, enough of an answer. And also a disturbing question.

The map was genuine. More than that, she knew now where the opening spell and mysterious word had last been used at the very clever hiding place. She'd been so close, but facing in the wrong direction!

But one of the first images to have been unrolled worried her greatly. Not long before she had found the parchment tucked into the old receipts, someone else had removed the map and placed a tracer spell on it. Then it had been replaced within the bundle of trade receipts again, very carefully so as to fit exactly in place.

She looked at the map, using wizard's sight to unravel the tracer spell. It was very powerful. Anyone attuned to it within several leagues would be able to quickly and accurately find the parchment. However, its very strength was also its shortcoming. The seeker had to be within those several leagues to find it.

No one apart from Feuery and the unknown hider was likely to have touched those records in centuries, except perhaps to trip over them with a muttered curse. Surely there was no point to putting such an elaborate spell on the parchment, unless it was anticipated that the map would be taken away.

By someone like Feuery. Someone *exactly* like Feuery.

The hairs on the nape of her neck rose as she looked at the bait in her hand. If she'd travelled to Rapanel by usual means, there would have been no end of opportunities to strike at her unawares along the way.

She shook off the feeling of shock, and tried to put herself in the mind of her unknown hunter. They would have assumed that she had slipped out of S'Than unobtrusively, perhaps sooner than expected. She could imagine their attempts to second guess her journey, for there were at least four ways she could have gone, and their frustration when, moving from one to the other, they'd failed to find her or any trace of her.

But sooner or later they'd known she would be at Rapanel. How long would it take for them to decide to come here and seek her out?

Possibly a month?

She shivered, but not from any evening chill. It would be prudent for her to expect her hunter was close.

Feuery took a bottle from her bottomless bag. It was a nice vintage of Western Downs wine. Pity, but it was the bottle she needed now.

She poured the wine over the edge of the parapet and after a last thorough examination of the parchment, rolled it up firmly and crammed it into the bottle. She sealed the neck tightly with wax and tied a piece of canvas around the mouth and neck for extra insurance. She wanted to ensure that it travelled a long way.

There was no point in dropping the bottle inshore. The coastal sea would merely toy with it casually before depositing it on some nearby beach. Quickly flicking through her book of spells, she found one that was perfect for the occasion. A pair of wings emerged fluttering from the bottle, and she sent the message in a bottle winging out to sea. The spell would fade within a few minutes, but by then the bottle should fall into the eastward current that flowed offshore. If not, it would be some time before the sluggish coastal waters washed it ashore.

A spy spell on the pavilion was next. If there was anyone close on her trail following the parchment, they would surely go to the last landward location of the tracer spell. And she'd know about it.

Determinedly, she went back to the city along the point's edge, avoiding the carriageway. She had no desire to meet her hunter on the way, but nor was she going to be frightened away when she was so darn close to discovering the cache!

* * * *

Instead of returning to the buildings where she was now fairly certain the cache was hidden, she went via the old docks to what had been the warehouse district below the main city. In the moonlight, the docks were scary. She'd seen a few ghosts in various parts of the town previously, and fervently hoped she wouldn't meet any tonight. She'd been to this part of Rapanel only a few times – partly because the area was so forbidding – and she had no intention of returning to any of the other places she'd stayed in the city. She needed a good night's rest, and planned to scry on what was going on in the city before tackling the search tomorrow. Experience had taught her that it was best to hasten slowly.

Above a warehouse, the private rooms that must have once belonged to a wealthy merchant provided a suitable location for a good night's rest. She woke early the next morning feeling refreshed and a little relieved she'd not been disturbed by a supernatural being overnight. However, a prickly, acidic feeling of being hunted hung over her thoughts and mood.

Feuery unpacked a small crystal ball from her pouch. Scrying is the art of viewing events or people through a magical medium. Crystal balls were favoured, but almost anything could be used by the talented. She wasn't talented at scrying, but it would at least enable her to survey the city a little.

Aside from an old man she spied living in an old chamber full of ancient, looted finery, she discovered little that was note-worthy. On a whim, she decided to check the pavilion, although her spy spell would also let her know if anyone was there.

She almost fell off her chair and lost the image she was looking at when she spotted a shadowy figure standing in the pavilion, looking out to sea. Her spy spell was still intact, but simply hadn't registered the intruder. That was a serious concern; only a powerful mage or a few magically-gifted crea-tures could avoid a spy spell so readily. Seeking a closer look, she refined the image on her crystal ball.

She caught a glimpse of the figure's face – and voided the spell instantly.

Shaking, she put her crystal ball away. The situation was far worse than she'd thought, or even feared. From the very brief peek she'd had, she knew that *thing* was born of no mother of this world.

Someone had set a hunter-demon onto her path. That was nasty. The use of such creatures was prohibited by the Wizards' Guild, so whoever had summoned it was playing high stakes, for only a high-level mage could summon and compel such a dangerous creature. For a moment she considered flight, but the odds weren't good. If she were to summon an elemental it would be like calling the demon, whereas if she fled overland, the creature would surely run her to earth on the way.

She forced herself to consider her options calmly. There weren't many. As a last resort, she could call for help from her sorceress mentor. After all, Trecina was a Wizards' Guild field agent, and the Guild would want to know that a mage, somewhere, was summoning such foul creatures. But trying to get hold of Trecina would be risky. Once again, the demon would be aware of her call and use it to find her. Furthermore, there was no certainty she would even be able to get in touch with Trecina.

Anyway, to call on Trecina for help would mean she couldn't handle it herself. And she didn't want to have to admit that to her mentor or herself. So she'd try to deal with it on her own.

But how? She flicked through her book of spells. Discouragingly, there were only a few amongst them that dealt with banishing demons. Feuery was fairly sure none of them would have sufficient power to deal with such a major summoning. While studying at the Wizards' Academy before her, ah, hasty departure, she'd attended several lectures in the Demonology Faculty.

Perhaps 'attended' wasn't quite the right term. The Demonology Faculty was notoriously secretive, and only selected post-graduate wizards were accepted for further tuition. She'd overcome that difficulty by reserving a good spot on the high beams which supported the rafters above the Hall of Pentacles, and had gained a good overview of the subject of Demonology.

Unfortunately, however, none of the lectures had included dealing with a hunter-demon.

Then a thought struck her: perhaps Wesithar's cache might contain notes on such spells. As a sorcerer who had lived during the Mage Wars, he must have had to contend with demons on occasion. Their widespread use during those Wars was the main reason their use was now banned by the Wizards' Guild.

Anyway, it was an extra reason for her to find the cache. And before the demon found her. That last bit was quite important!

* * * *

By now, the demon would most likely be a bit confused. It evidently knew the direction of the parchment, but obviously didn't fancy flying over deep sea looking for it. On the other hand, if the creature had visited the buildings where Feuery was fairly certain the cache was hidden, then it would probably know she had been there as well. The damn things had extraordinary senses, including the ability to trace psychic residue on the fabric of places. She'd have left a lot of psychic 'fingerprints' all over the city; something for which she was now grateful. Her innate curiosity had led her to explore quite a lot of Rapanel over the past month, which would have nicely muddled her trail.

However, if the demon hadn't been able to get to the parchment, then it would probably divide its time between keeping track of it, watching the area of the cache and keeping a broad watch on the areas outside the city in case she fled.

So it would be busy.

Good! she thought nastily.

If the bottle with the parchment drifted far away she'd have more time. If it quickly came ashore though, it meant the demon would shift more of its attention to the area of the cache and the city.

That would be a nuisance.

Feuery wondered briefly about using a simulacrum of herself to mislead the demon but quickly dismissed the idea. Any strong or sustained magic would quickly attract its attention. The demon had shown that it could void fixed, low-level magic; like the spy spell she'd left at the pavilion. And if it physically saw her ... She wouldn't be able to evade it, couldn't outrun it and doubted her best battle magic would do more than annoy it.

She shook herself. First things first. Don't assume anything except the worst. While the hunter-demon had shown no sign that it had sensed her, it was best to assume that it had and would be looking for her.

Here ... So she'd better move.

Ok, an' if I have to move, then let's have a try at the stash. The demon'll most likely be at the pavilion, or coming here or searching the city. Fair odds for me.

Especially now she was fairly sure where the cache was, and how to get into it.

* * * *

She cautiously made her way from the warehouse district of the city, up through a residential area and then on to a broad boulevard, keeping undercover all the way. To her left were the main markets and the banking and business centre. To her right were the innumerable offices and public buildings that had once housed the governing councils and their administration, with the military quarters pressed closer in to the rise that led to the scenic spot high above on the cliffs. Beyond the barracks were the rougher markets, taverns, bordellos and various similar businesses that wouldn't be found too openly in the commercial quarter. They led down to the port, which in turn led back to the warehouses further up-river.

A little less than half a mile along the boulevard, the carriageway divided to run each side of a long park, complete with a lake which was now empty, dry and dusty. In the middle of the lake bed was an island with two simple but elegant buildings of basalt and black marble. Once they would have been accessible only by boat or air, and must have appeared foreboding as they stood in their isolation and smooth, dark architecture. Now, of course, it was easy to just walk to them.

Feuery usually accessed the two buildings from the commercial side of town, where an old drain cut through the black basalt block retaining wall of the island that now rose nearly twenty feet sheer from the bed of the departed lake. Today, she avoided it. It was too obviously a form of entry to the island.

Fortunately, Feuery had earlier prepared another way on the other side of the island by dropping a rope tied to a dead willow stump into a stand of tall rushes that reached almost up to the top of the wall. That way had another advantage – the remains of an old ferry lay on the lake bed about halfway across, giving her some cover to get to the island.

It was also closer to where she needed to be.

She knelt cautiously near to the edge of the lake bed. A faint breeze rustled dry leaves and rattled rushes and branches, and set something creaking eerily in the government quarter, but otherwise there was no sign of movement anywhere. Feuery briefly considered scrying again, but quashed the thought quickly. The hunter-demon just might be able to sense her, and in any case she would be very vulnerable while her attention was focused on the crystal ball. She wanted all of her senses sharply attuned to the immediate problem.

She sped over to the old ferry, and surveyed the island carefully from the shadow of the boat's stern. Then she methodically scanned the city around her through the growing heat haze as the day approached noon.

Well, here goes, she decided.

She crossed the dry lake bed in a series of smooth stages, pausing to search all about her each time. A slight sunburn was starting to appear on her exposed skin, and she felt sweaty, hot and dusty; but she had no intention of hurrying at the expense of caution. Sunburn would heal; being torn apart by a demon wouldn't!

The stand of rushes created additional problems for her. Brittle, dead shafts crackled at the slightest touch. She was as quiet as possible; however, to her heightened senses and imagination she was sure her passage sounded as though it were accompanied by firecrackers.

Itchy from the bristles and dust of the rushes – on top of everything else – she clambered up the rope and carefully gazed over the top of the wall.

Still nothing. Hopefully, she might be lucky and the hunter-demon was occupied somewhere far away.

She quickly scampered over to the buildings. They consisted of two angular towers, with a circular courtyard paved in dark marble between them. A semi-circular wall gracefully marked the side she was on, curving up at each end to join the towers, but still about twenty-foot high at the lowest central point.

Standing against the wall on the courtyard side was a massive stone globe, about thirty foot in diameter, held up at the front by two arcing stone piers and set into the wall at the back. Two pairs of parallel lines had been inscribed into the stone, crossing high up on the front to form a square where they intersected. It pointed to a spot midway between the towers.

The globe was certainly impressive, but hadn't made much sense to Feuery each time she'd studied it. Why wasn't it set in the centre of the courtyard to impress both sides of the boulevard? It was almost as if the architect had deliberately sought to snub the governing sector. Maybe that was the case. But what was the reason behind the inscribed lines and the high-set square of their meeting? Feuery knew a lot about symbology, but this artefact resembled nothing she'd ever come across before.

She hoped her guess as to why the globe was set where it was, and about the inscribed lines crossing so high on the sphere, was right. Sure enough, at the back of the wall adjacent to the globe, she found what she had trusted would be there – a well-concealed doorway.

She cast the opening spell, and intoned what she hoped was the key-word 'Neaotark' after it. To her great delight, the stone shimmered, a centreline split appeared and the two large slabs of basalt slid aside.

She stepped into a surprisingly large room set inside the wall. In front of her, most of the room was occupied by the massive bulk of the hidden part of the stone globe.

As she'd anticipated, the two pairs of parallel lines also met on this side. Directly opposite the outside square, the lines again formed a matching square, but this one faced down toward her as she stood a dozen paces in from the doorway.

As she looked, the square began to glow an intense, clear blue. There was a rustling behind her. Glancing around, her heart almost stopped. The hunter-demon stood in the doorway.

She had an impression of a lithe, heavily muscled body – many times bigger than her – covered in indigo-coloured, feathery scales. A long arm, heavily taloned, reached for her as …

The blue seemed to explode from the square, engulfing everything. There was a moment of paralysed shock, and then the intense blue imploded back into the sphere, carrying them both with it.

Outside, the doors slid back into a seamless block of stone. Leaves shifted lazily in a light breeze. The sun continued to scorch the city.

* * * *

Feuery seemed to tumble for ages before recovering her senses. Somehow, she managed to finally stop cartwheeling.

Ah, that was much better. That just left the spinning and the falling. With each spin, flashes of brilliant blue light washed over her. By carefully balancing her arms, legs and staff, she eventually was able to stop spinning, but the feeling of falling remained, even though there was no longer a rush of air about her.

She looked around. She didn't seem to be falling, although her body stridently insisted she was. She told it to shut up and calm down while she worked out what was happening.

In fact, she seemed to be suspended more or less in the same place. But, what a place!

Looking in the direction of what she decided was down, she saw a huge ball of magic that bathed everything in brilliant blue light, with writhing tendrils of energy constantly flaring and falling back into the centre of the globe. She seemed to be floating – as if in water – but the air was fresh and easy to breathe. If anything, she felt exhilarated, hugely powerful and almost dizzy. However, she knew the feeling was the result of the massive magical energies floating around and through her, saturating everything in sight.

She'd never felt such a concentration of magic before. Every cell in her body seemed charged with it, and coronas of magical energy flickered across her hands and clothing. Her staff seemed to pulse to some strange rhythm, impossibly expanding and contracting in size.

There wasn't a visible end to whatever medium she was currently in. Looking away from the blue sphere, everything seemed to just fade away into an inky darkness.

There were two other things of note orbiting the globe with her though.

One – not too far away from her – was an absolutely black circle that looked to be about three times her size. She couldn't discern if it was actually a sphere or whether she was looking down on something flat that was smoothly spinning with her around the globe.

The other thing – further away and tumbling erratically – was the hunter-demon. Even as she watched it, two great orange wings unfurled from its back. It furiously beat them, throwing it into a wider orbit, but steadying its course.

Then the hunter-demon saw her.

The black circle suddenly looked very inviting, and Feuery started swimming toward it. It wasn't a very efficient mode of movement, but it worked. For once in her life, she was *really* reluctant to use magic. She sensed that there was such an excess of energies already that even a small spell could trigger a violent reaction.

Mind you, it was tempting to try. The demon was a lot faster at flying, but it was obviously taking some time to master flight in this place. With the demon's first effort it shot towards her; an action which also increased the height of its orbit and drew a cry of anger from it.

While Feuery crawled with painful slowness toward the black circle, the hunter-demon overshot her and plunged toward the blue globe of magic. It beat its wings furiously to stop, sending vortices of incandescent magic spiralling around it and shrouding the demon in an inappropriate halo of intense blue light.

It was close, but Feuery managed to reach the circle before the hunter-demon was able to get to her. She experienced the same peculiar imploding feeling as her outstretched hand reached for the blackness, until she finally found herself sprawled in a room of gleaming white marble.

The only items in the room were a massively heavy wooden table, on which were placed a leather satchel and a mage's staff. The staff was about six feet long; thin and crowned with a globe of stone. Two parallel pairs of lines were etched into the stone at the head of the staff.

Expecting a demon to land on her any moment, Feuery leapt up, shoved the staff through her belt, swung the satchel across her back and ducked behind the table.

Sure enough, on the wall that had been behind her was a square of blue-glowing light.

Taking a deep breath, she shoved the table toward it. For a moment, nothing happened, but then the table lurched forward with a long, drawn-out shriek.

Once again! She had to get the table into range of the opening. She gave a mighty shove, almost tearing her arm muscles in the effort.

The table – followed closely by Feuery – was abruptly sucked into the square of blue-glowing light to be thrust into orbit around the blue globe.

And so was the demon, much to its astonishment. It had just followed Feuery into the circular black opening and unexpectedly confronted the table on the way out. To Feuery's considerable satisfaction, the meeting appeared to have done neither of them much good.

The table splintered against the demon, in the process losing a leg that now spiralled erratically away. Against the greater mass of the table, the demon fell back into orbit stunned and dripped silvery drops that Feuery assumed were its blood.

By this point, like it not, she knew she would need to use magic. With one eye on the demon, which was slowly recovering and starting to free itself from the battered table, she quickly cast a spell and swam toward the blue globe as fast as she could.

For a fraction of a second that would remain forever firmly fixed in Feuery's memory, she saw a startled, handsomely-mature woman look up at her in astonishment from a spinning wheel.

Sorry Clotho, she chuckled to herself, but then became grimly serious. This had to be timed right.

Glancing back, she saw the demon had sighted on her and was preparing to pursue her; however, its movements were incredibly sluggish. Feuery witnessed its wings furl on the backstroke, and the gradual change of its expression as the facial muscles moved with glacial slowness from determined anger to shock at seeing the blur of movement she had become.

Feuery drew the wizard's staff she'd found on the table from her belt, and with some misgivings threw it into the globe of magic as she passed through it – only to fall into the room embedded in the wall back at Rapanel.

She wasn't going to hang about. Picking herself up, she cast the opening spell, careful to add the keyword, and legged it for all she was worth as the doors of the room opened. Immediately, she dived to one side, and ran as fast as she could across the island away from the doors in the wall.

Just as well. A colossal gust of magical energy poured out through the open doors, turning dust motes in the air into sparkles of … well, she wasn't exactly sure. However, the ground over which the magic passed had become a slab of fine china, with delicate designs of bizarre flowers that seemed to be frantically growing in that two-dimensional world. An eight-foot-long earthworm reared up, shattering the china, just in time to be turned into a waterspout. A second wave of magic followed the first, transforming the china ground into a fine dust-like talcum powder that exploded across the lake bed and settled gently on the wreck of the ferry. Feuery noticed a buried pot – probably someone's hastily buried hoard – lying exposed as the fine powder blew away. Silver and gold coins fell from its broken side.

A third wave of magic followed. The ground rippled and turned to brass, gleaming in the sun. A flock of tiny fairies, also glittering metallically in the sunshine, rose from where the pot had been.

Then the doors closed. Feuery stopped; partly to see what was happening, partly to catch her breath, but mostly to see if the hunter-demon was anywhere around.

It wasn't. The colossal stone globe was showing off though. It rose up, spinning furiously and making a noise like rhythmic thunder. It ascended above the towers, the rumbling noise growing ever deeper and imploded in on itself, ripping the tops off the towers as it collapsed to a point of brilliant blue light, and disappeared.

There was absolute silence across the city of Rapanel. Feuery stood transfixed for several moments until a faint tinkling sound attracted her attention. The metal fairies seemed to be holding a moot in barely audible bell-like tones. All of a sudden, they rose up and set off toward the west.

All but one. It hovered, watching for a moment as the others departed, and then flew over to Feuery.

It stopped a few inches in front of Feuery's face, and seemed to inspect her. The metal fairy was delicate, about six inches high, with wings that looked to be about ten inches long. Her skin was silvery, her hair gold and her wings silver with a fine tracery of gold. She wore a light robe that appeared to be made of burnished bronze, and her bright eyes and lips were copper-coloured.

Impulsively, Feuery raised her hand gently to the fairy. It drew back, but then darted forward to alight on the top of Feuery's forefinger. It seemed to speak to her in chiming, bell-like tones, looking at her enquiringly. Not knowing what else to do, Feuery smiled gently.

That was apparently enough. The fairy lifted up from Feuery's hand, and flew to her shoulder, where it snuggled into her hair and promptly fell asleep. It felt cool and calming.

'Guess we get to the language lessons later,' Feuery said softly to herself, receiving a tiny chime that seemed to be agreement.

Feuery went around the wall and picked her way through the rubble from the towers, across the pavement to where the globe had been. She looked down into the room. It was empty. The hunter-demon had vanished. The magic staff had been more than enough to unbalance the great magic held inside the globe, sending it … where?

No idea, an' I don't care. As long as it took the demon with it, she thought.

She found a shady spot among the ruins, and took a flask and snack out of her bag.

The fairy stirred, and drifted down to the food.

'Not backward in coming forward are you?' Feuery ferreted around in her bag for a moment, and took out a packet of caramels and lokum. The fairy sneezed on sniffing the powdered sugar – a plangent little sound like tapping a crystal – but then nibbled at the lokum. She was especially fond of those with pieces of pistachio, apricot and walnut mixed in, washed down with the diluted wine Feuery offered to her in a silver thimble.

'You've got good taste, but you're not going to be expensive to feed anyways,' Feuery said aloud. 'Be nice to know why you're tagging along with me though.'

The fairy smiled enigmatically at her.

'You got a name?' Feuery asked.

The fairy pointed to herself and made a chime. It sounded like '*T'zing*'.

'We need to work on communicating, short of me making my mouth metal to talk your language.'

Feuery pulled the wizard's satchel over to her, and started to sort through the contents.

* * * *

By the time she felt she'd done enough, the sun was low in the sky and the fairy had long since finished her meal and was snuggled comfortably into Feuery's shoulder.

There was more in the satchel than she'd expected. It contained two spell books. One book had 'basic' spells, but still above Feuery's level of magic proficiency. The other book – sealed with a strong guardian spell – comprised what was probably much higher magic. There was also an outstanding collection of scrolls and notebooks covering magic, fable, travels and history.

She'd also found a sheath of private notes in a blue leather binder that had been written by Wesithar to himself. It seemed it was a common habit for great wizards who used rejuvenation spells to make up such notes, but these were the first Feuery had ever found. Apparently, some longevity spells left temporary confusion after use.

Most wizards denied such spells existed, but given there were known to be centuries-old high mages, they must. They were of more than casual interest to Feuery. She enjoyed her life, and had long concluded the world held more opportunities for mischief than she could possibly hope to do justice to in an ordinary lifetime.

Poor old Wesithar, thought Feuery. *He'd trapped a mighty source of magic here in Rapanel that no one else could use, but that he was able to draw on freely. Then he'd been forced to leave, taking a substitute staff 'cos his was attuned to the magic orb. No wonder he'd been clumsy and frustrated with it at the end.*

Well, she had what she'd come for, and knew she had a really deadly enemy somewhere. *That was worth knowing. Now to find out who and why.*

Feuery took out her equipment to summon an elemental and nudged the fairy gently.

'Wanna come for a ride with me in the light of the moons?' she asked.

* * * *

Soon after Feuery and T'zing departed into the night on a wind-djinn, large raindrops began to splash onto the dry buildings and streets. The rains were returning to Rapanel.

Night Watch

'You need to be more careful.'

The new girl looked at him with her dark, smouldering eyes. 'I do appreciate your concern, but really, there's nothing to worry about. Certainly nothing for you to be concerned about, anyway.'

'Ok, I know it's none of my business, but there are some nasty types around here. I don't want you to get hurt.'

'I won't,' she said, with a tone of such assurance that he decided he'd said as much as he reasonably could.

Tinim was the landlord of the Duchess' Gables. It was a grand old inn in the pleasant and picturesque little village of Wenibi in the lower hills of the Paramounts – the mountain ranges that spanned the centre of the continent. The Duchess' Gables was the most prominent building in the village, which thrived for the three months of summer when those city-folk who could afford it came to the mountains to escape the heat and steamy rains of the plains below.

The new 'girl' had arrived a few months after the 'summer-folk' had left, but at a time when Tinim welcomed some help in running the inn so that he and his wife, Josera – neither of whom were getting any younger – could enjoy the quiet season. It would have been nice if their son or one of their two daughters had taken on the role, but like most of the younger folk, they had gravitated to the better opportunities and perceived glamour of the lowland towns. All doing nicely, but …

The new girl said her name was Demora and she was, in truth, no girl, but a confident and very capable woman, one of those blessed with the sort of mature looks, a full figure and a dignified personality that sat very comfortably with her years. Josera had not been impressed with her initially for reasons she couldn't quite pin down, but had been quickly won over by Demora's willingness to work hard and by her refined manners. She had an air of culture about her, which led others to speculate about her being a governess to the gentry, the adventuring daughter of a noble family or even more imaginative possibilities.

Demora politely declined to speak of herself or her past. With her gracious manner, mature beauty and cultured outlook she was a conspicuously elegant and refined figure within the community.

Therein lay Tinim's concern. Josera's too: she had been urging her husband to have a quiet word with Demora for a while.

Not all of the younger folk from the village ventured out into the wider world. And of those who did, not all made good of it. Inevitably, some chose to stay; while some who left, chose to return. A small proportion of those who chose to stay were the ne'er-do-wells, just as a very small portion of those who chose to return had merely learned bad habits from their experiences in the wider world.

While there were only five such individuals in Wenibi at present, they were a very bad lot indeed. The only bonds they formed were with their own company, where they fed on one another's nastiness. In the past year alone, two women had disappeared under strange circumstances. However, while suspicion fell on the members of the rat-pack, as it was locally known, nothing could be proven. Indeed, during the quiet season the village had no local law enforcement. Police constables came and went with the summer influx of the wealthy. And these five had clearly taken an interest in the 'new girl'.

The risks to Demora were made worse because she insisted on exploring the grand scenery around the village; often at night after the inn closed, or on her nights off. She maintained that she enjoyed the night, and her paintings certainly showed a fine eye for the contrast of light and dark, as well as a skill rarely seen in capturing landscapes on canvas. If her artworks leaned heavily toward ruins and eerie trees against a background of grand valleys and misted waterfalls on moonlit nights – well, that was indeed typical of the scenery in this part of the world.

Tinim and Josera worried on Demora's behalf, but could see that there was little they could do other than hope for the best. Surely a woman of Demora's age and experience would know to take care.

Surely …

* * * *

Two weeks earlier, a tall, heavily cloaked woman in the robes and veil of a Sister of Humility had taken lodgings at the Duchess' Gables. Most of the time, she kept to herself, sitting quietly at a side table in the common room, poring over what appeared to be religious texts. Not that she was reclusive. She was quite willing to talk politely (if a little shyly) with those folk who spoke with her, both at the inn and during her frequent walks in the village.

In a moment of ill-judgment, while chatting with the stable boy, she had mentioned in confidence that under her robes and veil she was horribly disfigured: an exorcism had gone dreadfully wrong causing terrible scarring to her face and body. She told him she had come to the village to assist her recovery. Unfortunately, she must have been unaware that the seemingly-innocent stable-boy was the village's inveterate gossip. Of course, everyone soon knew of the poor woman's plight, which drew her both a certain amount of sympathy from the villagers and a total lack of interest from the rat-pack.

Strangely, the Sister of Humility and Demora almost totally ignored one another. Beyond the absolute minimum amount of interaction necessary for each of them, the other may as well not have existed. They both were very discrete; although only one other person – the most recently-arrived guest at the inn – was aware of it.

But then, there was very little the newcomer missed wherever she was.

* * * *

The gnome had taken lodgings at the inn only two days before, telling Josera she was waiting for a companion to arrive, but since her friend was notoriously unpunctual, she might be staying for some time. Given that most of the inn was vacant – as was nearly every other form of accommodation in the village during the off-season – Josera assured her that wouldn't be a problem at all.

With her incredible charm, the new guest quickly endeared herself to everyone in the village. She didn't seek attention, but was the centre of it in the same way that the hub is automatically the centre of the wheel. With her prettiness, bright blue eyes and auburn hair, everyone in the village quickly came to recognise Feuery. Everyone (including the rat-pack) knew she was also a powerful wizardess as evidenced by the impressive battle-staff crowned by an enormous sapphire that she always carried. Consequently, it was understood that she was to be treated with great respect.

* * * *

Tonight was special, Demora decided. She wasn't needed at the inn this evening, and it would be a beautifully moon-lit night. Wreaths of mist curled sinuously through the lower valleys but the skies were clear. She'd waited a long time for exactly such a night to visit one of the more distant and spectacular ruins.

She left the village just after dark, before the two moons had fully risen, and arrived at the remains of the old estate a little over an hour and a half later.

Once, a stately home had stood there, with what would have been magnificent formal gardens. Now there were just piles of jumbled stone and charred wood largely overgrown with vines and bushes. The forest was well on its way to reclaiming the once beautiful, sweeping gardens. Small and not-so-small things scurried amid the ruins, and an unseen owl's hooting echoed eerily over the broken rubble in the pale light of the quarter-moons.

Demora seemed unconcerned. With her satchel of painting equipment slung over her shoulder and her easel tucked under her arm, she moved swiftly and with apparent unconcern toward her real objective.

Just behind the ruins was a rocky spur that jutted out over the valley below. On it was built a much older fortification. It rose above the ruined country house, and was crafted with strength and preservation spells that had well outlasted everything else.

The fort was comprised of a high stone wall – perhaps twenty-feet tall – that ran across the spur, with a massive double door of stout timber forming a courtyard that overlooked a magnificent panoramic view across the valley far below. The walls and the gates were still in sound condition; strange survivors across time that mocked the once far more impressive home now lying in overgrown piles below them. The interior of the courtyard comprised a laneway through four or five small, broken-down buildings; the walls still mostly intact but the roofs sagging and partly collapsed. The short lane opened into a wide, clear space with a set of low, broad steps up to a dais on the edge of the spur overlooking the valley.

* * * *

As she passed through the open gates, Demora noted that others had also recently travelled this path, but had given it little thought. Her attention was on the view that she anticipated witnessing from the edge of the courtyard overlooking the valley. Nor was she disappointed. The panorama before her was magnificent: ranks of sharp ridges dropping steadily away to the low lands, the valleys between them discretely shrouded, as if in modesty, by the mists. The two moons – great blue Oberon and petite pink Titania – lit the scene with an almost magical glow.

At that point, Demora's main concern was that she would be able to do justice to the glorious vista in her artwork, although the gathering of some low clouds threatened to darken the scene. Nevertheless, she reflected that this might actually help her to achieve her evening's main goal. She was a true artist, and appreciated the right ambience for her work.

Meanwhile, back in Wenibi, the rat-pack had quietly gathered and slipped out of the village soon after Demora had set out for the ruins.

* * * *

Feuery was uneasy, unable to settle in her room at the inn. Tonight had an indistinct but palpable ill-feeling to it. While she wasn't by any means a Seer, she was highly sensitive to the moods and unseen, silent echoes of the world around her. It was a sense that had previously saved her in many difficult situations and, yet, the same sense had also drawn her *into* many (often dangerous) adventures.

Feuery was conscious that a feeling of imminent terror and death hung over this evening – somewhere not too far distant

116

and not too far away in time. It was the feeling that a scream in the dark of night evokes – without the scream. Yet.

The sensible course would probably have been to securely lock the door to her room and curl up with a good book, but there was no adventure in that. At the right moment, Feuery also slipped out of the Duchess' Gables unseen and followed the echo of future fears.

* * * *

It led her along a path through the upland forests. At one time, this had been a well-maintained road. Occasionally, she came across sections that were still well cobbled where the workmanship or preservation spells had held better than elsewhere. For the most part, however, the forest was steadily reclaiming its land with the majority of the road well on the way to becoming overgrown, as saplings broke apart the pavement and runnels undermined it.

Someone had travelled on this path ahead of her. When Feuery occasionally paused to look at the trail with wizard's sight, viewing the magical manifestations that were left by strong emotions, two sets of trails glowed with the psychic residue of strong anticipation and excitement …

Neither trail was pleasant. The second of the two was a composite of a number of peoples' angers, hates, resentments and lusts. The first was a single individual, but with a medley of powerful emotions, difficult to identify clearly.

Even more perplexing was a third trail which had recently joined the path with a peculiar abruptness. It bespoke curiosity; much as her own trail would, and like her own, it hinted at great magical potential carefully restrained. Feuery gripped her staff more tightly and continued on through the deep shadows cast by the looming trees in the light of the two moons. Occasionally, she glanced back to make sure no one was following *her* on what was becoming a damnably busy road.

* * * *

Demora had set up her easel in just the right spot. Her palette, paint pots and brushes were neatly laid out on the tiny stand attached to it. She paused between each wash of colour on the canvas, allowing it to dry to just the right texture before adding another wash and gradually building a vibrant richness on the emerging painting.

The pauses gave her ample time to absorb the panorama, to decide on the next step of her creation – and to listen to the sounds of the night as predators stalked their victims and the hunted scurried or crouched, trembling in fear.

* * * *

The road led Feuery to the mouldering low wall that had once surrounded the stately home and its gardens. From the thick shadows of the forest trees, she scrutinised the ruins carefully. Satisfied that if she couldn't see anyone, then they probably couldn't see her, she furtively passed through the carriageway entrance to the estate. All three trails remained clear on the road; the first two sets becoming increasingly stronger, both because she was nearing their sources, and because the emotions were intensifying.

About halfway between the entrance and the crumbling ruins of the building stood the remains of two once-majestic statues, one each side of the road, set perhaps twenty feet from it. They were surrounded by straggly bushes and climbing roses – all tangle and prickles. One statue had toppled, the other had been broken – snapped off just above the base. The third trail veered off here from the road, heading towards the broken statue to the left. Curious to find out more, Feuery followed it.

In a neat pile tucked in under the rubble were a carefully folded robe and veil belonging to a Sister of Humility. A pair of sensible, flat shoes was placed beside them.

Some folk believe moonlight is good for healing injuries, Feuery mused. *Maybe she's doing a bit of therapeutic moon-bathing.*

Yeah, sure, she answered herself.

Then she noticed this third trail ended here as abruptly as it had appeared on the road. She usually wasn't prone to feeling afraid, but the hairs on the nape of her neck tingled.

* * * *

As she paused, waiting for one of her paint washes to dry, Demora heard a sound that was discordant with the other murmurings of the night. She smiled to herself. She had an unforgettable smile, especially in moonlight. Many who had seen it recalled it vividly to the end of their days.

* * * *

Feuery carefully picked her way past the ruins, following the remaining two trails by normal sight alone. She *really* didn't want to perceive them by wizard's sight. There was now such a strong feral eagerness, almost a bloodlust, overlying them that they were nauseating.

* * * *

As she'd expected, Demora heard the gates creak as they were closed and barred behind her. The timing was perfect – there was enough time for the base washes to dry thoroughly now. Afterwards, she could start adding in the detail.

* * * *

Feuery also heard – and saw – the gates close, with just a glimpse of shadowy figures pushing them to.

Darn! The walls look solid without anywhere to slip through or over. She'd have to use a spell to fly over them, but she'd so wanted to reserve her magic in case she needed it on the other side.

Muttering darkly, she scanned the wall for the best spot to levitate herself over.

'Like a lift?' asked a sultry voice filled to the brim with sexiness behind her.

Feuery turned to see a tall, elegant figure, framed by two enormous bat-like wings, smiling down at her.

'We've met in a sort of way, Mistress Feuery', the demoness said. 'My real name is Rielar.'

* * * *

Demora turned at the sound of the padding feet behind her.

Yes, it was the rat-pack, and what luck! All five of them were here, with predatory smiles as they closed in on her.

She'd suspected this was their haunt for tormenting, raping and murdering their victims and then disposing of the poor, broken bodies afterward by throwing them over the cliff to the tumbling river below. It's always nice when you're proved right.

Now, how was it supposed to go? Of course, she was obviously expected to scream and to try to escape so that they could enjoy the chase and capture as a prelude to their evil designs. It would be a shame to disappoint them. Rather like a last meal for the condemned.

She'd felt that tonight would be special. She smiled again before following the script. The moonlight gleamed off her teeth.

* * * *

Feuery and Rielar heard the first scream. It was unmistakably a woman's, but ... it seemed to lack conviction. It seemed almost like a stage scream at a rehearsal, inserted there because there was a space for it, but with more of a mind on the script that was to follow.

Irresistibly, but with surprising gentleness, Feuery was suddenly scooped up by the nightmare of all mages. There was a muffled boom as the two huge, bat-like wings beat down.

They soared up, over the wall and came down close to Demora's easel positioned on a small dais overlooking the valley. Feuery was carefully set down on a low stone bench. Another pile of woman's clothing lay neatly folded beside it.

Seems like the night for under-dressing, thought Feuery. *Hope it's not expected.*

Another scream from the direction of the ruined buildings shattered the night and was then suddenly cut off with a gurgling sound. *That* one had a lot more feeling behind it than the first scream. There was a sound of scurrying in the old buildings.

'Don't hurt 'er – not yet!' a rough voice commanded.

As if in answer, another scream rang out and then rapidly died.

Then: 'No, no!' The voice pleaded. It stopped on a third 'nooo …' that then trailed into silence.

'You got 'er?' demanded the rough voice. Indistinct shadows flickered between the buildings. 'I tol' you. Don't hurt 'er yet.'

There was a sound of running feet from the vicinity of the wrecked buildings, then a sullen creaking of timber hit by a moving body, followed by a coarse curse.

'Where are you?' called a deep voice, tinged by fringes of a high-pitched tone suggesting growing anxiety.

'We should see if we can help?' suggested Rielar.

'Who'd we be helping?' asked Feuery, but then shrugged. 'Might as well go and have a look-see.'

There didn't seem to be a lot of point in being circumspect. They strode down the stairs to the laneway, or at least one of them strode. Gnomes are built more to scurry in a dignified way, so Feuery did that instead.

They stopped in the laneway and looked in through the remains of the doorway of the nearest building. The dried-out husk of a body, fully clothed, lay looking up at them with sunken, desiccated eyes in a beam of moonlight. An evil-looking yellow-brown pool of thick liquid glistened near it.

Feuery knelt down, looking at what had once been the neck.

'Yes?' queried Rielar's rich, sexy voice quietly out of the darkness.

'Yep,' said Feuery as she stood up. She looked at the pool of liquid.

'What's that pool of vileness?' The tall, graceful figure moved closer, her barbed wings just clearing the sagging doorway.

'Let's call it off-cuts. More politer than some alternatives. They only ingest part of what they take – best bits. Finicky diners you might say.' Feuery looked around. 'Not sure I fancy playing tag with *her* in the shadows though. Could be an unfortunate misunderstanding, 'specially with her not knowing we're here. An' she *is* busy. Let's wait up at her painting-place for her. She'll most likely have calmed down a touch when she goes back to it, an' she'll have a chance to see us. Leastways, she should be pretty full by then.'

Another scream rent the air. Rielar's beautiful face winced. The scream sounded as though it was very close. 'Good idea! You lead. That way I'll be between you and … her.'

Feuery hesitated. No wizard could feel at ease with one of *them* close behind. But under the circumstances …

'Must say, I haven't met one of your folk before.'

'Evidently. You're still here.'

'So … ?'

'I'm a bit of an exception. Shall we go back?'

'Let's – you keep being an exception though, please.'

'By my count, that's four,' Rielar said conversationally as they returned up the stairs to the dais.

'Mine too. 'Course, some of 'em might have got away.'

'Do you think so?'

'Nope.'

'Me neither.'

'So that should leave just the one. Wouldn't wanna swap places with him just this minute.'

'I hope she doesn't play with him too long. We've been avoiding one another until we knew what the other one was up to. I'm interested in meeting her now she's 'come out of the closet' as it were.'

'Speaking of which, I can't help but notice …'

'Oh yes. Well, I had good reasons. I'm sure you'll understand.'

Feuery looked at the succubus – or rather, looked *up* at the succubus. She stood over six-feet tall, with her folded wings adding an extra two or three feet of height above her head. She was slim with iridescent red skin and a gorgeously angelic face – that of a predatory angel – framed by long, glossy black hair. Apart from a pair of high black boots, she was naked.

'Don't you get cold?'

'No. Probably because of the flames of Hell inside me.'

'Really?'

'No, but it's what people seem to expect.'

'Gather you're not here to see me profession'lly.'

'Oh, no! No disrespect intended, but you're not my type.'

'Meaning, you're not *my* type?'

'That's probably more accurate. Just please don't get ideas and start thinking I'm sexy and you'd like to get to know me better that way. I really don't need the distraction, and I'm sure you don't need … what might happen then. I'm afraid we succubi aren't very good at letting our admirers down gently.'

'Until afterwards, anyways. Lot lighter then I hear tell. I can manage not to get over-friendly that-a-ways, trust me. Good disguise I have to say, that Sister of Humility bit. Last place you'd expect to look for a demon is a dedicated demon exorcist.'

'Thank you. If I'd been called on professionally I could have sent any lesser demon packing a lot faster than the real Sisters do, I can assure you.'

'So are succubi pretty high in the infernal pecking order?'

'Very! Even the big fellas are reluctant to cross us because of the Sisterhood. It's one thing beating up on an individual, but we're united when it comes to *any* of us being bullied. Sadly, not with much else though.'

'Trust you're not going to have to kill me because you've told me all this?'

'Of course not! Otherwise I'd not be telling you.'

'Maybe you could tell me what you're doing here – especially, I note as a reminder, 'cos it's not about me – while we have a brew-up waiting for her ladyship. She might be awhiles; savouring the situation so to speak.'

'What's a 'brew-up'?'

* * * *

'That's very interesting', said Feuery twenty minutes later as they sat together drinking their cups of tea, lounging in the moonlight beside the easel. The double doors in the wall had shrieked open soon after Feuery had taken a small brazier, kettle, teapot and cups out of her bottomless bag. After a moment's reflection she'd put out a third cup for later, just in case. They listened to the departing sound of someone fleeing desperately through the night as though a terrifying fiend was close behind them, which was fair enough. Depending on how long the last member of the rat-pack would be permitted to try to escape, Feuery and Rielar decided they might be in for a lengthy wait.

'Her ladyship must really have it in for him', the succubus observed after a while. 'She's taking a long time.'

'Maybe she enjoys a strong adrenaline flavour?' Feuery replied.

'You won't tell anyone, will you?'

'It was only a spec'lation.'

'No, I meant about me. My quest.'

'Course not. Can't see no harm in what you've set on doing. 'Xact opposite in fact. Happy to give you some pointers, an' some references to some folk who might be able to help 'case you might need 'em. Can't help you in your search though. That has to be yours alone. You'll have to live with your choice – lit'rally.'

'I know. It's a bit scary. Exciting too, of course. I don't think any of my people have ever tried anything like this before. I'm grateful for whatever help you can offer me.'

'Works more often than not for most folk. Generally. More or less. Least enough that most folk keep on trying. So was being at Wenibi just to get more used to how this world works? How people behave an' such like?'

'Yes. I wanted a quiet little place to figure out how different things are here.' Rielar looked around. 'I'm not sure I chose the right place to start.'

'Not a lot of this sort of thing happens, most of the time. Though must say, I seem to have a knack for coming across similar.'

The succubus looked at Feuery with an earnest expression. 'I'm just so worried that if – when, I must remember to think of 'when' not 'if' – I find the right one I could mess everything up by doing something ungracious or offensive or uncouth. I don't want to make a fool of myself – especially not *then*.'

Feuery reached over and patted her gently on the hand. 'Don't worry. Most everyone in your situation has the same fears. You seem like a nice person – leaving aside the succubus bit for the moment. Just be yourself – maybe not the succubus thing, leastways not the last bits, the first bits should help a lot when the time's right – an' do what you think is right. Most of all, when you do find the right person, be prepared for getting off on the wrong foot first. Seems to be the usual start. Oh! Speak o' the devil (in a manner of speaking), here comes her ladyship.'

* * * *

Demora paused ever so briefly on seeing them – hardly enough to notice – before walking up the stairs as if she'd been expecting all along to meet them there. She was dressed in a gauzy winding sheet that clung to her body. A superbly *tailored* winding sheet designed to cling to and show her full figure to best effect.

She would, thought Feuery. *They're known for their composure an' dignity an' elegance. Very 'vein' as well, so to speak.*

'Tea's up,' she said aloud as they stood to greet Demora. 'Fancy a cuppa?'

'Just a small one, please. I've just eaten. I must admit I hadn't anticipated more company.'

'Oh, we were in the area and thought it was time the three of us had a nice chat. Private like – away from everyone else. Nice spot for it. 'Specially now you've cleansed it.'

'Sadly, it won't bring those poor girls back. But they're avenged now and it won't happen again.' Her tongue licked a fang. 'At least not by that lot.'

'There's a little crumb left on the side of your lip – that's it. You probably know I'm Feuery, freelance wizardess.'

Demora nodded graciously. 'Of all of us, you hid your power most effectively – openly in plain sight. But we all did quite well though. My full name is Demoratatiana Ir Feliskhar.

As you've probably surmised, I'm a vampire.' She turned to the succubus. 'I must say, you've made a remarkable recovery, Sister.'

The succubus inclined her head respectfully towards Demora. 'Rielar of Rivercut Abyss, madame. I am, as *you* may have surmised, a succubus visiting your world.'

'Holidaying evidently, as Miss Feuery seems to be quite relaxed beside you and apparently unconsumed.'

'My plans are more aligned with a quest. I'm hopeful of settling here if all goes well.'

'How delightful! Will you tell me about it?'

'Certainly! But we'd love to hear your own story first. If you wouldn't mind, of course.'

Demora settled graciously on an old stone bench, accepting a cup of tea from Feuery.

'No milk, sorry, but there's honey an' slices of lemon.'

'Thank you. Just a little lemon for zest. It's quite barbaric to pollute good tea with milk. Where would you like me to start?'

'P'haps about the reason why you came to Wenibi?'

'I never stay anywhere for too long. For reasons of health. We vampires need to feed in our specialised way only every few months. But after we do, the local folk usually become excited and tedious questions tend to get asked. Then it's the whole tiresome flaming torches and pitchforks thing. I prefer to avoid all that. Long ago I decided it was best to keep moving and have a nibble at lots of places. Wenibi just took my fancy.'

Rielar looked quizzically at her. 'And?'

'I'm sorry?'

'There's more to it than that though, isn't there?'

Demora studied the succubus with interest. 'You're perceptive. I suppose it helps in your line of work. Yes, there is. A few years ago, well – a century or so to be honest – I decided that since there were always some really nasty types in every place I visited, I could do the world a favour by selecting *them*.

I now consider myself as a sort of gardener, pruning away the bad shoots.'

'An' causes less of a ruction. Most-like folk would be just relieved that 'specially troublesome pests aren't around anymore. I'm guessing any official enquiries don't last long or look too hard as a rule.'

'There's that too, of course. Still, I'll move on from Wenibi now just to be sure.' Demora smiled. 'I think I might go over to Soleviar on the Blue Isle. I haven't been there before, but I'm sure folk will be much the same as anywhere: the worthy good, the steady industrious, the majority average and the troublesome, unsuspectingly tasty. Now, what of you, my elegant friend?'

Rielar explained her quest succinctly. Demora smiled when she'd finished. It was probably meant as a nice smile, but she'd forgotten to retract her fangs. In other company, it would have been more than a little disconcerting.

'An interesting idea. I hope it works out well for you.' She paused as a thought occurred to her. 'Would you like to accompany me to Soleviar? It would be nice to travel with someone who has nothing to fear from being with me for a change, and I can give you some instruction about this world along the way.'

'I'm not sure,' said Rielar doubtfully. 'I do really need to see if I can find what I'm looking for …'

'Gold's where you find it,' suggested Feuery helpfully. *'Specially if you look in the right places, such as bank vaults an' treasure rooms* she added to herself from personal experience.

'I'm sorry, I'm not sure what you mean?'

'She means that since you only know you're looking for a very special but yet-to-be-identified wizard for your quest, one place is as good as another to start,' Demora explained. 'Once you're a little more comfortable with this world, you'll be better placed to refine your search.'

'You're both right. Thank you. When were you thinking of leaving?'

'I prefer to travel at night. Would right now be convenient? I know one isn't supposed to exercise after a substantial meal, but it's a little different for vampires. If you're agreeable, we can pick up our essentials from the Inn quietly on the way. I'd like to leave a note for my host and his good lady. They're decent folk, and treated me very kindly. I wouldn't want them to worry.'

'If you'd like to write it now, I can slip it in under their door. I'll be staying until my friend finally gets around to arriving. I'll just sleep in tomorrow morning, an' act mystified.'

'Would you? That would save us some time. That is, if Rielar doesn't mind going so soon.'

Rielar shrugged. 'One time is as good as another for me. I'd have liked to have gotten to know you better though', she said to Feuery.

'You can find me again when your quest is successful. I'll give you some addresses. And if it's not – no disrespect, but I'd sorta be grateful if you didn't look for me.'

'Yes, I understand.'

'I am hopin' it'll be successful for you. I'd like to have an opportunity to talk with you some more also.'

'Let's be off then, so that you may meet again sooner', said Demora briskly. 'Do you need to eat before we go, Rielar?'

'Oi!' Feuery protested.

Reilar laughed. 'No, I'm fine thanks. Like you, I need 'special' food only every so often, and Feuery is, of course, exempted.'

* * * *

After the good-byes, Feuery sat on the dais and watched the two figures fly away, Demora and Rielars' bat-wings silhouetted against the two moons.

I hope things work out for her, she mused, finding an unexpected romantic streak within herself. Then she returned back to the Duchess' Gables, carrying the note Demora had written to the innkeepers explaining that she was going to accompany the Sister of Humility in her quest to find a healer. It was, in its own way, quite true … but that's another story.

Meeting my Succubus

He'd been around the entire island during what was left of the day. Bizarre as the place was, there was nothing to explain why his flying-bubble spell had failed, dropping him into the surrounding lake as he passed over it that morning.

At least he was dry now, and he still had his staff and bottomless bag safe. Pity about his sword though. It had plummeted forty fathoms deep when he'd plunged into the lake.

He gazed out over the endless rows of posts while sitting collecting his thoughts under one of the twisted and stunted trees on the craggy little hill above the western beach. Inevitable, given that there was almost nothing on the island to see *but* the posts. They covered it in all directions. Everywhere except the pebbly beaches and the hill on which he now sat.

All of the posts were six or seven feet tall, and about a foot in diameter. Each was firmly placed into the rocky ground, and all were set about six feet from any other post. Some were carved of wood or stone; others were of bronze, steel, iron, brass or copper. Occasionally, there were some of silver, and at least one or two he'd seen were gold – or at least gold-plated. Others were of bone or ivory, and there were some that were made of materials he couldn't readily identify. None of the posts were tarnished or weathered in the slightest. Each post was inscribed with flowing script unlike anything he'd ever seen before. All different, but all horribly unpleasant.

The only magic on the island seemed to be whatever it was that was hindering all of *his* magic. His spells wouldn't work at all: whether basic or complex or powerful. Only his innate magical senses seemed unaffected, for he could still use his wizard's sight, even if almost all it revealed was ... posts.

Was it some type of magical concentration, perhaps like the stone circles to be found in the Druid-lands? Stone circles, mistletoe, garlands – and some of the nastiest rituals to be found anywhere. But, if such quaint and gruesome 'folk customs' had been inflicted here, then surely they'd have left some form of psychic residue that he'd have noticed. Mind you, his wizard's sight had shown there were lots of places where some terrible evils had occurred, but not at the individual posts. Nevertheless, the island had an underlying, brooding miasma of vileness.

Could it be an artwork? For a moment he imagined gay spring festivals with dancing, revelry and song culminating in the unveiling and judging of each year's entries of inscribed pillars. The vision evaporated quickly. It just didn't fit with the macabre mood of the island or the feeling from the inscriptions on each post.

Maybe it was a cemetery or cenotaph island? Some sort of memorial? It seemed the most likely explanation, although there was no sign of the people who might once have revered the island's strange assemblage of elaborate posts. But then again, there was a sense of agelessness about the place, as accentuated by the perfect preservation of the posts. Whomsoever those folk had been, they may well have lived on one of the distant shores and long since vanished into a forgotten past.

Q'tel shook himself clear of his thoughts. His more immediate need was to secure shelter for the night. For all he knew, ghouls (or worse) prowled the island when darkness fell. Something had left those traces of great evil amid the posts.

He shuffled through his bottomless bag, being careful to test whether any items taken from it could be returned to it again. He discovered that they could. Bottomless bags were their own more or less self-contained magical items, and shouldn't be too affected by local magic, but it was prudent to be sure. He'd never before encountered a place like this that absorbed or neutralised magic.

His travelling pavilion would be useless since he needed to cast a spell to activate it. Pity! It would have provided a luxurious and completely safe retreat for the night. That really left only one option. He grimaced. It would have to be the darned Cubbyhole. *If* it worked. But it should: it was its own form of pocket dimension, something like a bottomless bag, and required no activation spell.

He drew a length of fine grey cord from a small velvet pouch and spread it wide in a circle, about three feet in diameter. One end was braided as a loop through which the other end could be drawn. He placed the cord against a fairly upright and flat rock face, the cord sticking to the surface. A hole, the diameter of the circle, appeared in the rock. Gingerly, he clambered in – feet first – thankful he was slimly built, even though at nearly six and a half feet tall he was nearly at the limit the Cubbyhole would accommodate. He tightened the cord so that it closed the opening behind him.

Like being interred, he thought. Even placing a small spy spell outside wasn't an option here. He made an unsatisfactory mattress of his cloak and an uncomfortable pillow of his bottomless bag. Eventually, while still trying to twist and shuffle into a position resembling comfort, he dozed off.

* * * *

After what felt like an eternity of restless dozing interspersed with unsettled tossing and turning amid horrific nightmares, he fretted the cord open slightly to what he hoped would be morning. Bright sunshine peeped through the tiny spyhole. Very slowly, he opened the entrance of the spell.

He looked out from the confines of the Cubbyhole. With no threats apparent, he thankfully climbed out.

Deep grooves had been freshly scored overnight in the rock all around the Cubbyhole entrance. The stones on the ground in front of it had also been disturbed. *If rocks weighing more than a hundredweight each being ripped out of the ground counts as disturbed,* he thought wryly.

He quickly scouted around, keeping a wary eye around him while trying to work out his next move. The lake was too vast to swim, even ignoring some of the creatures he knew lived in it. They'd also be a serious risk if, by some chance, he could make any sort of raft. And given that he had only a dagger with him after losing his sword, cutting logs for a raft was out of the question.

He suspected it would be a very, very bad idea to try to use the posts. Even if any were suitably buoyant, he had nothing to lash them together with anyway.

His thoughts were shattered by a scream; half fear, half fury. A dark, fluttering shape was plummeting toward the island.

The scream stopped abruptly. The creature was frantically gaining some control by quick-wittedly gliding, angling its fall sharply away from the island and toward the sea. It shot over the beach and disappeared in a plume of spray, just beyond where the waves started to break.

Without conscious thought, he'd begun running toward the beach as soon as he'd observed the direction of the creature's descent. He ploughed through the lightly breaking waves and swam as hard as he could toward where the – whatever it was – had fallen.

After only a few powerful strokes, his hand touched something that felt like soft chamois-leather. A wing possibly? Paddling furiously, he felt for the head, quickly recognising that whatever the creature was, it was humanoid and very definitely female.

An angel? No, the wings would be feathered. Maybe it was one of the winged folk with their bat-like membranes? *They're scrawny little sods*, he thought. Yet 'scrawny' wasn't a likely description for what he'd briefly felt.

There was no time to work it out now though. He knew the types of predators in the lake; from the shoals of tiny (but voracious) snaggletooth sharks through to the giant wal-otter via several sizes of mosasaurs and crocodilians. Holding the creature's head above the water, he clumsily swam for shore with frantic haste.

He splashed through the waves of the shallows with the inert body in his arms and struggled across the beach, collapsing beside it in the dunes. She wasn't very heavy, and the entire rescue had only taken a few strenuous moments.

After catching his breath, he took his first real look at his rescuee. The sounds of wind and wave, the feel of the breeze on his wet clothes, all faded to the far distance. Time seemed to pause as he looked at her, his breath catching in fear.

Her face was gorgeous, of course. Finely featured with arching eyebrows and delicate but full lips – the face of an angel with serious attitude. She had a slim, very attractive and beautifully-proportioned figure with iridescent reddish skin. Long, glossy black hair framed her face, cascading sinuously over her shoulders. Stark naked, sleek as a stiletto, with her huge, reddish-black, bat-like wings untidily jumbled around her. Two exquisitely shaped little horns rose above her temples.

A succubus. She was a succubus.

A succubus!

From the very first day of their studies, every apprentice wizard is warned about succubi – or incubi for the girls. They were known and feared as demonic creatures from another plane; always able and willing to slip through to this world for a snack when conditions were right.

A dormitory full of healthy youth under the enforced celibacy that was required of apprentices by the Wizards' Guild definitely met the criteria of 'the right conditions'. Hence, the emphasis their lecturers had placed on driving home the very direst warnings of the inherent dangers. The warnings didn't just consist of 'don't or you'll go blind' tales: one in ten wizards was reputed to fall victim to succubi and the occasional incubus. There were plenty of precautionary examples. Horror stories for the magically gifted.

The favourite prey of succubi and incubi were wizards; the more highly talented and skilled the better apparently, but anyone would do fine if the opportunity presented itself. And they were very, very good at exploiting opportunities. Once a succubus homed in on you, your chances of survival were slight.

Q'tel was a *very* highly skilled and talented wizard. How difficult would it be to home in on the only other person on a tiny island?

He released the breath he'd inadvertently been holding. *Well, right now she's just another being who needs help* he thought resignedly. He couldn't just walk away. Since he'd rescued her from the sea, and given he was the only one here, he was the only one who could help, eliminating all other alternatives.

Probably best not to think of it that way.

He checked her pulse. It was steady but fast. Perhaps that was normal for her kind. Despite his extensive studies and training, he lacked any formal knowledge about the health, metabolism and needs of succubi. Rather, his training was *heavily* loaded toward avoiding them and their wants.

Should he give her mouth-to-mouth resuscitation? It didn't seem necessary as she appeared to be breathing well, if shallowly. But it was probably wise to check in case it did become necessary. He drew closer to her face, noting the fine features and full red lips …

'Don't even think about it,' she said in a husky voice, her eyes opening to look directly up at him. They were huge – a delightful golden-pink, piercing in the intensity of her gaze.

He drew back, unsure what to say as raw fear seized his thoughts.

She sat up with some effort, straightening her wings as she did so. They towered over her head, with a vicious-looking claw at the high joint.

'I have the cracker of all headaches', she observed conversationally in a rich, sexy voice that despite himself sent tingles down his spine. 'What happened? Where am I and who the blazes are *you*?'

'I pulled you out of the sea before you drowned. Shouldn't I have?' His answer surprised him. He was fighting the urge to run, but her tone had nettled him.

She glared at him, but then suddenly smiled. It was the sort of smile that lit up the world around her. *Goes with the territory I guess; tools of the trade, so to speak,* Q'tel speculated cynically. *At least I'm seeing her as she truly is. She couldn't cast a glamour to appear in another form while she was unconscious. Nor, for that matter, can either of us cast a spell of any sort here on this island.* It was a comforting thought. Without at least some of her powers, she was much less dangerous.

'I *am* being ungracious. Thank you for your help. But I'd really like to know: what happened, where am I and who the blazes are you? I'm Rielar of Rivercut Abyss. Use my name against me and I'll eat your chitlins.'

Well, it was progress of a sort, he thought wryly.

'I'm Q'tel. I dropped in, as it were, yesterday much as you just did. Any magic you have will be inoperative here. As to where you are, all I know is that it is an obscure island I hadn't heard of before somewhere in the Perched Lake.'

'Wherever that is.' She glared at him for a moment before standing gracefully in one swift moment and turned to face him.

'Are you a mage?' she asked innocently.

'I have no magic,' he answered truthfully (at least as it applied at that very moment).

'You must be a Darkling!'

'I'm a half-elf.'

'You look like a Darkling. You have the blue skin and white hair and all.'

'My mother is a Dawn Elf. They're the First Elves, so all the elven folk are in their lineage. But they don't like inter-marriage with other kindreds. When she had me she was exiled. I've inherited most of my looks from her.' *And most of my magic from my human father*, he thought, *but we won't go into that now.*

She shrugged dismissively. 'What do you mean by my magic won't work here?'

'Some pre-spelled items seem to be ok, but magic can't be initiated on this island.'

'You seem to be pretty knowledgeable about magic.'

'I acquire spelled items when and where I can. And yes, I know a few spells, but they won't work here. So of course I know a bit about magic. Most people do.'

'You're lying,' Rielar said, 'but about what I'm not sure – yet.' She raised and straightened her wings, then looked surprised.

'Can't retract them?' Q'tel inquired.

'Shut up!' She concentrated for a moment, looking exasperated before suddenly beating down with both wings, sending sand swirling around her. It was an elegant hop, but certainly not flight.

'See what I mean? You fly by magic; at least in this world. Like I said, you can't initiate it here.'

'How'd you get here?'

'Flight spell I acquired in Soleviar to the south. It required a cantrip – a minor spell to maintain more substantial magic – to be repeated every so often to keep flying. When I crossed the island, it failed.' *'Acquired' meaning that I cast it myself, but close enough,* he thought. 'What are you doing here?'

'I know what a cantrip is,' she replied scornfully. 'And as to my business: it's none of yours.'

He turned and walked away, almost as much to his surprise as hers.

'Where are you going? I was talking to you!'

Q'tel turned to face her squarely, careful to keep his face neutral. 'No you weren't, you were talking *at* me. Interrogating me, actually. I'm happy to have a conversation with you, and if we're to be completely honest, we probably need each other's help in getting off this damned island. But there's nothing in it for me if you aren't prepared to tell me anything. That's not helpful.'

'Do you know *who* I am?' she asked softly, a dangerous undertone to her voice.

'Yes, you told me. Rielar of Rivercut Abyss, wherever that is, and what you *are* is a succubus. You can fly, you can materialise through walls, you can transform your appearance, and you have supernatural speed, agility and strength. Probably other things as well, but you also have a problem. Two, in fact.'

'Go on,' Rielar said tersely.

'You can't do any of those things here and now, any more than I can cast magic. Yes, I am a mage, but right now without your supernatural strength and all the rest, I'm probably more of a threat to you than you are to me; if it comes to that. Your second problem is that you're too arrogantly self-centred to recognise when you're in serious trouble. You're stuck here on this island with me just as much as I am with *you!*'

He was surprised he'd almost shouted the last words. Angry – and angry at himself for being angry – he muttered bitterly, 'Save yourself next time' and stalked away.

Q'tel returned to the hill where he'd previously left his possessions before running down to the beach to help her. He pulled some bread and cheese out of the bag, and a flask of irial tonic. He nibbled and sipped distractedly while poring over the few references he had of this part of the world. He kept his knife handy and sat with his back against a rock wall, although he was sure he was more than a match for the succubus physically under the present circumstances. Despite all that had been drummed into him throughout his training, he feared her much less than whatever it was that had torn up the area around where he'd slept last night. If anything, her attitude simply annoyed him.

* * * *

You're not thinking straight, Q'tel told himself. *Stop being so emotional about her. She can't help being what she is.*

Sure, he answered himself, *and what she is, is insufferably arrogant.*

He was too annoyed, too tired, to concentrate. He was about to give up on the references in disgust when someone cleared their throat delicately.

It was Rielar. She stood about fifteen feet away, looking contrite. *Don't trust a succubus,* he reminded himself. *They can portray anything they want on the surface.*

'I've come to apologise,' she said stiffly. 'I shouldn't have been so rude to you. It hasn't been the best of days. I *do* appreciate your rescuing me, and you're right – we need each other. I'm sorry.'

He looked at her suspiciously. Her apology had been almost forced out, unwillingly. Somehow, that was a lot more reassuring and believable than if she had used honeyed contrition. It

140

was almost possible to believe she meant it. He sighed. Trust – to some extent at least – had to start somewhere if there was to be any chance of them working together.

'Me too,' he muttered. 'I'm sorry for getting angry. Would you like something to eat and drink?' *Other than wizard*, he added to himself.

She hesitated before nodding. He reached for his bottomless bag, but then hesitated. 'I'm sorry. I'm not sure what you'd like.

'A nice haunch of tender young apprentice, raw, and a cup of virgin's blood would be nice.'

She laughed – a delightful, cheerfully infectious laugh – at the horrified look on his face. 'I'm sorry. I couldn't resist it. Anything you can offer is fine by me. Any of that bread and cheese you can spare would be wonderful. And an apple, if you have any. I'm very fond of apples. I can't get them back ho … where I came from.'

Why the correction? Q'tel wondered but replied, 'You're in luck then.'

He watched her as she ate, delicately at first, but increasingly with a strong appetite – almost voraciously. He unobtrusively brought out some baked potatoes, seasoned and wrapped in vine leaves, and a small loaf of seed bread, all of which she enjoyed. Apart from hospitality, it seemed like a good idea *not* to be in company with a hungry succubus.

'You were obviously famished,' he observed as she slowed down, savouring an apple.

'I'd flown a long way before, you know. I guess before my downfall, you might say.' She smiled lightly.

'Mind if I ask where you were heading?'

She looked at him thoughtfully over the apple, before taking a small bite and answering. 'Like you I was travelling from Soleviar. To a place called Heliovorn.'

'That's over the other side of the Zeiden Sea. It's a long flight, plus the weather can be treacherous at this time of year.'

'So you know of it?'

'I certainly do! It's my hometown. That's where I was heading too.'

'Ah! Could you tell me something about it? Please?'

'There's a lot to tell. What would be most interesting to you?'

Rielar gazed at him thoughtfully, evidently weighing up how much she could tell him without exposing too much of her interest.

'I understand that it's a very cosmopolitan city.'

'It is that. It was one of the first cities to re-emerge after the Mage Wars. A lot of folk of all kindreds gathered together there for mutual protection during the Troubled Times that followed the Wars. You can meet most types of folk there. Tolerance and cooperation are sort of a cultural legacy.'

He looked at her quizzically, wondering about her motives. It was difficult to think clearly. The poor sleep he'd had last night after a very active day yesterday was starting to take its toll. He yawned, trying to stifle it so that she wouldn't notice.

'It must be a very strange community.' She showed no sign she'd noticed his sleepiness.

'No one even thinks about it much. It's just part of life. You can have your lunch at a tavern owned by a dwarf, the meal cooked by an elf and served by a human whilst sitting next to an orc, a gnome and a sprite – or folk of any mixture of them. That's just normal in Heliovorn. It's a lovely city. The Guild Museums, the Academies, the wonderful markets where you can buy almost anything from all over the lands. And of course, the festivals and trade fairs. Most caravans to and from almost everywhere pass through Heliovorn.' Q'tel was finding it increasingly difficult to keep his eyes open.

'You make it seem more like a carnival than a serious community,' Rielar chided softly.

'Not at all. Heliovorn is renowned for its finished goods and the Guild Academies. Some of the finest fabrics, metal wares and lots of other goods are produced in Heliovorn. And of course, most of the Guilds do much of their research there. Best healers too ...' It was becoming *really* hard to stop his eyelids drooping.

They chatted about life in Heliovorn for a little while before the succubus announced, 'I think I'll have a look around this island. I'll meet you here later?'

'Sure. I'll persevere with scanning my references to see if I can find anything that may help.' Her intention was welcome – although he'd also have liked to continue their conversation. She actually wasn't too bad, when she left off being the Princess of Darkness. He could almost like her, but he was so tired ...

I'll just close my eyes for a few moments, he thought after she'd gone, *that'll refresh me. I won't go to sleep. Mustn't go to sleep ...*

* * * *

His dreams twisted, running away on him. He was back in the Academy, but while the sounds of other folk were all around him as if it were a typical, busy day, there were no people to be seen anywhere.

Except ... he felt someone was following him but when he turned to look over his shoulder, there was no one there. A moment later, it was as if that same someone was ahead of him; always just out of sight behind the next doorway or turn of the stairs.

Nor did he seem to have volition as to where he went. It was as if he were being steered at random through all the places so familiar to him. And time seemed so strange. At one point, he appeared to drift through the Academy as a fresh-faced novice still in awe and confusion, while in the next moment, it was with the easy familiarity and confidence of the High Mage he'd become.

His dream paused at the oddest points; bringing to mind incidents he hadn't thought he'd ever recall. Calming a frightened new apprentice who'd become lost in the great building and escorting him to the correct class so he wouldn't be in trouble with the tutor. Catching and soothing a frightened baby dragon that had just escaped from its cruelly cramped and filthy cage while the crowd in the marketplace fled in all directions. Nursing an assistant archivist afflicted with a minor demon accidently released from an old tome in the archives of the library.

And some he did remember, but didn't want to. Tripping on the Academy stairs and landing ungraciously on a visiting dignitary. The practical joke a colleague played to have him attend a formal function with the back half of his clothes transparent. Undressing at a mages' convention in the suite of a renowned enchantress as she walked in because he'd got the wrong room after having one too many drinks.

Then his dream abruptly brought him to his recognition ceremony of the High Investiture.

His dream paused for a while there, with a sense that the same someone behind him was listening intently to the Calling and Citation. Oddly, he viewed the whole thing as a spectator, one of those backed close against a side wall in the crowded hall, while he saw himself mount the podium to receive the investiture.

But the figure that mounted the podium with embarrassment and pride wasn't him. It wasn't anyone. The robes he had worn that bright summer morning, gilded by the golden light streaming through the stained glass windows above the vast, full hall, were empty. A phantom in his shape received the award and was invested in honour.

Then, in the midst of his acknowledgement speech (with its carefully chosen words to allay the concerns he knew many felt about a 'Darkling' receiving such an honour), the compulsion that had taken hold of him steered him to the Reliquary. There was a series of images of the work he had done to earn the award; years of work compressed into a coil that unravelled in moments. There it all unfolded before him again: the seemingly endless translations of the ancient fragments of scrolls; the risks – and injuries – he had taken to work through the guardian spells on many of them; the often perilous fieldwork to find ancient documents and bizarre ingredients; and the long experimentation to re-create the elixir at which the records and legends hinted.

All of that also suddenly faded. He sped through the Academy again, as if at the behest of the strange presence that was always just out of sight before or behind him but indisputably there, to his second award, back in the same Hall.

On this occasion the figure that took the stand *was* him, complete with the bandages he'd worn, as kind, careful hands helped him up to the podium. This time his speech was a simple 'Thank you.' There was nothing else he could say, and the Hall rose in a standing ovation.

Now he was outside the Academy, watching himself while he earned that second honour. There were the oh-so-familiar, horrible, confused images; the children behind him, the wolfen beasts in front, his flaming bolts of magic fire and lightning at first and, at the end, only the flashing sword. And everywhere blood; brilliant red on the snow, snow still falling all around and the cold, cold, pitiless cold permeating everything.

Then he was back at the podium, but the Hall was empty. His hands were held immobile on either side of the lectern. He was being interrogated: What were his motives? What did he expect of life? What was his favourite colour? What were his personal hygiene habits? Who did he love? The increasingly personal questions seemed endless, the answers sucked out of him. *None of that had ever happened …*

* * * *

He awoke, shivering, with tears in his eyes, feeling more drained and exhausted from the nightmare than when he had inadvertently dropped off to sleep.

Night had fallen, but the scene was lit by a fire someone had kindled in front of him. His first thought was that he was still dreaming within a nightmare; his second was the wish he could return to the nightmare in preference to what materialised before him.

Rielar stood on the other side of the fire, her back to him. She faced a horde of demons that roared, slavered and gibbered, making feint rushes, but always falling back from her. She was barely moving, but even a glance from her seemed enough to make even the most ferocious of the horrors – some twice her size or more – shrink back, snarling in fear as much as in belligerence or defiance.

What was going on? In his sleep, he'd slumped over on his side, his head resting comfortably against his bottomless bag. Yet, it had been over on his other side when he'd dropped off to sleep. And his cloak covered him against the cold night air, rather than being securely stowed in his bottomless bag as he knew he'd left it.

Q'tel raised himself onto one elbow, careful to ensure he made no sudden movements. Nevertheless, a demon with eyes of fire and teeth and jaws like a deep-sea predator saw him stir. It was enough to trigger the hideous creature into a frenzy. It rushed forward at incredible speed, aiming to run under Rielar's guard.

She was faster. A whip (*where'd she get that from?*) cracked across the back of the demon, splitting its knobbly hide deeply. Rielar whirled with blinding speed, a slim sword now in her hand skewering the screaming creature. She thrust the toe of a long black boot under the impaled demon, and in one swift movement perfectly coordinated with her sword arm, flung it back among the sea of demons.

Those creatures nearest immediately tore the hapless demon apart. The others on each side continued their restless seething, waiting for an opportunity.

It never came. A raging bellow split the air and set the rocks shaking. The mass of demons instantly dissolved, running, hopping and slithering into the darkness, all the while screaming and hooting and trumpeting, and leaving Rielar standing alone before the fire.

Q'tel slowly stood up. The magic was back! He could feel it coursing through him again. Darn! That meant the succubus was also powerful, and that she wouldn't need him now. He gathered a powerful protective spell about himself, in order to mull over the most ferocious of his attack spells. If he had an opportunity he'd use the translocation spell he now always carried with him for an emergency. If this wasn't the one, which crisis would be?

Q'tel's chance to get the spell didn't eventuate. There was another earth-shaking bellow; much closer this time. As the echoes faded, a flame demon leapt over the rocks to land heavily facing Rielar.

Demons just love grand entrances Q'tel thought inconsequentially.

The flame demon stood well over twenty feet tall. Its huge, fiery wings spread on either side of it seemed to fill the world. Wreathed with fire and smoke, it held an enormous trident and a whip that looked to be a cable of molten metal. Arcs of blazing fire danced across the weapons. Q'tel stood frozen to the spot. This was an adversary with fighting skills and magic well beyond his; most likely beyond the capabilities of any wizard he knew. Only a few of the Great Mages could stand up to such a foe with any confidence.

His only hope now was to find and activate the translocation spell. But before he could move, the fire demon spoke in a deep voice that reverberated through the air and rocks.

'Why are you here?'

'Ur …' Q'tel began to reply before realising that the question wasn't directed to him.

'I tarry in this world on a quest, oh Great One,' Rielar answered evenly. Her boots, sword and whip had vanished, leaving her facing the terrible creature naked with open hands. 'While passing over this isle, my magic was nulled and I plunged into the sea.' Rielar's tone was respectful, but her voice firm.

There was a rumbling sound that Q'tel interpreted as being the flame demon's laughter. **'Like a moth that ventured too close to the flame. Do you know where you are now?'**

'Yes, Great One. Your penitentiary.'

'Aye. Here to learn penance in this bleak world are those who thought they would be able to thwart my will. By day they are imprisoned within their posts, each to their own. By night they may wreak whatever havoc they will on one another for their sport and mine. My presence is the only means by which the nullity on magic is lifted. Are you in need of penitence for intruding on my isle, little huntress?'

'No. That would hinder my quest. In any event, my presence here was unintended, and no slight upon Your Mightiness.'

'What is this quest you speak of?'

'One entrusted to me by a significant member of my Sisterhood. It requires an understanding of this world and its magic.'

The flame demon seemed to hesitate at the mention of the Sisterhood. **'Then best you be about it. What is that?'** The handle of the demon's whip pointed at Q'tel.

'A mage of this world, whom I have chosen to accompany me to assist in fulfilling my quest. I will take it with me.'

'I will have it!'

'No, it's mine!'

'You seek to thwart my will, succubus? Take care!'

'It is mine. Selected with care and required for my quest. It is you who should take care, Great One. A slight towards a succubus fulfilling her duties is a slight to all of the Sisterhood.' There was a tense moment as they glared at each other.

'Bah!' rumbled the flame demon. **'Take it with you and begone!'** It turned its back on her contemptuously.

Rielar leapt over the fire to Q'tel. 'Hold your staff and bag tight. I'll carry you.'

'To a better picnic spot?'

'Idiot! We don't have time for this. He may change any of his minds at any moment.'

Rielar wrapped her arms around Q'tel as he grabbed his bag and staff. Her wings swept down with a muffled *boom!* as they leapt into the air.

Rielar sped both of them away; across the lake and away from the island which was now devoid of posts. Below them, the horde of demons crowded on the beaches furthest from the flame demon, gibbering and jeering as the succubus and her charge faded into the night.

* * * *

The sunrise was just breaking, casting shades of salmon-pink, pale yellow and peach on the delicate early morning clouds. Rielar alighted beside a gnarly, lone tree on a grassy hill overlooking the eastern edge of the Perched Lake. She gently set Q'tel down on his feet.

'We'll rest a little while here,' she said, still holding him with one arm around his waist. Her wings disappeared as she spoke.

'When do we get to the bit about your breakfast?' Q'tel inquired.

'Well, I'm hoping you still have something left to eat in your pouch. Yet that wasn't what you meant, was it?'

He shook his head grimly, acutely aware (for a confusing range of reasons) of her body pressing against his.

'I'm not going to hurt you. Not now, not ever. I promise.'

'It was you who searched my mind and my memories, wasn't it?'

She looked at him directly, her beautiful eyes seeming to fill his world. 'I did. I had to. Time was short, and I had to know. I'm sorry for violating you, and I promise I'll never do anything like that to you ever again. Not ever.'

'Is it something to do with your quest for your sisterhood that I'm to help you with?'

She stood silently for a moment, still with her arm around him.

'Too much room here for misunderstandings,' she murmured, half to herself. 'We need to get past that. Look, the significant member of my Sisterhood who set me on this quest was *me*. This is my quest, and I promise you it will cause you no harm. Not ever. Quite the opposite, in fact.'

'You're making a lot of promises!'

'They're all part of the one promise I make to you and I hope you will make to me. Forever,' she murmured softly, gently but irresistibly drawing him closer. She brought her face near to his.

No! Not me! I'm not meant to die like this! But her lips gently met his, her sweetly scented hair swirled around his face; her warm, soft body pressed against him.

In the clear light of the early dawn, he fell prey to the charm of the succubus.

* * * *

'Who's that odd couple?'

Feuery glanced around the square. 'This is Heliovorn, Elusive. You'll need to be a bit more specific. Any amount of odd couples 'round here.'

As if to illustrate the point, the two speakers were, respectively, a tiny blonde brownie and a little auburn-haired gnome. Both girls carried the characteristic staves of wizards, and an air of assurance and experience far beyond that which one would reasonably expect given their apparent youth.

But of course, that was different. It would be *others* who were odd, not *them*.

'I meant the Darkling over there; the one holding hands with the red lady in the white robe, the one with the long black hair. She's a stunner! Mind you, he scores all the points too.' Elusive discretely nodded toward them.

'Them? That'll be Q'tel an' his wife, Rielar. Lovely people, an' absolutely dote on each other. For real too. Not just for other people's look-see.'

'The same Q'tel …?'

'… who re-discovered the secret of the all-healing potion. Yep! An' he improved the old formula. Lot of people walking 'bout today have him to thank. Bugger to make it up as a potion though, an' I should know since I was the first one to snitch a copy of the improved formula outta the Guild. Also, Q'tel of the Children of the Gorge fame among other things.'

'I heard a bit about that. What happened?'

'Q'tel is one of those mages like you an' me who believes if you need to find or find out sum'it, then do it yourself. He was up in the mountains awhiles back on some quest or t'other an' came across a caravan ambushed by wolfen-riders. He took a wagon-load of kids who had been separated out by the wolfen under his wing. He fought off swarms of wolfen an' orc wolfen-riders for two hours all by hisself until help arrived.

The Wizards' an' Mercenaries' Guilds point to it as a textbook example of lone combat.'

Elusive looked at Q'tel with renewed interest.

'Oh! An' he's not a Darkling, no matter his looks. He's half Dawn Elf, half human. His mum is Haelela, one of the top alchemists, an' his dad is Somervoar the wizard.'

'What about *her*?'

'Rielar? She's a succubus. That's her nat'ral looks, just with her wings tucked in.' She chuckled. 'Seems like Q'tel finally convinced her to wear some clothes. She couldn't see the point of it, but is probably doing it to keep him happy. She's studying at the Wizards' Guild, wants to be a Healer like him. Doing very well too. Very interested in our world I might add. She often gets me to tell her 'bout things; taking notes 'cos she wants to understand the new home she's chosen. Bit of a ker-fuffle enrolling at the Academy, considering how wizards feel about succubi. *An'* some folk were worried she was some sort of spy, but Q'tel's standing an' Trecina weighing in for 'em eventually did the trick.'

'Trecina argued in favour of a succubus?' Trecina was a high sorceress who periodically assumed the role of Feuery's mentor. That was until Feuery became bored and slipped away on an adventure; sometimes on the same day as her tuition re-started. Their mutual friends might have observed that Trecina often spent more time trying to find Feuery than tutoring her. 'But succubi ...'

'Not generally known for their romantic and domestic side? Rielar is a bit different. She's smart.'

'What do you mean?'

'You do know that succubi an' incubi target mages 'cos they feed off the magic as well as – the rest?'

'Of course! That's one of the first things the Wizards' Guild drums into every apprentice. And for good reason.'

'Rielar wanted a bit more than that. Figured that if a quick snack is good, why not go to the kitchen?'

'Huh?'

'Succubi and incubi aren't there 'cos someone decided people shouldn't take a hand in their interesting dreams. They *need* magic, just like we need salt an' vit'mins. Very similar – only need a little bit. But once they start feeding, it's hard to stop 'pparently. Bit like chocolate. They sniff out good sources of magic through dreams. Dreams cross over between the worlds, an' they use the right sorta dreams to track the magic they need. Trouble is the traditional way of getting that magic is kinda rough; terminal as a matter of fact on the source. But they figure that's ok. After all, it *is* traditional, an' there's always more where that last one came from.

'Rielar looked at it different. She figured: why not *make* a beautiful dream an' have a personal supply of magic all the time? Without any of the nastiness; she's actually a really decent person. Never take too much, but it's always there for a sip. Never enough for the giver to even notice. So she went looking for a good source. Found him too. No 'one night stands' for Rielar, you might say.'

'That's terrible! Poor man! Why doesn't someone tell him?'

'Oh, he knows. *She* told him. She's smart like I said. No surprises. He just sees it as a special need she has he can help her with, an' does so gladly. Boosts his standing as a mage no end havin' a loving succubus as his partner. Plus, he has the most devoted and capable companion in life anyone could ever want. Damned – 'scuse the term – fine bodyguard too, if he ever needs one! But then, so has she well-as.'

'Feuery, that's horrible! How could anyone live like that?

Feuery looked reflectively at the two lovers tenderly holding hands across the square. 'Seems to me it's not that fars off lots of relationships an' better'n, more honest surely, than most. Good relationship is 'cos you're there for each other going through the tangles an' bogs of life well as the sunny bits. Bein' there for each other. *Knowing* when an' *how* to be there for each other. Giving what you can when the other needs it, an' accepting what they can give when *you* need it; 'cos it has to be shared fair, two ways both-wise when the need arises. She was looking for a good partner, 'specially someone caring, an' she's determined to do her best to make it work out for keeps. He probably hadn't figured it out for hisself (males usually don't), but he needed a good companion – someone special – also. He's got the best deal around for him. Just 'cos she's a succubus, in't automatic she can't care. They both have carin' in bucket loads.'

She chuckled. 'Not sure either of 'em figured on falling in love so much though. Look at 'em. What flows between 'em is like a river both ways now. But fallin' in love is a serious breach of ethics for a succubus so Rielar in't welcome where she came from. Don't think she minds much. She'd made up her mind to leave all that behind an' start fresh over anyways. I think Trecina was counting on that before she supported Rielar enrolling for magic training. Makes Q'tel even more caring-protective of her though, an' bonds 'em closer. An' Heliovorn's an accommodating place, 'nough even to accept a succubus. Works for them, an' that's what counts.'

'Feuery! Did you …?' Elusive inquired since Feuery's proficiency with love potions was well known.

'No. I didn't! My love potions in't for playing politics, 'twix folk nor powers. Starting down that ways leads to all sorts of trouble! Anyways, no potion works if'n the folk aren't that-a-way inclined, ne'er mind what you hear. All their own work. Cross my heart!'

'Mind you,' she continued with a mischievous grin, 'I'm *really* looking forward to seeing their kids when they get around to that part. Should be a revelation!'

The Golden Marigold

'They're behaving well tonight, love.'

Sedena's quiet observation as she passed Burtag a tray of tankards was correct. He glanced at the crowd in the common room. He'd been expecting trouble tonight – but he always expected trouble. He knew his customers all too well; anticipation often forestalled serious strife.

The locals weren't usually a problem; they knew what to expect if they annoyed Burtag. No one crossed him twice. Half-orc, half-dwarfs aren't commonplace: in Burtag it resulted in a person of near-human height with the stockiness of a dwarf and the great strength of both his parents' kindred combined. He'd once punched the boss through a shield while, at the same time, his other hand snapped the haft of the battleaxe wielded by the *other* drunken attacker.

Fortunately, his disposition was generally placid, which may explain the great fondness his wife Sedena – a delicate half-elf, petite even for her kind – held for him. Their Sunrise Tavern was by far the least rowdy in the far northern port of Nothor. And they intended to keep it that way.

Burtag and Sedena had even banned the trollops and gamblers of the town from doing business in the tavern. The reduced trade was far less of a concern than the problems *that sort of* trade brought with them. Anyone was welcome to eat, drink or stay, but the rougher and seedier occupations were expected to go elsewhere.

All in all, Burtag was feeling quite comfortable this evening. The Vikings had been here before. The punctured remains of a shield and a broken axe hanging on the wall had once belonged to them. Tonight, they were enthusiastically eating and drinking themselves toward near-oblivion before rowdily adjourning elsewhere to wreak havoc. That was fine by Burtag. The crewmen from various ships in port seemed content to enjoy the best meals and finest ales available in Nothor, and the locals here tonight were settled. The only group he didn't like the look of were six sailors from a ship that had docked earlier today. Not that they were doing anything wrong – yet. But they were unusually reserved and silent. Mariners *not* letting off steam while on shore leave were usually building up a good head of it for explosive release.

One spark, thought Burtag from long experience, *that's all it takes for trouble to erupt.*

As if on that thought, two more than adequate 'sparks' innocently walked in. For a moment, he thought they were two young human girls. He glanced behind them expecting to see someone accompanying them.

Oh! A gnome and a brownie, he corrected himself as they walked over to him in the suddenly hushed tavern.

'Hi 'ya,' the gnome greeted him. She was barely level with the top of the bar and Burtag had to lean forward to see the brownie at all. 'We'd like a room for tonight, an' dinner. 'Specially dinner. Baths'd be nice too.'

He looked at them uneasily. Two exotic, pretty and apparently unattached girls were the type of guests he didn't need. *Girls with wizard's staves,* he also noted. *Expensive* staves, for each staff had a huge jewel at the head to help focus spells: a sapphire on the gnome's, an emerald on the brownie's. The gnome was dressed all in blue, with big blue eyes and tidy auburn hair. The brownie was blonde with mischievous green eyes, and dressed in muted yellows and buff with an elaborate silver and gold hair clasp above her ponytail. *Trouble for sure*, Burtag assumed. But he couldn't help liking them with their fresh air of openness. He glanced to Sedena, who nodded ever so slightly, *Ok*.

'I'll put you in the room next to our apartment,' he said. 'It's a little small, but comfortable.'

'Like them, I'll bet,' a voice called out.

Burtag scowled in the direction the voice had come from among the rough laughter, but he couldn't identify the culprit. The two girls showed no sign they'd heard the remark.

'Just the two of you?' he asked. He'd learnt that it was wise not to take anything at first sight.

'Three,' the brownie said helpfully. Her hair clasp stood up. A little gold and silver fairy barely six inches tall curtsied gracefully with a greeting chime like the ringing of finest crystal.

'T'zing don't count, Elusive, on account she's so tiny,' said the gnome.

'Of course she counts Feuery, 'cept maybe *on* the account,' the brownie replied mildly. 'Don't forget Hector either.'

'Hector *definitely* don't count, on no account. Don't eat, don't sleep an' surely don't bathe. No need. Just a dust an' polish every so often.'

Burtag swallowed. Maybe it was better not to know about Hector. 'So two it is. Ah, the baths will take a little while. Do you want to settle in your room, or would you like some dinner first?'

'Dinner would be great! Better still with a nice green tea', the gnome, Feuery said firmly. 'The room can wait. We only have what we have on us anyways. It's good to travel light.'

Apart from their staves, each girl was carrying only a flask, a short cylindrical container and a large, shapeless bag. They were also each holding one handle of a rather long bag between them. Even a quick glance revealed that each item was beautifully made and finished, even the sacks.

Wizardry, I shouldn't wonder, thought Burtag. *Expensive, too. Looks like Elven craftsmanship.* Aloud, he continued 'It's roast weslock tonight, with fresh vegetables. Hope that suits you?'

'No idea, not knowing what a weslock is. But we'll take your word for it. If'n you're not game to try new things, best to stay home.'

'We can show you some new things,' a voice quipped. Burtag was almost sure this time it was from one of the six new sailors. He noted uneasily that their silent sullenness had been replaced by a feral animation.

'Anywhere you want us to sit?' the brownie asked brightly, ignoring the comment and laughter.

'Perhaps near the kitchen …'

'Here's a nice table,' the gnome said suddenly, making for one in the middle of the tavern.

Burtag groaned. He'd wanted to put them off to one side where he could keep a protective eye on them. The table the girls had chosen, and at which they were now having an animated discussion, was the centre of attention for the whole tavern. He was about to ask them to move to a less obvious spot when Sedena gently touched his arm.

'Let them be. They know what they're doing,' she said quietly. Burtag didn't, but shrugged and did as he was told. Sedena was often more aware than he was of the undercurrents in the tavern.

Seemingly oblivious to everyone else, the brownie pulled a skull out of her bag and set it on the table. 'There you go, Hector. Time you had an evening out too.'

The skull's eye sockets lit up with a green glow that seemed to peer around the room inquisitively. Having satisfied itself the surroundings and company were acceptable, it began a quiet but intense conversation with itself, in two different voices, with a third one joining in from time to time.

The gnome conjured a ball of blue flame about two inches across, which the metal fairy played with back and forth over the tabletop like a kitten plays with a ball of yarn.

With their two companions happily occupied, the two girls began chatting in soft voices that could nevertheless be heard by anyone who chose to listen. And who wasn't listening?

'You wanted to know all about death-trap spells on the way here?' Feuery asked. 'You know, before those bandits interrupted us? Briefly – granted – but they caught my attention at the time.'

'Not so much as your dust-devil spell caught theirs. But yes, I did. You'd started to tell me about Yanniker's Dissolving Snare,' Elusive replied.

'That's right! Now I rememb'r. Cloud of acid that clings to the intruder. Unless you have a counter-spell, an' that'd have to be one of the *really* powersome ones, the Snare strips all the flesh off a body to Hector's specifications in thirty-six seconds. Most-like a mighty long thirty-six seconds at the receiving end though. Probably remember it for the rest of your afterlife.'

'Heh?' said the skull, pausing in his conversation with 'himselves' at the mention of his name.

'Talking '*bout* you, not *to* you Hector. As a f'r instance, respectfully. Sorry to interrupt.'

Elusive looked thoughtful. 'Could be useful. Can you teach me it?'

'Guess so. I'll have to get you some crystallised ammonites though. Only have enough left for about six spells now. I might use one tonight. Just to show you, of course.'

'Would you? What others would you suggest to me?'

The gnome considered the question thoughtfully. 'Can't really go past the Burning Net. Personal favourite of mine actually, an' easy to cast. Not very nice, but them what sneaks about can't really complain if'n they're not careful. Nothin' against sneaking about when the need requires but it always pays to be careful. There's also Jecub's Infernal: throws the victim into one of the demon worlds. Not permanently. After a couple of hours they get returned. Well, whatever's left of them gets returned. Mostly. But I'll have to get you some ammonites for that too.'

'Speaking of which, how's that going? You know, since we last spoke about it?'

Feuery was spared a retort (as was Elusive) by the need to retrieve T'zing and her ball of fire. In a swoop of enthusiasm, the fairy had dropped the ball onto the floor where it was steadily burning its way through a slate tile. The fairy was fascinated by the bubbling lava and acrid white smoke. So was the tavern's clientele.

Feuery unconcernedly scooped the ball up with her bare hand and replaced it on the table.

'Need to be more careful T'zing. Keep it on the spell I cast over the table so's it don't hurt the furnishings.'

'Typical fairy! No forethought for the consequences. It's all fun until someone loses an eye,' opined Hector disapprovingly in a sepulchre voice.

T'zing's reply-chime was sharp, high and discordant.

'That's not very lady-like,' said Hector primly, with an undertone of malicious satisfaction. 'In any case, quite impossible for me. Sadly.'

'Cut it out you two. People will think you're a bit strange if you're going to behave like that in public.'

'Here you are girls,' Sedena said with a smile, placing two platters piled with food and two mugs of steaming tea onto their table. 'Anything I can get for your friends?'

'We'll share with T'zing if she wants some, an' Hector's on a diet. Thanks', said Feuery with a winning smile. 'Sorry 'bout your tiles. I'll cover the damage.'

'Wouldn't hear of it,' said Sedena, fully aware that everyone in town would inquisitively drop in to see the evidence as the story circulated. Trade would be good.

'Weslock' turned out to be slices of some sort of huge sea hare, marinated in wine (and absolutely delicious) with fresh, steamed vegetables. The two girls lingered over their meal until most of the other patrons lost interest in them. Many were surprised to see the table was vacant a little later. The eccentric entourage seemed to have disappeared as if by magic. Which was fair enough – it had.

* * * *

'Feuery?' Elusive cautiously prodded Feuery.

'Wazit?' mumbled Feuery sleepily.

'Hector says it's time.'

'A li'l bish long'r …'

Elusive sighed. When she was awake, the gnome was one of the sharpest beings around, but getting her to relinquish sleep before she was completely ready was always a chore.

'Now!' Elusive said forcefully, 'or I'll slip Hector in under your bedcovers.'

Feuery sat bolt-upright, a horrified scowl on her face. 'Don't you dare do that again', she demanded. 'He's already too much on the-look-and-tell side of things he shouldn't do neither of. No manners at all. Bad enough that last time.'

'Haw, haw, haw! What did the lich see? Wanna know?' the skull guffawed snidely.

'Nuff out of you. You're always putting tickets on yourself, claiming that you're a lich.'

'Well,' said Elusive reasonably, 'since you're up and awake now we may as well get on with the job.'

'Awright,' grumbled Feuery, 'just don't use that tactic on me again. What is the time? Barely feel like my eyes closed.'

'Mine what I don't have any more don't ever,' Hector leered, 'but since you ask, it's just gone one hour short of middlenight. Our host and his charmingly attractive wife have just closed up the inn.'

'Ok. Let's get everything set up.'

'Are you finally going to tell me what this is all about?' asked Elusive.

'Only if you put Hector away first. He's a blabbermouth.'

'I am not!' Hector said indignantly. 'I'm a chronicler of events. If no one reports happenings, then they may as well not have happened.'

Feuery and Elusive glanced at one another sideways. Their businesses involved lots of happenings, most of a nature which it was better no one ever knew about. Elusive swiftly put Hector back into his travelling bag, ignoring his strenuous objections.

'Much better. You indulge him too much. It'll go to his head.'

'I suppose so,' sighed Elusive, 'but he can be so charming when he tries.'

'As skulls wi' glowing green eye sockets go, I suppose. Now, help me sort out the flying carpet an' I'll tell you while we get ready.'

'You've changed carpets!' Elusive exclaimed as they unrolled it. 'It's not as nice as the last one.'

In fact, the carpet wasn't 'nice' at all. It was, or had once been, a jaundiced yellow, on which the weaver had endeavoured to create what might have been a swan, in shades of violet and magenta. It looked like a dejected duck from a morosely psychedelic nightmare. Extensive blotches of rusty, red-brown staining failed to add further charm. And to top it off, it was frayed and threadbare with numerous roughly mended tears.

'What happened to your beautiful blue one?' Elusive inquired.

'Had to sell it after it was compromised by that Enchanted Fleet business. Got a decent price for it, but not what it was worth on account it had to be sold quick-like. This was the only replacement I could get at the time. From the estate of a late wizard.' Feuery replied.

'What's all that staining on it? '

'Told you it was a *late* wizard. He challenged a royal griffin to an aerial duel. You know how touchy *they* can be. Guess he was trying to make a name for himself. It worked, but 'idiot' probably wasn't the name he'd intended.'

'It does fly, doesn't it?' Elusive asked doubtfully.

'Of course it does! It's a magic carpet after all. It flies, just not all so well.' She almost mumbled the last sentence. 'It's a bit of a short-range number, that's why we didn't fly up on it.' Seeing the look on Elusive's face, she added, 'I've tested it. It'll be ok. Anyways, it was all I could afford.'

'But you had buckets of profit from the Enchanted Fleet business!'

Feuery sighed. 'Had. Reinvested almost all of it in this job.'

'Not on this carpet, you didn't. I hope!'

Feuery drew a crystal on a chain up from inside her blouse. 'No, mostly on this. Now do you want me to tell you what we're doing, or not?'

'Of cour ... What's that noise?' Elusive looked up, startled, as loud shouts and heavy thuds suddenly rang out from next door.

'That'll be those sailors most-like. You know, the mouthy ones with the shifty leers? The ones what looked like they couldn't take a hint? Guess they didn't. They were very careful to make sure they got our room number, but maybe somehow the room numbers got mixed up.' Feuery shook her head sadly. 'Doubt Mr Burtag will be interested in what they had in mind. Still, sounds like he's found 'nother way to entertain 'em.'

* * * *

The two girls stepped quietly out of the open window onto the slowly rippling magic carpet.

The night was dark and overcast, so they flew just above the rooftops until they came closer to the docks and their numerous, well-lit and noisy taverns. Here they raised the carpet higher so they were beyond the range of the flickering torches and sputtering lanterns of Nothor's nightlife.

'Glad we don't have to go through that,' said Elusive, looking down on one of several fights that had erupted outside the taverns. It seemed to be operating on 'the-more-the-merrier-bring-your-own-cudgel' principle. Patrons from other taverns came out to see what the noise was all about and then usually joined in. Slatternly-looking women of several kindred gave shrill vocal support from windows overlooking the fight.

'What's that about, do you think?'

'Just high spirits most like. Who says people don't know how to make their own fun these days?'

'I can think of better ways to spend an evening.'

'Me too! For example, ours,' said Feuery happily as they flew over the docks and came out over the harbour. About twenty vessels were anchored there, spaced widely apart, all well lit by lanterns to discourage raiding and pilfering by their neighbours. In the lamp light Elusive could identify several local fishing boats, the Vikings' longship and the low, lean silhouette of a Brethren raider. The rest were a mystery to her; various sized and shaped boats with masts and rigging.

'Hmm. That'll be a Sea-Elf Runner over there. High-class goods. We'll avoid it else we're likely to be shot full of long-bolts. They'll see us if we get closer. An' they tend to ask questions like 'so you were innocent?' *after* shooting. Usually don't miss, neither.' Feuery angled the magic carpet sharply to one side, going around the edge of the harbour across the mud flats.

'Phew! What *is* that *smell*?' Elusive quickly pressed a handkerchief tightly across her nose and mouth, but her words conveyed the expression of disgust on her face.

'Sea pumpkins. Lots of 'em grow in the shallows in spring an' summer after the ice melts an' the hot sea currents reach up here. But first the mess from the previous winter has to defrost an' muck down. That's what you can smell. Later, the first cold snap kills off everything but the seeds, which grow next season. One of nature's glorious cycles. The smell only lasts a month or so, an' then things go back to the usual *eau de harbour* whiff of salt an' rotting fish an' seaweed.'

'Picked the timing well, didn't you?'

'I didn't get to choose the time! The smell'll ease off some once we get past the flats an' over the deeper water. A bit anyways.'

'Oh, good,' said Elusive faintly.

'Now, you know what we have to do?'

'Yes, we've been over it three times', said the brownie wearily.

'Well, let's make it four.'

'You bring the carpet to the big mast, I fasten Hector up there …' Elusive said in a sing-song voice.

'He knows what he has to do?'

'He knows, but he's not being very cooperative tonight. I think we hurt his feelings. He can be very headstrong.'

'I guess he hasn't too many other options. But will he do what he's been told to do?'

'I think so. He'll do something anyway. I had to bribe him.'

'How do you bribe an animated skull?'

'For some reason he wanted to be put into the compartment with the medicines, so I said yes.'

'Hmm. Can't see he's up to any good, but also can't see what he'd do bad there. I'd skin him if he plays up, 'cept he hasn't any skin left to start with. Then what?'

'We go to the back of the boat ...'

'Stern of the ship.'

'Whatever. I don't speak foreign languages like sailorese. Just encourages them in my opinion. *If* I may continue? We wait until the crew gather to see what's at the top of the mast....'

'Masthead.'

'*The pointy top end of the biggest stick the cloth thingeys hang from!* And when you give the word, we cast the spell together.'

'You sure you know the spell? It works a lot better if two wizards cast it together.'

'Of course I know it. It's one of the simplest spells.'

'One of the oldest too. Can't rightly pinpoint when it was developed, but the earliest record ...'

'Which boat is it?' At this point, Elusive had no intention of letting Feuery go off on a tangent.

'Ship. That one. *The Golden Marigold.*' Feuery pointed to a nondescript schooner, typical of those used up and down the coasts everywhere. This one had workman-like lines rather than elegant ones, but seemed solid and sturdy, if a little neglected.

'Not much golden about it,' said Elusive, peering into the darkness.

'You'd be surprised. Shouldn't be taken in by appearances. It's what's inside that counts. Anyone not knowing you're a wizardess an' one of the best sneak-thieves around would just think 'what a sweet li'l brownie girl.''

'I am!'

'I meant the rest as well. All in all. I'll just drop the carpet down to wave top height to run in so's the watch won't see us, even if'n it is a dark night.'

She lowered the magic carpet so that it skimmed just above the waves.

'Feuery?'

'Um?'

'Don't you ever worry something might come up from below and grab the carpet? I've seen sea-weasels do that to sea-birds. One *clomp* and bye-bye birdy.'

There was a moment of silence.

'I guess I do now. Thanks.'

Feuery lifted the carpet a little higher and coaxed a touch more speed from it.

She brought them in over the bow of *The Golden Marigold* and angled the carpet steeply to follow the rigging from the bowsprit to the foremast, and thence over to the mainmast.

'Ok,' she whispered, 'set Hector up there.'

'He isn't cooperating,' Elusive whispered back, urgently. 'Says he'll bite me if I bother him.'

'Gimmee that bag,' Feuery said in a no-nonsense voice. Her hand dived in and pulled the skull out in one swift movement.

'Ousch!' exclaimed the skull loudly, 'Thash not nicsh.'

'Quick! Cast the holding spell. He's been into the medicinal brandy somehow. That's why he wanted to go in with the medicines.'

'Shpir'tsh for the shpir't, thash the shpir't!' carolled Hector exuberantly.

Elusive pulled herself together and cast. Hector stayed affixed to the mast as Feuery let him go.

'Let's get outta here. That drunkard was supposed to wait for our signal when we were ready.'

There were calls from below, and more lanterns were hurriedly lit. Above the growing ruckus, two voices could be heard clearly. One voice was the ship's captain demanding to know 'what the behevens was going on'; the other was Hector who had decided that a brisk sea shanty was appropriate given his new location.

Muttering darkly, Feuery lifted the carpet straight up, and away from the furore. She sped toward a patch of the harbour where there were no ships, and then brought the carpet back down as close to the sea as she dared. Sea-weasels and worse fought for front seat in her mind, coupled with dark thoughts about Hector.

'Sorry,' whispered Elusive. 'I've never seen him do anything like this before.'

'He's never had the *chance* before, but in't your fault. Something always goes wrong, and Hector was a disaster waiting to happen. At least he's got their attention.'

Indeed, the dramatic oration the enchanted skull had launched into – following on from several minutes of singing and realising that he could only remember the two line chorus from a sea shanty – was getting attention not just on the schooner, but also on several nearby ships. Lights were being lit and hoisted aloft everywhere, and queries megaphoned across the water.

'We're still going ahead with it, aren't we?' asked Elusive anxiously.

'You bet!' growled Feuery grimly. 'It's going to be the most public theft ever though.'

* * * *

Feuery steered the carpet in low under the shadow of the stern of the ship and slowly raised it past the rudder until it was just level with the railing of the poop deck.

'There're a lot of them,' Elusive commented worriedly. 'Rough-looking lot. Is that usual for a boat this size?'

'Ship' this size. Only if'n it's a privateer or a pirate or a slaver. Need lots of crew to cope with the rough an' tumble.'

'You mean this is …?'

'Don't rightly know for sure. But for the present moment it needs a lot of crew to guard the cargo. Valuable, like I told you.' Feuery glanced at the two stern cannon in front of them and the swivel guns mounted around the deck and frowned, 'Mind you, they don't usually put boomers back here. This in't just a' ordinary trader. Possibly a privateer. Never mind, folk still sleep.'

'Feuery?'

'What now?'

'Wasn't your plan for us to cast a sleep spell on everyone while Hector distracted them?'

'Yep. Darn fine job he's doing too, if not exactly to plan.'

'And then we put them into the little boats, and steal the big boat?'

'Ship. *Ship*, not boat. They've even helped us – see? The ship's boats are still all tied up alongside, not hoisted on deck. Must've left 'em out after provisioning today. Bit sloppy, but thanks fellas.'

'Yes, but just how are you and I going to get thirty or so snoring sailors *into* the little ships? They're mostly on the big, or even bigger than big, side. We're on the little side.'

There was a thoughtful pause.

'Whoops!'

'Ah.'

'Guess another strategy might be useful.'

'Do you have one?'

'Give me a minute.'

'Better not be longer. Some of them are starting to climb up toward Hector.'

'Ok,' said Feuery decisively. 'Bit drastic, but needs must. Here's what we're going to do ...'

* * * *

Captain Harpinor was livid. Whoever the fool at the top of the mainmast was – and it was impossible to see any details from the deck – they weren't just drunkenly disruptive, but also infuriating. The yodelling and monologue that followed it had been bad enough, but for the past few minutes the twerp had been reciting the most disrespectful limericks about mariners he'd ever heard, and in his long career he'd heard a lot.

Tomorrow, he promised himself, *there would be one helluva memorable flogging.*

Captain Harpinor had great faith in the therapeutic benefits of a good flogging. Not that they seemed to do the flogged a lot of good, but they certainly made Captain Harpinor feel much better.

With his concentration divided between puzzlement as to the identity of the drunk up on the mainmast and anticipation of tomorrow's flogging, it took him a moment to realise the purser was urgently trying to get his attention.

'Fire, Captain, fire! In the storeroom, above the magazine!'

'Flood the magazine! B'sun! Fire crew!'

There was a horrified scream from the main-top, followed by an exact mimic of it, like an echo with feeling.

'Yourshelf! An' the sheahorshe you ride – rodeded - *roded* in on!'

'It's a lich! It's a lich!'

'Shee Missh Schmarty-pantsh Feuery? *They* know a lish when they shee one! *MWWAHAAHAAHAAAH!*'

Sudden, uncharacteristic fear gripped the Captain. He'd been warned about sabotage on this mission, but a lich? And one so powerful that it descended from the night-sky and ignited a fire deep below decks from the maintop!

Unbidden, the thought rose in his mind, *It's here to harvest us! We'll be slaves to it for eternity, undead servitors.* **It** *won't worry about the ship blowing up when the fire reaches the magazine.* Despair and a rising sense of panic joined the fear, linking hands and forming a wild dance inside his head; its cadence in time with the lich's cries of 'Die, burn, die! Hic! Burn!'

'Cap'n! We can't get below decks to open the sea-cocks! It's a raging mass of fire!'

'Abandon ship! Everyone for itself!'

* * * *

From the boats and hatch-covers hastily thrown overside to serve as life rafts, the ship became a growing inferno. Other ships in the harbour pulled away as fast as possible, urgently rigging sail, or using sweeps where the wind would have brought them closer to the imminent ruin of *The Golden Marigold*.

And above the entire horrible scene, the hideous voice of the lich was now screeching the *Drunk Sailor's song* – enthusiastically, because he'd managed to remember most of the words to *that* one.

Then the ship suddenly disappeared. No explosion; no billowing, seething cauldron of flame and smoke and steam. It simply wasn't there anymore. All that remained was a small sudden inrush of water jostling for the vacant spot that the ship's hull had displaced, and a half-hearted wave – a foot or so high – with just a hint of foam gleaming in the lights of the lanterns as the waters met. A very eerie silence spread softly across the harbour and town as the spectators gaped in disbelief.

* * * *

Dawn broke over the bay as the sun rose over the mountains to the east.

A tired Feuery joined an exhausted Elusive at the foot of the mainmast. T'zing merrily flitted through the rigging, occasionally joining them in passing.

'Finally managed to drop the spare anchor,' Feuery said wearily. 'Just in time too. There's a wind blowing up. How'd you go?'

'Couple of rats and mamoks is all that's left. They weren't fooled by my panic and illusion spells. More sensible than people, rats. And the mamoks were too dopey from so much magic to notice. No sign of anyone else. T'zing is really handy to have around. She can check out places a person can't even get into.'

'Have'ta say you adding the illusion of heat to the flames was pretty impressive. Not many wizards I know that could do that. Is the cargo ok?' Feuery knew it would have been securely locked up. She also knew Elusive was both inquisitive and proficient with a lock-pick.

'Thank you! Sure is!' Elusive brightened a little. 'And it's all ours?'

'An' the ship. All the commission decreed was to stop the cargo getting to the Vikings. Surely done that being as how we've been magiced clear over to the other side of the continent. No one cared much 'bout what happened to it afterward. An' this way, no one's going to salvage it 'cept us. Where's Hector?'

'He asked to be put into a bucket of icy water with some willowfine in it. Said it felt good for his head. He's to call me when he drinks enough to expose his mouth.'

'Hope he's suffering,' said Feuery with great satisfaction. 'Self-inflicted injuries, hangovers. Let's see if we can rustle up a nice pot of tea.'

* * * *

'Bit chilly, even with the sun up', observed Elusive as they sipped their hot mugs of tea beside the ship's wheel. Biscuits would have been nice as well, but all they could find was hardtack. After a cautious nibble or two and an exploratory dunking in their tea the ship's biscuits made quite satisfactory splashes when thrown overboard.

'We're pretty far north. Same latitude, more or less, as when we were on the other side of the continent. However, over here you don't get the warm ocean currents coming up from the tropics.'

'That was a powerful translocation spell.'

'That was a powerful and *expensive* spell. One-off use also. Crystal shattered when it was done.' Feuery ruefully held up the chain from which the crystal had hung. Only a few shards remained in the clasp. 'Worth it though.'

'Pity it didn't take us to a nicer spot.' Elusive looked across the bay to the snow-covered hills and mountains. She was sure she'd seen ice floes further north too. 'Wouldn't want to be caught here in a gale.'

'No, the spell had to be used on the same line of latitude from Nothor to here. The mage who made the crystal for me was most particular 'bout that. Said it had to align with two fracture points in space – there and here. Also said not to cast magic near what it was used on – that'd be *The Golden Marigold* – for awhiles. Mumbled something about it being magically unstable for some time. Mind you, I don't think he knew exactly what he was talking about neither, but the spell worked fine,' she added.

'So, here we are with one working schooner full of gold and no crew to man it. What was the treasure originally for?'

'The Grand Magister at Sarfin took it into his head to acquire Saar'filian from the Fair Elves. Didn't want to make open war with them though, can understand that. Peaceful folk for the most part, Fair Elves. However, they take less kindly to swords an' spears pointed at 'em than most anyone else I know – barring Dawn Elves of course. So, he was going to pay the Vikings of the Eastern Fjords to raid Saar'filian 'til the Fair Elves gave it up as being too troublesome. Not sure how he intended to get the Vikings to stop then, but most likely he didn't think that far ahead.'

'I saw the treasure. It's a huge payment!'

'Thorvold, the Viking Warlord, figured the Elves would be tough to beat. He demanded weregild in advance for the warriors he figured he'd lose, as well as for payment for doing the job. Reckon the Fjords'd have to have lost just about every warrior, all the boys down to about age five *an'* half the ol' ladies to cover the weregild he demanded. From somewhat else I heard he had organised a commission on the side with the Brethren too. The Fair Elf navy at Saar'filian has been cramping their style something dreadful.'

'You have to wonder how some folk can be so greedy,' Elusive said ruefully, shaking her head at the avarice of such people. 'He would have been getting triple payment, plus whatever they could loot out of Saar'filian.'

'I know, it's terrible,' said Feuery sympathetically. She had unsuccessfully tried to find out how the Brethren payment was to be made. Their success last night probably meant that stealing the Brethren payment as well was an opportunity that was (sadly) foregone now. She'd just have to be satisfied with getting the Vikings' payment and weregild, plus the ship and the commission from the Fair Elves. Oh, and, of course, the gratuity she'd negotiated with the Guild of Merchants who were keen for the Fair Elf navy to keep trade routes safe. Pity there hadn't been time to cut any other side deals.

'So, *The Golden Marigold* – is she full of the payment for the Vikings *and* the weregild?'

'Yep. The payment is in gems 'n' white gold. The weregild is in gold an' silver. We'll take the payment with us in our bottomless bags when we leave, an' stash the heavy stuff for later. I brought along a spare bag too, so we can take a fair bit of the gold with us. But there's a limit to what even a bottomless bag will hold. We'll have to hike out, but we can use the carpet for any difficult parts of the trip.'

'This Thorvold and the Grand Magister – can't see them being very happy about last night.'

'The elves will be happy. Can't please everyone.'

They sipped their teas quietly for a moment, each lost in her own thoughts.

'Feuze …?'

'I told you not to call me that!'

'There was something else I found; in a little storeroom with lots of old clothes and personal bits. Most of the clothing was good quality, although bloodstained and cut about.'

Feuery grimaced. 'Most likely *The Golden Marigold* has done a bit of pirating. Stuff left from its victims.'

'There was one magical item that had just been chucked into a corner; not just the usual charms and stuff.' Elusive pulled a long, round canvas bag over to where they were sitting. 'I'm not sure what it is. I thought you might know.'

Feuery opened the mysterious bag and looked in: her eyes appearing unfocused as she viewed the item with wizard's sight, following the lines and twists of magic around and through it. Elusive looked on with envious admiration. All wizards were taught to use magical sight, but Feuery was exceptionally adept.

The little gnome looked up after a moment, her eyes readjusting to normal vision. 'You struck lucky. It's an enchanted pavilion. Once it's been set up, you're safer inside than in a citadel. With a bit of luck it'll be well set up inside too. When a mage goes to the trouble of making one of these, they usually appoint 'em well.'

Elusive looked up at the sky, a gust of cold wind flinging her ponytail about. 'It might be useful now the sky's getting darker and the sea's picking up. Looks like there might be a storm coming. Maybe we could set it up over there on the deck?'

'Look, I'm just about done in, and you're not looking your usual fresh self. We could both of us – an' T'zing – do with a good kip. Let's take the treasure that'll be coming with us when we leave over to shore, set up the pavilion an' have a good night's sleep. We can come back tomorrow and secure the ship an' the rest of the heavy treasure.'

'You mean just leave the boat?'

'Ship. Someone I know who's been soaking a self-inflicted sore head is going to act as look-out while the rest of us who've been busy working have a well-deserved rest.'

Feuery stood up, and almost tripped over a sack. It rattled. 'Wazat?'

Elusive looked embarrassed. 'Um. Bones.'

'Bones?'

'Um, Hector asked if I could create something for him to give him some mobility …' her voice trailed off.

Feuery looked at her sternly. 'If you're thinking of making him a body, there'd be some bits you'd wanta leave off for starters. Save trouble generally, an' save me taking 'em off of him when he plays up. For seconds, you be careful. That's getting into necromancy territory.'

'It was just an idea …'

'The sort of idea you think regretfully about later even though it seemed like a good idea at the time. Don't do it! Now let's get our stuff. You can set Hector up there on the binnacle with orders to let us know if'n we have to get back in a hurry.'

* * * *

By the time they'd loaded the majority of their treasure into their bottomless bags, had a short but fierce argument with Hector (who hadn't wanted to be disturbed) and ferried themselves over to the meadow on the magic carpet, the storm was sweeping in toward them. The bay was a churning mass of foaming waves, strong gusts of wind were howling through the rigging on *The Golden Marigold* and the sky was a solid sheet of writhing storm clouds. The air became bitterly cold. Light sleet and rain were just beginning to fall as they activated the pavilion and hastily crowded into it with their gear.

Elusive gasped. The interior was brightly lit and far bigger than the outside would've suggested. The floor was a light, resilient material that soaked up the water dripping from them. The centre of the pavilion was taken up by a low table, around which three couches were placed with the promise of anticipated comfort, while off to her left was a little kitchenette complete with bench, cupboards, a sink and an oven. To her right were a row of screens, which Feuery immediately inspected.

'Two sleeping alcoves with raised palettes, an' pillows an' soft blankets. Probably look good anytime, but just now hard to imagine anything better. The last is a li'l toilet an' washroom. This place is just right for two people. Better still, two folk an' a metal fairy. Wonder who made it? I could find out, but I'm too tired right now.'

'Do we need to lock the door? Or something?'

'Just order it secure. We can still look out, which is why I wanted to position it so the door looked out over the bay, but no one could look in. Very comfy. Lots of little spells in here too. Bet the water in the washrooms is hot, an' the beds will probably be heated too. You did well.'

They quickly settled in, and almost as quickly turned in for the night, as the full force of the storm swept in over the bay.

* * * *

'Feuery, wake up! T'zing is all worked up about something!'

Feuery reluctantly surfaced. 'Wha'?'

T'zing fluttered excitedly around Feuery's face, sounding like a school reunion of excited musical triangles.

'Ease up T'zing! Can't follow you when you're so skittish.' Feuery sat up and listened carefully to the fairy's chimes.

'I really don't understand how you get the sense of what she's saying,' said Elusive, yawning. 'I can recognise some of the 'yes-no-here-there' basics, but the rest is just chimes. Nice ones though,' she added hastily as the fairy looked at her reproachfully.

'Me neither, but T'zing understands me an' I'm getting better at discerning her meaning. She says something's happening at the ship.'

'But we haven't heard anything from Hector yet!'

'Most likely it'll be Hector that's happening', Feuery answered grimly.

* * * *

It was just before sunset, with enough light seeping through the storm clouds to give grey definition to the hills behind them. The storm was easing with fewer rain squalls, but the seas and winds were still high. Breaking waves and flying spindrift covered the bay. *The Golden Marigold* should have been pitching and tossing wildly at the end of its anchor chain, but it wasn't. Instead, surrounded by a yellow-green phosphorescent glow, it floated serenely above the crests of the highest waves, seemingly oblivious to the winds.

As they watched from the pavilion, the ship rose even higher, the anchor chain straining before parting with a sharp *crack!* audible even over the howling winds and the rolling thunder. The ship shivered as it lifted suddenly, then settled, its bows turning to point toward them.

'Unstable magic, just like the mage warned', muttered Feuery. 'Wonder what tipped it over.'

'Look!' cried Elusive, 'Up there at the mainmast head! It's Hector!'

'He's made himself a little nest of bones. See the way he's nestled into the 'v' where the two thighbones cross?'

'How'd he do it though?'

'You can ask him. He's coming our way now.'

The Golden Marigold, sails still furled, *was* making its way toward them. It crossed the massive breakers where the sea sent great clouds of spray high against the rocks, and stopped at the edge of the dunes.

'Wotcher!' shouted Hector gleefully from his lofty perch.

'Neat trick. How'd you do it?' Feuery shouted back.

'My ever-so-kind *former* mistress Elusive felt sorry for me and put some all-healing potion into my recovery bath. It was just what I needed to achieve my proper status as a full lich! *MMWWAAAHHAAHHAAAA*! Now I'll celebrate by crushing you with my new self, a former and future pirate ship!"

The Golden Marigold surged forward and dropped toward them – then abruptly stopped.

'Before you start threatening decent folk, be best to know what you can and can't do,' advised Feuery. 'You can't leave the sea now; beaches are your limit. Not mine though.' She cast a pulsing stream of blue energy at Hector.

It struck the ship's rigging, the rippling blue writhing through the yellow-green phosphorescence. The sails broke loose from their fastenings and dropped, filling with a solid *BOOM*! while turning bright blood-red. Hector screamed. *The Golden Marigold* shook violently. A cannon broke loose, crashing heavily inside the hull. A family of three mamoks sped out of a porthole and hovered uncertainly before making a beeline for the pavilion. Elusive hastily stepped aside as two of them shot inside. The third paused and burrowed into Elusive's abundant hair.

Hector bellowed in fury at Feuery. *The Golden Marigold* pulled away, back over the bay, and then turned and sped out to sea. It dwindled rapidly and disappeared into the low clouds.

'Darn! There goes our treasure', exclaimed Elusive in the relative silence. 'And our big boat.'

Feuery shrugged. 'Fair price to pay to be rid of Hector. We got the best of the treasure anyways. An' some mamoks. No need to come back here again neither.'

'But what just happened?'

'I cast a spell on him so that wind attracts the sails, 'stead of pushing 'em along. Also, the ship has to always stay airborne. Should keep him outta trouble.'

'Aren't you worried about what Hector might do with the ship?'

'Most likely not much now. Scare some folk, start a few dark legends, try to be evil in a looking-up-girls'-dresses sort of way. Hector's too flaky to be a seriously bad lich. He's trying to be what he's not. Catches up sooner or later; sooner most-like for Hector, I'll bet. Probably sell the ship for booze or run into an iceberg if'n my spells fail. Elsewise, great stuff for some colourful stories: a flying merchantman with blood-red sails that always heads into the wind, cap'ned by a ghostly skull on two crossed bones. Scary stuff, 'less you know Hector.'

Elusive giggled. 'He always wanted fame!'

'And now he'll get it. Come on, let's finish our sleep an' then go home-ways in the morning.'

The Azure Needle

The blizzard was finally easing.

For three days and four long nights it had battered the proud mountain ranges and deep, dark gorges, burying them under snow and sleet as gales shrieked through the passes and tore at every exposed rock and crag.

At the first hints of the storm, the yetis and ice-worms had hidden deep in caverns and crevices. Likewise, the rocs and gryphons had sensibly flown far way to avoid it altogether. Even the barbegazi communities who inhabited the few relatively sheltered valleys had withdrawn inside deep caverns to shelter from the ferocious tempest.

But now the sun was striving to shine through the last vestiges of trailing clouds, its weak rays softening the gleaming, fresh snow on the mountain wilderness. As if to celebrate the storm's passing, avalanches sporadically rumbled throughout the mountains, sending plumes and scurries of snow and ice shards from the high peaks and crags.

Yet few creatures – even the most ravenous following the days of enforced fasting – ventured forth. They restlessly waited in their dens and caves and rocky crevasses for the mountainous landscape to return to its former merely hazardous conditions.

However, not everyone was prepared to wait patiently for the scene to settle. In fact, some folk did *not* consider patience to be a virtue; rather they viewed it as an onerous and quite unreasonable imposition.

On a huge snow bank on a sloping ledge at the foot of an immense cliff there were signs of sudden activity. A cloud of snow abruptly erupted outward with a mushy (but startling) noise somewhere between a wet *whoosh!* and a soggy *bang!* It triggered a small avalanche that cascaded noisily to the valley far below. Several other avalanches joined in sympathetically across the nearby mountains.

As the echoes and the swishing of the falling snow gradually faded, two figures appeared at the gaping hole left in the snowbank.

'Not bad,' said a thoughtful, appraising voice, slowly. 'That should'da sent snow clear over Heliovorn. Though not quite enough to reach Sarfin. You might wanta work on the *oomph!* behind your spells in future.'

'Oh, stop exaggerating Feueze. I didn't want us to spend half the morning picking our way through the loose stuff. Looks like a nice day. Shall we use the magic carpet?'

The first speaker was Feuery, an auburn-haired, blue-eyed gnome wizardess and adventurer-at-large. The second was her friend, colleague, understudy and enthusiastic (junior) partner in – when the need or opportunity arose – crime. Elusive, a blond, green-eyed brownie (sometimes known as halflings) was also a wizardess, although not as accomplished as her friend.

The combination of the two young women generally spelt trouble for the unsuspecting.

Feuery looked around thoughtfully. 'Nah,' she eventually decided. 'Lot of crosswinds still. Bit dangerous, plus the carpet's a bit dodgy. It's a long ways down in all directions up here in the mountains if'n it plays up. We'll try to pick up that trail again an' see if we can get into a valley that'll lead us out.' She looked disapprovingly over the mountains around them. 'Untidy way of leaving things this. Feels like all the bits left over when the world was made. Just sorta dropped around any-old-how, like no one cared less at knock-off time.'

'They were probably tired, you know, what with Creation and all,' suggested Elusive charitably. Elusive's reasonableness rarely failed to annoy Feuery. It was a steadfast aspect of their relationship and one that Elusive cherished and honed like a fine blade.

Feuery wrinkled her nose in disagreement. 'Still, that's no excuse. Good workers tidy up after 'emselves.'

Having just spent the duration of the blizzard with Feuery in the safe but close confines of their enchanted pavilion, Elusive was well aware that the gnome had remarkably little inclination to tidy up after herself if there was anyone else available who might do so (and usually, in desperation, did). However, those same three days and four *very* long nights had also temporarily sated Elusive's desire for bickering, so she kept her observation to herself.

'Any chance of summoning something for a ride?' she asked instead, hopefully.

'Can't think of anything we could call at the moment. Air elementals are usually the best bet, but they'll be too busy playing up there in the winds to wanna do anything else. Look at 'em.' Feuery gestured to the fine, high wisps of purest white streaking across the deep blue sky. 'They're having the time of their lives. Too cold here now for water elementals to be ought but grumpy, an' fire an' earth elementals aren't much good for travelling. All the winged folk with any sense would've buggered off after a storm like that. That just leaves infernals, an' you just 'bout need a lawyer in every pocket to deal with them – even for me. Anyway, the exercise will do us good.'

'Some mages keep a couple of elementals or infernals handy, don't they?' Elusive hinted hopefully.

'I don't hold with that, me. Not right to keep thinking creatures bottled up at your beck an' call. Next thing, folk'll be thinking it's ok to do that to other people well-as. People who don't do the right thing by other creatures who can't speak out for 'emselves surely can't be trusted to do the right thing by folk who can be bullied into *not* speaking out for 'emselves neither. Best not to encourage that type of thinking an' doing. Come on, let's get packed an' moving.'

* * * *

'I don't like the appearance of that. It looks sorta glassy.'

The two girls stood looking across the edge of a wide sheet of snow that angled sharply down from a high cliff face to end at the edge of another, very high, drop-off. They'd made surprisingly good time, quickly picking up the trail and following it around a series of ledges with high cliffs above and below them. The main delays had been the need to carefully pick their way along the narrow sections of the ledges, and frequent stops to grip anything available when sudden, sharp wind gusts threatened to tear them off the trail.

'We're not going back, and we're not going to wait it out', said Elusive decisively. 'I'm game to give it a try,' she added.

Feuery shrugged. 'Ok, but tie the rope around your waist. I'll anchor it here. Once you get to somewheres stable, I'll cross to you, an' then we do the same again. One of us always anchoring t'other, just in case.'

'How come I have to go first?'

'Because you're the one who wanted to try it. I'm just taking care you don't rush in an' get yourself hurt. Anyways, you're the lightest one.'

Elusive opened her mouth to say more, but then decided against it. This was exactly why she didn't want to wait it out. At least this way she could walk away from a bicker, even if walking away was out over a precarious snowfield. Not ideal, but definitely preferable.

Bargain, she thought sourly as she grumpily tied the rope around her waist.

Feuery carefully paid out the rope as Elusive gingerly crossed the snowfield.

'Not much more rope left. You found a solid spot yet? A big rock'd be a good idea.'

'No, but I think it's quite saf …'

Elusive's voice was lost in a tearing groan that quickly became an earth-shattering rumble as the snowfield tore loose from the slope. Almost instantaneously, Feuery cast the spell she'd had ready and darted backwards around a slight corner of rock to the relative safety of the ledge as tons of snow, ice and rock fell into the abyss below. A cloud of shattered ice and mist enveloped everything in front of her.

As she listened to the fading din of the avalanche, her racing heart gradually slowed.

'Would you mind pulling me down now? Not that I want to rush you, but the view is pretty scary from up here.'

Feuery looked up to where Elusive now floated at the end of the taut rope immediately above Feuery's head.

'Hope you're not whingeing. Could've been a lot worse.'

'Oh, I know. Believe me, I'm grateful, but I think you might have overdone the strength of the weightless spell.'

'I was hurrying things a bit,' Feuery grumbled as she hauled the brownie down. It was hard work pulling against the weightlessness spell until Elusive was low enough to de-spell herself.

'Thanks Feueze,' she said sincerely before breaking into a wide smile. 'And look … tah dah! I've found us a clear passage across!' She gestured theatrically across the rocky expanse where a few tenacious patches of snow and ice were clinging stubbornly to the mountainside here and there. 'Hey, careful!'

Feuery had suddenly darted past her and was bounding across the rocks toward the top of the slope, where several massive boulders lay at the base of the cliff.

'Now what's she up to?' Elusive muttered to herself as she cautiously followed behind Feuery.

Feuery was kneeling beside what looked to be a bundle of clothing tucked into a space between two boulders, when Elusive joined her. With a start, the brownie realised it was a body.

'Been here a long whiles I'd say. Not much ice on him, so I'm guessing he was in under a rock that just went over with the rest.' She began checking over the body.

'Feuery! What are you doing?' Elusive inquired.

'Like to know who he was. Judging by the clothes he looks as though he was a philosopher, which is a bit strange for around here. Yep – see? He's still wearing the Philosophers' Guild amulet.'

'Maybe he was seeking solitude, enlightenment and wisdom far away from any distractions?'

'Well, he certainly found solitude. Maybe enlightenment too, but can't see him sharing it now. As for wisdom, bet he'd think twice afore venturing here again if he had the choice. Also, he might have something interesting on him.'

'You can't go robbing dead bodies!'

'Bet I can! Less fuss than live folk, as a rule – such as now, case in point. Look, *he's* not complaining, an' *I'm* not, so you're outvoted two to one. Ah! What's this?' She drew out a heavy leather pouch from an inside pocket of the green cloak wrapped around the body. She undid the tight knot on the drawstring, and tipped the contents cautiously onto the cloak of the dead man.

A long, slim sliver of brilliant blue crystal twinkled in the sunlight. Beside it lay a small pair of long forceps.

'Wow! I can feel the magic contained within it from here,' Elusive exclaimed. 'What is it?'

'Not so certain,' said Feuery. 'Rings a bell, but not very clear. I wonder …' She cautiously touched the crystal.

Light erupted from the crystal, engulfing and dazzling them. The world seemed to lurch and it took a moment for both girls to recover their senses.

'Yep. Wondered 'bout that. Now we know not to touch it. Guess that was why he had it safely wrapped up an' the reason for the forceps. Think I know what it is now. Very rare, most likely won't see another one like this again in an elf's lifetime.'

'I can see another one right now,' said Elusive distantly.

'Huh? You're kidding me?' Feuery scanned the ground around them quickly.

'Nope. It looks exactly the same, just a bit bigger.' Elusive pointed behind Feuery.

Feuery turned. They now stood on a gentle, grassy slope on the side of a wide valley ringed by steep mountains. In the middle of the valley was a city of elegant white buildings neatly laid out in concentric circles pierced by wide avenues radiating from the centre – to which Elusive now pointed. At the very centre of the city was indeed another azure-blue, needle-like crystal with the same proportions as the one they'd just found. However, this one must surely have been over a thousand feet high.

'If you're planning on starting a collection, you'll need a bigger bag to put them in,' Elusive remarked drily to her friend.

* * * *

'Feueze,' whispered Elusive. 'Why are we creeping like this? The city is obviously deserted.'

By now, they'd made their way well into the city proper. Feuery had insisted they be as furtive as possible, which for a gnome and a brownie was very furtive indeed. Nevertheless, not only had they not seen any inhabitants, but also they'd seen no other creatures at all. Not even an insect, nor heard so much as a bird call. The only sounds were their own faint foot-falls, an occasional rustle of their own clothing, and the gentle sighing of breezes through the buildings around them.

'What made it deserted in the first place is what worries me,' Feuery said grimly. 'It's not natural; trees an' grass an' bushes are fine, but nothing else. No folk, no birds, not even insects.'

'It is a bit eerie. This is Luminosa, isn't it?'

'Seems so. The fabled city of the Arch Mage Philineso – one of the greatest mages, historians an' philosophers of all time. Legend has it that he established this place afore the Mage Wars as a paragon of society, inviting many of the most promising scholars an' students of the day to become residents, an' he hasn't been seen since. Nor them.'

'It would be nice to see someone now.'

'Even if'n we did, bet it'd be a stranger in town who didn't know where anything is anyway. That always seems to happen everywhere, every time.'

'Can we at least stop for a few moments and have a rest and bite to eat? It's been hours since we had breakfast.'

'Ok. A nice cuppa surely wouldn't go astray, grant you that.'

They settled down for a short break in a small garden in what appeared to be a market square; the great crystal obelisk now rearing majestically over them.

Elusive glanced up at it uneasily as she munched a sandwich and Feuery phistled about making tea; a protracted procedure that was always accompanied by a certain amount of tinkling, clinks and the faint burbling of water coming to the boil.

'There's something really creepy about this place,' Elusive remarked as Feuery finally settled down with a steaming cup of tea and some ginger biscuits. Feuery was very fond of ginger biscuits, especially when she felt free to dunk them in her tea first – which was always, regardless of the company. 'Something about it keeps grating on my nerves. Something just out of reach of knowing.'

Feuery took her time in answering, mainly due to having to juggle a soggy biscuit that was threatening to seek refuge in the depths of her tea. Unlike Elusive, Feuery was completely at ease.

'Well ...' she began.

'Shhh!' Elusive interrupted urgently.

That got Feuery's attention. There was a long silence during which she alternated between alertly scanning their surrounds, battle-staff in her hand at the ready, and watching Elusive with growing fascination.

First the brownie lass closed her eyes and appeared to be listening intently, slowly cocking one ear, then the other. Then she abruptly stared with narrowed eyes toward a point in the empty marketplace, intently scanning it before she resumed her listening process.

Finally, Feuery could take no more. 'What the blue blazes are you doing?' she demanded.

Elusive seemed to emerge from a dream. 'Not exactly sure. Hold still! I want to try something.'

She leaned forward and twisted Feuery's nose – hard.

'Ooowww! Gerrorfme! That hurt!' Tears streamed down Feuery's cheeks, and it was all she could do to restrain the fireball she'd primed against imminent danger. Assault by brownie hadn't been high on her list of possible dangers about which to be vigilant. But, on face value, so to speak...

'Look around you. What do you see?' said Elusive serenely.

'*You'll* see stars if you try that again! Not much with my eyes running like a tap ... Oh!'

All around her were dim shapes, like the ghosts of ghosts, going about their business as folk normally would in a market. A spectral mother carrying a small child haggled with an ethereal stall-holder standing beside them. Two phantoms of men clumsily carried a heavy crate of fruit through the throngs of shadowy figures. To one side, the ghostly outline of a workman angrily threw a stone at a transparent dog chasing a wraithlike cat across a pavement of just-smoothed concrete.

'They're all still here ...'

'I thought so,' said Elusive with satisfaction. 'I thought I could just hear something – like a faint susurration – rising and falling at the edges of my hearing.'

'How come I didn't hear 'em?'

'You're a gnome. We brownies have better hearing – although yours is pretty good too,' she added generously.

'So how'd you know the watery-eyes thing? I'll have some more to say 'bout that soon, by the by, just noting.'

'Old trick we use in the forests to keep a watch out for invisible lurkers and spirits. Tears help you to see things you don't usually see.'

'Ain't that the truth. Didn't know it was so literal though.'

'Do you know what's going on?'

Feuery thought hard. 'This is a bit like when I stepped out of Time with Janice the Time-Witch,' she said slowly. 'I think we're both still here, but they're on an ever-so slightly different plane to us. 'Nough to share the place, but out of our phase. Something very strange happening here. I think we need to have a good look at that crystal. The big one.'

'Well, if you've seen enough ...'

'Hang on! There's a procession coming into the market. Banners an' guards an' some lady lying on cushions on a canopied litter carried by centaurs, everyone's bowing, an' everything's in full colour!'

'Oh! I wish I could see that!' Elusive exclaimed.

* * * *

'You didn't have to be so rough, you know. That was much harder than my tweak.' Elusive had a moist handkerchief pressed against her face, muffling her words. She definitely sounded hurt in more ways than one.

'Not something I've had a lot of practice at.' Feuery's tone was cheerful and had a faint undertone of satisfaction. 'You did say you wanted to see the procession.'

Elusive's glare indicated this was a minor detail in no way justifying the speed, firmness and above all *enthusiasm* with which Feuery had fulfilled her wish.

Feuery ignored the look with just a touch of smugness. 'Anyway, we're here,' she said, quite unnecessarily as she gazed up at the immense azure blue crystal. 'Question now is if'n it's a portal to somewheres else, or a shell to sum'it inside. An' where the key is, of course.'

'How about the first question being whether we want to tinker with it at all?' Elusive asked sulkily.

Feuery looked at her in surprise. 'Of course we do! How else we going to know? Anyway, bet you High Waring to a troll's toenail this'll be the only way out of this valley. Don't know 'bout you, but I've got better things to do than spend the rest of my days listening to ghosts murmuring. An' while I like your company – most-times anyways – it'd just be the two of us stuck here.'

'How do we find the key?' asked Elusive hurriedly.

'First we have to find the door. 'Course windows are usually a better option when you're dealing with locked up places. But can't see 'em being a big part of the architecture here.'

'Time to use the magic carpet?'

Feuery frowned. 'No, I don't think so. The philosopher we discovered the first needle on must've found a way somehow.

191

He didn't have any flying stuff on him. 'Course, some of 'em get so good they can levitate, but it's more likely that the entrance is around ground level.'

The two adventurers started scanning the spire using their wizard's sight which enabled them to view the world according to its magical energies. Feuery was much more proficient at it than Elusive, but it was the brownie who made the call.

'Here Feueze! At the top of this ornate ramp. Very standard opening really.'

'Which probably means it'll be a difficult lock. Well, let's give it a go.'

She studied the concentration of magical energies Elusive had found.

'Colour coder,' she said eventually. 'Very popular system 'round that time.'

'Should be easy then. Just shoot random colours at it until it works.'

'Sure. Do that an' we'll get a demon come out, or a fireball or worse. It has to be the right colours in the right sequence. Get two – maybe three – attempts afore things turn nasty.'

'Oh!'

'But which colours, an' what order …?' Feuery lapsed into thoughtful silence, while she pondered the riddle of the lock.

Elusive kept quiet, amusing herself by looking out over the city of Luminosa. *Ol' Philineso hadn't stinted,* she mused. The city was beautiful, with everything well designed and built in a classic style. It had a feeling of space and airiness, but grand majesty as well. The overall effect was delightful while, at the same time, being functional and impressive.

Still, the procession had demonstrated that there was a strong hierarchy in the city, in which everyone was aware of place – especially those at the top (who, no doubt, had a very firm sense of their place). Wonder who that lady was, or is. Hard to tell when the worlds are out of phase. Could be the past or present – maybe even the future. Whatever the situation, she'd surely have been about as high in the city's pecking order as could be. Maybe even linked with Philineso because he wouldn't be willing to share the power and glory of his position with anyone who wasn't really special …

Then suddenly, she knew the answer to their question!

'Feueze …' she began excitedly, just as Feuery turned to her with an excited 'Got it!'

'The banners!' they both said elatedly.

'Ok, blue, yellow an' green, blue on the outside. Usual thing is start at the centre. Mages most-always think of themselves as being the centre an' 'spect everything else to start from there. Hope I remember the shades alright.'

A gleaming white mist formed around Feuery's hands as she faced the closed entrance. Abruptly from the mist a shaft of green light speared out, followed in quick succession by yellow and blue. It seemed to Elusive that Feuery had exactly captured the colours they'd seen earlier on the banners.

Nothing happened.

'Ok, let's try t'other way round. Philineso had a reputation for being fascinated by opposites.'

The mist re-formed, blue, yellow and green light bathed the entryway – which adamantly remained tightly sealed.

'Maybe yellow, green, blue,' suggested Elusive.

'Or green, blue, yellow or sum'it,' said Feuery edgily. 'Too many different combinations that we'll maybe have to ask a demon its opinion. Opposites, opposites,' she mumbled.

'Shall we try again tomorrow?' suggested Elusive. 'It's getting dark and I'm a bit worried about what keeps this city so sparkling clean and tidy. Gnomes and brownies might be on the unwanted clutter list.'

'Hmm. I think I've understood the key now,' answered Feuery slowly. 'Doing the reverse. Clever really.'

'But we already tried reversing the colours.'

'There's more than one way to reverse some things, including colours. Go to the opposite.'

The mist formed around Feuery's hands again. Red, purple and orange light lit up the spire's entrance.

'What are you doing?' cried Elusive, 'That's nothing like the colours on the banners!'

The magic around the entrance swirled and expanded, then seemed to hesitate before a wide, high passageway opened into the crystal.

'Opposites,' said Feuery contentedly. 'I do love puzzles. I really do, 'specially ones like that. Opposite of blue is orange, green is red, an' so on. Tricky getting the right shades though.'

'Mind against mind, that sort of thing? Challenge of intellects?' Elusive suggested.

'Mainly 'cos if I figure 'em out, I get to go somewhere someone didn't want me to be. Has to be a reason for locking something away, an' oftentimes it's 'cos it's valuable or interesting. Let's go and see what this one is. With luck it'll be both.'

* * * *

The two girls entered the passage cautiously, but had only gone a few paces before they felt something move. The walls around them disappeared. Elusive screamed.

Feuery reached out and held her arm reassuringly. 'It's ok. Believe me, you get used to this sort of thing after awhiles. Downside of taking an interest in the business of high mages. Just go with it an' keep your thoughts calm.'

'It's alright! It just surprised me, is all!'

Suddenly the view in front of them cleared. They stood on what appeared to be a solid cloud bank. To their right, a vast storm raged. Another storm seethed to their left. The space between the storms blazed with flaring lightning bolts and pulsing St Elmo's fire.

'Very pretty,' said Elusive. 'Especially the colours. Pity they clash, so to speak.'

The storm to the right roiled swiftly in every shade of blue, with a vicious electric blue predominating. It rose majestically, appearing to want to crash down and smother the other storm.

The storm to the left was a churning maelstrom in shades of orange, with an electric, vivid orange predominating. Even as they watched, the blue storm sank back as if defeated, and the orange storm cloud began to rear upward with a new surge of energy. All of this activity took place in absolute silence.

'What by all the stars is happening?' Elusive breathed softly.

When Feuery didn't answer, Elusive glanced at her. The little gnome was standing quietly, but swaying slightly. Her eyes were closed, her breathing slow and shallow.

Oh no! She's gone over to deep Wizard's Sight and become caught up in it. It sometimes happened. A penalty of seeing the world according to its magic was that sometimes the magic became – sticky. A wizard could become twisted up in whatever they were viewing and with whatever was happening about it. And sometimes they didn't re-emerge. It was dependent on what they'd encountered, and how strong-willed they themselves were.

Elusive hoped Feuery hadn't encountered a lot more than she could handle. Those storms boiled with magical energy.

She gently eased Feuery onto the cloud bank, and made her as comfortable as possible. Then, she stood guard – although against what she really had no idea. Or how she'd deal with it if whatever it might be happened. Those were details somewhere ahead on the stream of time. What mattered most now was to keep an eye on her friend. At least there was an interesting light-show to watch.

Nevertheless, after an hour or two even the most fabulous battle between two magical storms, with spectacular displays of duelling lightning, paled in interest. Elusive had a quick snack between checking Feuery and trying to discern whether either of the storms could be picked as a potential winner. Feuery's near-coma state hadn't altered. Meanwhile, the cycle of first one storm and then the other gaining brief ascendancy, before retreating, kept on repeating.

Just as Elusive was beginning to wonder if – and how – she would need to follow Feuery into the magical maelstrom to retrieve her, Feuery gave a deep shuddering sigh, and her eyes opened.

'Feuery! Thank goodness! Are you all right? I've been so worried about you!'

'Good reason too. I've been worried about me.' Feuery's voice was thick and slurred, and although she was looking around her, it was evident she was conscious of very little through her daze. 'Give me a minute or two. Not sum'it I'd want to do again – leastways, not for a long time. Any chance of a cup of tea?'

Glad to have something focused to do, Elusive immediately set about making the tea. The fact that Feuery didn't direct operations – she was usually very particular about how her tea was made – was an indication of her current condition. Using wizard's sight was always a little disconcerting, but extended use left the operator feeling befuddled about what was real while trying to readjust their senses. Very few wizards could have coped with nearly two hours of being immersed in a world where all their senses were aware of only the flows and flares of magic.

'Ok,' said Feuery as she sipped her tea. 'For starters, the big blue crystal we went into is the Azure Needle: one of Philineso's greatest works. It's a grand terminus to lots of places, an' it was the main way in or out of Luminosa an' this valley. All the little ones are just to get back in. Sort of like tickets for very exclusive travellers.'

'But what we're looking at here,' Elusive gestured at the warring storm clouds, 'doesn't seem like a staging centre. If it is, the conductors here must get *really* upset if you don't have a valid ticket.'

'No. Well, you know how the Mage Wars ended a couple o' centuries ago?'

'Of course! Then, during the Troubled Times that followed the Wars, the Guilds and Protectorates formed to bring back some order into the world.'

'Yep, that's right; while still leaving room for you an' me an' a few folk like us to make an' enjoy a bit o' disorder. Well, looks as though the Mage Wars aren't over; they're still being fought here.' Feuery said, pointing at the storms.

* * * *

'Philineso an' his partner, Ambridia the Sorceress, were challenged by a High Mage called Rasar to a duel – winner take all. From the bits I picked up when I was … scouting, I think Philineso had opened a portal into Rasar's place. Lots of the mages during the Wars set aside their own little pocket-dimensions where they could feel safe, an' Rasar didn't take kindly to having Philineso an' Ambridia climbing through the window of his bedroom, in a manner of speaking.'

'When I say 'challenged' that might be a bit loose actually. Rasar was pretty hot under the collar an' this is where they met.' Feuery looked pensively at the raging storms. 'Been going at one 'nother now for close on five hundred years.'

'Five hundred years! Wow! That's an enormous amount of magic,' Elusive exclaimed.

'I know. Terrible wear an' tear on the mages using it, an' the energy has to come from somewhere. As they get more n' more tired, they're drawing on the nearest energies they can locate, whilst using the magic to sustain themselves. They'll end up pulling their places in on themselves, which is why Luminosa is out of phase with the real world. Rasar must be doing the same to his place. Eventually, everything they set up will just get sucked into an' used up in the battle.'

Elusive thought back to the marketplace scene they'd witnessed of a woman holding her child, and a dog chasing a cat. Common everyday things that deserved better than to be swallowed by a senseless war between a trio of self-centred mages.

'So what are we going to do about it?' she asked slowly.

'Right question! Good girl! Got a sense of what's really important an' responsible about you. Even if you're a mite too particular 'bout some li'l things, like me not being super careful with leaving a few things lying around.'

'So what *are* we going to do about it?' As far as Elusive was concerned Feuery's approval was nice, but didn't go anywhere near making up for the numerous disagreements about having to pick up after her.

'I think,' said Feuery slowly, 'we'll send 'em off to somewheres that they can have it out with each other for as long as they want, but not bother anyone else.'

'Oh yes,' Elusive replied sarcastically. 'We'll just suggest that to them then, shall we?' Feuery sometimes left others around her feeling incredulous about her twisting logic, or, conversely, her direct approach to dealing with complicated issues.

'Good idea! Let's do it.'

Before Elusive could properly fathom Feuery's agreement, the gnome was striding forward toward the battle of the storms. The solid cloud on which they'd been standing lengthened out just a few paces in front of her.

Elusive made a noise something like '*gleep!*' and raced after the little figure in blue.

'What do you think you're *doing?*'

'What you said – suggest to 'em that they move on.'

'But you can't. Why would they listen? You can't!'

'It was your idea. Darn good one too. Don't know what you're fussing about. I agreed to every detail.'

'I was being facetious! The lightning will fry you before you get anywhere near them anyway.' Elusive suddenly looked down and back. The surface on which they were standing was now a rough disc hanging in the air.

'What are we standing on?' This immediate thought jostled her audacious advice regarding the warring mages aside briefly.

'Firmament. Appropriate name. There's so much magic sloshing around here even we can make it. Wouldn't want to try it anywheres else though. An' you're right about the lightning, but that's easy fixed. Leastways here in this place.'

Feuery cast a complex spell. A dark green nimbus cloud sprang up around them.

'Learned that one from the Lady in Green. Well, from a spellbook she'd left lying around when I baby-sat her twiglings one evening. Too powerful for me usually, but fine to cast it here.'

Elusive had a fairly shrewd idea about how the high-level spellbook of a powerful, centuries-old sorceress would have been 'left lying around'. However, there were more pressing matters now than enquiring more deeply into Feuery's larcenies.

'Feuery, give it up! This is way too dangerous.'

Feuery gave her a sombre look. 'I know it's dangerous Elusive,' she said quietly. 'But right here an' now, there's no one else, an' someone has to do sum'it afore these idiots take their folk somewhere that's likely to be not at all nice. Sometimes you get to be a pivot of events without being asked. But if'n you slip out from under, then there'll likely be a crash that can hurt lots of folk. You don't have to come with me – an' I won't think any less of you if you don't – but we're both safer together an' I'm determined to do this.'

She resumed steadily walking toward the space between the storms. Elusive gaped for a moment, and then hurried to catch up. It was far from ideal, but right now Feuery was probably right. She was safer tucked in close beside her friend than anywhere else.

* * * *

Elusive almost changed her opinion when a ragged sheet of lightning crashed over both of them. However, it was deflected away by the surrounding green glow. After this happened four or five more times, she found herself barely jumping at all in fright.

They came to a standstill about midway between the storms, at a point when one was receding and the other ascending, so that both were roughly at the same height, with the crests of the storms only a few hundred feet above them.

Feuery raised her arms and a bolt of brilliant green light flared upward between the piled thunderheads, disappearing into the distance far above them.

Both storms seemed to pause. Elusive attributed it to astonishment that something new was intervening after centuries of alternately surging struggle. Even the lightning died away. Globes and sheets of St Elmo's fire lingered for a short while. But then, perhaps in embarrassment like someone continuing to sing after the orchestra has stopped, also faded away.

There was a long hiatus.

'So, you think you can enlist a dryad against us Rasar?' a Jovian voice boomed.

'She's not mine fool. Must be a pathetic attempt to try to deceive me,' another voice thundered in answer.

'Actually, not with either of you,' said Feuery, her voice sounding very faint and tiny in the dramatic scene. 'Not ag'in you neither,' she added hastily. 'Just had a thought though that might be of interest to you.'

'It's a gnome!' exclaimed a voice that sounded as though it belonged to a goddess. 'How'd it get in here?'

'More to the point, what does it want?' said the first booming voice, with a hint of displeasure, but possibly also with just a touch of curiosity.

'There are two of them,' the second voice that had spoken earlier retorted.

'This I know. Do not presume to correct me.'

Both storms began to churn ominously again.

'The Wizards' Guild sent us with a message for you,' said Feuery calmly. Elusive's eyes widened at the bald-faced lie, but sensibly she kept the surprise off her face.

'The what?' asked the female voice curiously.

'The Wizards' Guild. The Great Convocation of High Mages.'

'Never heard of them,' sneered the second voice thunderously. 'Dispose of them and have at you!'

'As I understand it, you've all been rather busy for this past couple of hundred years, so that's to be expected,' said Feuery smoothly.

'Who are these High Mages?' asked the female voice suspiciously.

'Well, there's Ivarn of the 3Rs, who's the current president. An' Insariar the Insidious is vice-president.' (*True enough* Feuery thought to herself, 'vice' was what Insariar was *good* at.) 'An' Parax ix Olar is Treasurer …'

'Parax was killed,' said the first voice thunderously.

'What's that to a necromancer?' Feuery pointed out easily. 'Hid himself in a' orb for awhiles, an' then returned, determined to make the world a better place for High Mages.'

There was a thoughtful silence; the sort that accompanies a growing realisation that other people – in this case very powerful High Mages – have been busy while you've been preoccupied.

'What is the message you have for us, gnome?' asked the female voice curtly.

'They've been really interested in your battle, an' would welcome the winner – or winners as the case may be – to take a senior role in the Convocation. When you're ready of course. That's the first part.'

'Go on.'

'The second part of the message is a respectful suggestion. The Guild is greatly impressed at the mighty magical powers you've all been able to wield. But they suspect that you have grown so powerful that all that is preventing you from resolving your duel is insufficient energy for the mightiest one to determine the final outcome.'

There were murmurings – if thunder can be considered a murmuring – along the lines of 'Thought so myself', 'Quite true' and 'It'd be different if ...'

'So,' continued Feuery smoothly, 'they recommend – with full respect – that you may like to consider Ackaban's Wondrous Resolve. Just in case you hadn't yet thought of it.'

There was a long silence.

'Ah, did you say ...?'

'Ackaban's Wondrous Resolve.'

There was another long silence broken by Feuery striking her palm against her forehead. Only Elusive seemed to notice the slap was disproportionately loud – magically enhanced no doubt and theatrical.

'I'm so sorry,' Feuery declared contritely. 'Ackaban would've done what he did after you began your battle, so's you might not have heard of it.'

'Done what?' Suspicion and curiosity tinged the air almost tangibly.

'Ackaban emerged from the Mage Wars as the leading Elven High Mage. Not content with drawing on energy around him, he transported himself to a distant star so he'd have a near-endless supply of energy for his magic. Some say he became a god then. The Convocation thought if you moved the Azure Needle close to a star, then the mightiest among you would have the means to resolve your dispute.'

The silence this time was thoughtful and prolonged. The temptation of being offered limitless power was almost overwhelming.

'Have you got a portal spell handy?' whispered Feuery to Elusive.

'Me? I wish! Do you think I'd still be here if I did?' Elusive muttered back forcefully.

'Probably, 'cos you've got more curiosity 'n' a sackful of cats. Pity! We'll just have to use the one I nicked from Trecina an' hope for the best, being as how it's a fairly short-range one.'

* * * *

'Are we agreed then?' a mighty voice rumbled around them.

'We are.' The words seemed to reverberate everywhere.

''Scuse me? The Convocation also suggested you might like to use one of the mountains hereabouts as a source of energy for the move. Just a thought?'

There was no direct answer, but the storms roiled might-ily, and for the first time ever started to combine to produce a common mighty magic.

This was around the precise moment in time in which Feuery frantically triggered a portal spell, and hastily scrambled into it. Hard on her heels was Elusive, who could move very fast indeed when the occasion warranted it.

* * * *

They both tumbled out of the portal spell not very far from where they'd first arrived in the valley of the Azure Needle.

In the twinkling starlight, the city of Luminosa with its sparkling clean, empty streets, plazas and marketplaces lay below them.

However, the valley was not quite the same as before. On the far side, one of the great mountains that had sealed it in from the world was twisting and swirling as though it were a living thing in great pain. Streams of sand cascaded down from the summit accompanied by a swishing, rumbling and continuous thunder. At the same time, raw energy was wrenched from the dying mountain, curling in a sinuous, glowing stream towards the apex of the Azure Needle.

When all that was left of the mountain was a vast sand dune over which the lesser hills and plateaus beyond could just be discerned, the Azure Needle began to shudder with some sort of mighty internal force. The vibration quickly increased and was accompanied by a rising, shrill whistling.

The Azure Needle then vanished from sight.

'Bon voyage. That's not something you see every day,' observed Elusive casually.

'Hope it's the last we see of them,' Feuery agreed. 'Just goes to prove that power an' wisdom don't necessarily go hand-in-hand. They became so caught up in their battle an' the thrill of wielding vast magical forces they lost sight of everything else. Then we come along an' suggest a way they can get at even *more* power. Hardly fair, but they'd lost sight of everything else in their pursuit of power; like what they were doing to other people. I won't be losing any sleep over 'em.'

'What will happen to them now?' asked Elusive.

'Hard to say. Maybe one side or t'other will win. If'n that happens, our world is going to seem like a mighty small pond to come back to. More like they'll just keep on doing what they've become accustomed to do until the star they picked explodes.'

'Stars don't explode. Do they?'

'It happens. All sorts of theories as to why. Never heard murder-suicide by High Mage mentioned as one of the reasons, but fair chance this time.'

'Is that what happened to Ackaban?'

'Who?'

'You know – the great Elven Mage you told them about.'

'I made up that bit about him. The others were real mages. Most likely they knew them at one time or another, so that put their minds at ease that what I was saying might be true. But far as I know, there's never been a High Mage named Ackaban. The elves are pretty secretive about their mages, so fair chance that he – or she – could have existed. 'Specially if'n you've been out of touch with the happenings of the world long enough.'

Down below them in the city of Luminosa lights began to appear in the streets. Figures could just be seen moving as the two phases of existence once again merged back to normality.

'Now what?' asked Elusive. 'At least we now have a way out over the sand dune.'

'All in good time. Afore we leave, we'll do a bit of trading. There should be a decent profit to be made from selling the first goods from the fabled city of Luminosa at the Heliovorn markets. No idea what they'd fetch there, but I bet we could sell pickled rhubarb as a novelty if it came from Luminosa – at least for a little whiles. But that's for seconds.' She paused.

'Ok, I'll ask – what's first?'

'Somewhere down there is a palace that used to be occupied by a great mage an' a sorceress, both of whom are currently occupied on a li'l venture elsewhere. An' there's two people in town – no names mentioned 'cos they'll be us – who haven't been taught to be scared stiff of offending the mage an' sorceress. Such as by having a good sticky-beak through their palace an' collecting a few select souvenirs, like gems, magical artefacts or ol' spell books not being used.'

Feuery unrolled the tatty old magic carpet. 'Let's see if'n we can find anything interesting lying around afore other people realise that Philineso an' Ambridia are well an' truly away. Should be good prospecting in a scavenger's market!'

Bickering genially over what they would find in the mages' palace, the gnome and brownie steered the wobbly carpet over the avenues and boulevards of Luminosa as a new day dawned over the city.

Anthor

Anthor was restless. He slithered quietly through his palace, barely noticing anything.

He passed through the Feathered Hall. Most days, the Hall would serve to enhance his mood with its ever-changing, brilliant displays in which millions of semi-sentient, highly empathetic feathers growing from the walls and ceiling acted in unison, creating patterns of dazzling colours and subtleties. Today the Hall was a neutral grey colour, with only the merest flicker of subtle brown shimmers to indicate it was discretely aware of him. He grunted sourly. It was either an accurate reflection of his emotional state, or the feathers knew when it was wise to be unobtrusive. Possibly both.

The Crystal Globe reflected prettily as he passed by. He glanced at it. It was one of the most fabled fortune-telling oracles in all the worlds, and many an emperor about to embark on adventure would have given half of all they commanded to look upon it for even a few seconds. Great Mages had schemed and used mighty spells to try to gain a peek at it. And today, what did this great wonder show in its innumerable crystal-line facets? Tomorrow's weather forecast for the major towns of Th'eia. He snorted sardonically. His own senses could do better than that. The Crystal Globe was playing it very safe indeed.

Nor was the Kaleidoscope any livelier. The patterns were slow to change and form, and were little more sophisticated than those displayed by a cheap 'scope from a child's holiday gifts. A far cry indeed from its usual displays, where even Anthor, with all his vast experience, could imagine that he'd been transported into the depths of a dynamic galaxy at the moment of creation. He barely glanced around as he headed for the palace entrance.

Proximity to a Great Dragon inevitably changed even inanimate objects over a long enough time period. Much of his palace had become semi-aware by now. And today they were choosing caution in response to his own foul mood.

It was all stale, washed out, insipid. Anthor needed to get out for a while – out into the world.

At one point, he had spent a lot of time in the world, or more accurately, many worlds. However, for the past couple of centuries or so his mood had been contemplative and he had largely kept to himself and his own thoughts. Now, he was becoming increasingly tired of their company and his own.

He needed something fresh; something to stir and energize his thoughts. Not that he expected to find it.

As a brash young firedrake, his eager world had been full of novelty to satisfy his curious mind. As a mature dragon, the worlds had constantly piled new wonders on him, and he had avidly soaked up and savoured new concepts, feelings and thoughts to repletion. Now, as one of the Great Dragons, he had become wise from his many experiences, and had used that wisdom to filter all he had seen and done and felt in order to distil understanding against which to balance his vast powers.

But all he was doing now was recycling what he'd mused over far too many times previously. The rise and fall of civilizations, the merger of continents – even the birth of a star had become passé with too much hindsight.

Anthor knew he was experiencing a major life crisis. Intellectual growth was as important to higher draconian life and maturity as physical growth (indeed, the form of a Great Dragon was dictated by it). But, as in all things, there were limits. Worthwhile learning which enhanced a being's life experiences seemed to be increasingly more difficult to come by as the millennia passed.

He now understood why some of the Great Dragons before him had chosen to simply subside back into the nothingness that was everything, while others had cast aside their physicality to soar as disembodied spirits among the stars and the cold, dark voids between the galaxies, desperately seeking elusive answers to unasked questions. Others had turned inward; their bodies turning to stone while their minds exulted in their own inner nirvanas. Many options were open to him, but none he could envisage appealed to him – at least, not yet.

More insidiously, he could also feel the Dark Dragon lurking inside himself; that force inherent in all his kind that, unbidden, could twist his nature into a pure essence of evil to be launched upon the worlds so as to re-make them in a new and horrifying form. That same fate had occurred to others before him. He had witnessed the cinders of their former worlds. Designated as the Great Dragon of the Rising Sun and Guide of Wisdom, Anthor shuddered at the knowledge of these hidden, pernicious desires within his own soul. The dark miasma inside him repelled and disgusted him, but he was aware that it was always there; waiting silently, ready to emerge. Increasingly, he caught himself exploring its fringes, like a human painfully probing at an aching tooth due to some unwitting, sub-conscious desire.

Enough! The more he brooded and dwelt on that poisoned uncleanness, the more it would pervade him. He wanted to be free to feel life in all its diversity. To be part of it again, and not to slip beneath the waves of darkness imaginary that threatened to turn real.

He flowed to the grand entrance of his palace, and launched himself from the high mountain top. The urge to spread his wings still twinged he noted wryly, despite the fact that he had outgrown the need of wings many millennia past.

He soared upward, unexpectedly enjoying the cold, thin air, and viewing the wisps of cirrus clouds below him and the curving world below them.

A pounce of sylphs arced up toward him. Sylphs lived long lives and Anthor knew many of them from old. They soared about him, teasing, feinting at and cajoling him. He took no offence as they had no malice toward him; merely light-hearted spirit, *joie de vivre*, and relishing the occasion of sharing their world with a respected, rare visitor.

He glanced at the many forms of the sylphs: here, one appeared merely to be comprised of wisps like the clouds below, and there, one was like a tall human in full armour wielding a long *bec de corbin* and a slim knight's shield embossed with flowing designs. Sylphs could take more or less any form they desired, but generally preferred to remain gleaming white, with hints of pale blue shadow in honour of their favoured home in the clouds.

A slim, playful young female in diaphanous, swirling robes flew daringly close – barely an arm's length from his great, scaly head. For the briefest instant, their eyes met. Anthor observed fresh innocence and lively intelligence in the sylph who was still finding her place in existence. Despite his grim mood, his mind smiled as a ripple of warmth passed through him. In turn, the sylph saw …? Fear momentarily flitted across her face, but that was almost instantly replaced by a strange comprehension which combined deep time, hard-earned wisdom, immeasurable understanding and compassion beyond comprehension.

She faltered in the air, and slipped beyond Anthor's vision, yet his 'dragon-sense' continued to be aware of her as she hovered in the air with incredulity blazoned across her face.

Few beings are Touched by a Great Dragon. Fewer still receive blessing from one and always their lives were changed thereafter. Whether that change was for better or worse was up to them and their fate. Anthor wondered briefly what the sylph would make of his gift, which he'd bestowed on her on a whim; yet with shrewd judgment it could be put to good use.

With a sinuous twist, Anthor dived, quickly leaving the swift sylphs far behind. He plummeted like a comet, twisting the air around him in order to avoid a sonic boom distressing the world, before levelling out above a vast plain of tall umber grasses and hardy steppe herbs.

While flying just above the highest plumes of the flowering grasses, he retained (but shrank) his physical form to barely more than a yard in length from the tip of his nostrils to the feathery tuft at the end of his tail.

Movement? With the tiniest flick of his tail, he curiously veered toward a band of centaurs. In fact, it was a war band led by an impressive stallion and a dam-mare. Several ridgerunners – probably their colts – flanked them protectively, while half a dozen armoured stallions and mares stuck close behind the two leaders. He saw no fillies, but wouldn't have expected to. The lithe fast young females would be out scouting; fearing little danger as a result of their speed, agility and deadly lances and bows.

Casually wondering what the war-band's prey was, Anthor threw a tendril of future-sense forward and another of hindsight backwards.

Ah, that was it! The centaurs were mercenaries commissioned by Queen Aureliara to dissuade incursions by Darksiders onto the borders of the settled lands. The Dawn Elves took their obligations to those they conquered seriously. Those obligations were virtually the same as those they extended to their own folk, including security. The vanquished were also expected to assume the same rules and responsibilities as those the Dawn Elves lived under, invariably leading to more frictions than the obligations engendered – naturally. Most folk seem to be easily able to accept largesse, and yet, perversely, be willing to forfeit all advantages over sometimes minor, symbolic impositions.

Not that the Dawn Elves seemed perturbed. They only conquered those beings who sought to invade them, and any revolts were suppressed with clinical efficiency. In times past, they had applied the same principles to their own folk, and would no doubt do so again if the circumstances required it. The immediate exile of any Dawn Elf who dared to take a partner of any other kindred – even one of the other Elven folk – demonstrated the rigorous maintenance of their standards.

Did Anthor really understand the Dawn Elves? He had to admit he did not, and a prickle of excitement went through him at the prospect of a possible venture to relieve his mental lethargy.

No, not now! His study of the Dawn Elves would certainly be undertaken, but in due course, for his mood now was else-wise. He sought something more basic that went to the core of his being, although he wasn't sure what. He'd know it if he found it, and would continue to yearn for it if he didn't. To better understand the Dawn Elves would be fascinating, but the time for that wasn't now. Something deep within him required healing first.

He left the centaurs in peace: even those wary folk were unaware he'd been close upon them.

As Anthor sped across the plains, he observed in passing the little wrens and parrots that lived there; the fleet, tiny crea-tures in the tangled tussocks and even some wild mamoks dwelling in the remains of some ancient sorceress' tower. At a distance, he saw mammoths too, but he'd seen plenty of mammoths before. He enjoyed their company, as he did all of the elephant-kind, but he had business to attend to, even if he was unsure what it might actually be.

Gradually, the steppe vegetation began to give way first to bushes and stunted trees, and then to the fringes of a great forest. He knew these parts well, and wondered what drifts in his sub-conscious desires had impelled him to travel here of all places.

Nevertheless, for a time he cavorted through the forest, dashing among the branches and trunks of the trees, twisting around bushes and skimming over tiny, meadow-like clearings. He hadn't played so much for many long years, and enjoyed the child-like joy it brought him.

Next, Anthor's travels bought him to the ruins of a town. He recalled that it had been named Chancifor. His frivolous mood instantly vanished.

While honoring the memory of a family who had once lived there, he had appeared to protect the town on several occasions during the Mage Wars. Although no one had ever threatened Chancifor by searing fire and shearing blade during that time, the failure of trade as a result of the Wars had less spectacularly (but just as surely) sealed its fate as sword and fire would have done.

Now, the stone bones of the town lay amid the forest from which it had been carved. The folk who had lived there had long since dispersed across the lands. Did any of their descendants still remember those times? Did they still tell tales of lost Chancifor? He hoped so.

Anthor alighted in what had once been the town's central square. A young oak now struggled to grow amid the ruins of what had once been a fountain. Wiry grasses, weeds and straggly shrubs tormented and all but obscured the once meticulous flagstones. A crow cawed nearby; another further off answered it, their calls mournful and bleak.

Anthor heard neither of the birds. Rather, he *was* aware of a concert playing in the past square. *Sweet Requiem.* That had been the name of the piece – appropriate now indeed – scored for violins and woodwind, with a cello providing a deep counterpoint to the sweetness of the lighter strings. He listened, and as he listened the strains began to sound more real, while around him he felt the fellowship of his long-gone friends delighting in the sweet entrapment of the music.

The music eventually faded to a soft ending and Anthor opened his eyes, unaware that he had even closed them.

A girl stood at the edge of the square looking intently at him. He looked at her carefully, not wishing to frighten her. To his surprise, she held his gaze easily, neither challenging nor staring, but rather appraising him closely.

Her eyes were bright blue, intelligent and large. Her hair was a deep auburn red, her skin almost golden, and she held a wand in her hand. She was sensibly dressed in light clothing in shades of red-brown and muted orange, highlighted tastefully with deep blue piping, but she was barefoot and hatless.

'You made the music?' she asked suddenly. She had a pleasant but firm voice that seemed devoid of fear or surprise, but instead was as casual and friendly as someone inquiring 'Did you call?' to a friend.

'Not made, but I brought it here. From a previous time.'

She continued to gaze at him.

'From a time long past,' he added. For the first time in longer than he could recall, he felt the need to explain himself further. 'When Chancifor was a thriving town – um – I had friends here.'

'Other dragons?' she asked.

'No, mostly humans – like you. Oh, and elves. Some gnomes, of course, but many other folk as well.'

She smiled as though enjoying some secret personal thought. The sort of smile that stems from knowing something another does not.

'I would know about this place and them,' she said. It wasn't a demand, nor quite a request, but more a statement of fact with an assumption that he would be pleased to comply.

Anthor frowned inwardly. Not since he had been a yearling had another led a conversation with him, prompting his responses. Still … there seemed no harm in it, nor did it feel seemly for him to assert command.

He wondered if this 'slip of humanity' would accept his authority anyway – even if he did resume his full size. He didn't want to alarm her though. In fact, at the present moment, he welcomed company as a refreshing change to his long, self-imposed isolation.

So he told her all about Chancifor and, as he spoke, he realised how enjoyable it was to share his knowledge with another being. The town had meant much to him once, and during his monologue he better understood how much it *really* had meant to him.

He spoke of how the town had been founded for the collection of araj essence from the woodland streams, for, at that time, the essence had commanded high prices. High enough for folk to establish themselves in what had then been a wilderness, and to which (in their absence) it was now returning. How the easy way of life, the peace and beauty of the forest, together with the relative isolation, had attracted first a few – then many – of contemplative and creative mind and inclination. Over time, Chancifor, while far from the glittering opera houses and staid, formal galleries and regimented academies of greater, more sophisticated urbanities, had come to surpass them all in terms of the richness and variety of art, sculpture, music and eccentric topics of study that flowed readily within, and from, the town.

Anthor told her of how the wood elves had first shunned the town, but had gradually left the forest to adopt it; the only significant gathering of town-dwelling wood elves anywhere. Their creativity contributed to the general pool, making Chancifor a truly unique location as a result of its style and innovation. But not only wood elves chose to make Chancifor their home. Many other kindreds such as the amazing ballet troupe of half-orc sisters and the master-sculptor, Eramius the Troll, whose fine miniature works were widely sought (still!) across several worlds, and the surpassingly delicate porcelains of the Kratgar Ogre family who had, at one time, made their homes in the town.

He then recounted to her some tiny part of his knowledge of the Mage Wars. For Anthor had closely (and sadly) witnessed them from the first vicious duels between rival mages, through the labyrinthine intrigues and vast, bloody battles, to the last shuddering, sporadic clashes between the few surviving mages and their remaining followers. The Mage Wars had never come to Chancifor – he had seen to that. However, they had wreaked such havoc upon the world's peoples that most cities and towns had fallen, whether or not they had been directly involved in the Wars.

And then he fell silent, for he felt his own soul had been scoured by the bitter memories.

'Can you bring them back?' she questioned.

It took a moment for her question to work its way through his tumultuous thoughts and hot, leaden memories.

'Sorry?'

'Can you bring them back? Can you return Chancifor to as it was before?'

'You mean you'd like to see what it was like in those days? I suppose I could share my memories with you, or even take you back in time to it …'

'No, you don't understand. Please listen. Can you bring it back to what it was – now – so that tomorrow it will still be here as it was at its peak?'

That got him thinking. Of course he could. He had ample magic to do it. And the thought she'd thrown across his awareness was so very appealing.

'Yes, I could,' he answered, 'but I won't. It would be impractical and unethical.'

'If you could, then I would think you should,' she replied shortly. 'The world needs its Chancifors.'

'Yes, it does. But think a moment. What made Chancifor so special was those folk living in it. People – not inert matter – make places what they are. Whose lives do I bring forward from their chain of relationships that stretched before and after them, wrenching them from their linkages? Would they thank me – or you – if, for our ends, or even the noble end of recreating such a concentration of creativity and beauty, we were to wrench them from their time and the futures they still held to be placed alone in a strange time like a bouquet on a pedestal?

'And then what? Chancifor's prosperity was founded on araj essence. When the trade died, so did the town. Araj is now supplied readily and more cheaply to the world by the exiled fairy-folk, who learned to spin the essence from any clear mountain stream, often in close proximity to their markets. Should I prevent that, and disrupt countless lives, to enable Chancifor to be once more?'

Her face fell as an inner dream crumpled. He felt sad for her, and sad for himself also. He'd have liked the opportunity to reverse time and events to have Chancifor back to the way it was when he'd visited it so often in the past.

'I can show you it as it was. I can even take you back to it for a while if you wish,' he offered gently.

She looked up at him with eager hope. 'If the town had been more protected – then, could it still be here?'

Puzzlement grew in Anthor's mind. *Why was this chance finding of a human so intent upon making Chancifor live again?*, he wondered.

'Do you know me?' he asked.

'No,' she admitted. 'I think you're one of the greater dragons. But you do seem to be quite nice.'

That's something, he thought to himself wryly. Aloud, he said, 'I am Anthor, the Dragon of the Rising Sun of the Five Great Dragons at the Foci of the World.' He refrained from accompanying this grandiose statement with thunder and harmonics as was usually expected. Not here, not in this company. In any case, such a portentous statement would of itself suffice to silence any of the regal courts of the mighty, or bring conventions of mages to respectful silence and attention. Little else would.

'That's nice,' she said, offering him her hand, although it was far from clear to him what he was supposed to do with it. He settled for touching it lightly with one of the sensitive tendrils at the front of his snout. That seemed acceptable to her.

'I'm Curiosa,' she added.

'You haven't heard of me?' he ventured uncertainly.

'Oh yes. You're the Great Dragon of Wisdom. One of the five Great Dragons who guard the Five Great Virtues of the World. Renewal is attributed to you too. I guess that's why you're associated with dawn and the rising sun. I like mornings. They're a fresh start that we all get every day of our lives, and each one holds promise that something amazing can happen. Sort of like the gift of a potential miracle each and every day we awake. Yet most people don't seem to think of them like that. Instead they're grumpy about waking up, and throw their expectations over the day instead of looking forward to it with seeking eyes and open hearts. Of course, the days don't always turn out to be amazing, but it would be boring if every day was so wonderful.'

She appraised him carefully for a moment. 'You're quite a little bit smaller than you're described in all the books and lessons. I suppose legends grow in the telling,' she added as an afterthought, as if it really wasn't his fault.

Now Anthor *really* studied her. He'd wanted a fresh, new experience and he'd just had it. Curiosa lightly – almost dismissively – accepted she was in the presence of one of the most powerful, most magical beings in the world and just didn't deem it all that important – even if he was 'nice'. That hadn't happened to him before; he'd never expected it to happen and he wasn't sure whether to be pleased or annoyed. He *was* disconcerted.

That was a new experience as well. What was the other thing that had been discordant in her words? He realised his thoughts were rattled. He tried desperately to gather them. Oh yes, '...*the days don't always turn out to be amazing* ...' Not '... *they're usually disappointing* ...' or '...*only a few days are amazing* ...', but rather '... *if every day was so wonderful* ...'

What was he dealing with?

'... it have survived?' Her voice again interrupted his train of thought.

'I'm sorry. I was preoccupied. What was your question?'

'I *asked*,' she said archly, 'if Chancifor could have survived if someone had protected it *properly* back then.' 'Twice,' she added.

Anthor mentally shook himself. Again. 'I did,' he replied simply.

She pointedly glanced around the square at the ruins.

'I couldn't protect the town from the collapse of trade,' he said defensively. 'The Great Dragon of the Rising Sun' within him roared in fury for feeling he owed her an explanation, let alone an apologetic one.

She stared at him accusingly for a long moment, but then seemed to wilt. 'No,' she said. 'I understand. Nor could I do better. It would have been nice …'

She sat wearily on a fallen block of stone and seemed to disappear into her own thoughts.

'So is nearly every day amazing for you?' he asked. The idea intrigued him.

'Of course. Today, for example, I met a Great Dragon. That didn't happen yesterday or any of the days before. And yesterday I saw a butterfly come out of its chrysalis. There's always something new. And today I had an important idea too. It didn't work out, but maybe tomorrow another one will.'

The suspicion of an idea came to Anthor.

'You're not human, are you?'

'That's a bit nosey, isn't it? I didn't ask you if you were a dragon.'

'You had a few hints that I might be,' he suggested dryly, rattling his scales a little. 'Sorry, but I would like to know. Are you a Demi-goddess?'

She laughed, a merry little sound that lightened the sombre mood of the ruins. 'No, of course not. If I was, do you think I'd need your help to revive Chancifor?'

'They come in all types. Not all of them are good at everything they get into their heads to do. So what manner of being *are* you?'

'You're the Dragon of Wisdom. Surely you should know?'

'I could very easily. But it's more polite to ask you than walking through your mind to find out, or following your time-path back to an answer. Humans seem to object to such actions. But then, I'm not sure if you are a human.'

'Then that makes two of us. I think I am – partly anyway. My mother was; at least she was before she changed. I'm a dryad, Great Mr Nosiness,' she said, but with a smile that took the sting from her words.

'Ah! A human at times, a life-spirit of the woods elsewise. But why do you have an interest in the town? Dryads are not usually known to be urban folk. Quite the opposite, in fact.'

'I'm not your typical dryad,' she sniffed. 'Trees aren't generally great conversationalists, and once you've watched squirrels for a year you can predict squirrels *amazingly* well. There are so many wonderful things and events and people in the world. I want to know as much about, about *everything*, as I possibly can.'

'I think I can begin to see the reason why you were given your name. Curiosa: the inquisitive one.'

'You got it! And a dryad must eventually settle around her Tree. Then the world shrinks, and don't please tell me of the richness of detail to be found in that little world. I *like* hiking up mountains above the tree-line, and I'm not supposed to enjoy being out of the sight of trees. No more soaring with sylphs! Do you have any idea how glorious the sky is above the clouds? Sorry, of course you do. But apparently I should feel nervous if I can't wiggle my toes in the dirt – which is nice, by the way, but very overrated, and not something any sensible person would want to do *every* day. I want to swim among coral reefs, and the closest tree there would be a coconut or a mangrove pod floating past. Algae doesn't cut it. Whoever heard of a Lichen Dryad, or the Dryad of the Moss? I don't feel as though I was meant to be a dryad, but I am!'

'I think I'm beginning to understand.' He looked at the young oak tree growing as best it could in the old fountain. 'A nice central abode with a thriving, creative community all around you would at least be some continuing interest for you.'

'It was a thought. A hope, even. It's probably the best I can hope for, even though it means I can't go out and do things for myself, but I could at least share in the active world! Don't get me wrong. I love trees and I'm looking forward to the Bonding with my own Tree. I can't help that. It's part of me, but trees are so, so ... *static!*'

'Known for it,' agreed Anthor. 'Rooted to the spot as it were. So you figured if you had to be in one locality, then why not try to make it as dynamic and interesting as possible.'

'Yes, but every idea I have for how I can do it doesn't seem to work.' She looked over to him and suddenly smiled brightly. 'Never mind, things will work out somehow. But I'm being very rude. We're just talking about me. What brings you here?'

'Just a whim,' he reflected. 'I thought I had a problem, but really, I don't. It's all about how you look at life.'

'Very true,' she agreed. 'If bad things are going to happen to you – and they happen to everyone at some time because that's life – you still have a choice about how you handle them. Nothing can change that. Take them seriously, but not personally. If you let them get you down, then you're just helping them and making it harder for yourself. And you still have to deal with them anyway. You have the choice not to let them win by changing you and making you forget that the wind on your face still feels nice, and the rose that blooms today is just as pretty and scented as the first one that ever captivated you. You're laughing at me. I can *feel* it!'

'Not *at* you – *for* you, and for me. And now wise little Dryad Curiosa, 'twere best you sleep now, to see what marvel the new dawn promises.' Anthor's voice changed, deepening as he spoke, filling the ruins of the town and reverberating through the forest around them as he resumed his full size and drew on his vast powers.

Curiosa slept peacefully.

* * * *

Dragons don't hum when they're happy and content, instead they purr. Anthor's palace fairly rumbled in response to his current feeling of satisfaction. The Feathered Hall had shone with vivid colour and vibrant motion this morning, and he'd made sure he'd made the time to pause to appreciate and enjoy it. Likewise, he'd spent time marvelling at the Kaleidoscope, whose rippling displays of colour and pattern thrilled him more than in an Age – and that was no figure of speech for a Great Dragon! The Crystal Globe had offered him visions of unparalleled clarity, with much food for thought.

The sense of well-being that flowed from Anthor's palace that day was felt well beyond into the wider worlds, for such is the nature of the Great Dragons. Many a being awoke that day feeling unusually invigorated, refreshed and eager for what lay ahead.

To think that I'd been concerned that I'd find nothing new, he pondered. *And who'd have thought it would eventuate from an intriguing little slip of a sapling dryad. The world is full of countless wonders. I'd forgotten that. Each of us casually assumes that we're the only ones who think certain things over. So it's always a shock to realise that not only are others doing the same, but sometimes they're doing it better than we are.*

You just need to look around you, with an open mind – which is very different from just looking with your eyes open. Even the blind can see if they open their mind. Maybe especially the blind. But just looking with your eyes is to only use them as sensory tools to help prevent you from tripping over things. Opening your mind opens understanding.

He vowed to himself that forgetting even the one world is full of wonders wouldn't ever happen to him again.

Deep in his psyche, the Dark Dragon snarled in the far chasm in which it now hid among the discarded shards of unpleasant memories, and vowed it damn well *would* happen again. Yet, it snarled it very quietly so as not to attract Anthor's attention.

* * * *

As the morning sun was peeping through a gap in the trees, Curiosa awoke on a drift of soft leaves in the deserted ruins of the town square. Anthor had vanished.

She sat up in shock. She had Bonded in her sleep! She didn't know how she knew, but she had no doubt it had happened. This then was her new domain, from which she was now fated to go no more than a few leagues. Disappointment washed over her while, at the same time, she felt guilt-ridden because she knew all dryads longed for their Bonding. *The dragon must have caused it to be*, she thought bitterly, even as she acknowledged his reasons may have been wise: to force her to make a decision she knew was near but had shied from herself.

Perhaps it is for the best, she mused resignedly.

But where was her Tree? She knew instinctively it was the determined little oak that had been growing in the old fountain, but the wrecked stones no longer housed a tree among them now. And if she'd Bonded – as she knew she had – she should have been encased within the warm, safe home of her Tree – such as it was.

Perhaps I'm supposed to be the moral of a story, she thought bleakly. *I tried to seek what I couldn't have, so, in the end, I and my poor, straggling little tree are left with only the impoverished soils and emptiness of a deserted town – the judgment of the Dragon of Wisdom for being presumptuous.*

She stood up, feeling resigned to finding her Tree, yet determined to make the best of what she had. However, she suddenly felt an unfamiliar presence on her left hand.

There was a ring on her left ring finger – just like a wedding ring – but displaying a complex jewel.

She peered closely at the ring. A clear, bright crystal was set into the plain metal, and within that crystal was a tree – her Tree! No longer simply an oak sapling struggling to survive in a poor environment, it was now a thriving, mature giant. Her eyes and being were drawn into it, and had anyone other than a couple of mice, a late-settling owl and a pair of courting song-birds been present, they would have seen her vanish from view.

Her Tree! She swam within it, flowing along its capillaries, feeling the warmth of the sun on its/her leaves, enjoying the rich, moist nutrients all around its/her roots. She revelled in the swish of sap, and the creaking of strong timbers as it/she stood proud in their own little world.

How long she stayed would be difficult to say, at least from the point of view of the Dryad and her Tree. However, a mouse certainly had a nasty shock when, later that morning, Curiosa re-appeared as if from out of thin air. Satisfaction and joy seemed to radiate from her.

She admired the ring in the bright morning sun, enjoying its sparkle and reflections, but this time she didn't merge with it. Instead, she silently (but most sincerely) thanked and blessed Anthor for enabling her to become the first truly free being amongst all of the dryads. The ring held her Tree, and she bore *their* ring, and the Tree bore them all. At any time she could return to her Tree; even if she was on the highest mountain top, or soaring high above the clouds with a friendly sylph, or swimming in the tepid waters of a coral reef. And her freedom was virtually absolute. In the normal course of events, her Tree couldn't be felled. Neither forest fire nor crackling lightning bolt could threaten it. It dwelt safely within an ideal environment free from droughts, storms or pests. And like all dryads, at any time she could return to her Tree for safety, nurturing and to enjoy the mutual comfort of belonging and togetherness.

She exulted in her life and good fortune, silently blessed Anthor and with a sprightly spring in her step set out for more adventures.

Islands of the Sun

Je-nee banked gently and looked down on the lands far below. While earlier it had seemed like an exciting way to spend the morning, the prospect of skiing the up-draughts over the mountains had entirely lost its appeal.

Glancing back at her from the speeding, excited pounce of sylphs Je-nee had just left, Sesarias motioned for her to catch up to re-join them. However, Je-nee gave him a swirl of negation and indicated that they should continue. She needed some time alone to think.

Poor Sesarias, she thought. *We've been so close that comments have started to circulate about what a lovely couple we'd make. That was, up until ...* Until the dragon.

It wasn't that her fondness for Sesarias had in any way diminished. However, since looking into the eye of a Great Dragon as it passed through the high domain of the sylphs on whatever business Great Dragons had, the world seemed to be so much *more* to her She was restless with a desire for experiences she couldn't quite identify, but knew they *must* exist.

She'd done her best to put her restlessness aside; to continue on with life as a carefree young sylph, soaring through the vault of the heavens among fleeting cloud and streaming wind; golden sun by day and silver stars and the tinted moons at night. Some days, she thought the uneasy yearning was fading, but today it was stronger than ever.

Then, unbidden and unexpected, the opportunity she hadn't known she was waiting for called to her as she glided through the clear, fresh air over the snow-peaked mountains among the wispy white cirrus clouds, with the marvellous world that was Th'eia below her, just waiting for her ...

She dived eagerly to meet it.

* * * *

'It's not my fault!' asserted the little gnome wizardess in a defensive 'the-best-form-of-defence-is-attack' tone, her blue eyes blazing.

'Feuery! I didn't say it was', replied the even tinier Elusive with a carefully veiled 'yes-it-most-certainly-is' inflection that stopped just short of inviting a heated response. She was a tawny-blonde, green-eyed brownie dressed in shades of fawn, and Feuery's friend, protégé and partner in adventure and crime.

'It was bound to happen sooner or later. And odds were that it wouldn't be somewhere convenient like the main square at Heliovorn,' she continued. 'Mind you, it couldn't have been anywhere *much* more inconvenient.' She looked around the thick forests surrounding them. 'Do you think there're wolves here?'

Feuery, her auburn hair contrasting with the rich blues in which she habitually dressed, didn't answer. If there were *only* wolves in the forbidding forest over which their magic carpet had chosen to expire, they'd be lucky. They'd been fortunate to make a soft landing on the relatively clear hilltop. From the looks of this forest, they were going to need a lot more luck than the day so far had granted them.

The two of them looked despondently at the carpet; now magic-less and likely to disintegrate under any good housewife's beating. It had never been intended as anything more than a temporary utility. However, like most temporary things, its use had been extended for just one more time – many times over. And now, as it turned out, that had been one time too many.

'Nearest town is a good twenty leagues away – more in that forest,' said Elusive helpfully. '*We* might be able to buy a *good* carpet there – if we make it that far.' She didn't think it was a good idea to mention to Feuery that it had been the gnome who had bought the recently-expired carpet.

'Were there any pearls amongst the loot?'

'Sorry. What?' Feuery's mercurial twists of thought tended to catch everyone by surprise. Even Elusive, who wasn't bad at them herself and could generally keep up with Feuery on that score.

'Do we have any pearls? Air elementals are partial to powdered pearls. They use 'em for glittery effect by swirling the dust through 'emselves. Make-up for translucent beings, I guess. I usually keep some pearl-powder handy. However, I most-like won't have enough if'n we get a sharp one at bargaining when we Call a sylph.'

A quick trawl through the treasures stashed in their bottomless bags turned up a few pearls inlaid in rings and bejewelled items. Quite a few, in fact.

Elusive objected. 'Feueze! These are really high-grade, valuable gems. Ok if they were seed pearls but ...'

'You wanna spend a week playing tag with wolves an' gaunts in spooky forest glades? Looking forward to being invited to dinner by a troll – bring-your-own main course? I'm not! Needs must, an' right now we need a ride to somewheres that in't here; preferably a decent town. Air elementals are the best option for a ride, but they'll want payment. Haven't met one yet who could refuse powdered pearls. Now, give me a hand getting 'em out of the furnishings while I use the mortar and pestle.'

When Feuery was satisfied they had enough powdered pearl (an operation that nearly brought Elusive to tears and rebellion as valuable and beautiful pearl after pearl was ground to dust) she cast the summoning.

A minute or so later a gust of wind whipped up from the direction of the mountains. It tore across them, sending their clothing fluttering and wildly tossing their hair. It circled the trees around the edge of the hilltop, setting branches flailing and creaking, filling the air with leaves. A peal of sibilant, joyous laughter echoed around the surrounding forest.

'Frisky one. Eager too! Must really want these pearls,' observed Feuery knowingly. 'Good, it's a buyer's market. This'll be easy to negotiate.'

The wind swept back around, abruptly depositing leaves and twigs in a pile before them as it died away. A figure formed in the air, gradually becoming more solid and defined as a slender young woman with long, flowing hair and shimmering robes that rippled gently, even though the wind had died away everywhere else.

'Hi-ya,' said Feuery. 'We were wondering if you'd be ok to take us for a ride in return for … pearl?' She held out a small handful of powdered pearls; about a third of the total they'd prepared previously.

Again there was the joyous peal of happy laughter. The powdered pearl was swept out of Feuery's hand and swirled glittering into the air, where the dust compressed and fell back onto the palm of her hand as a single, huge pearl.

'Give it the rest of the powder,' suggested Elusive, looking over Feuery's shoulder at the pearl. 'I like its style. Sensible. More than some I could mention.'

Uncharacteristically, Feuery was lost for words. However, the sylph swept closer before she had a chance to recover.

It hovered in front of Elusive.

'Sshee, not it. *Sshee*, Je-nee the Sswifft of Aeolian Sssongsss. Ffee for trassportingss is partner.'

Feuery's eyes flew wide open and she readied her battle-staff.

'Don't tempt me,' murmured Elusive. She addressed the sylph: 'That's a bit of a steep price. She's high maintenance anyway, believe me. Lots of little and 'not-so-little' quirks as well. She has some bad habits also, like being messy for one. I want to be friends with you afterwards. Is there anything else we can trade – other than a rather foxed gnome – if you're not interested in pearl?'

Feuery's face looked like a thunderstorm just before it breaks. However, before she had a chance to express her feelings, there was another long peal of silvery laughter from the sylph.

'Missundersstandingss. Not gnome, not brownie to have and to keep. Ssylph *partner with* sstone folk. Travel, adventure, experienssse!'

'You wanna be *partners* with us?' Feuery asked in surprise.

'YESSS! Ssee world, new thingss, meet peoplesss, exssitement!'

'Ah, could my friend an' I just confer for a moment?'

'Ssertainly.' The sylph swept high into the air, swirling leaves around them.

Below her there was an intense, whispered conversation; every word of which was clearly heard by the sylph. She wasn't eavesdropping at all, but speech is, when all's said and done, just skilful movement of air, and sylphs are *very* good with air.

'Stone folk?'

'That's what sylphs call us. Because we're bound to the ground.'

'Oh. Have you ever heard of this happening before?'

'Well, a fire elemental once enlisted as a mercenary with the Tunk of Ferik's army. Very good at fire raising, an' handy around the camp at mealtimes with cooking fires I understand. But I've never heard of a sylph wanting to partner with any of the kindreds. Not something elementals do as a rule. Most elementals generally avoid the kindreds unless summoned, 'less someone unscrupulous puts a binding on 'em. Bad form to summon 'n' bind, but if'n they're there, it's a bit of a temptation for some wizards.' Feuery's tone made it clear what she thought of such wizards.

'I didn't think they took much notice of anything on our side of things.'

'Me neither, but this one is.'

'So, what do you think?'

Feuery looked reflective for a moment. 'Lots of things. Once there was a gnome girl who felt life was smothering tight 'round her. Angry all the time. Seeker for the Wizards' Guild found her. Took her out of the cold North where most all folk think about is turnips an' cabbages – plus there's thirty-two different names for the different types of mud an' twelve for cold up there. Put her where she found all sorts of new an' interesting things, like magic spells an' commercial opportunities. Still finding new an' interesting things; no end of 'em. Reckon everyone deserves a chance to spread their wings; winds in this case. Up to them then as to whether they like it, an' what they do with it. Having the chance is what's important.'

Elusive mused that if Feuery was permitting a personal glimpse of herself, then her transformation was still a work in progress; with a *long* way to go if the 'angry all the time' was an attribute that was supposed to have been left behind. Still, she couldn't deny that her own collaboration with Feuery was certainly the most interesting thing she'd done in her life (even counting being accepted by the Wizards' Academy). And, by far the most profitable. It was almost as though the little gnome was a direction-finder or a catalyst for exciting adventures and events. Somehow, she always seemed to be in just the right place at the right time; ready to take a lead or an opportunity no one else seemed to actually have seen. It was as though she could sense adventure in the air and instinctively knew how best to respond.

'Ok. I'm game!' Elusive said brightly.

Feuery gave her a sharp look. Evidently Elusive had been expected to try to reason her out of the idea so that Feuery could argue it through, or, ultimately, pull rank. The brownie smiled inside and mentally notched up a small point.

The little gnome glared at the brownie for a moment before turning to look up at the sylph. 'Ok Je-nee. Let's talk business.'

* * * *

So far it hadn't been a good day for Feuery. Apart from the ex-carpet, the pearls fiasco and Elusive being her usual quietly insufferable self, Je-nee had proved to be an unexpectedly hard bargainer. Now, the sight of Feuery homing in on their wares would usually fill those merchants who knew her – or who had heard stories – with consternation, and those who'd dickered with her were often left wondering what had happened to leave so little in return for what they'd forfeited. Nevertheless, Je-nee had somehow managed to join the team of two wizards as a full and equal partner; both in terms of decisions and shares of spoil. It had taken all of Feuery's considerable skills to get it down to that.

Most sylphs were happy to accept a handful of pearl dust, she reflected sourly.

Feuery had a sneaky feeling that it wasn't that Je-nee was greedy. It was more that the sylph was determined, and with that determination came an iron-clad requirement for full respect.

Greediness would have been easier to manage. But Feuery was gradually coming to terms with dealing with a kindred spirit in a very different physical form.

Yet it didn't make it any easier.

Elusive, on the other hand, was having a thoroughly enjoyable day. She respected the gnome mightily, and was as (or more) fond of her than most people are of their siblings. However, she was also (like most siblings) more than happy to see Feuery taken down a peg or two in a harmless sort of way when the occasion presented itself.

In any case, being carried by a sylph was an extremely swift and easy way to travel. Now she knew why Feuery favoured it.

Je-nee was ecstatic, eagerly awaiting the next exciting experience. Today was turning out simply *marvellously*!

On the whole, the mood of the newly-formed group was very good, with just one spot of grumpiness. That isolated spot of grumpiness had auburn hair and was dressed all in blue.

The trio flew south-east over the forest; the two wizards carried securely and comfortably in the arms of the wind.

Feuery had been right on one point at least. Wolves would have been a minor inconvenience compared to some of the forest's inhabitants they glimpsed from safely high above.

* * * *

'Turn to the left an' head for that pass in the mountains when we get to that river ahead,' Feuery said suddenly.

'Why?' The question was voiced in stereo.

It had been so *much easier working solo.* Feuery unpursed her lips.

'Cos when I was staying with the Fair Elves I heard whispers of some islands in these parts. Little ways offshore; supposedly directly out from the mouth of this river that flows through that pass. The tales didn't come up often, an' when they did, always as sum'it hushy-secret. The Islands of the Sun they're called. Guess that's 'cos they're seen as being the nearest to where the sun supposedly rises. No imagination, some folk. Sometimes folk mention 'em as the Isle of the Sun, which is a bit strange 'cos there's apparently more'n one. Anyways, no one would talk openly 'bout 'em, an' no references I could find. But some of the Fair Elf sailors hinted after a few wines an' gentle encouragement (an' a few more wines) that they'd been on ships that their navy keeps on a guard picket around the islands. Not cheap that, so it must be important.'

She paused, thinking hard. *Ask, don't tell.* 'Wondered if it might be worth us having a look-see, careful-like?' she suggested casually.

At this juncture, a long discussion followed – mainly involving Elusive and Je-nee as the suggestion was enjoyably dissected and used as a 'getting-to-know-one-another' opportunity. Feuery couldn't help noting the two seemed to get along together very well indeed. Personally, the liberal lashings of small talk and forays into side issues bored her, but the other two seemed to be thoroughly enjoying themselves. There were also lots of questions, to which Feuery could add little she hadn't already mentioned. However, in due course they reached a consensus that a reconnaissance couldn't hurt – providing it didn't delay them too much.

Exactly what it might delay them from wasn't clear to Feuery, but she wasn't going to ask and risk setting them off again. As it was, they didn't have too far to go back after overshooting the river.

A 'little ways offshore' proved to be an understatement. The coast of the great continent was barely more than a faint haze in the distance behind them and a severe storm was brewing ahead of them. By this time, the consensus was under severe strain when Elusive spotted a tiny smudge on the horizon almost under the leading edge of the gathering storm.

Instantly, shared curiosity quickly displaced any grumbling as they veered smoothly toward it.

* * * *

It grew into a cluster of three craggy, luxuriantly forested islands; a large one to the south and two smaller islands perched very close to it to the north-west and north-east. Ordinarily, the islands would have looked idyllic, with clean fringing beaches of white sand and shallow seas all around. Now, however, a huge ocean swell, whipped up by the storm, broke in mighty waves and sheets of spray and foam against the seaward eastern shores, and a light rain, like the forward scouts of a vast army, began.

'There's a boat down there. And look! Another one on the other side!' Elusive shouted above the rising wind gusts.

'Ship not 'boat', Feuery corrected. She had a nasty suspicion that Elusive persisted in misusing nautical terms simply to be annoying. In fairness, it was more that Elusive, who like most brownies came from a rural and forested area, simply couldn't care less about the precise wording, and the nearest familiar term handy was what she used. If it floated on water and wasn't a duck, a log or a raft, it was a boat.

'Fair Elf frigates on guard picket. An' that's not all. Je-nee! Get us down to the island – fast!'

'Wh …?'

'*NOW*!' There was unmistakable urgency in Feuery's voice.

Je-nee banked and dived, heading for the main island.

'Land us somewheres with overhead cover,' Feuery commanded. She pointed slightly ahead, to their right. Two dark shapes, wings beating fast, were closing on them, trying to cut off their escape. To their left, another pair vectored in on them.

'Who …?' began Elusive, perplexed.

'Fair Elves, on hippogriffs. Guards. An' that's *still* not all. Look behind us,' said Feuery grimly.

Elusive did, Je-nee glancing back and up as she steepened their dive. A fire-drake – with rider – was diving steeply toward them from behind.

'Je-nee, if'n you can go faster, sure would be appreciated. Might not hurt you, but they're deadly with those longbows, an' there won't be a warning shot. Being flamed by a dragon would smart sum'it terrible too, most like for all of us.'

'But, but … they're Fair Elves!' Elusive almost wailed indignantly.

'Sure are. What I said. Weren't you listening?'

'But Fair Elves are really nice!'

'Most folk are; even orcs on occasion in my experience. Right time, right place. But here, it's the wrong place, an' probably no right time ever. We're breaking their rules – so welcome to the *other* side of the Fair Elves. The reason Fair Elves can be so nice an' civilised is 'cos they're confident they're not under threat. An' the reason they're confident is they make sure no one forgets what happens when you do the wrong thing by them or their laws. Word gets around somehow, such as from Fair Elves – even when there *aren't* any survivors. Doing well Je-nee! They're not gaining, but if you can push a bit more speed …'

The sylph, somehow, managed to increase their pace. For a moment, the two wizards could hardly breathe as they accelerated, rapidly leaving their pursuers behind. The island came up at an alarming speed.

'Easy girl,' Feuery gasped. 'A bit lower, an' can you turn me about to face 'em?' The gnome frantically scrabbled for something in a small pouch at her belt.

'Yesss.' The sylph's voice was faint.

She braked their dive, sending the treetops below them shivering even against the gusts of the incoming storm. She hovered just above the trees, angling so that Feuery looked directly up at the rapidly approaching elven guards on their exotic winged steeds.

Feuery hastily cast a long powerful spell, ending it by throwing a handful of black dust upward as hard as she could from her precarious position. Then she slumped back, exhausted from the effort involved. The dust spread and grew with amazing speed. It formed a heavy cloud that billowed out and up, obscuring their pursuers and expanding to take in much of the sky immediately above the islands.

'Quick now! Keep low an' head for those crags on the next island. Not even elves could see through *that* cloud, an' they won't dive through it an' risk hitting the trees.' Feuery's voice was weak.

'Why the next island? It's tiny, and there's nothing there,' asked Elusive.

'Then no reason for us to try to hide there, is there? Always do what's the least expected. I need to rest, an' I suspect I'm not the only one, right Je-nee? We can do that while they're ratting around searching for us on the big island 'cos the big island is where it would make most sense for us to try to hide. Just keep low to the ground now so no one on a ship sees us.'

Je-nee sped across the main island at treetop level, dodging sharp crags that speared up out of the thick, tangled forest below. Elusive felt sure she saw ruins briefly; however, they were travelling too fast for her to be certain. They swept down from the forest canopy low and fast over a beach and then skimmed over a short stretch of shallow water to the beach on the next, most easterly, island.

'Over there! Sharp turn to the left! There're caves in the cliffs.'

The island consisted of a ring of sheer cliffs with a thick forest in the centre. A break in the cliffs opened onto the beach over which they'd flown, but on the eastern seaward side, the ridge rose up steeply. There were numerous caves dotting the cliffs; probably more than they could see because veils of vines hung from the heights, and the thick foliage of many trees growing near the cliffs could have hidden countless openings.

'Pick one of the caves that's high off the ground, but not too obvious.' Feuery's voice was barely audible.

Je-nee landed them smoothly on a narrow ledge about forty feet above the forest floor, gently setting them down at the mouth of a low wide cave. Feuery tottered and lost her balance, crumpling into the drifts of leaves on the cave floor.

'Big spell,' she mumbled apologetically as Elusive rushed to her side in concern. 'Just need to eat an' rest.'

'I alsso,' Je-nee whispered. 'Iff I go, you will bide here?'

'Not going nowheres, an' we'll be fine. You go, an' see you here later.'

'Good. Resst well.'

The sylph faded. A gust of wind raced over the treetops and disappeared with the faintest swirl.

'Where's she going?' Elusive asked as she helped Feuery inside.

'To eat an' rest. It's the same thing – near 'nough – for sylphs. Little darling near exhausted herself getting us away from those guards. I never knew a sylph could move that fast, 'specially carting two folk. She'll go above the clouds, 'way above *all* the clouds, where the stars are bright an' clear an' don't twinkle, where the sky is a darker blue than the blackness it becomes, an' bathe in the heat of the sun that travels between the worlds. Funny thing is she thinks *our* lives are exciting! Suppose they are, actually, but not sure if she realises hers is too. It's the usual way of folk to see things; or more rightly, often *not* to see things, 'cos they're too close an' familiar. She'll be fine. Chirpy too, I'll bet, when she gets back.'

Elusive carefully checked over the cave, setting wards front and back against intruders from either the cave mouth or the deep, narrow fissure that disappeared into the range at the back. There were insects everywhere – more than she'd ever seen anywhere before – but a simple repulsion spell soon fixed that. The insects could have their cave back tomorrow. Tonight, it was needed by two tired wizards.

She settled Feuery so she was comfortable, and then prepared a hot meal on an enchanted brazier that provided heat, but neither glow nor odour. Unfortunately, the ceiling of the cave was too low to set up their magic pavilion.

She had to rouse Feuery for the meal, after which the gnome quickly fell into a deep sleep, wrapped in a thick blanket and with her favourite pillow from her bottomless bag. Soon after, the storm broke in full force over the islands. It slashed at the crags with lightning and filled the world with deafening thunder; drenching the forest and blowing away the last remnants of Feuery's concealing cloud – only to replace it with what seemed an even more solid mass of roiling, dark storm cloud.

Elusive took a seat toward the mouth of the cave. Far enough out that she had a good view of the storm-lashed landscape, yet sufficiently well in not to be readily seen herself (if anyone was out on such a night) or get too wet. It was a long night with many hours spent listening to the sounds of the gusting rain, growling thunder, howling wind and the protests of the tempest-whipped forest. Yet, even more disturbing were the chaotic murmurings of her own thoughts and imaginings as she fought back sleep. In the deep darkness that presages dawn, she fell into an exhausted slumber.

* * * *

Elusive woke to bright sunshine, the faint tinkling of bells and a fluttering about her face. She sat up. A beautiful little fairy – barely six inches tall and all silver and gold with copper-coloured eyes and lips – smiled at her delightedly.

'T'zing! Great to see you again!'

T'zing was a small metallic fairy who had chosen to leave her fairy shimmer to travel with Feuery – although her motive for doing so was a mystery to both Feuery and Elusive. T'zing would merely smile enigmatically if asked, so perhaps she wasn't actually sure herself. Equally mysteriously, she had abruptly departed some weeks ago on a venture of her own. Elusive was overjoyed to find she'd returned.

The brownie lass then did a double-take. Another fairy – steel-grey and bronze complexioned with eyes the colour of brass – hovered just behind T'zing. Slightly larger, this one carried a miniature crossbow with a quiver of tiny darts and a needle-like sword – a little epee – at his waist. The reason for T'zing's mysterious disappearance suddenly became clearer.

'Are you going to introduce me to your friend T'zing?' Elusive questioned.

At T'zing's request, the newcomer hesitantly came forward. T'zing pointed at Elusive while making a sound that might have been 'Elusive' if verbalised by a xylophone, and then wrapped her arms briefly about herself with a warm smile. She then pointed to the new fairy and chimed 'Chai' before embracing him tightly. He, in turn, looked happy when she took hold of his hand, while he put an affectionate and protective arm around her. The fairy had evidently found (or reclaimed) a mate.

'Pleased to meet you,' said Elusive happily, 'Congratulations and my blessings to you both.'

How did a creature made of metal blush? Elusive wondered. She was sure she'd observed T'zing do so in a pleased sort of way.

Then she remembered Feuery. She scrambled over to her, all the worries of the previous night returning.

The gnome was still soundly asleep, but even a quick glance told Elusive she didn't need to fret. Usually Feuery met each new day head-on at a disgustingly early hour (which she expected everyone else to do as well); however, occasionally she indulged in lengthy sleep-ins. Elusive had learned not to encourage the former, and not, if at all possible, to disturb the latter. This morning, the gnome was sleeping curled up with her face buried in a pillow, with just the faintest hint of a satisfied smile showing.

It was a 'do not disturb, let snoozing gnomes lie' morning. Elusive started to wash herself, but stopped at the sudden realisation that a male was present. Embarrassed and confused, she didn't quite know what to do. However, after realising the problem, T'zing discretely escorted Chai out with an amused chime.

After a very quick sponge-down, she quickly dressed and set about making breakfast. The aroma of roasting chestnut immediately brought the metal fairies back: T'zing liked chestnuts. So did Chai it turned out, after T'zing had introduced him to the taste, and Elusive set a second one to roast for them. Elusive couldn't imagine why roasted chestnuts were so appreciated by beings formed of metal, but Feuery had pointed out that people, who are mainly water, enjoyed salt, iron and other minerals, so why shouldn't someone of metal enjoy chestnuts? Like many of Feuery's explanations, it wasn't really an answer, but as an explanation it *was* unanswerable.

The smell of frying bacon, beans and toast was making Feuery twitch in her sleep. However, she obstinately clung to her dozing until Je-nee made a dramatic entrance. The sylph suddenly appeared in the form of a strong gust of wind which swept through the cave – tumbling the fairies, setting Elusive's abundant hair a-whirl and causing the brownie to reach defensively to her staff. The sudden gust all but stripped the blankets off Feuery.

'Waz't' game?' Feuery growled grumpily, her hand pawing ineffectually for her lost blanket before she irritably sat up.

Je-nee chose that moment to materialise. This morning, the translucent young woman of yesterday appeared again. But

242

this time, Je-nee firmed up to the point that only a faintly trans-lucent glow – almost like an aura surrounding her – was all that distinguished her from a normal human form.

Feuery looked around at the small group: the two glitter-ing fairies with their sparkling iridescent wings; the radiantly glowing sylph, her long blonde hair tossing in a perpetual personal breeze; and Elusive holding her staff aloft with its magnificent emerald head gleaming in the shade of the cave. A tableau of note, even by Th'eia's standards.

'Any chance of a cuppa tea?' she asked hopefully.

* * * *

Introductions were made over breakfast. Feuery translated the chimes of the fairies, although they understood perfectly what the others were saying.

'Are we now sset to adventure?' Je-nee asked eagerly.

'Few little details to sort out first,' Feuery replied, helping herself to a third cup of tea and two more ginger biscuits. 'Couple of hundred Fair Elves with 'intruders wanted, dead or dead' orders being one, 'xactly what we're looking for being another.'

T'zing tinkled enquiringly in response to Feuery's statement.

'There will be that many, T'zing. Right 'nough, might not seem so, but there'll be two shifts of the aerial picket at least. So I figure there'll be minimum eight hippogriff riders an' two dragon-knights, or sim'lar. An' those frigates will have a squad of marines, as well as upward hundred an' fifty sailors for each ship. If'n I was in charge an' keen, I'd be starting to methodi-cally search each island, keeping the aerials on the look-see for anything they flush out. An' they *are* keen! They weren't aiming to warn us off yesterday; that was serious hunting with intent to puncture an' fricassee. An' while there's not a lot of us to be found, remember these *are* elves. Good elf hunters can track down most anything.'

There was silence as everyone absorbed this information.

'Oh, I forgot to mention. There'll be some elven mages; 'least one, or maybe even two, well-as. Have to be with as big a force as this.'

'Wonder what's so important,' she added musingly, almost to herself. 'This picket must be costing the Fair Elves a fortune. Not much fun for the elves 'emselves neither, sailing round in circles an' flapping about the same sky, day after day. No wonder they're bad tempered an' keen for someone to take it out on. Just a shame it's us. What's here to make all that needful? An' why haven't they set up a base camp here, 'stead of all the bother of operating off the ships? Fair enough, elves are discrete, but we'd have seen sum'it of a camp if'n there was one.'

'Are we getting a bit out of our depth here?' suggested Elusive carefully.

Feuery looked at her blankly. 'Huh?'

'Well, there might be something dangerous here. Also, do we really want a fight with the Fair Elves?'

Feuery considered these points carefully. The others watched her, knowing that if Feuery agreed the situation was too dangerous they would soon be sneaking back to the mainland, leaving the mysteries of the Islands of the Sun to the elves.

The little gnome nodded sagely. 'Course, that's the up-side, you're right. Dangerous things are always interesting, and we haven't had cause to outsmart Fair Elves afore. Just noting we need to be careful is all.'

Elusive stared, open-mouthed at Feuery. The little gnome was completely serious.

'Sso, what sshall we do?' asked Je-nee before Elusive could get over her astonishment sufficiently to reframe the discussion.

'Glad you asked,' replied Feuery, much happier that the world had resumed its proper order in which *she* gave the directions. 'Now gather 'round an' listen up.'

* * * *

Elusive paced restlessly just inside the cave mouth. It had been *hours* since the sylph and fairies had left on their missions, and she was beginning to feel very concerned that they'd heard nothing from them.

Feuery evidently wasn't worried. After instructing the two scouting parties when they eagerly set off, she'd insisted on tutoring Elusive on the intricacies of composing spells, until the brownie girl could no longer concentrate.

Then Feuery had busily occupied herself translating and cross-referencing some ancient scroll or other from the extensive collection she held in a bottomless bag, while Elusive vented her energy on setting the cave to rights. The results were difficult to see, but at least she felt better for it.

Now, for the past half-hour, Feuery had simply sat, cross-legged, staring at a swirling globe of quicksilver slowly rotating in the air in front of her.

'Aren't you worried about them?' Elusive eventually burst out angrily.

The little gnome seemed to slowly come back from somewhere.

'If'n I had cause, I'd be. Been checking on 'em though' she pointed at the ball of quicksilver 'an' they're fine.'

'Meanwhile I've been worrying myself sick about them! Why didn't you *tell* me?'

'You didn't ask, an' I've been too busy making sure they're ok to notice you fretting. Thought you were just phistling 'round, tidying up, usual-like. You do a lot of that.'

Mainly in your company which is usually what made tidying up necessary, thought Elusive sourly. She was building up to really nice bicker …

'If'n you want, I'll show you how to scry with a seeing-globe.'

Now, that was a very different matter entirely. Scrying, or farseeing, is the magical art of seeing somewhere else. A crystal ball is the most commonly used. However, there are a wide range of possible methods and equipment – even humble tea-leaves could work for those with the gift. The easiest scrying was to see events at a distance; the most difficult was to see into the future. Wizards who are gifted at scrying are known as seers and greatly respected, but some specially-made magical items could allow most wizards to become quite good at viewing distant events (but not into the future – that requires great innate skill). It was a rare opportunity to use such items because they were valuable and much sought-after. Elusive's irritation was put on hold for the moment as she sat down beside Feuery.

'It's easy if'n you concentrate. Lots easier an' clearer than a crystal ball or dropping ink in water. The quicksilver's spelled to find what you're seeking, but the trick is to help it with a clear thought. Might be best to start with T'zing. You'll have a nice sharp image of her. Je-nee mingles with backgrounds sum'it terrible, an' Chai's new to us so not so easy to form a picture to start with. I'll help you.'

'Where are they?' Elusive asked eagerly.

'The fairies went to the elven flagship to scout it out. Done well too. I haven't seen any Elven wizards yet but we now know how many elves there are near enough, an' what they're doing – which turns out to be not much at all. Bit odd that, 'specially since their Admiral is Elven High Lord Emathier. Capable an' keen: one of the Elven High Council. Fearless, incorruptible an' very brave. Rude, arrogant, conceited sod well-as; an' just between us I don't think he's all that bright. But then, he an'

I did get off to a bad start an' it's kept right on going down-hill from there. Snubbed me an' T'zing sum'it nasty when I was arranging the *Golden Marigold* deal. Almost walked out on him, but Lord Evanthiel (his papa) stepped in. True gentleman, Evanthiel. *He's* ok.

'Now, what's T'zing up to?' Feuery mused.

It was a reasonable question. Beside an ornate, closed door emblazoned with a magnificent enamelled coat of arms, they could see a pair of elven thigh-boots – evidently freshly cleaned and polished. And what boots! Fine, soft white leather of the finest quality, faced with silver plate greaves bearing an elabo-rate design traced in gold and highlighted by a multitude of tiny (but finely cut) and flawless emeralds cascading across the silver. The pair of boots would have been worth more than the total annual income of many small villages.

T'zing had just finished pouring something thick and yel-lowish into one of the boots from a cup that was almost the size of her, and was making room for Chai. He too carried a cup, and began tipping something black into the boot. Then both of the fairies flitted down the corridor and flew out of an open porthole. They were followed by the wizards' bemused gaze in the spelled perspective.

It almost seemed as though the fairies were trying hard not to laugh.

T'zing and Chai flew a short distance along the side of the ship before smoothly entering into a vent to the ship's chandlery. It was full to overflowing with rope of various sizes, tightly folded silken sails, baulks of timber large and small, tools, bundles of signal and ceremonial flags, kegs of nails and several barrels to which the fairies immediately went to refill their cups. In fine elven script, one barrel was marked 'tallow' and the other one, 'pitch'.

Feuery leaned back, distracting Elusive so that the vision was lost.

'Li'l buggers! So much for forget an' forgive. Don't annoy a fairy!'

'Will they be ok? They're taking a huge risk!'

Feuery snorted. 'Even an elf would be hard pressed to see a fairy who don't want to be seen. They'll be fine. Wonder what else they've been up to? Bit of an accident waiting to happen really – two fairies an' a whole unsuspecting ship full o' serious elves. Maybe best not to know. Glad I asked Je-nee to look over the *other* ship though. It'll likely have the mages on board, an' *they'll* be more alert to enchantment. T'zing was using a liquefaction spell on that stuff. Stays sloppy until someone puts pressure on it, and then it sets hard. Sorta pressure you might get, for 'sample, from someone forcing on a tight boot. Didn't know she could do spells?'

'There's lots of things we don't know about T'zing. And even more we don't know about Chai,' Elusive reminder her.

'In't that the truth? When we get the chance, maybe we'll see if they can pick up some of our magic spells. Fairies *are* magic. However, quite a numbers of 'em can cast spells too – more'n just a couple they seem to have naturally. Never thought to ask if'n she could learn spells, but T'zing seems most-like to have picked up that one from somewheres.' Feuery's eyes twinkled mischievously. 'Tempting to see what happens when he puts the boots on. Better still when he tries to get 'em off.'

'Can we look in on Je-nee?' Elusive asked. 'Just to make sure she's ok?'

'Sure. At least *she's* sensible, more'n some fairies I could put names to.'

It was a difficult task to fix a vision on the sylph. In the first place, Je-nee was all but invisible. In addition, Feuery was being careful to avoid their scrying attracting the elven wizards' attention on the second frigate.

They finally succeeded in locating the sylph by her actions rather than by actually seeing her faint outline.

Je-nee was in a storeroom amidships, opening sacks. *Really* opening *many* sacks in order to spill a fine white powder in great drifts across benches, tables and the floor. When she seemed to be satisfied with the mess she'd made, she swiftly moved through the ship; opening some hatches, doors and portholes methodically, while closing others. Her final exploit was to furtively close a door opposite a large, well-appointed cabin in which Feuery was horrified to see *four* elven wizards – one of whom was a High Mage. Feuery immediately recognised the High Mage as Lady Ilith Silverstem – one of the most renowned mages of any kindred. She was also a member of the High Council of the Fair Elves and highly regarded within the councils of the Wizards' Guild.

Feuery was shocked to see such an esteemed and powerful Mage here. Even more surprising was the fact that one third of the Fair Elven High Council was currently on guard duty at this remote (almost unheard-of) cluster of little islands far from anywhere. What was going on at these Islands of the Sun that the Fair Elves considered them to be so important?

Amazingly, Je-nee didn't attract their attention. The elves seemed to be deep in discussion about a vision of their own in a swirling ball of amber-golden sap – evidently the equivalent of Feuery's hovering ball of mercury.

'That'll be us they're looking for,' Feuery said grimly. 'An' they're getting way too close for our comfort if their intentness says anything.'

'Should we stop scrying?' asked Elusive.

'No point. They're scanning the islands, looking for us. It's a random process if'n the seer doesn't have a guiding image of who they're looking for. However, these mages are pretty darn good. We'll hold the image here for now an' see what they're up to. Might get some warning if'n they find us. Wish I could disrupt their spying though. They seem to think they're onto sum'it, an' that has to be us.'

The elven wizard who was directing the scanning pointed to the image and asked a question that was inaudible to the two spying wizards. High Mage Lady Ilith said something in reply and sat down to join the scrying. The three wizards at the table peered intently into the spinning amber ball while the fourth watched them closely from where he stood beside a large open porthole.

'Not good,' muttered Feuery. 'She's taking the lead. They *must* think they're onto us. Might haveta get ready to move fast. Damn! Wish we had a good magic carpet now. Where's your sylph when you need her?'

As it turned out, she wasn't very far away.

The circle of elven mages was suddenly startled, and then quickly obscured by a mighty gust of wind that filled the corridor and room with a fine white powder. The vision disappeared as if it had been dropped into a bowl of milk.

Elusive gasped.

'What the blue blazes!' Feuery exclaimed.

She switched her view, desperately seeking Je-nee. She finally found the sylph hovering in the air beside the bowsprit, immediately in front of a large door that opened to the heads. Je-nee was convulsed with silent laughter. There was pandemonium on board as sailors ran toward the stern, shouting and gesticulating in a manner most unlike the measured, dignified demeanour usually characteristic of Fair Elves. Clouds of white powder were puffing out of hatches and open portholes – an indicator of the chaos inside the ship.

'Flour!' exclaimed Elusive suddenly. 'Je-nee made a wind tunnel through the ship after opening those sacks of flour. I guess she then sent through a gale – tightly focused down the wind tunnel.' She started giggling, as much in relief that the elves' scrying had been disrupted as at Je-nee's imaginative practical joke.

'I'll take back the bit 'bout sylphs being more sensible than fairies,' said Feuery. 'But best thing now is the elves' scrying ball won't work. The flour'll gum up the sap sum'it *awful*. I should give Je-nee, T'zing an' Chai a lecture on how scouts are *supposed* to be serious, but today's scouting worked out well.'

* * * *

That evening, Feuery convened a council of war (or, more accurately, adventure). Je-nee and the two fairies were in high spirits, and only a little subdued (and that only briefly) by Feuery's lecture on the seriousness of the situation. In any case, the heat had been removed from the telling-off by the timely clouding of the elven scrying.

Elusive completely failed to support Feuery's lecture by continually breaking into suppressed giggles. Feuery almost regretted allowing her to scry on the scene that had unfolded when Admiral Emathier was called urgently because there appeared to be smoke coming from the other frigate. His first action was to be properly attired, including hastily stepping into his magnificent boots.

The response from the flagship had been somewhat delayed.

'Ok,' Feuery summed up after the excited reporting and semi-suppressed snickers concluded. 'So let's summarise. There're two dragons with three riders an' ten hippogriffs, all stationed on the other small island in a little camp way over on the western side. 'Bout as far from us as you could get, which suits me just fine. There're seventy marines between the two ships, an' 'bout three hundred sailors an' officers all up. Plus a High Mage, an' three other wizards as well. A small army – 'nough to take on some of the smaller city-states.'

'The sseass are sstrange alsso,' said Je-nee. 'Many mossos-saurss and kritoidss – ssome huge. Very many of ssea-weassellss. Many more than ussual.'

'How come you know about sea-life?' Feuery asked with interest.

'Sstorm-ssurfing. Ffun sskimming wavess. Ssee many thingss.'

'Hmmm. Haveta get you to tell me more 'bout it sometime. As to the local gathering, could be an ocean upwelling against the islands. Brings nutrients up from deep down. Fish come in shoals, an' things that eat fish, an' things that eat things that eat fish. Anyone with ideas 'bout bathing off the beaches maybe would decide to re-think.'

'No. Many more than natural, even for rich waterss. Ass if the ssea-monssterss gather here.'

They all looked at Je-nee, but she made no further comment.

'Something else is strange,' Elusive suggested slowly. 'This morning there was no dawn chorus here.'

'Remind me again what a dawn chorus is?' Although she had grown up in a small village, Feuery was, by inclination and determined perseverance, very much a city girl.

'Birdsong – baks too – greeting the morning. Setting their territories; seeing who the neighbours are and whether anything changed overnight. Maybe even just plain happiness at another day. But there wasn't one here this morning, which is really strange, because you'd expect these islands to be full of birds.'

'No sseabirds alsso. None on the clifffss, no nessstss, none ssoaring,' Je-nee added.

Chai made a series of tones.

'Almost no sign of animals on the islands either? You sure? There's always rats, leastways.'

The fairy shook his head and spoke in his clear ringing. T'zing nodded, supporting him with a forceful chiming directed at Feuery.

'I believe you! Just lots an' lots of insects then?' Feuery frowned. 'Sum'it very strange here. So I recommend we take extra care 'till we figure it out. Anyways, the elves were hoping to scry us out. But, Je-nee stopped that idea, 'less they have another scrying ball. Good chance they won't. Good ones that any wizard can use (even not being a seer or diviner) are expensive an' hard to come by ...'

T'zing belled an enquiry.

'Never you mind where I got mine from. It was just lying around anyways; shame to see a magic item like that not being appreciated. Disrespectful to fine magic. Moral duty to give it a good home. The Wizards' Guild Museum at Heliovorn will hardly miss it I'm sure. So, what do you think they'll do next?'

'Perhapss,' said Je-nee after thinking for a moment, 'they will ssend sscoutss?'

T'zing and Chai chimed in – literally – with thoughts that it was more likely to be a warband. That way the elves would ensure that when the intruders were found, they stayed found.

'I don't think so,' said Elusive thoughtfully.

'Oh? Whyzat?' enquired Feuery.

'Because I think they're scared to venture onto the islands. Otherwise they'd have been here last night and today; searching before we could really hide ourselves away. Instead, they tried to scry us. Even if they were sure who we are, scrying is *so* unreliable unless you know more or less where to look, and who to look for. Even then it's a real art – more skilful good luck than anything else (unless you are a Seer). We'd have been in real trouble if they'd set half a dozen hunting parties out looking for us. Elves are the keenest trackers and hunters around. But, for some reason, they don't want to come onto the island. They want to find us so they can set the dragons on us, but they don't want to set foot on the island themselves. What can be scaring them so much they won't even set up a base camp on these islands?'

There was a pause as everyone absorbed this perspective, and its implications. Feuery glanced at Elusive with the hint of an approving smile.

'There iss the flyerss' basse on the little island,' Je-nee pointed out.

'I can't see how you could practically keep a dragon on a boat,' Elusive replied. 'Not for long, anyway. Have you ever seen what's involved in mucking up after a dragon? Be thankful if you haven't. *And* they have a tendency to – um, how can I put it? – jettison unnecessary weight as they take off. Not what you want on a boat. Look where the base is too: at the furthest place on these islands that isn't actually sea. Anyway, dragons and hippogriffs are just what you need to get away quickly if required. Think about it: what could be on this island that two fire-drakes and a squad of hippogriff riders may need to flee from quickly? I think if they can find us, they'll use the dragons on us, but they won't put foot on the island. At least, not unless there's no other choice for them.'

'Any thoughts why?' Feuery asked quietly.

'No,' Elusive admitted, 'and I can't decide if I wish I did know, or if I'm glad I can't think of why it might be so.'

'Whatever is on these islands, it in't throwing out magic, else-wise we'd have had real problems scrying today. I think tomorrow we'll let the elves alone. They've been stirred up plenty today, so we should start looking around a bit ourselves. I think Elusive is on the right track. Time we figured out what's here that's making the elves so rambunctious an' trigger-happy an' scaredy-cattish. We'll take turns on watch tonight, an' be ready to skedaddle fast.'

It was a disturbed night for them all – full of restless sleep, fretful watches and shapeless foreboding.

* * * *

Feuery was up before dawn and greeted T'zing and Chai, who'd performed the last watch. She made sure Elusive was up as well; something she considered to be part of her duty to the brownie. It was a mystery to Feuery why Elusive was bad-tempered most mornings, but she put it down to a minor personality flaw.

There was no sign of Je-nee. The sylph needed little rest between her periodic respites in the stratosphere, and she had left during Feuery's middle watch to scout the islands; under strict instructions from the gnome to look and listen *only*, before reporting back. Night or day made little difference to the air elementals, and they could be virtually invisible to everyone (with the exception of a wizard actively looking for them). Sylphs, it was becoming apparent, were simply wonderful scouts, and on top of that Je-nee was a lovely person. However, learning to live in a confined space with a restless air elemental was a new and educating experience for them all. At least it made Feuery much less inclined to leave her scrolls and papers lying around, as was her usual habit.

The sylph blew in just as the first rays of the sun transformed the greys of the dying night to the soft golds and pastel yellows and pinks of the freshly-born day.

'There are many ruinss in the ssentre of the big island,' she reported. 'Jungle around iss very thick with many nassty bugss. Again, I ssaw no birds, no bakss, no batss, no lizzardss, no furry creaturess. Just inssects everywhere and the ssleek, sslithery creaturess of the deep sseass. Elven patrolss are already fflying the sskiess, sseeking, ssearching.'

'Guess there's a temple in the middle of the ruins?' Feuery was trying to get the quicksilver ball working, but without much success. It was almost as if the ball was distracted and she was having to get its attention.

'No, no temple. Just lotss of ruined sssity. Beautifful once.'

'There's *always* a temple. Why'd anyone live in a place like this, ways out here if'n it wasn't for someone or other's greater glory?' She frowned as the quicksilver continued to be unco-operative. Annoyance – never far below the surface for Feuery – was beginning to show.

'Great fishing apparently, or so I've heard. And the air's clean and healthy,' suggested Elusive. 'Very relaxing place. Good for the nerves. At least, it would be if it weren't just *some* folk who get to sleep in occasionally.'

Feuery ignored her. She was just starting to get an image.

A dark purple, scaly hand with long yellow-grey talons shot out of the quicksilver, groping for Feuery's face. Only her quick reactions and habitual caution – especially when using magic – saved her. She dodged the hand and flung herself side-ways, bringing her staff up. Elusive stifled a scream and struck out with the nearest thing at hand, which happened to be the frying pan she was holding.

There was a solid *Clunk!* as pan and arm met. The hand instantly grabbed at the frying pan, so Elusive let it have it as a faint *Swish!* went past her ear. A tiny crossbow bolt fired by Chai buried itself in the scales, sending a ripple along the scaly arm. She saw Feuery – a grim, angry look on her face – raise her staff as the great sapphire at the top pulsated menacingly with magical energy, and was vaguely aware of a movement behind her.

Je-nee suddenly appeared in front of the arm and the sylph seemed to both fade and swell in size. There was a sudden roar as air was sucked from all around them and directed in a jet directly in line with the arm and the quicksilver. The fire flickered and went out as leaves, twigs – even small branches – swirled into the cave from the forest outside, causing their possessions to fly all around the cave. The roaring became a near-intolerable screaming. Elusive gasped for breath, vaguely aware of the arm wildly flailing about as it was pushed back into the quicksilver; then the world faded out …

Elusive came to with Feuery rubbing her wrists and neck to help restore circulation. For a brief instant, she glimpsed real concern on Feuery's face, before the gnome saw she was ok and returned to her more usual look of quiet peevishness.

'Take it easy for awhiles,' she advised Elusive. 'But we'll have to move pretty darn quick now. Looks like they found us. Much good it did 'em, but they'll have the dragons on us soon's they get sorted out.'

'What happened?' Elusive asked groggily.

'Someone tried to send a demon onto us. That's against the Wizards' Guild rules. *Really* playing dirty! Not like the Fair Elves at all. They must be feeling really desperate to do that.'

'But ssurprissed now,' said Je-nee solemnly.

Feuery laughed. 'Thanks to you. Blowing the demon back on 'em surely musta been a surprise – and also having a gale inside the ship! I'd give a lot to see what it's like over there right now. But we need to get a move on since they know where we are. Listen up everyone! We'll start at those ruins Elusive an' Je-nee saw on the main island. Good places for eldritch horrors an' deep, dark mysteries, ruins. Treasure also, with a bit of luck. Should be lots of writings inna place like that too. Interesting stories, maybe? Pack up everyone. Time to find out what's going on here at the Islands of the Sun.'

'I'm going to miss that frying pan. It was my favourite, not to mention being the only one we had with us. The demon took it with it,' said Elusive ruefully.

'Will they usse the frying pan to sseek uss?' asked Je-nee, still trying to get a better understanding of the magic of the 'stone folk'.

'Nah. It's iron, an' iron's hard to magic. That's why spells on swords an' such-like are so hard to do – an' costly. Have to cast 'em while the iron's forging, before it realises what you're up to. Never heard of an enchanted frying pan though.' She paused. 'Now there's a thought. Sum'it practical an' useful for enchantment ...'

'Let's move it,' said Elusive brusquely. If Feuery went off on a tangent they could be stuck here for ages while she resolved (what was to her) an intriguing train of thought.

* * * *

Escorted closely by the two fairies, Je-nee carried Feuery and Elusive to the island with the ruins, crossing over the narrow strip of water between the two islands as swiftly as possible through the early morning mist.

Through the breaks in the mist, Elusive looked down at the little, rippling waves gently lapping at the sands. The beach – at least on this side of the island – was mostly made up of millions upon millions of delicate, tiny shells. She'd grown up inland, so as a child hadn't seen ocean beaches, and had always assumed they would be all pebbles and silt like those of the lakes at home. Right now she'd have loved to fritter away a sunny day just meandering along the beach, looking at the little shells and feeling the sea breeze on her face.

It's so easy to simply look there where the land and sea meet and think 'just a pretty beach, Elusive mused philosophically to herself. *All those little lives involved in making up a beach over how many years? It was one of those things that Feuery said was a type of hidden magic all on its own, even without magic. Wonderful things were all around them in the world. You just needed to look at life with your mind open, not just with your eyes.*

Maybe she'd have the chance to quietly walk along the beach later. That was if their luck held and if they achieved some sort of understanding with the Fair Elves, and if they could look around the island and if ...

I guess that's a lot of 'ifs', so maybe, for the moment, best to stick with 'if our luck holds' as the all-important prerequisite, pondered Elusive. She forced herself back to the present. This was no time for daydreaming.

Fortunately, their luck held. From the dappled shadows under the trees lining the beach of the largest island, they watched a dragon spiralling around high above, while two pairs of hippogriff cavalry made erratic passes over the islands. They caught a brief glimpse of one of the frigates sailing in the direction of the other ship.

'Hope Je-nee managed to dis-mast 'em,' Feuery said nastily. 'Sure looks like that one's going to the rescue.'

They quickly set off toward the ruins, the sylph keeping watch above them while the fairies scouted ahead through the thick, tangled forest. This turned out to be no mean feat since, in the deep shade of the trees, the understorey consisted mostly of an interlocking maze of vines cascading untidily about with tendrils and stems disappearing into the thick canopy above. The gnome and brownie had a difficult time navigating through the dense vegetation, and, in places, even the fairies had to find ways around the thicker knots of vines and trunks.

'I can see why the elves aren't searching down here on the ground for us,' Elusive said crossly, as if the hard going was intentionally their fault.

'Could be, could be so, but I'm still thinking you were right first-off about them not wanting to set foot on the islands 'cos of sum'it that's here. Darn!' Feuery replied as she struggled out of the clutch of a vine with inch-long spines. 'I'm hoping these aren't poisonous.'

'Why would they be? Nobody would go in here if they could avoid it. Couldn't we just ask Je-nee to carry us over this forest? We're getting nowhere fast at present.'

'So long's we stay low, should be ok. We'll get the fairies to call her for us when they get back.' Feuery twisted under some stems to settle thankfully against a tree trunk, but then jumped up again with alacrity as a centipede as long as her hand scuttled away into the leaf-litter.

'What gives here?' she mused. 'The folks were right. All I've seen so far is insects. Not only neither birds nor baks, but also no sign of anything else that doesn't have more legs than you can shake a staff at. An' way too manys of *them*. In't natural at all. Be even nice to see a rat 'bout now, an' never thought I'd say *that*.'

Long minutes passed. Insect life buzzed, scurried and tottered all around them.

'Shouldn't at least one of the fairies have come back by now?' Elusive eventually asked as time dragged on. It was hot and stuffy in the thick forest. She was starting to perspire, and the sweat was irritating the scratches from the thorns.

'Yep, long past,' Feuery replied grimly. She rose, then abruptly stopped, staring intently to her left. '*Climb, now!*' She was like a blue blur scampering up the nearest tree trunk; her auburn hair looking like the head of a meteor that had changed its mind about the whole business of falling to earth.

Elusive needed no second warning: if Feuery was scrambling, then it was a good idea to follow her lead. She too scrabbled her way as fast as she could up into the lattice of branches and vines.

A *thing* – a horrible thing – slithered through the vines. It was about fourteen feet long, with a mottled grey-brown, barrel-like body that was almost of uniform thickness, except for the last two feet of a stubby tail. Its hide was composed of thick, overlapping plate-like scales. It moved on a multitude of wickedly clawed feet on incongruously short, stubby legs, but it was nevertheless *fast*. The front end seemed all cavernous mouth and serrated teeth, yellowish-white against a reddish, liver-coloured tongue and maw. It sized up each of them intently, deciding on Elusive as the nearest prey, and promptly scaled the tree she was perched in easily – much faster than the brownie could have run on level ground. Any brownie with that thing behind them would have been running pretty darn fast!

Elusive scrambled backwards along the branch, but abruptly stopped as the beast reached it and fixed her with an intent stare. Feuery heard a soft rhythmic sound like a swift tattoo on a drum. She realised it came from scales around the creature's eyes rapidly fluttering hypnotically. It slowly crept along the creaking branch toward the mesmerised brownie.

Team vacancy coming up, thought Feuery. *Gonna be difficult to fill here too, so's best do sum'it about it.*

She scrambled onto a branch just above the predator and its imminent prey. The land-shark's mouth opened wide and a ripple ran along its body as it coiled in readiness to seize Elusive.

Without conscious thought, Feuery jumped to land between them, thrusting her staff nearly its full length into the beast's maw. The jaws snapped shut onto the metal of the shaft, the teeth just missing Feuery's fingers by a fraction of an inch.

She cast her spell frantically. Brilliant blue light shone through the gaps between the creature's teeth, lighting the forest in a harsh, broken glow. The creature convulsed, tearing the staff from Feuery's hand before rearing back to fall slowly sideways off the branch and land heavily below, accompanied by a crackling and splintering of branches and lianas.

Feuery turned to Elusive. The brownie crouched, mouth slightly open, staring ahead.

Out of necessity (but with a tiny touch of quite unworthy satisfaction), Feuery slapped her lightly across the face.

'You ok?'

Elusive shook herself. 'I think so. Feueze, it was horrible....'

'Just be glad you missed the ending that could have been. It woulda been a lots more horrible. Stay here while I get my staff.'

The land-shark lay where it had fallen, steam wisping up from between the scaly plates. A quite nice roasting smell filled the area, like the faint whiff of a family barbeque. Feuery reluctantly went to the head where the end of her staff was just visible under the bulk of the beast.

'You're going to need to help me on this,' she muttered quietly to the staff as she grasped it.

The head of the lifeless beast suddenly reared up, taking years off Feuery's life and causing some anxiety for her bladder. With a tearing, crackling sound, the staff burst out of the creature's mouth.

It was absolutely clean; the great sapphire at the head glowing brilliantly.

'Glad *you* enjoyed yourself,' Feuery grumbled as she tucked the staff into her belt and started back up the tree. 'Didn't need to give me a start like that though. Mind you, I'm not complaining this once, but keep it in mind.'

Elusive helped Feuery clamber onto the branch. She seemed to have recovered from the hypnotic effect of the land-shark's attack.

'Thanks Feueze. I get the picture now, but it'd be nice if you told me later what actually happened. Let's hope we don't meet another one of those.'

'It was a whopper right 'nough. Shouldn't hit 'nother one, I reckon. They have big territories at the best of times, an' that one shouldn't even be here. They come from the jungles ways down south on the continent of Fyraviar. Never thought I'd see one. But thanks very much, once is 'nough. Wonder who put it here. Not the sort of critter Fair Elves play alongside much, but then, never heard of a Fair Elf sending a demon neither.' She still sounded self-righteously offended by the sending, as though a basic moral principle had been broken. And it had. Use of demons by mages against other mages – or anyone else – had been banned after the chaos of the Mage Wars.

'Maybe they have a colony here. That sometimes happens with creatures being located far away from where they're most commonly found,' Elusive suggested.

'Not for long these wouldn't. These islands are big 'nough for two, maybe three of them. Not enough for happy families long-term. Not much in the way of food for them anyways: I think that one must have survived by scavenging the beaches with nought else to eat but insects. An' it surely didn't swim here. Great! Almost no critters around on these islands, an' we have the luck to find *that* one 'stead of a sweet li'l bunchy-bear or a googum. Maybe we can find some answers up ahead.'

'Speaking of which, wouldn't it be better travelling up here? We still have canopy cover to hide us from the dragons and hippogriffs, but the branches are clearer going than on the ground.'

'Seems so. We have some fairies an' a sylph to find. They maybe need help, considering we haven't seen them for a long while. An' they'll definitely need help if they're ok, 'cos I'll have words to say about not seeing 'em in altogether too long.'

With a combination of scurrying, swinging and leaping from branch to branch, they made good time, before suddenly running out of trees at the edge of the forest. They quickly half-climbed, half fell down the last branches – which obligingly drooped down almost to the ground – emerging onto a pavement through which saplings and tufts of grass struggled. Fallen columns and the remains of dry-stone walls lay all about. Ruins and clumps of trees – some that were substantial copses on their way toward being small woods – dotted the area.

Keeping a wary eye above for the elves, they quickly made their way from cover to cover, ready to hide instantly should hippogriffs or a dragon appear.

'I can hear something ahead,' whispered Elusive, 'but I can't tell what it could be. Just a sort of swishing, clacking sound, and an occasional thump.'

'So let's find out,' Feuery replied shortly. She was not in a good mood. She felt hot and was itchy from the bristles of the leaves, scratched from thorns and annoyed that what should have been a simple exercise had gone wrong so soon. The demon-sending was still infuriating her also. If anyone was going to play unfair, she should have had first turn. Something or someone to take her annoyance out on would be nice.

They followed the strange sounds to an almost intact set of six columns, on each side of which a thick copse of tall trees and the ubiquitous vines had taken hold amid the ruins.

Long strands of a fine web stretched between the trees, across the space between the columns. Within that web, Chai hung suspended about twenty feet off the ground with T'zing flitting around him. All across the web were creatures about the size of an outstretched human hand, crawling toward the fairy. He was methodically loading, aiming and firing his cross-bow. With each shot, one of the creatures fell from the web to join a growing pile of twitching bodies on the ground below. T'zing repeatedly darted in, dodging long, thin legs that groped up at her, wielding Chai's epee and skilfully adding to Chai's carnage. Nevertheless, for each creature the pair killed, three more emerged from the foliage at the ends of the web strands. If the situation continued in the same way for long, it was clear Chai would soon be overwhelmed by sheer numbers.

However, before the two wizards could act, Je-nee returned. She swept down in a graceful arc from high above, the form of the woman dissolving into the air as they watched. She darted through the web, setting it vibrating so much the spider-ants had to hold on desperately, and plucked Chai cleanly away and placed him smoothly on Elusive's head.

'Sswiftly! Dragonss come!'

Je-nee swept back to them, regaining a more solid form while deftly picking up the two wizards in her arms. Feuery grabbed a surprised and affronted T'zing on the way, while Elusive cupped a hand protectively over Chai.

'Where we going?' Feuery called. They crossed the ruins swiftly, dodging columns, ruins and the thick patches of invading forest. However, the sound of the dragon's pounding wings could be heard close behind them.

'Ssaffe place, undergroundss. Sserioussly impresssive place too.' Je-nee banked around a pile of rubble that may once have been a fine public building and swooped for a space that had long ago been a vast plaza. A wide flight of stairs, almost closed off by the remains of a colossal fallen statue, led down. Feuery eyed the ruins of the statue intently, hoping to gain a clue as to the nature of the Islands of the Sun. However, apart from seeing it had been beautifully crafted, the jumbled piles of cracked stone covered in vines gave her little clue of its original form.

Je-nee gently dropped all of them at the very edge of the entrance. 'Ssmall folkss, ssqueezze through eassily. Be quicking!'

They needed no further urging: there was the sizzling sound behind them of a dragon drawing in air for a fiery blast. They scrambled over the rubble as a blast of heat swept over their backs and lit up the area in brilliant red.

They emerged from the rubble of the fallen statue onto a wide, sweeping staircase, easily broad enough to take a troop of cavalry abreast.

'Knew there'd be a temple,' Feuery said with considerable satisfaction. She liked being proved right.

'I guess that's one way to describe it,' Elusive said distantly as she looked at the scene spread out before them.

The stairs led in a very long, smooth curve down to their left onto a wide avenue flanked by massive colonnaded arches stretching as far as their eyes could see. It was all made of a glowing white stone that cast an ethereal light over the scene. The huge hall was wider below ground than the plaza above it, and stretched far into the distance. The walls above the arches curved up to a high, majestic ceiling far above. Grand statues stood within each arch – superbly carved, graceful, grandiose, and heroic. They were among the best of elven art Feuery had ever seen, and she was very knowledgeable about art. When your trade is adventuring, you pick up an awful lot about the value and significance of things, even if you hadn't (as Feuery had) been born with the insatiable curiosity of an entire generation of cats.

'What *is* this place?' Elusive wondered aloud.

'Pretty darn impressive, is what it is. Might be for audiences to a mighty ruler, maybe a triumphal processional, maybe the final route to the tomb of someone who was *really* important way back whens.'

'What do you think it is?'

Feuery took a moment to consider. 'I think it's all three, most like. Notice the statues?'

'It would be difficult not to. They're magnificent!'

'Anything else?'

There was a ringing as Chai answered.

'Chai's got it. They all represent the same person.'

'What …' Elusive looked more closely at the sculptures. Chai was correct. Each statue was of (or had as its central character) one figure who was unmistakably the same person: here standing in an heroic pose as though leading an army on a battlefield; there gazing seriously at a scroll beside a carven bench with scientific instruments; the next one reclining graciously on a couch while beautiful elven women vied to offer him plates of fine foods and goblets of wine.

That central personality was a Fair Elf of heroic size, outstanding physical perfection and almost unbelievable handsomeness. He appeared in various guises: always confidently (bordering almost on arrogant) riding various mounts from horses to hippogriffs and dragons; in grand uniforms; in simple academic robes; standing by a ship's wheel; on thrones; or with sceptre, sword, staff or scroll suited to the occasion portrayed. He was often depicted grandly alone; sometimes the focus of a group of admirers eagerly seeking his least glance.

'What does it all mean?'

'Shortage of models to pose for the statues maybe? Notice he's never shown holding a shovel or sitting at a spinning wheel or anything useful? Someone grand. An' by the looks of him he knew it.'

'He musst have been highly resspected and loved to be sso honoured!'

'Maybe Je-nee. But the big question is whether or not being respected an' loved was the general feeling of his folk or if'n it was by hisself. Makes a big difference.'

They set out to explore further, Feuery leading confidently. The others stayed close to her and a little behind – even Je-nee – as if seeking to be protected by the little gnome.

'Do we have to go right down the middle of the avenue in clear sight?' Elusive asked plaintively.

'Of course. Why not? Nowheres to hide in here, 'less you wanna pretend to be one of the admirers in a tableau. Just noting, mind you, it would be hard to carry that off; all these figures are Fair Elves. We may as well show we're not scared if'n anyone is watching. Can't see anyone else is likely to be here, but let's keep up appearances.'

'But I *am* scared!' There were nods and murmurs of agreement amongst the fairies and sylph.

'Course you are. That's what this place is all meant to make you feel. Overwhelmed an' insignificant. Don't take any notice. You'll only encourage it.'

The hall stretched for well over a mile, but it took them *hours* to navigate it – mainly because Feuery's curiosity soon got the better of her. Instead of marching to the end of the hall along the centre of the avenue as they'd begun, she soon insisted on constantly detouring to read many of the inscriptions they came across along the way. Every statue and set of statues had a facing inscription, detailing the significance of the event portrayed. Periodically, steles formed the faces of the columns of the arches, each adding yet another facet to the atmosphere of greatness all around them. Since they were inscribed in an ancient form of Elven, the gnome's perusals were often lengthy as she translated the archaic script for the group.

At first bemused, and then irritated by the delays, the others eventually found themselves becoming increasingly interested in the stories revealed by the ancient inscriptions.

'All of the writings are in the first person,' Feuery said after translating a particularly long passage. 'It's all 'me' an' 'I', so's no clue as to who Mr Majestic actually was. Unusual that. Most elves (not Darklings of course) define themselves by reference to their clan or people, not 'emselves. Almost like he built this place by hisself, for hisself. Mind you, if you believe what's written here, he may's well have. Obviously did everything else.'

'I did like the story back there where he rescued the stolen children from the ogre war band though,' admitted Elusive. 'Very cleverly done and so brave.'

'I mosst like hiss adventure to recover the losst sceptre off the Elvess from the demonss of the world of Dea-kar. Such daring! I did not know there was ssuch a terrible world!'

'Well, the *world's* real 'nough,' Feuery replied thoughtfully. 'We used to trade with it afore the Mage Wars. Mostly peaceful folk – though I guess they may have had their own good-for-nothing's too of course. Far as I can see, everyone does.'

'Thiss brave elven hero musst have made them change from being the cruel and war-like creaturess they were when he dealt with them!'

'Hmmm. Maybe. I'd like to see what *they* wrote about his adventures there.'

In a mischievous tone, T'zing added her opinion of one of the sets of statues. Chai looked uncomfortable. But then again, he had been *very* uncomfortable at the tableau represented by the story Feuery had translated for them (with a lot of accompanying comments and discussion from the girls).

'Don't think oysters are *that* good, T'zing. Even magical ones. Not speaking from personal experience, 'course, but that story mighta been a bit fancied up.'

It had been a large tableau, with many eager attendants to the hero. All very pretty ones too and definitely not over-dressed.

They eventually meandered their way to the end of the hall, arriving at another monumental stairway that curved up and off to the right.

'Ah,' Je-nee breathed. 'The temple.'

'Thought you said there wasn't a temple?' Feuery asked.

'Not in the ssity. You assked about ssity. Iss on the easstern island. On the other sside of the sseaward clifffss from the cave where we sstayed ssafe. Not in ssity. I ssaw thiss temple while sscouting. We musst be below it now.'

'You an' me need to talk more 'bout reporting: how to. Anything else we need to know?' Feuery remarked irritably.

'What do you need to know?'

'Fair point. How's about you tell us what you saw out there?'

'A temple ssitss within the clifffss looking out toward the eastern sseass. It iss carved into and ffrom the clifffss of the issland itsself. Cannot be sseen from above, cannot be sseen from the ssides – only from the easst.'

'Like maybe by the rising sun?'

'Exssactly.'

'Ok.' Feuery mentally rifled through her memories of sun-gods and cults. There was quite a lot she could recall, but nothing triggered a memory of any situation like this. Surely, a temple that was so open to the rising sun *had* to be something to do with sun worship. 'Did you get a closer look at it?'

'Oh yesss! But all empty. Not even debris. There are two great doorss leading into the clifffss ffrom the back of the temple. Even I could ffind no way through. I think they musst open only from the insside.'

'Must be darn well made if'n you couldn't find a gap through,' mused Feuery. '*Really* airtight. An' everything sparkly fresh just like it is here. Looks like the cleaners did a real good job only last night. Yeah, sure! This place is full of maintenance magic. Old spells, but still powerful. They built things to last back then. Leastways, they built this place to last.'

She looked back down the avenue, frowning a little. 'How many elves did it take to make this, an' how long did it take 'em? 'An' now, all they're concerned 'bout is keeping it hidden away – from 'emselves well-as everyone else. Don't add up; leastways 'till we find the missing piece that puts all the pieces together.'

'Where's all this taking us?' Elusive asked pointedly. The interest built up during their tour of the great esplanade in honour of the unnamed elven hero was being replaced with a growing sense of foreboding as they neared the end. There were no shadows in the hall due to the bright light from the very stone from which it was made. However, if there had been any, she'd have been looking warily into them for lurking danger. It was that sort of feeling: as if a trap or ambush was about to be sprung.

Having some shadows to focus her apprehensions would actually have been better than trying to cope with her fears in the wide, brilliant expanse around them.

Shadows could be good to hide in too. The thought lingered in Elusive's mind.

'No idea. The elves are running mighty scared of what's in here even though they built this place 'emselves. An' elves – including Fair Elves – don't scare easy. Bit strange, being as how everything in here is about Fair Elves. One of 'em, anyways. The rest are just underlinings for that one. To all appearances, some high an' mighty ruler was being honoured more'n anyone else I ever heard of – by the Fair Elves or by anyone else. Else-wise, lot of work by some cult that somehow skipped the history books. Must've had a fine sense of drama an' particular tastes in decorating an' a narrow focus of interest, but you get that with cults. The answers should be up the top of this stair with a dab of luck.'

'Feueze, I think we should get out of here – quickly. This is something that's too powerful for us to meddle with.' Elusive could no longer contain her growing fears. 'Anyway, I don't want to make enemies of the Fair Elves.' The fairies chimed in with their support for discretion, Je-nee also seemed to waver, which for her was very literally. Perhaps there were limits to adventure.

'Bit late for that if'n they've recognised us, an' no never-mind if they haven't.' Then Feuery said what Elusive feared she would. 'Can't hurt to look. You can stay here if you like. I'll just nip up the stairs an' have a sneaky-peek look-see.'

* * * *

Elusive took a deep breath and opened her mouth to argue. There was something very wrong; something subliminally *evil* about this place. She could feel it, even if she couldn't nail down exactly what it was. Glancing at the others, she sensed T'zing and Chai felt the same. And to the extent it was possible to tell, even Je-nee was looking as if she was uncomfortable. Feuery *had* to be made to see sense.

Then Feuery took the wind out of her sails.

'Course, not now. Like as not, just be getting near evening, an' it's a good rule of thumb to stay out of tombs at night-times. Nice bright morning; things always look better in the morning. If you like, we can talk it over more when we're fresh.'

She said it all with a winning smile and a disarming earnestness that bathed them all with reassurance. Elusive saw T'zing (who should have known better since she'd known Feuery's wiles for almost as long as Elusive had) and Chai relax with visible relief. Personally, she knew Feuery was up to something. Whenever Feuery suddenly became charming and accommodating, it was time to be careful.

Still, if it delayed them proceeding now ... And Feuery just might see more sense in the morning.

'I'll set up the pavilion, shall I?' Elusive offered.

* * * *

Elusive's pavilion was truly a magical wonder. Few of them had ever been made, and then always by (or for) only the most powerful of mages. Nevertheless, since they were virtually indestructible, it was inevitable that over deep time (possibly due to the Mage Wars), some had become separated from their owners and fallen into wider circulation. Elusive had salvaged this one from the spoils of a pirate hoard, where it had been dismissively tossed in a corner due to ignorance that it was worth more than a squadron of pirate ships were likely to plunder in a year. Feuery had tried to investigate its history, but even the spell she had for that purpose became a jumbled mess of confused images; no doubt affected by the strong magic inherent in the pavilion itself.

When activated with the right spell, the pavilion became a small tent from the outside. Inside, it was a fully equipped (indeed, almost luxuriously appointed) dwelling with two bedrooms, a bathroom, self-replenishing stores and ample living space. Once the pavilion had been sealed, those inside could see out the main entrance, but nothing in the outside world could see in or enter.

It even had hot and cold running water. Apparently, you had to supply your own maids, which Elusive frequently felt meant *her* in Feuery's view.

But, as Feuery had pointed out, sooner or later those inside it had to come out. It wasn't an escape spell, merely – if 'merely' was the right term – a perfect hostel that required some sense and pre-thought to use.

But tonight it was exactly what was needed. Elusive and the fairies barely paused before dashing in as soon as the pavilion was erected.

Je-nee had other plans.

'I go to resst,' she said quietly to Feuery.

'Already? Thought you only needed to do that every coupla weeks.'

The sylph smiled. 'I have been bussy thesse passt dayss. Not tired now – too much. But tomorrow? I think very bussy again. Besst I reffressh perhapss. I will return jusst before firsst light of the morning.'

'Good idea! Sensible.' Feuery looked at Je-nee meaningfully. 'Find me first when you get back, ok? Might be important.'

'I sshall. You will be here?'

'Oh, you know me by now. Might go for a l'il walk early-ish. Let the others have a l'il sleep-in.'

The sylph looked sideways at Feuery and then smiled. 'Thank you for ssharing ssurprisses.' She then became wispy; a breeze which flowed back down the hall.

Feuery noted Je-nee had gone *back* the way they'd come, not the shorter route up the nearby stairs. But then, she recalled, not even the sylph had been able to find a way through the doors at the end of the temple. What brilliant engineering or magic had been used to make the doors airtight after so long?

Why? Hopefully she was getting nearer to some answers to the many mysteries around them.

She shrugged and went into the pavilion.

Elusive had disappeared into her favourite room, from which splashing sounds suggested she was thoroughly enjoying a bath.

T'zing and Chai were setting up camp on a shelf in the main living area.

'What do you two think you're doing?' Feuery inquired.

The two fairies looked up at Feuery in surprise, mid-way through spreading out a tiny blanket from the store of linen Elusive had had made up for T'zing by the Fairy-folk community of Heliovorn.

'No way you're going to stay out here. You need your privacy now. You take that room there, the one I usually use. I'll sleep on the couch. I'm probably going to be up late anyways, studying. An' remind me that we need to get a little doll's house made up for you later. Proper one, your size, all things working. No arguments from you.'

They didn't argue with her. Both fairies seemed a little embarrassed in a pleased sort of way. They flew into the room Feuery usually occupied and quickly set about making themselves – or perhaps more accurately, each one trying to make the other – comfortable.

Elusive was surprised when she finally emerged, glowing from the luxurious bath she'd enjoyed. She didn't disagree with the arrangement. Far from it, in fact. But she had a nagging feeling it would have been far more in character for Feuery to have offered the fairies *Elusive's* bedroom.

Still, sometimes it is wiser to keep quiet while you're ahead. At least it was some reassurance that Feuery, as usual, 'let' the brownie see to making a meal for all of them. *That* was normal! In any case, Elusive enjoyed preparing a proper meal from the extensive contents of the pantry in the pavilion. Their bottom-less bags held a fair stock of provisions, but the pavilion's pantry was like a well-supplied marketplace.

'Do we need to set a watch?' Elusive asked as she and the fairies cleaned up after a fine dinner; three courses with fresh fruit, cheese and nuts to follow. 'And just what are you reading now? You always seem to have your nose buried in a book or scroll.'

Feuery looked up from the tome she was rifling through. 'Just refreshing myself up on the customs of the elves – the ones from a long time ago. As to taking watches, shouldn't think so. Least ways, I'll be up for awhiles, an' Je-nee'll likely be back afore midnight. She can take over from me then. You folk get a good night's sleep, or equivalent valuable use of time.' The last comment to the fairies caused T'zing to blush.

After everyone had departed for bed and things had settled down, Feuery sat quietly thinking for a long time, the books and scrolls around her apparently forgotten.

Eventually she rose and listened carefully. All was quiet. Convinced she wasn't likely to be interrupted, she took some ingredients from the large pouch at her side. She drew a design in chalk on the kitchen bench. Lighting a candle of swirling blue wax, she carefully set it in the exact centre of the design. She dropped a pinch of a fine powder into the flame, carefully enunciating a spell as she did so.

Satisfied with her actions, she pinched the candle out and returned the ingredients to her pouch, painstakingly wiping away the chalk. Elusive was wrong in thinking Feuery was messy by nature. When it came to magic, Feuery was very, very tidy and meticulous indeed.

She discretely checked on the results of her handiwork. Everyone was soundly asleep, and very likely to remain so well into tomorrow. She wrote a quick note, apologising for her precautions and left beside it an amulet containing a very precious portal spell that would, if necessary, return Elusive, T'zing and Chai to safety at Heliovorn. She sincerely hoped she'd be back before the note and spell were found. The spell was very valuable, but more pointedly, her non-return would probably mean she was dead – or worse. That was a definite consideration in her preference for the portal spell not to be used.

She slipped out of the pavilion, carefully re-setting the security spell behind her. She felt bad about being sneaky, but Elusive had certainly been right: this was well and truly out of their depth. Feuery just hoped it wasn't completely beyond hers.

Once more – possibly for the last time – she looked down the avenue with its monuments. Undefined thoughts flooded her mind as she purposefully set off up the stairway in the perpetual, eerie glow of the cold, stone hallway.

With her magic staff in her right hand she felt reassured, although she had a strong feeling there was little it could do if this situation went badly.

* * * *

At the head of the stairs, there was a wall with a small, heavily locked door. Feuery inspected it carefully in the eerie light. It was definitely Fair Elven workmanship, and old. However, compared to the rest of the fine architecture around her it was almost shoddy.

The Fair Elves had added this wall much later than the original construction; but still a very long time ago. And the work had been done quickly; there was little evidence of the usual care and fine attention to detail that the Fair Elves were renowned for.

Whoever had built this later wall and door hadn't wanted to be around here any longer than was absolutely necessary.

There'd been no skimping or shortcuts on the locks though. Obviously, the intention was that no one could get into whatever chamber lay beyond the wall. There were mechanical locks and magical locks, and locks that combined mechanics and magic. Unlike the hastiness with which the wall had clearly been constructed, skilled artisans and high order mages had spent a lot of time on the locks – both in making them and setting them.

It took Feuery nearly half an hour to open them all and ensure they would stay open.

* * * *

The chamber inside glowed like the rest of the complex. The walls were covered in carefully executed, flowing Old Elven script. Feuery sighed at the prospect of having to do yet more translating. However, she stoically set about the task, while carefully trying to not be distracted by the centrepiece in the middle of the room.

It took Feuery a long time to decipher the Old Elven engravings; a task made more difficult by a need she felt to keep looking over her shoulder to reassure herself that she was still the only one present in the chamber.

The translated scripts eventually confirmed more or less what she'd expected. They also provided the answers she'd wanted about the Islands of the Sun, which was more than she'd initially hoped for. And of course, there was the evidence of the centrepiece itself.

She then sat thinking while time passed slowly until the dawn was close.

The company could have been a lot better, but at least it wasn't *too* distracting. Quiet, too. Like the grave.

Tomb-robbers, she decided, *had it easy. They only had to deal with the dead and the undead.*

The most difficult thing to understand was how the Fair Elves – surely amongst the most intelligent and civilised of the kindreds – could have got it so wrong. Twice. Three times, if you counted their present attempts to seal off the islands.

Just goes to show, she thought in the gloom of the chamber, *if'n someone is too close to sum'it, their judgment gets all distorted. Easier to see from a distance, most times. 'Course, not being emotionally all tied up in sum'it helps too. Shows how, when sum'it goes wrong, trying to make it right without thinking through what you're doing just keeps making it even wronger.*

In the end, it looked like all the Fair Elves could really think to do was hide away the mess they'd made, pretending it wasn't so and hoping that no one ever found it.

Feuery could understand that, but it didn't make it any easier. It all made for a difficult decision for someone, and she was unhappily coming to terms with the fact that the someone would have to be her.

When she was satisfied she'd understood the situation, and had come to terms with what she knew she'd have to do, she dis-spelled the vast doors that sealed the chamber from the outside temple.

Being air-tight was just on the side, she mused. *The trick had been to make 'em so that no light could get through, 'cepting the glow from the stone (which didn't count).*

Again, Feuery made sure the doors would remain open so that the pale glow of the light of the chamber spilled out into the temple's courtyard for the first time in millennia. In the grim pre-dawn darkness, she made her way down a narrow path to the beach, toward a sea full of monsters.

That in itself was a great relief compared to the quiet and bright light of the chamber, the beautifully flowing inscriptions and – most of all – the centrepiece.

She took off her boots and socks to enjoy walking along the beach just where the water and sand met. The water was just a little chilly so as to be refreshing and the sand was soft so, with each step, she sank a little way into it. As the dawn slowly neared, she could see the backs of mosasaurs and kritoids breaching the still sea. At one point, a little sea-weasel came close inshore to stare at her with big, brown, intelligent eyes. Feuery shoo-ed it away before something bigger made breakfast of it.

Everything deserves a chance, she thought sadly to herself, *but sometimes there could be too many chances, an' then it was best for everyone if things came to an end.*

* * * *

That's where Je-nee eventually found Feuery (and observed her strange pensive mood). The two of them made their way back up to the temple, deep in conversation, to wait for the sun to rise.

Then Je-nee also understood, and felt sad for what shouldn't have been – and very sorry for Feuery as well.

* * * *

Back at the temple, Je'nee and Feuery stood either side of the catafalque (except it wasn't exactly a catafalque, because catafalques are meant for the dead). They were watching the still, but perfectly preserved, figure on it: a Fair Elf of heroic size, outstanding physical perfection and almost unbelievable handsomeness.

As the sun rose above the horizon, its rays speared through the temple to cascade across the still figure. At Feuery's signal, Je-nee leaned forward. Her mouth met his, and his chest rose majestically as she breathed the rich, warm air of life into him.

The figure shuddered, shivering as the golden light and warmth of the early sun streamed over him.

'Ta,' remarked Feuery casually to Je-nee. 'I wasn't looking forward to doing that bit myself.'

'It wasn't that bad,' Je-nee replied, experiencing a twinge of guilt as she thought of Sesarias.

'Medical need. Think of it that way. Rather like having to take a swig of medicinal brandy.'

The Fair Elf sat up stiffly. Resplendent in the sunshine, he looked around the chamber.

He seemed to have been expecting someone other than a gnome and a sylph, which was understandable.

'Where are my priestesses?' he demanded in a rich baritone voice used to giving commands and directions.

'Just us,' said Feuery in Old High Elven. 'Been awhiles, hasn't it?'

He glared at her.

'Fetch me my sceptre. Then I shall require some explanations.'

'Already have,' Feuery said sadly. There was a depth of compassion in her voice that few who may have considered they knew her would have believed possible. She held up a sceptre of plain white gold and touched it to his forehead.

* * * *

A few moments later T'zing – closely followed by Chai and Elusive – came up the stairs in a state of high anxiety and even higher dudgeon. The *really* unexpected sight of a weeping gnome being held reassuringly by a comforting sylph did at least forestall the self-righteous tellings-off Feuery would otherwise have received for her trickery.

* * * *

Realising that Feuery and Je-nee were currently sharing a common grief and that explanations would have to follow later, Elusive shepherded the fairies discretely away to collect their equipment and pavilion. Whatever was going on, she sensed events were drawing to a close and that being ready to depart quickly would be prudent.

When they returned a little later, Je-nee acknowledged them with a nod. However, Feuery remained in some inner world, seemingly oblivious to them.

'I think we'd best leave?' Elusive remarked quietly to Je-nee. 'I don't know what's happened, but this isn't exactly a good place to hide from the elves.'

'Yes,' agreed Je-nee. 'It iss time to not be here.'

'Is Feueze ok?'

'Sshe will be, I think. She has done ssomething – ssomething terrible – because thosse who sshould have done what had to be done did not. I will leave her to tell you – iss besst – when sshe iss ready. Now, let uss be gone.'

Led by Elusive, they stepped out of the temple into the courtyard. She *really* wanted to get as far away from these brooding islands and their mysteries as soon as possible. Feuery stumbled in a daze. Je-nee still had an arm around the gnome to help her.

The Fair Elves were waiting for them; spears levelled and bows drawn. High Lord Admiral Emathier stood squarely and haughtily before the troops to confront the adventurers. Lady Silverstem stood to his right with the elven wizards behind her, their staves held easily for ready use. Dragons and hippogriffs wheeled lazily in the sky above.

'What have you done?' demanded Emathier imperiously. 'Speak and be heard, and then I will pass my judgment and sentence on you.'

'There must be an accounting,' affirmed Lady Silverstem icily. 'For the trespass, sacrilege and misdeeds against the Fair Elves you have committed.'

Elusive's jaw dropped. She stood stock still, not knowing what to say or do. There were a lot of sharp spears and arrows currently pointed at her by tall, strong elves in full battle gear, and she was very conscious of being one very small brownie.

Elusive heard a faint murmur behind her, and saw a swirl of air from the corner of her eye as Je-nee departed swiftly. Then a firm hand pushed her aside. Feuery stepped forward. Her previous remoteness had vanished. She moved stiffly, her eyes fiery. Elusive recognised the signs: her friend had been propelled out of her dispirited exhaustion by outraged indignation, apparently directed at the elves.

Elusive had no idea why Feuery was so angry. However, knowing her friend, the brownie had no doubts that the reason would become evident soon enough.

'Sorta a trial?' Feuery demanded.

'Yes, of course! Very much a trial. Although hardly necessary (except for the niceties) on capital charges.' Emathier's voice was clipped, but with an undertone of satisfaction. With his troops behind him and with clear, black and white issues before him, he was enjoying being in total command of the situation.

'Ok. But I'll try not to be too hard on you. There's some chance you mighta had extenuating circumstances, I suppose. Hard to see it now, but you should get the opportunity to have your say once all the facts are out.'

Emathier stared at her in disbelief. Lady Silverstem stirred uneasily. She may have had a premonition of what was about to occur; but then, she *was* a High Mage.

'Wha ...' Emathier began.

'You shut up!' Feuery said shortly. 'You'll get your chance to talk later. Prosecution always gets first go.'

She paced angrily for a moment, collecting her thoughts while everyone watched her in stunned fascination and disbelief. Then she sat cross-legged about ten feet in front of the elves and spoke in a firm, clear voice as though delivering a lecture, or reciting a fable to a group of children.

'Long ways back – long afore the Mage Wars and even afore the kindreds began to meet up with one another – the folk we now call the Fair Elves all lived in a great forest on the mainland north of hereabouts. Even back then, they had their High Council to govern 'em (even if it would have been a pretty cinchy job back then).

'But one of the High Councils couldn't get along. Maybe they had too little to do so they bickered among 'emselves most times. Hard for the elven folk then to understand, 'cos each of the High Councillors was the best of their calling, an' each one was a great person each by hisself as well. Just like now: a warrior, a' artisan, a scholar, a mage, a traveller, an' one called from the folk. That's who made up the High Council in those way-back-when times. No king then; that came later 'cos of what happened – to keep the Councillors in order. All men then too, not like now 'cos this was before the Fair Elves learned it takes all kinds of different thinking to make good decisions.'

Emathier rallied. 'What has this …'

'I said you get your turn later,' Feuery snapped. 'Fair Elf lore says facts haveta be clear. Nothing to say they can't be said by a gnome, so you listen up. An' once a trial starts – an' this one has – no one's allowed to disrupt it (save for sensible emergencies).'

'That's not the way we do it now …'

'No, it isn't. This is the *old* way, the Elders' Ways. An' anyone can call on the Elders' Ways an' they take precedence over all others, right Lady Ilith?'

There was a murmur of support among the troops. Aside from being good entertainment due to their commanders being clearly discomfited, it was both a real novelty and pleasing to hear from one of another kindred who was familiar with their own ancient ways – even if most elves themselves weren't really all that clear about the old ways. But the ancient lore was there to be deeply respected by all Fair Elves, and that meant a lot to them.

'That's true, but I believe it *meant* anyone who is a Fair Elf ...'

'No it don't. The lore says *anyone*. Makes no never-mind that the lore was made afore the Folk came outta the Forests an' found out there were other types of people too. Not up to us now to start revising the beliefs of the Elder Ones 'cos it suits someone – such as some present company.'

This time the murmur of the troops was strong and sympathetic. Lady Silverstem decided not to push the point. High Lord Emathier looked bewildered. The High Council traditionally deferred on matters of the lore to the Mage and the Scholar, but that was supposed to be so that the High Council was always in the right, as, of course, it should be. After all, that's why it was the High Council. Now the Lady seemed to be agreeing to being pushed into this upstart gnome's nasty web of baffling words. He felt confused, and when Lord Emathier was confused, then anger soon followed. Most folk had learned it was wise not to confuse Lord Emathier.

However, the upstart gnome continued. 'So the squabbling of the folk in the High Council had to end, an' the High Councillors knew it. Then someone – maybe the Mage (but could've been any of 'em) – had a BIG idea. Since they were the best of the Fair Elves (everyone said so an' *they* themselves knew it to be true), why not the six of them merge into one great person to be truly representative of the Fair Elves? All the best bits in one person. You not heard this before?' Feuery suddenly and disconcertedly asked an elf spearman in the front ranks, one of the many listening intently to her.

'Never,' he breathed. Many around him nodded.

'But you have, haven't you?' Feuery asked Lady Silverstem.

'There are ancient stories ...'

'This is nonsense!' Admiral Emathier shouted. 'Tales told to children. Stop filling my troops' minds with nonsense! This fiasco ends now!'

'Let me tell the story, then I dare you to say the words written – well, actually carved – in that temple behind us by the Elder Ones are nonsense!' Feuery replied hotly. 'Ancient High Elven, the *really* old tongue (bet you skipped those lessons). But the wizards here, especially Lady Silverstem, can translate for them what needs it … later. Already been settled this is a trial under the lore of the Elder Ones, so's one more disruption from you an' you get restrained. Gagged too by rights for too many interruptions,' Feuery grumbled.

'So a mighty magic was cast,' she continued, 'to join the six High Councillors into one being. Much like the First Folk – the folk even *before* the Elder Ones – made the first Unicorns. I know personally that so-called legend is true, believe me. An' the magic worked. From the Six came one great Fair Elf, with all the skills an' knowledge an' understanding of the Six combined. He was called The Son and he embodied the best of the best of all the Fair Elves: a powerful ruler of heroic physique, outstanding physical perfection an' almost unbelievable handsomeness. Plus, bucket loads of wisdom, bravery, insight an' learning.'

She made a wry face. 'An' I thought this place was called the Islands of the *Sun* 'cos it's close to where the dawn seemingly starts every day. Not even that. Isle of the Sun was closer even, 'cos the *real* name – the first name – was '*Aisle of the Son*' after the showpiece down below here. Shows what happens when you jump to obvious conclusions without checking *all* the facts. But anyways, all of that came later, after the Fair Elves found out they'd made a big mistake an' had a big problem.

'It wasn't just the good bits that made up the Son, but all the bad ones of the Six too. An' like the good bits, they were greater than they had been in each one of the individual Six. 'Course, each of the Six probably figured they didn't have any bad bits 'emselves. Folk rarely do, so it was an easy oversight for 'em to make I guess. Still, pretty sure they would have thought they'd figured out the faults in the others.

'Anyways, all the good and bad poured in, an' the good made for *very* good, but the bad became truly horrid. Some of the bad bits, like lechery, maybe could be lived with after some careful management an' provision of certain services – there's some statues to that effect downstairs. But the arrogance, spite, ambition an' ruthlessness were lots harder to manage. It's easy to be ruthless if'n you know you're always right. Way too easy.

'An' worse still, the Six being One didn't stop the bickering *at all*. Times when the Son was just plain mad; six personalities all feuding away inside the one head. In between times, when his head was clear, he did some wonderful things. Maybe not so many as he *said* he did, but some at least. But the not-so-wonderful stuff the rest of the time made lots more of trouble than the good things were worth. Making The Son was Mistake Number One.

'So the Fair Elf mages took it on 'emselves to spell him to a long sleep. It wasn't the Son's fault he was as he were; so killing him wouldn't be fair, an' he had done marvels in his good times. Made a great temple for him to sleep quietly here – maybe a memorial too. They probably weren't quite sure.'

Feuery looked around, catching the eye of as many of the troops as she could with a wry smile on her face. 'Bit like giving a maimed soldier a medal an' sorta sincere-sounding thanks for near getting killed, an' figuring that squares the account, eh fellas?' There was a murmur of agreement. Lady Ilith winced. Wherever this gnome was taking them with her harangue, they were along for the ride. The gnome now had the full attention and sympathy of the troops.

'Story don't end there though. Never does; just like it don't ever end like that for a poor maimed soldier holding a medal and a fading echo of thanks.'

She stood up, carefully brushing sand off her clothes.

'No one seemed to recall – or if they did made no never-mind of it – folk *dream* when they sleep. Not just dream neither. Too much to sort out and too much confusion causes dreams to turn into nightmares. *How many thousands of years can a nightmare last?* We're talking here 'bout the kind of nightmare that leaves you shaking an' in a cold sweat an' mixed up about reality when you finally wake up. When you really, *really* want someone dear – or *anyone* even – to hold you tight. An' to tell you everything's ok, don't fear, it was just a bad dream. Yet *he could never, ever wake up, an' there was never, ever anyone to say it's ok.*'

There was a long silence in the temple courtyard.

High Mage Ilith – Lady Silverstem – despite herself dis-covered her eyes were moist and blurred. 'It was never meant...' she tried.

Feuery cut her off. 'Course it wasn't meant. You Fair Elves are a decent people by an' large. But you didn't think, neither. Sometimes that's worse than meaning to do sum'it nasty. That was Mistake Number Two.

'For millennia, this poor bugger lay there with a headful of pain an' trouble. There were times he would've roused himself enough to try to call for help. I couldn't figure why there were no birds an' almost no critters on these islands. 'Course it's 'cos being Called to beat yourself to death trying to open the doors to a tomb isn't a real good survival strategy long-term for any bird. The same goes for the land-critters: even those that came in by the rifts in space he opened time-to-time in desperation trying to get help from anywhere when he could. I wondered how the land-shark came to be here. The Son must have reached far and wide at times seeking anything that could try to open his tomb and end the nightmares. The only chance of survival the creatures he Called in had was if'n he lapsed back into his deep pain afore they got to the doors.

'The only ones Called who regularly escaped being killed trying to free him – 'til they starved or got eaten by one another – were the sea creatures. Not much they could do by way of opening a tomb high up on a cliff. An' the only ones who might've been able to do it, such as a kraken, were too big for the shallow seas hereabouts. Ironic isn't it? The Fair Elves set up a slaughterhouse for the creatures of the air an' land an' sea just by not thinking things through, an' then by being unwilling to look at what had been done.

'An' you had plenty of time to look. Ever since, after the Mage Wars, some of your own folk had the notion to bring The One back. Figured maybe they needed a great protector from fable; even if the Fair Elves barely felt the Mage Wars. Like a lot of folks who get big-hearted romantic ideas 'bout making the world better, they didn't bother too much about doing their homework. It's a pity the legends passed down were based on the wonderful things The Son did, an' overlooked why he suddenly stopped doing them. Still, there must have been enough Elves thinking that bringing The One back would make everything wonderful that the High Council decided to blockade the Islands. The High Council knew the true story an' didn't want The One back. 'Course, it might have been more sensible to make sure everyone understood there *was* a problem with The Son, or better yet, deal with the problem instead hiding it away as too shameful an' leaving it to someone else. As it turns out, that someone else had to be me.'

'What did you do to The Son?' Lady Silverstem asked hesitantly.

Feuery looked her firmly in the eye. 'I let him go,' she said. 'There was a sceptre – his Authority to rule. Some Elven

Mage had enough wisdom somewhere way back when to add a little something extra to it: the ability to end it all. Had to be used by someone without malice, and done with compassion for what the wielder genuinely believed was best for The Son. It helped maybe that I could see clearly without myths an' fables an' legends misting the picture. *I did what a Fair Elf – any Fair Elf who coulda used it shoulda had the sense an' the kindness to do a long time ago.* Mistake Number Three. That's why it's not me on trial here, but *you* – the Fair Elves – for allowing him to suffer an' keep on suffering for no good reason. Just 'cos no one thought everything through properly. Unless you have some really good thoughts 'bout now, I reckon you're guilty.'

'I've heard more than enough of this defamatory gabble.' Emathier stepped forward. 'If you have truly ended the need for the watch to continue here, then very well. But it changes nothing. Trespassers here are sentenced to death, and that's all that counts. We don't need the story of this spreading.'

'Oh, shut it!' said Feuery irritably. 'No need to make a bigger fool of yourself than life has already made you.' She pointed up. Instead of dragons and hippogriffs, more sylphs than could be counted circled above, watching with interest. 'Thought you'd play at something like this. So I had Je-nee summon her folk. Darn fine witnesses, an' can't be threatened. Do anything un-Fair Elfish now, an' everyone in all the lands knows all 'bout it this afternoon. Might be some serious questions asked by folk you wouldn't want asking such questions.'

She turned to Lady Ilith. 'We're leaving now. I suggest you claim 'Right of the Mage' and take command. The troops will still listen to *you*. I've made the case an' I'm not hearing anyone – 'cept an Admiral who don't count – showing it in't so. So I call justice: the decision here is for you who are here to go back an' tell all the Fair Elves what happened. They need to know; plus all your folk need to think on better ways of doing some things. Hiding history away – even if it in't pretty history – means folk never learn lessons from it. It's hard enough to get folk to learn from history anyways, even if it's bright an' clear.'

She looked around the temple. 'Not sure what you can do with your li'l outpost here. Might be wonderful place for holidays – 'cept for the storms, 'course. Best cover up some of the statues down below from the kiddies, mind you. Maybe could be a good place for people to come to understand themselves, an' where they came from. Looks like maybe it was a temple before. Should be again, so that folk can learn to remember an' to think – an' remember to think. A bit of thinking to remember before doing things wouldn't go astray neither.'

She turned to Lady Ilith with a puzzled look on her face.

'One thing still on my mind though. Question for you, Mistress Silverstem, not the Fair Elves all. What were you playing at sending a demon on me? Not only against the rules, but a bit foul, especially with you being a Fair Elf an' all.'

Lady Silverstem looked at her aghast. 'I thought *you* sent it against *us*! It suddenly appeared in a gale of wind as we were scrying for you!'

'No, it …' Feuery suddenly grinned. 'It must have invited itself to the party. Even when he was most desperate, The Son would never have called on a demon. Too much of the Fair Elf in him to even think about Calling for that sort of help. Then here you an' I are scrying all over the place. Guess the demon felt the magic an' was curious an' followed it hoping for a snack of wizard.'

She shrugged. 'Anyways, we were on other business afore we looked in here. Best we get back to it. We'll be right for a lift to the mainland,' she added, glancing up at the sylphs.

Je-nee appeared beside her. 'Enough of myssteriess here? Where's our nexxt adventure?' she asked eagerly.

Glossary

Angels – very magically powerful, winged beings of magnificent human or elven appearance, but possibly of elemental origin. Dedicated to promoting the causes of either Light and Order, or Darkness and Chaos. They are rarely encountered as they are only few in number and preoccupied with opposing their opposites.

Araj essence – a versatile ingredient of magic potions that can often replace substances less readily available, or of distasteful origin or nature. Once distilled from only a few woodland streams, exiled fairy-folk have learned to refine araj essence from the sparkle of any clear mountain brook, making it more readily available (if still expensive).

Baks – tiny flying mammals that behave very like (and compete with) birds. Unrelated to bats, they have fine, interwoven fur for feathers, and are often colourful and quite intelligent.

Barbegazi – stocky dwellers of high alpine areas and remote mountain valleys, where they grow mainly oats, rhubarb and cabbages. They are similar in size and appearance to dwarfs, but are more like gnomes in disposition. Barbegazi have pale blue skin and hair that blends with their habitat, and extremely large feet for running swiftly across the softest snow. Rarely seen, but occasionally some venture to (and even settle in) the lowlands, where they then constantly complain about the heat and humidity.

Brownies – amicable gnome-like folk, slighter and more rural than gnomes. Most humans refer to them as halflings as they are generally about half the height of humans and similarly proportioned. Usually extroverted and fun-loving, brownies are often found where humans live in the more temperate lands.

Bunchy-bears – koala-sized bears with a caramel-coloured fur and green eyes that are native to the realm of the Fair Elves. By day, they forage for fruit and the succulent tips of certain leaves, but congregate at night in groups of up to twenty to cuddle together. Noted for their placid and friendly disposition (if not threatened).

Centaurs – formidable but civilised beings with the bodies of horses and the torsos, heads and arms of humans. Centaurs are one of the few kindred of Th'eia believed to also regularly travel across planes to their own world (or worlds). Strongly independent and highly principled, many are mercenaries but are discriminating in the commissions they accept. Centaur wizards are rare, but most centaurs are part-magical by nature, giving them amazing physical skills.

Elves – a diverse kindred, typically taller and more slender than humans, and who live much longer lives. Most Elven societies tend to matriarchy, but gender equality is strong. An intelligent, capable and generally sophisticated folk, usually possessing greater dexterity than humans. There are great physiological and cultural differences between the five main Elven kindred:

    Darklings – live mainly in the cold and impoverished high latitudes. Their habitat overlaps with trolls, goblins and other folk commonly referred to as the Darksiders, with whom the Darklings alternate between war and alliances against other kindred. Hard folk from a harsh environment with an unforgiving society, Darklings may be found throughout the lands and are treated with reserve and suspicion. Their capital is the fortress city of Vrishtan.

Dawn Elves – relatively few in number, but claim to be those from whom all other elves originated. Their traditional lands lie in the valleys and western slopes of the Aulandria (otherwise known as the Skybound) Mountains, to the east of the Darklings and west of the vast forests of the Fair Elves on the far side of the mountains. Bounded by the mountains to the east, Darklings to the west, Darksiders to the north and humans to the south, the Dawn Elves' survival has been precarious. They are rarely seen in the wider world; however, in recent times under their Queen Aureliara, they have exerted disproportionate influence with their small (but capable) army and careful diplomacy.

Fair Elves – widely regarded as the most aloof and civilised of the elven folk, the Fair Elves homeland is in the forests to the east and south of the Skybound Mountains, across to the great ocean that separates the continents of Neswin and dry, mostly inhospitable Arenisia. Fair Elves are spread widely across the lands, mixing freely and urbanely with most kindred. Most are very tall and fair-haired, with a pleasing complexion and appearance.

Sea Elves – uncertainty regarding their numbers, for at any given time most are found on the swift, graceful sailing craft coursing Th'eia's many seas and oceans. The most widely travelled of all elves, their landward settlements are few and usually small, serving mainly as shipyards and trade points with other kindred. The smallest of all the elves, few are as tall as the average human.

Wood Elves – the most widely distributed of all the elven folk, but are by far the most reclusive, living in mostly small, self-contained communities in woodlands and forests throughout Th'eia. Physically, they differ from the Sea Elves mainly in terms of their height (they are about average human height). Wood Elves are often widely encountered, for many choose to escape the insularity of the Wood Elf communities.

Darksiders – a generic term for the kindred of the cold, dark lands in the high latitudes, but who have widespread communities in the harsher environments – hot or cold – in many places across Th'eia. Almost constantly at odds with one another, occasionally a strong leader succeeds in semi-uniting them for a common purpose. Often this involves waging war on elves, humans or dwarfs to expand territory or simply for slaves and plunder. The term 'Darksiders' is quite vague – it may include not only goblins and orcs (who may interbreed with other kindreds), but also trolls, Darklings and ogres – and sometimes even humans.

Demons – a generic term for (frequently) dangerous inhabitants of other planes. Some (such as charls) are more or less innocuous creatures employed by higher wizards for specific tasks, but others (such as Hunter-demons) are very treacherous as a result of being intelligent, bloodthirsty and resistant to magic. The majority of demons (such as succubi and incubi) are not summoned, but find their own avenues to Th'eia, usually with ill-intent. Most fearsome of all are the Demon-Lords who are highly skilled in magic, and are often ambitiously keen to expand their empires to Th'eia. The extensive summoning of demons for use against enemies during the Mage Wars led to the strict prohibition of that practice by the Wizards' Guild after the Wars. Nevertheless, some folk (especially the ruling caste of the Darkling Empire) consort with demonic worlds.

Dragons – occupy many niches on Th'eia, and come in an amazing variety of forms: with or without wings, with no or multiple limbs, fire- or frost-breathing. The most important difference is that some are self-aware and sentient, while others are not. The most typically encountered type are the non-sentient forms – wyverns, wurms, forest, sea and swamp dragons. Some are kept as pets by the rich and powerful, whereas others are pressed into city guards and armies as mounts, guardians or simply beasts of burden. Over eons, a few evolve to become Great Dragons of vast wisdom, experience and power. Five Great Dragons have taken it upon themselves to be the Guardians of the Five Great Virtues of the World. However, they rarely interfere directly in Th'eia's doings, reasoning that to do so would merely make them rulers with all the challenges and difficulties that this role entails. Consequently, they tend to avoid this fate, recognising that with great power comes great responsibility. The fear of all sentient dragons is that their inner darkness will consume them; a risk that all dragons watch for carefully. Sentient dragons rarely form close friendships with any of the kindreds, and then only in unusual circumstances with very select individuals.

Dryads – female life elementals of forests, although some may evolve from humans or elves who have very special affinities with forests. All dryads bond with one special Tree, merging their life-forces with that of the Tree's. Within their domains and centered on their Tree, dryads are immensely powerful and guard their woods zealously. Their power and well-being swiftly fades as they progressively travel away from their Tree.

Dwarfs – shorter than humans but much stockier, although some – particularly some of the women – are very similar in appearance to gnomes. Most dwarf communities specialise in mining and metallurgy, in which roles they are considered superior to all but a few elves and the occasional human. Whilst generally living within their own communities, they trade and mix freely with other kindred.

Elementals – Despite being common and a subject of great interest to the learned, surprisingly little is known about the nature of elementals. Some are raw forces of fire, water, air, earth, life and death, while others are equal to demi-gods and -goddesses in their wisdom, intelligence, experience and magical powers. Nor is the line between elementals and kindred clear. While most elementals can take form at will, others such as dryads and some sylphs may take and hold humanoid forms and be indistinguishable from the kindreds. It may be that elementals are brought into being by the interaction of magic with the world, but exceptions have been recorded where individual kindreds have transformed into elementals.

Fairies, faeries or fay – a generic term for folk of many appearances, aptitudes and personalities who usually (although not always) originate from Faerie. In the purest sense, a fairy is a tiny, pretty humanoid with butterfly wings.

First Folk, the – ancient legends tell that before the kindreds came into being the First Folk existed, living in a perfect world before vanishing from Th'eia. Generally regarded as old wives tales to amuse children.

Furies – flying demons from another plane in the form of dark, wiry creatures with extremely bristly, near-black fur. Utterly ruthless, armed with poisoned fangs and fearsome talons on their hands and feet.

Galumphers – large, heavily-built beasts of burden and mounts for the larger folk of Faerie. Often used in the Wild Hunt or in hunting packs sent to chase down those who have offended the rulers of Faerie.

Gaunts – Wiry, semi-intelligent creatures about the size and shape of a baboon that hunt in packs. Gaunts have huge mouths with teeth designed to rip flesh, and are feared for their habit of eating their prey alive.

Ghouls – cursed predators and scavengers, retaining in corrupted form the bodies they had before being cursed. Although they appear to be undead, they are, in fact, living creatures, and are feared wherever they are encountered. Ghouls aren't particular about what they eat if it helps to sate their voracious appetites.

Gnomes – rarely more than two-thirds the height of a human, gnomes form small communities either in association with other kindred or alone, but may be encountered virtually anywhere. They have a tendency to seriousness, and are acknowledged as being Th'eia's most skilled artificers of fine 'engines' – that is, any fabricated mechanism. Most are very reserved and avoid seeking attention. Gnomes are perhaps the most enigmatic of the kindred, for despite their many capabilities and firm views on right and wrong, gnomes universally shy away from wielding power or authority.

Goblins – the most numerous by far of the orcish kindred, goblins are about the size of gnomes, but much wirier, tougher and stronger, with numerous nodules in their tough, bronze-green skin. They have large noses, ears and lips, with tufted dark hair. Originally from the great swamps fringing the northern Wastelands, goblins may be found (usually causing trouble) almost anywhere. Some tribes even migrated to Faerie, finding conditions there to their liking, although what the folk of Faerie think about this is unknown. Even orcs consider goblins unsophisticated and a trial to have to deal with.

Googums – small mammals that look like balls of greenish fluff with big, dark eyes. They are thought to have originated in the Jemamian Islands. Like leprechauns, googums can teleport themselves over a distance of up to fifty feet, and may do so several times in quick succession. As they have very fast reflexes, they have no known enemies and tend to be of an inquisitive and friendly nature.

Great Ones – those of the kindreds who over deep time have become, what in any other world, would be considered to be demi-gods and -goddesses. Sometimes it is because of the skill they have developed in magic; sometimes from being magical themselves over a long period. They are rarely encountered, often unpredictable and should be treated with great caution – even by the greatest mages and the most powerful magical creatures, including dragons, unicorns and demon-lords. Some are broadly puissant, others phenomenally powerful in their specialisation.

Greps – solidly-built predators about the size of a dwarf, but even more muscular. Greps inhabit dark forests and hunt individually – often in loose association with others – using brute strength and enormously powerful jaws to subdue prey.

Gryphons (alternatively, **Griffins**) – huge, winged creatures with the heads and forelimbs of eagles, and the body of a gigantic lion. They are intelligent, and become more so with age. The only kindred successful in forming an alliance with gryphons has been the Fair Elves, making them a powerful and much-feared aerial cavalry. Gryphons generally live on high mountains in small family groups, and may frequently be seen soaring high overhead. They are bitter enemies of harpies who raid gryphon nests at any opportunity.

Harpies – part vulture, part human, harpies were thought to have been created through magic during the Mage Wars as a counter to Furies summoned from another plane. However, harpies proved unamenable to discipline, quickly escaping to the wild to out-live their creators and plague the open spaces of Th'eia. They are fierce carnivores and skilled aerial ambush hunters. They are overwhelmingly female, with only a few of the smaller and weaker males allowed to survive for breeding purposes. They have the heads, faces and breasts of women, but the rest of the body and wings are those of a vulture. Two harpies can overpower a strong human warrior.

Hippogriffs – horse-like creatures with the wings, head and forelimbs of eagles. Much sought after as mounts, but difficult to catch and to train. Hippogriffs rarely breed in captivity. Usually restricted to remoter areas, they are understandably very wary of other creatures.

Humans – Although there are far more variations of humans and their cultures on Th'eia than on Earth, the physical and cultural differences between them are considered by other kindred to be so slight as to be unworthy of comment. If distinction is required, it is done by reference to their homeland or to their trade or vocation.

Jiingans – emaciated-looking, cat-like creatures of human size who fly with huge dragonfly-like wings. Jiingans frequently scent out prey hunted by Faerie, locating, harassing and bringing it to bay to be taken by stronger members of the chase.

Kritoids – marine predators up to thirty feet in length, shaped like streamlined jellyfish and swiftly propelled by numerous tentacles on the fringes of the main body. Kritoids are part-plant, part-animal, and there is speculation that they were created by an unknown mage during the Mage Wars, although for what purpose is unclear.

Land-sharks – very large, ferocious predators with multiple legs, like a millipede. Known to grow to nearly 20 feet in length in their native forests of eastern Arenisia, they often mesmerise their prey by hypnotically rattling the scales around their eyes. They prefer to inhabit thick, heavily-overgrown forests.

Leprechauns – Brownie-sized folk renowned for their intelligence, avarice and for being universally magically-gifted. Leprechauns are now rarely seen on Th'eia, after the Great Dragon Sirax banished them to a separate plane and put a curse on all of them (whereby every leprechaun is compelled to surrender their personal horde if, on returning to Th'eia, he or she is caught by one of another kindred). Consequently, most who are seen are extremely cautious, under diplomatic immunity or are adventurers with no hoard but keen to acquire one from Th'eia's treasures. All leprechauns are able to teleport at will, unless held firmly.

Liches – undead spirits, with or without physical form at will. Extremely powerful magically, many liches are the remaining spirits of necromancers who sought to cheat death. Some become death elementals; all should be feared and treated with great caution – even by High Mages.

Mamoks – small, slim mammals with thick, speckled chocolate-coloured fur. They favour similar habitats to rats and mice, but are fastidiously clean, much less destructive and carry no diseases. They form nests by re-moulding wood to their requirements, and feed primarily on background magic. Considered lucky to have in residence, they live to a great age. They are so fast as to be almost impossible to trap or catch, and have few young in a lifetime. They are also extremely trusting and endearing if they take a liking to someone.

Mosasaurs – sleek, vicious and fast marine predators, ranging in size from a few feet to over fifty feet in length. True living fossils from an earlier age, they thrive in the seas of Th'eia.

Ogres – it is generally accepted (albeit reluctantly) that ogres are one of the kindreds along with humans, elves, dwarfs, goblins, gnomes and brownies. However, ogres are distinctly different from all other kindred: they are huge beasts, standing more than twice the height of a tall elf, and with a total mass of more than six or seven men or dwarfs on average. They are also solitary beings. Females live within large territories under the wider domain of a dominant male, from whom they must protect their young – even if they are his own offspring. Ogres are extremely aggressive and often resistant to magic. They are regarded as being semi-intelligent, but there are exceptions.

Orcs – an intelligent, warlike and vicious kindred related to goblins, but far more organised, capable and focused on their main pursuit, which is battle. War is at the center of their culture, and they are capable of superb metal-work in its pursuit. Generally, orcs are about the size of large dwarfs, and like them are massively-built and muscular. An exception are the Great Orcs, who may stand as tall as a Fair Elf, but are thickset (although agile). Female orcs are rarely encountered and, while the orc dens are known to lie north of the Darkling lands, orcs travel widely and their war-bands may be encountered anywhere. Many individuals hire themselves out as guards and mercenaries, and many turn to brigandage and piracy.

Pegasii (singular *pegasus*) – winged horses that live in most mountainous areas. They are notable for their many colours, swift flight and intelligence. Pegasii won't tolerate any of their kind being harmed or taken into captivity, but will sometimes enter into the service of Great Ones or High Mages. They have no natural enemies.

Rocs – huge birds with a superficial resemblance to crows. Rarely seen, except at great distances. They nest in the high mountains, venturing down to the lowlands where they hunt prey as big as elephants. Rocs frequently raid rural areas for cattle and other livestock, but rarely bother with anything less than horse-sized beasts. They are thought to use magic when hunting, as they are rarely seen or heard during these raids.

Rusalki – the watery ghosts of women drowned by false lovers, bound eternally to stay in streams and pools. Rusalki are supernaturally strong, and vindictive to the living, especially males.

Sea-weasels – marine weasels that originally followed their relatives – the otters – to adopt aquatic life and took to it enthusiastically. Sea-weasels are found in the inshore waters, rivers and lakes throughout the tropical and temperate parts of Th'eia – some sub-species growing to over eight feet long. They are swift, agile and intelligent creatures, able to easily outwit most of the other creatures with whom they share the waters.

Snaggletooth sharks – a small schooling shark, usually less than two feet long. However, a school can overcome all but the largest prey by the ferocity of their attack. Fortunately, they are slow swimmers, preferring to rise as a ravening pack from the watery depths to attack most things passing above them.

Spinners of Fate – Clotho, Lachesis and Atropos: Clotho spins the thread of each and every life, Lachesis measures it, and Atropos cuts the thread to end that life at the time and place ordained by Lachesis. The Spinners of Fate are universal entities above even the Great Ones and deal with all types of lifeforms.

Spriggans – humanoid creatures of Faerie, extremely thin and spindly, but strong, quick and agile. They have the ability to change their size, from less than that of a brownie to gangly forms over twelve feet tall.

Sprite – Faerie creatures who are like fairies, but more solidly built. The have the appearance of tiny brownies or gnomes, and are among the most frequent of the creatures of Faerie to forsake that plane to seek to settle on Th'eia. Sprites (albeit in small numbers) are commonly found in most Th'eian towns.

Succubus (plural **succubi**) – are demons from the World of Rifts. Their natural form is that of a gorgeously angelic woman with a long, gracious barbed tail, bat-like wings and horns on each temple. However, succubi can appear in any form they choose and are excellent mimics. As well as being able to fly, they are supernaturally strong and agile, and can materialise through solid walls. They are also highly intelligent and strongly resistive to magic. They detect erotic dreams and home in on the source, preferring magicians so that they may also feed on the magic. An *incubus* (plural *incubi*) is their male equivalent.

Sylphs – air elementals who usually (but not always) appear in a translucent humanoid form. Inhabitants of the higher atmosphere, where they surf the jet streams and feed on ultraviolet light. Some may venture down to perform paid services, or even (rarely) to mix with the folk of Th'eia.

Trolls – it is universally agreed, these creatures are not considered to be Th'eia's kindreds. Rather, they appear to be an earlier form of life that has persisted. The most usually encountered variety are the common troll: scrawny and tough creatures with a ragged, dusty hide and ropey tails known for hunting anything edible in wastelands. 'Depraved' is the most common description applied to trolls; however, they are intelligent and can converse with those kindred they aren't yet trying to consume. Less common but still frequently encountered are rock trolls, which are similar to Ogres in size. While not as aggressive, they are even more formidable as their outer hide is made up of plates of rock. Rock trolls are often employed as beasts of burden, until they lose interest and wander off. Rarest of all are the mountain (or high) trolls. Little is known about mountain trolls, but they do appear to be more intelligent that other types of trolls.

Twiglings – baby dryads who emerge from special seeds. Beyond that, dryad reproduction is a mystery to all but dryads.

Unicorns – are guardian spirits in the form of huge equines. Their purpose is to limit the intrusion of those they consider undesirable to Th'eia from other planes.

Undead – creatures that are neither fully alive, nor fully dead, in that their physical life has ended, but for whatever reason a spirit remained. Depending on the strength of that spirit, various physical forms may be taken, and some have magical or magically-enhanced attributes. Undead are usually vengeful of the living, and often crave warm, living blood. Liches are among the most powerful and feared, but some undead can find gainful employment among the living performing specialised tasks.

Valkyries – every major battlefield on Th'eia is attended by Valkyries, who appear as buxom women in archaic armour and riding pegasii to the dead and to the magically-gifted. Valkyries conduct the spirits of the slain to whatever afterlife is ordained for them. While no one knows why, there is general agreement that the work performed by the Valkyries prevents vengeful ghosts from wandering the world.

Vampires – rarely seen; greatly feared. They may take the guise of any of the kindreds and are supernaturally fast, powerful and agile. They have the ability to sprout bat-like wings and fly, and can also easily teleport. Extremely difficult to kill as the entire body must be fully destroyed. Their total population size is unknown, for they are necessarily secretive and keep a low profile. Likewise, it is not clear how they came to be in existence. They are not, however, considered not to be of the undead but, rather, a strange derivation of the kindreds.

Wal-otters – giant otters the size of a killer whale and well adapted to aquatic life. They may be found in both marine and freshwater seas and lakes. Very intelligent creatures. There are many stories among mariners of aid that wal-otters have given to stricken ships and sailors. How true these stories are is open to debate.

Werewolves (also *were-creatures* generally) – folk of any kindred who may shift their form to that of an animal (usually impressive and dangerous animals such as wolves, panthers, bears and such-like – a were-googum has never been recorded). In that form, they become viciously animalistic, immensely powerful and are protected against harm or injury to a far greater extent than would normally occur. Changes are generally controlled, but may be brought on by certain events such as the phases of the moons. After too many changes, however, the person loses the ability to control the change or, even worse, it may become permanent.

Wing-folk – seemingly frail, slight humanoids with a general appearance of attenuated fairies, but with huge, bat-like wings. They rarely mix with other kindreds and do not appear to practice magic, but maintain cordial relations with others so long as there is no encroachment on areas they consider their own. Most live in the great forests of the spire lands.

Wizards – folk of any kindred who have the ability to manipulate magic. Wizards have numerous titles depending on how they use magic, and there are many associated levels of proficiency. However, the terms used for wizards should only be considered to be a broad guide because any individual may learn about any of the many forms of magic and the different schools to use it. Generally, *mages* are those kindred who become broadly proficient in magic, with the very skilled known as *High Mages*. *Sorcerers* and *warlocks* are mages who also become talented in one or more forms of specialised magic such as battle magic or demonology. *Druids* deal almost exclusively with life energies, while those who become adept with death magic are known as *necromancers*. *Seers* may originate from any school of magic and tend to focus on foretelling. *Witches* (male or female) usually apply a very practical form of magic and are involved in helping their communities. A few particularly talented and learned wizards may become virtually as powerful as the Great Ones, and are sometimes known as Arch Mages. However, most wizards are employed casting endurance spells on building sites, preserving foodstuffs for trade or performing prosaic tasks such dealing with crop infestations, spelling consumer goods, healing and general odd-jobbing about towns. Occasionally, a wizard will take to adventuring to delve into Th'eia's many ruins and mysteries. Even more rarely, a magician will hire themselves out as a mercenary or ship's guard. Some wizards of certain aptitudes have the ability to shapeshift. They do not choose a form: it is determined by the peculiar flows of magic that enabled the ability. As with were-creatures, excessive use of this form of magic may result in the change becoming permanent.

Wolfen – huge, ferocious wolves that hunt in packs. A favoured mount of orcs and Great Orcs.

Yeti – huge, white-furred dwellers in the high mountains. Little is known about them or their affinity as they are of a shy disposition and shun contact with other creatures. They appear to have advanced teleportation and other magical skills.

Yompers – one of the creatures that normally accompany a Faerie Hunt, yompers are lanky, long-limbed creatures that can pursue other creatures with incredible speed, leaping obstacles easily and reveling in the chase.

About the Author

Allan Williams has had careers in multicultural relations, social issues and conservation. In moments between, he has pursued abiding interests in fantasy, science fiction, geography, history and mythology. However, most of all he is fascinated by the ways in which people interact with one another and with the world around them. From 2012, he has been inspired to write his own stories about intriguing fantasy worlds and folk, with the (possibly naïve) hope that our planet may make more sense if viewed from another world's perspective. He is still hopeful.